The Elfin Series
Book 1

Elfin

Quinn Loftis

Acknowledgments

There are so many people that I want to say thank you to, so many people who made this book possible. Thank you to the Wolf Pack, you girls are amazing! Thank you to the Quinnesentials, the street team who so diligently promotes my books. Thank you to all my ARC readers who take their time to read and then post reviews. Thank you to my editors, you all are amazing and I couldn't do this without you. Thank you to my family for all your support and encouragement. Most importantly, to those who take their time and money to read my books. I'm humbled and honored by you all! From the bottom of my heart , thank you.

Dedication

For my best friend and husband, thank you for your support, your input, your critiques, you encouragement, and most of all thank you for being all the inspiration I need to write a love story. You are my soul mate, the only one for me and I'm honored to be your wife. Thank you to my precious son for smiling at me when I truly need a smile and just being the awesome kid he is.

Important Elvesh Terms

A'maelamin (My beloved)

Amin mela lle (I love you)

Im harma le (I treasure you)

Amin naa lle nai (I am yours to command)

Arwenamin (My lady)

Sereg'wethrin (Assassin)

Lle amin (you are mine)

Melethron (lover, masculine)

Sh'mai (Beloved of my soul)

Almare (Bliss) Plant being used to make Rapture.

Lotse (flower) *lótë*

Tirith (Guardians loyal to Triktapic- Tyndril and Tao)

Elfin

"Humans are not to see the Elfin in their true form. They are not to know of our realm. If a human does see an Elfin in their true form their life is forfeit." ~ Book 1 Law of the Elfin

Prologue

"You summoned me?" Trik knelt before Lorsan and his mate Ilyrana, the leaders of the dark elves. He kept his eyes on the floor as he waited for his King to address him and tried not to show his irritation at having to wait.

Lorsan stood, tall like most males of his race. He wore traditional black fitted pants and a black fitted shirt made of a supple material that moved with the body so as to prevent any hindrance of movement during battle. His warriors donned black vests while he wore a vest of gray. His boots came up over his pants and laced up his calves. These were also crafted in such a way as to provide maximum efficiency in battle. They hugged the foot and calves so well that one wearing them couldn't even tell that he sported any footwear at all. His hair was long, hanging down past the middle of his back and dark as midnight. His eyes were catlike shaped and glowed a deep shade of gold. He was handsome according to the females of his race though a human might find him quite disarming.

He folded his arms across his chest as he continued to stare at his most faithful warrior.

"Tamsin is planning something." Lorsan's mouth tightened as he said the name of the leader of the light elves. His eyes narrowed as he looked down at Trik. "I need to know what it is."

"Forgive my boldness but why do you believe he is planning something?" Trik asked.

"Oh for goodness sake, stand up," Lorsan told him in exasperation. "Since when do you submit to anyone with such grace? It doesn't suit you and frankly it bores me."

Trik stood slowly with the grace of a cat unfolding itself from a long nap. He looked at Lorsan with a smirk and brushed his long, dark hair from his face; hair so dark that it held a purple hue and shimmered in the firelight from the torches that lined the walls of the throne room.

"Far be it from me to be the one to bore you. How shall I entertain you my Liege?" Trik asked giving a dramatic bow. "Shall I dance? Perhaps sing you a song, one of the old ones? Enchant you with one of the many stories of how the dark elves have corrupted the innocent and bathed in the blood of our enemies? Or maybe you would like me to wow you with magic and mind blowing feats of daring?" Trik rose from his bow and winked at the smiling Queen, obviously enjoying his flippantness.

"What I would like, Triktapic is for you to do what you do best. Be invisible. Follow Tamsin's warriors to the human realm and find out why they have been spending so much time there."

"Do you want me to bring one of the pasty ones back?" Trik asked. Lorsan snorted at the nickname his most trusted spy had given the light elves, poking fun at their immutable pale skin.

"No, I don't want to draw their attention just yet," said Lorsan. "Just hide and watch. Leave immediately." Lorsan dismissed him with a wave of his hand.

Trik let out a chuckle at his King's seemingly careless brush-off. He walked slowly toward the door waiting for the inevitable.

"Oh and Trik," Lorsan's voice carried through the room echoing off the high ceiling.

"Liege?" Trik asked not bothering to turn back around.

"Try not to get yourself killed. I would hate to have to train another spy and assassin."

"Since you put it that way, I'll have to stay alive. We both know that there is none such as I," Trik chuckled.

Lorsan let out an exasperated breath. He knew Trik was right; there was no other elf that even came close to matching Trik's talents, if that's what you wanted to call them. When it came to covert operations and undetected killing, no elves, light or dark could compare.

"And stay away from the human females," he heard Lorsan's raised voice as he shut the door behind him. Just before it closed, Trik responded. "No promises there."

Chapter 1

"Halloween is here and once again I'm struggling to pick a costume. Once again I am trying desperately to ward off Elora's attempts to turn me into some sort of gothic princess or dark fairy. If you happen to see me strutting down the street in a halter top with wings, glitter in my hair, and three inch heels, please shoot me on sight." ~ Diary of Cassie Tate

"I'm not wearing that Elora. You might as well take that pattern and stuff it back into the bag of long lost costumes that should never see the light of day." Cassie climbed into her best friends beat up Dodge Neon. The door creaked ominously as she opened it. Chipping red paint sloughed off, revealing a layer of blue beneath it. Who knew what color lay beneath the blue. Elora's car had been painted several times by her older brother, Oakley, when he had started working at the auto body shop his senior year and the original color was since long forgotten. Few little sisters would have voluntarily allowed their brothers to practice painting on their vehicle, but Elora didn't have much of a say in the matter. At least he had finally covered up the skull and crossbones he had jokingly, and quite poorly, painted on the hood.

"I'm telling you now, as your friend, if you try and wear a costume like you did last year, I will personally put you out of your own misery, not to mention my own," Elora said in her signature dry voice. She rolled down the window, letting the crisp fall air blow through the car that had, despite the increasingly cool temperature, still grown hot from sitting in the asphalt parking lot that boasted absolutely no shade for the student parking.

"Seriously?" Cassie's jaw dropped open. "That costume was so creative."

Elora rolled her eyes as she started the car. She shifted into drive and pressed the pedal to the metal, coaxing the sputtering little engine to deliver its maximum effort, which resulted in a loud squeal from the tires as the girls pulled out of the school lot. Cassie latched onto the door unconcerned about the loud noise; well acquainted with her friend's maniacal driving skills.

"You were an ant." Elora's face scrunched up in distaste.

"Yeah, but I wasn't just an ant. I was an ant *on a picnic table.*"

"Exactly," Elora responded deadpan. "You were wearing a table. I'm sorry Cass but I draw the line at wearing furniture. We're seniors this year; we have a responsibility to blow the minds of all the underclassmen peons."

Cassie laughed. "What about Charlie's Angels? They are some kick butt females."

Elora raised a single pierced eyebrow at her best friend.

"Do you really see *this*," she motioned to her face and then her body, "as Charlie's Angels material?"

Cassie looked over at her friend. There was no doubt that Elora was beautiful, but not in a typical way. She was heavy into the Goth scene. Her hair was dyed jet black, with the exception of the bright red chunks she put in it. She wore it in long layers with bangs sweeping across her face intentionally creating a mysterious air. She had a stud resting in her left brow; four piercings in her left ear, five in her right, a stud in her right nostril, and, of course, a stud in her tongue. She wore dark eye shadow that gave her purple eyes, made possible by colored contacts, an enigmatic sparkle. She was naturally fair skinned, so she didn't bother with any powder on her face and her skin was flawless anyways. She wore black, black, and more black and she rocked it. Black miniskirts with black fishnet tights drew attention to her insanely long legs on her five foot, seven inch frame, which was completed by black combat boots and an off the shoulder shirt revealing a black halter top. Around her neck dangled various crystals, all of which were, according to her mother, effective to promote healing, positive energy, or some other such nonsense. Various rings, ranging from skeletons to talons, adorned nearly every finger.

Cassie's mouth quirked up. "I see your point."

"Just leave the costumes to me. I'm sure my Lisa can help me come up with something dark and sexy." Elora turned onto Cassie's street and her tires screeched to a halt in her driveway.

Lisa was Elora's mom and that is what Elora had always called her. Elora wasn't into titles that she claimed society put on people to set them apart, when, as she put it *"we are all human beings who picked their noses as children in front of people without shame and then in secret as adults."*

"Who says I want to look dark and sexy?" Cassie asked.

"I do," Elora answered giving Cassie a *what kind of question was that* glare.

"Just remember that we are not standing on a corner trick or treating for the wrong kind of tricks and treats, okay?"

Elora rolled her eyes but then added, "That was actually a pretty good analogy."

"So glad I meet your approval."

"I'll call you later tonight. No doubt you are going to need my help on our English project." Elora began to back out of the driveway. Cassie motioned for her to roll down her window.

"I have to go up to my dad's work remember?" Cassie yelled to her.

"Why do you have to go again?"

"His assistant is out for the week and he asked me to do some of the filing and whatever other meaningless tasks she does," Cassie said in exasperation.

"Okay. We'll work on the paper tomorrow. It's not due until Friday anyway," Elora waved as she continued out of the driveway and peeled and puttered off down the street.

Cassie looked at her watch and realized that she was already late. She walked over to her less than impressive, not to mention ancient, Honda Civic, digging her keys from her backpack. Once she had them, she tossed her backpack into the back seat, slid into the driver's seat, and started it up. She backed out of the driveway in a much more reasonable fashion than Elora just did, and headed towards her dad's work in downtown Oklahoma City.

"Dad, I'm here." Cassie hollered as she walked into the reception area of Woodland Oil Company, Inc. From what little she knew of her dad's work, he handled the company's financial stuff and had the words "President of," in front of his name. She walked past the reception desk and down a long hallway passing office after office on either side. Her father's office was the last one at the end of the hall.

She knocked and opened the door when she heard his voice. William Tate, III sat at his paper-covered desk, tie loosened around his neck, his salt and pepper hair rumpled from continually running his hands through it.

"Come on in, Cass," her father said and she noticed how tired he sounded. He always sounded tired, Cassie thought to herself. He worked way too much. Though he never complained about it, Cassie could tell the long hours were wearing him down. She made a mental note to bug him later about taking her on a vacation. It was for his own good.

"Hey," she said with her brightest smile, hoping to bring a little energy into the stale room. She wanted to wrap him in a hug when he returned her smile and he immediately looked at least ten years younger.

"So what do I need to do?"

William stood and his six foot, three inch form seemed to make the large office shrink a bit. With a flat stomach, large muscular arms and powerful legs, William Tate was an avid athlete. He tried his hardest to make time to do push-ups and sit-ups in his office throughout the day. Aside from his graying hair, he looked much younger than his forty-six years. He laid the papers that were in his hands down as he came around his desk and motioned for her to follow him back down the long hallway to the reception area. His assistant, an older, frumpy woman named Martha, kept her desk in meticulous order. He pulled a box of papers out from under the organized desk.

"These need to be filed alphabetically into these file cabinets." Then he pulled another box from the other side of the large file cabinets.

"These need to be shredded," he motioned to the box. "The shredder is actually in the break room which is out those doors," he pointed to the main office doors. "Down the hall, on the left."

"That seems like an odd place for a shredder," Cassie said absently.

Her dad let out a huff of laughter. "You don't have to tell me. But do you want to be the one who tells Martha where she should put her shredder?" He turned to go back to his office then paused. "You'll be okay out here by yourself?"

Cassie rolled her eyes. "Dad, I'm eighteen. Technically I no longer require supervision."

He let out a groan. "Don't remind me," he said, leaving her to it.

An hour and three paper cuts later, Cassie finally finished the filing. She stood and stretched her legs and then her arms. She looked down at the box full of papers to be shredded and quickly decided that she was not going to be able to carry it down the long hall. She looked around the office for some sort of cart.

"Bingo," she smiled as she pulled a rolling cart from a closet to the right of Martha's desk. She hefted the heavy box onto the cart and then steered it from the office and down the long hall. Cassie had to admit that it was kind of creepy being alone in a large building, knowing there was no one else inside. It reminded her of a movie that she once saw where the lead character woke up from a lengthy coma and staggered from the hospital only to discover that there was no one left alive in the city.

She found the door that her dad had been talking about and poked her head inside to make sure that it was indeed empty. She saw that no one occupied the room and proceeded to pull the cart inside and over to the shredder sitting at the back of the room. She began the monotonous task of pushing paper into the machine and listening to the grinding sound it produced as it cut the paper into tiny pieces that would be impossible to read. Just as she grabbed the last of the papers, she heard raised voices that sounded as if they were coming from just beyond the wall to her right.

Cassie froze. Without thinking, she tried to quiet her breathing, which had inexplicably begun to speed up. Cassie stood and walked over to the wall and pressed her ear to it. The voices were intoxicating, smooth and intriguing, like melted milk chocolate. She found herself wanting to get closer, wanting to find out who could have such a voice. Before she realized it, she found herself walking back out of the break room and to the very next door in the hall. The wall of this office was made of glass instead of painted sheet rock. The blinds that hung in front of the glass were closed, blocking her view to the inside of the room. She walked a few steps down the hall, passing in front of the glass. When she reached the end of the glass, she saw that there was a small, roughly four inch opening where the blinds weren't quite covering the window. She peered in through the opening and her breath caught in her throat.

A long table filled the room and was surrounded by chairs, half of which were filled with men, though they were far from normal looking. These men were beautiful, regal, and masculine all at the same time. Each had long hair, board straight and shiny, with unorthodox coloring. The hair of one of the men was stark white, though he looked as if he were in his early twenties. Another sported hair of pale blue, while another's was light purple. This was bizarre in and of itself, but that was far from their most unusual feature. Cassie's mouth dropped open when she noticed that their ears were pointed at the tips. Not *sort of* pointed, like some people have, which are often described as 'elfin' in appearance. No, these ears were well and truly pointed, strikingly different from anything she had ever seen before. Cassie blinked her eyes and rubbed them fiercely, trying to make sure that she wasn't just seeing things that weren't really there. She looked away from their ears and instead studied their faces. Again she noted that they were inhumanly good looking. Everything about their faces was perfect. High cheek bones, straight, perfectly proportioned noses, pale, smooth, flawless skin that seemed to shimmer under the florescent lights. Then she noticed that their eyes, like their pointy ears, seemed unbelievable. They sparkled, containing unnatural colors that appeared to match the color of their hair.

One of the beautiful men stood from the table and she saw that he was unusually tall. His fitted clothes left no wonder to his body structure. This man's hair shimmered a dark blue, and his eyes were a matching sapphire. He was muscular, but far from bulky. He was built for speed and agility. He wore loose fitting brown pants that looked as if they would allow him to move without hindrance. The material of his white shirt appeared to be the same as his pants and while it also seemed to be fitted for allowing maximum movement, was tight enough to reveal a flat stomach. His chest was broad, but not too thick. His arms, even covered by the sleeves of his shirt, were obviously muscular.

He began to walk around the table and she noted that his movements where so smooth as to be catlike in their grace. He walked confidently, owning the room and commanding the attention of the others. As he drew closer to the back of the room, nearer to where

Cassie stood on the other side of the glass, she held her breath, wondering if he could hear her. He stopped only feet away from her on the other side of the glass and his eyes snapped up, meeting hers. His piercing stare seemed to root her in the spot, even though everything inside her was telling her to run as fast and far as she could from the room, and the beautiful men that occupied it. His lips began to move and the motion of another man standing behind him broke her eyes from the intense stare. She saw that the man was moving towards the door. Cassie made a quick decision, albeit the wrong quick decision. Instead of heading in the direction of her dad's office, she turned and ran in the opposite direction, grabbing the first door she came to. The door opened into an empty office next to the conference room. She rushed inside and pulled the door closed, pushing the lock in place, not bothering to check and see if the room was empty. Once again, not her brightest moment.

Her breath came in rapid pants and her heart was beating so hard it felt like it was going to jump straight out of her chest. She pressed her ear to the door, listening to see if she had been followed. When she didn't hear anything she turned, pressing her back to the door and tilting her head up. Her eyes closed as she let out a long, nervous breath. She stood there for several moments composing herself before she felt someone's eyes on her. Letting out an inward groan before she opened her eyes, she nearly whimpered knowing that she was going to find someone staring at her. Deciding that there was nothing left to do but face the individual, she opened her eyes and slowly scanned the room. They stopped on a figure with his arms crossed, leaning against the wall that separated the room from the conference room where the impossibly beautiful men sat. He looked as if he didn't have a care in the world and didn't appear to be surprised to see her there.

She couldn't move or speak. Like the men she had just seen, he was gorgeous, unbelievably so. For a moment the person seemed to flicker and someone else stood before her, equally gorgeous, and then he returned to his original appearance. She frowned, puzzled by the strange occurrence, but was quickly distracted when he spoke to her.

"Well hello, beautiful." His voice was deep, resonating to her very soul. It was smooth and as flawless as his form.

Cassie still couldn't speak. Her mind was too busy taking in his appearance. His hair, dark as midnight, fell across his forehead and was long enough to tuck behind his ears. Long lashes framed his silver eyes, which shined when they caught the light. He had high cheekbones and a straight, aristocratic nose. His lips were red and full, and appeared to Cassie as if they were made for all things pleasurable. He was tall and, like the other men that she had seen, muscular but not overly so. If his looks were not enough to disarm her, then adding the clothing would take care of it. If she had to describe his clothes in one word it would be 'medieval.' He wore black pants that appeared to be the same material as the others, fitted to his form, a black shirt that was molded to his arms and over the shirt he wore a black vest that looked like it was designed for protection more than style. He had on black boots that came up over his pants and laced all the way around his claves.

Her eyes ran slowly back up his body and when they returned to his face, she saw a smug, knowing smile. She blushed at having been caught obviously ogling him.

"Had your fill?" He asked her and the teasing was evident in the mischief dancing in his unusual silver eyes. He continued to watch her and seemed to be waiting for something but Cassie's mind was lost in a fog of desire and longing.

"I'm wondering if someone as beautiful as you can speak," he said. "And if so, will the intelligence level be so wanting that it ruins the outer package."

That caught her attention and pushed through the fog.

"Are you asking if I'm an idiot?" Cassie asked incredulously after finding her voice.

He smiled a slow, Cheshire cat smile and the look in his eyes made her shiver.

"She speaks," he uncrossed his arms and one hand came up to cover his heart as he pushed away from the wall and took a step towards her, "and her voice is a caress to my soul. I suppose if you have a voice like that then I could tolerate you not being the brightest bulb in the box."

Cassie's mouth dropped open at the insult. She too pushed away from the door, not considering the fact that she was in a locked room with a guy that she didn't know who looked dangerous and unpredictable.

"What makes you an authority on intelligence levels?" She snapped.

He took another step towards her, his eyes never leaving hers.

"I'm a genius," he answered with a look that said "duh."

"Oh. Well in that case, you being an ass is totally okay." Cassie let out an exasperated breath as she continued to watch him.

"Perhaps I am being a tad rude." He stepped closer still and was suddenly only a foot away from her. He swept down in a dramatic bow and stood back up, looking at her with smoldering eyes that had her holding her breath.

"My apologies, my lady. Will you let me start our introduction over?"

Cassie could still hear the playfulness in his voice but there was something else as well, something that made her feel like he really wanted to know her. He reached his hand out, waiting for her to place hers in it. She looked at the hand and then back up at him. Something in her screamed, 'don't do it' and yet she slowly lifted her hand and placed it in his. He wrapped his strong fingers around it and his eyes squeezed closed. She felt a jolt of power burst up her arms. She wanted to pull away, yet she also wanted to wrap herself in his arms, to have him touch her, kiss her, love her.

Her eyes, which had closed at some point, popped open. *Love? WTH*, she thought to herself. *Cassie get a clue, he's dangerous, it's written all over his lovely form. Yes, he is, but I still want him.* She frowned at the petulant voice her subconscious had suddenly become. She shook her head, trying to clear it. She felt her feet moving forward and realized that he was pulling her to him. She was standing mere inches from his face. She tilted her head back to look up at him and found his silver eyes staring back at her. His brow was furrowed and she could see the questions on his face.

"You saw me?" He asked her disbelievingly. "My true form, you saw it."

"What do you mean?" She asked, her voice wavering under his intense scrutiny.

"Cassie, beautiful Cassie, what are you? How could you possibly see my true form?" He still held her hand in his and with his other hand he ran a finger down her jaw causing her to shiver again. She wanted to take a step back, needed to take a step back, but she couldn't move.

"How do you know my name?" She asked.

His lips lifted in a crooked smile. "I saw it in your mind." He said it like it was the most normal thing in the world.

Cassie tried to pull her hand away but he tightened his hold.

"You think you can read my mind?" She asked slowly, as if speaking to a child.

"Not think, know," his finger was now trailing slowly, so very slowly across her bottom lip. "I know that you think my lips are made for pleasure."

Cassie felt the blood rush to her face in embarrassment. "Oh," she squeaked out.

She cleared her throat and tried again. "I don't know what you're talking about." It came out more as a question than the firm statement she had been going for.

His finger continued to run gently across her jaw and down her neck to her collarbone.

"I know about the time you fell out of the tree in your front yard and broke your arm because you were trying to rescue the neighbor's cat. I know that you aren't sure you even believe in prayer or the One you pray to, but it comforts you. I know that you think that your best friend is prettier than you are and I know that you do not see yourself clearly if you think that."

Cassie's breath was coming in short gasps as she listened to this guy she had just met, and didn't even know his name, tell her things that there was no possible way that he could know. She felt like she was suffocating; she couldn't get enough air and her sight started to fade.

"Come on beautiful, breathe for me." His voice sounded far away though she knew he was standing inches from her.

She felt his breath on her face as he spoke. His scent swirled around her and as she breathed in and out, she felt like she might be drunk on the smell. She felt him brushing her hair away from her face and then tilted her chin back to look up at him. She blinked as she looked at his inhumanly handsome face. She saw his features flicker again. For a brief moment, he had long; pitch black hair, pointed ears, and eyes so silver and clear that they shimmered like diamonds. His face shifted slightly. If she thought that he couldn't be even more beautiful, she was wrong. Then, in the blink of an eye, she was again looking at the man with shorter dark hair, regular ears, and eyes that were a more subdued, yet stunning grey.

"Wwwhat was that?" She stumbled over her words. Finally getting her feet to move she pulled back from him staring up at his widened eyes. When he continued to stare at her instead of answering her, she gathered her thoughts. She turned to look back at the door where she had entered. She could hear the other men out in the hall, speaking in low tones.

"They are going to find me soon. I need to go." She looked back and nearly jumped when her face almost ran into his chest. She tilted her head to look up into his face.

"They won't look for you in here," he told her confidently.

"They will eventually. It's pretty obvious since its right next door to the room they were just in and I hid so quickly," she reasoned.

His lips formed a wickedly crooked smile. "They won't find you because I won't let them."

"And who *are* you, exactly?" Cassie raised a single eyebrow in question at him.

He leaned forward until his mouth was mere inches from hers.

"I'm yours," he whispered.

Cassie snorted out a short, abrupt laugh to cover up the gasp his words caused. "Does that work on all the girls?"

Suddenly his head whipped up as the handle of the door began to jiggle. Cassie's body tensed as she turned to look at the door, ready to bolt like a frightened animal.

"Cassie, are you in there?" Cassie let out a relieved breath as she heard the voice of her father.

She took a step towards the door but was stopped abruptly when an arm snaked around her waist. She let out a gasp of air as her back came in contact with a very firm chest. She felt his breath on her ear as his lips grazed her skin.

"I *will* see you again, beautiful."

She closed her eyes briefly as she tried not to enjoy the sensation of being held so confidently. When he released her she headed quickly for the door and as she unlocked it and began to turn the knob, she felt his breath on her neck again and then a whisper.

"Trik, my name is Trik."

She turned to look over her shoulder at him but there was no one there.

Chapter 2

"Light elves have one mate—their Chosen. They love that one with totality and unquestioning faithfulness. For all the darkness that lives inside a dark elf, for all the evil that is innately born in them, they too have but one mate. And whatever the reason, the ferocity and intensity they love their Chosen with is neither lessened by their evil, nor sacrificed because of who and what they are." ~Myrin, Advisor to Lorsan

Trik stood leaning up against a large tree in the deserted park, the lateness of the night having driven the humans to the perceived safety of their homes. He debated whether to go and report back to Lorsan or wait until he had his emotions under better control. He didn't want to get into what had happened with the beautiful girl, Cassie. He had plucked her name from her mind when he had touched her. As soon as his skin had made contact with hers, it was evident to him that her beauty wasn't just skin–deep. She was beautiful down to the deepest part of her soul, and that should be enough to make him stay away. But he knew he wouldn't, especially since she had seen the light elves in their true form. For all the good in the light elves, they still lived according to their laws and a human who had seen them in their true form had forfeited their life—whether it was their fault or not. As soon as she had walked into the room where he had been spying on the light elves and turned to look at him, she owned him. There was no way that he would let Tamsin and his band of goody-two-shoes touch a single hair on her head.

He shook his head and chuckled as he remembered the look in her eyes when he had told her that he was hers. What he hadn't said, and what would have probably sent her running straight into the arms of the ones searching for her, was that not only was he hers, but she was his. And that was why he couldn't go see his King right then.

He pushed away from the tree and decided to head for one of the many businesses that his people owned. It would do him good to surround himself with some good old-fashioned greed to remind him of who and what he was. Like the light elves, the dark elves had many businesses in the human realm. It was a good way for the elves to justify coming here to keep tabs on the various other species that had decided to make this realm their home. But where the light elves businesses had to do with the wellbeing of the earth, the dark elves' businesses had everything to do with self-indulgence, feeding off of the baser needs of humans and the potential for darkness and evil deep in their hearts.

Deciding he needed a distraction from the beautiful human, Trik headed in the direction of the stores just beyond the park. He found what he was looking for in a large glass front window where he could see his reflection. Elves could travel from realm to realm as well as to other cities using mirrors, or glass as long as there was a reflection of themselves in it. They needed only to think of where they wanted to go and then step into the glass. He pictured the lights of Vegas in his mind and took a step forward, his leg slipping easily through the glass followed by the rest of his body. On the other side, he stood in front of Iniquity, one of the many casinos in Las Vegas that his people owned. The bright lights flashed across his face; the city noise and chatter of humans was music to his ears. He could feel the greed, the lust, and the depression that swirled around the city in a thick fog. He inhaled a deep breath, smiling as he thought to himself; *this is where I belong, not drooling over some human girl.* Yet even as the thought passed through his mind, he knew he would see her again. He headed into the casino looking to find one of the few humans he dared to call a friend and hopefully a good card game.

"So why exactly were you hiding in that conference room?" Cassie's father asked as they walked out to the parking lot after having locked up his office.

Cassie had been trying to figure out what to tell her father. She didn't want to freak him out, nor did she want to sound like she was off her rocker, but she didn't want to lie to him either.

"Are there any unusual people who work in your building?" She asked carefully.

"What do you mean by unusual?" He asked as they arrived at her car.

"Like long, shiny hair, unusual colored eyes, and pointy ears unusual?" Cassie cringed as she said the last part. She knew how it sounded, and the look on her father's face just confirmed the sanity, or lack thereof, in her statement.

He thought for a moment before he replied. "The owners of our company *are* a little odd looking."

Cassie jumped on that statement. "Odd, how?"

Her dad scrunched up his face as he tried to describe them. Of course, a man trying to describe anyone in any amount of useful detail was a little bit of a stretch.

"Well, they don't have long hair, or pointy ears, but they are…" he scratched his forehead and searched for the words, "well, for lack of a better term, beautiful."

Cassie's mouth dropped open and her mind jumped to the tall, incredibly handsome, and yes, *beautiful*, guy who called himself Trik. She remembered how his appearance had seemed to shift before her very eyes, though both forms were unbelievably beautiful.

"They don't have long shiny hair?" She asked.

Once again her father looked at her as if she had grown a second head.

"No. No long shiny hair. Are you sure you're alright?" He asked her cautiously.

Cassie thought for a moment before she answered her father. "I'm alright," she nodded, "maybe they were just dressed in their Halloween costumes or something." The tone of her voice made it very clear that she didn't believe her own words.

"Maybe you need to get more sleep," her dad offered.

Cassie nodded in agreement, though she knew that what she had seen had nothing to do with sleep. She climbed into her car telling her dad that she would meet him at home.

"Be careful," he told her as he always did when she was getting in her car.

Cassie sat on her bed as she dialed Elora's number. She had gotten ready for bed, allowing herself to gather her thoughts and try to gather the words she would use to describe to Elora just what she had seen tonight. The phone rang four times before Elora answered.

"What's wrong?" She asked.

"How did you know something was wrong?" Cassie asked.

Cassie could swear that she could almost see Elora rolling her eyes.

"It's eleven o'clock. You only call me this late if there is some sort of issue. So let's get on with it so we can get some sleep."

Cassie was used to her friend's abrupt and oftentimes rude behavior. Others might have gotten offended, but Cassie knew that Elora didn't mean anything by it, it was just the way she was.

"I think I'm going crazy," she began, unable to hide the nervousness in her voice.

"You are going to have to give me more than that," Elora told her dryly.

Cassie jumped into the details of her night without hesitation, making sure not to leave out even the smallest of details. When she finished she sat quietly, waiting for her friend's reaction. After several heart beats of silence, Elora finally spoke.

"So what I hear you saying is that you saw some incredibly handsome men with pointy ears, shiny hair, and freaky eyes in one of the conference rooms of your dad's building?" She summarized and Cassie let out a breath of relief as she heard the belief in her friend's voice.

"Yes," she answered simply.

"Then you ran into another incredibly handsome guy who seemed to flicker between two different appearances?"

"Exactly," she answered again.

"Well, I have two theories," she paused in thought. "We could be dealing with one of two different beings—Elves or Fae."

Cassie choked as she swallowed. "You're telling me that you really believe that there are things out there other than humans?"

"Definitely," she answered matter of fact like. "Do you have another explanation?"

"Halloween costumes," Cassie answered lamely.

Elora snorted. "You believe that about as much as you believe in Santa Clause."

"But you would have me believe that there are two other species besides ours that exist?"

"Yes. Can you honestly tell me that you think, in this whole wide world, we are the only beings besides the animals?"

"How could they have kept themselves a secret for so long?" Cassie challenged.

"Oh come on Cass, just because we haven't seen them doesn't mean that others have not. Let's just go with this theory for now. I will do some research and ask Lisa. Now, you said this Trik character said that he would see you again and that he was *yours*?"

Cassie nodded absently, only to realize that her friend could not see her through the phone.

"Yes," she answered.

"That means you need to keep your eyes open. If you see him again, ask him what he is."

"Just like that? Isn't that kind of rude?" Cassie huffed.

"How else are you going to find out if he isn't human?"

"Fine," Cassie said dryly. "I'll ask the incredibly hot weirdo just exactly what he is. That should go over real well."

"Good. We aren't going to figure out anything more tonight so try and get some sleep." Elora told her before she abruptly hung up.

This was another of the quirks that Elora constantly exhibited; she didn't believe in goodbyes, so she simply did not say them.

"Yeah, fat chance on the whole sleep thing," Cassie told her empty room.

She lay back on her bed, not bothering to get under the blanket. She closed her eyes and Trik's face appeared despite her attempt to push him from her thoughts. Deciding that it was useless to try to prevent it, she decided to enjoy the view.

Chapter 3

"The old adage, *if you can't beat them, join them*, to me is just a way of saying that you're weak. My motto is, *if you can't beat them then you aren't fighting dirty enough.*" ~Trik

Trik played poker well into the early morning hours. After he had taken enough of the humans' money, he looked at his friend and made a motion with his head to leave the table. Now they sat in a quiet bar enjoying the only time that the city was somewhat subdued. Tony sat across from him looking like a model from a GQ magazine in his custom suit. His blonde hair was fixed in a messy style, which probably only took running gel slicked fingers through it a couple of times. He was tall, though not as tall as Trik, and it was obvious that he worked out. He had a strong jaw line and his nose was slightly crooked from being broken two too many times. Fighting had been his thing in high school; not street fighting, but organized fighting for money. He had been good, undefeated for the four years that he had fought. He was young to be the manager of a Casino, especially one as large as the Iniquity. Tony had turned twenty-one only a few months ago and his father, who had worked for the dark elves for the past thirty years, had been only too happy to pass the title, and the stress that went with it, to his only son.

"So are you going to tell me what brought you to my lovely city?" Tony asked as he lifted his glass to his lips, taking a sip of Cognac, the gold liquid glistening in the glass as the lights hit it.

Trik smiled. "A woman."

Tony chuckled. "Isn't it always? Some hot little elf number trying to tie you down?"

"If only it were something so simple." Trik ran his fingers through his dark hair. He was still in his human guise. Though he had known Tony since he was fifteen, when Trik had seen one of his fights, he had still never shown Tony his true form, for doing so would be the equivalent of signing his death warrant. Tony's father, who also knew the true identity of Trik and the other elves with which he did business, had also never seen any of them in their natural forms.

Tony sat up and leaned his forearms on the table. "Whoa, you're really rattled. I don't think I have ever seen you look so, so…." He struggled to find the right word, "human." He finally settled on the only word that would really describe his friend's frustrated look and agitated movements, all of which were very un-elf like. "Come on Trik, spill it. I can tell that you need to talk about it and you obviously don't feel like you can talk to any of your people or you wouldn't be here."

Trik let out an exasperated breath. "She's human."

"Damn," Tony muttered as he sat back in his chair, taking another sip of his drink.

"That's only part of it," Trik told him with a sardonic laugh. "I'm pretty sure she's my Chosen."

"Double damn," Tony added.

"Oh, and one more thing…she's in high school."

Tony choked on the sip that he had been taking when Trik had shared that last bit.

"Please tell me she's legal," he said as he slung the spilled liquor from his hand.

"I have no idea of her age."

"How did you meet her?" Tony asked.

Trik let out another chuckle that made Tony's skin crawl at the menace behind it.

"Those damn light elves. She saw them in their true form and she was running from them."

"I thought you said that there was only *one* more thing back at the whole high school issue," Tony said sarcastically.

"I lied," Trik growled. "Her father works for one of the light elves' conglomerates. They will have no trouble finding her."

"So why aren't you with her?"

"Tamsin won't act until he has spoken with his counsel. That should buy me at least a night to decide my next move."

"Have you decided?" Tony asked.

"If she *is* my Chosen, then I have no choice but to protect her."

"How do you know if she is? I'm assuming there isn't a big arrow that points to her, flashing Chosen over her head."

"She saw through my guise. She saw my true form. In all my centuries in this realm, no human, as in none, zip, zilch, nada, has ever been able to do such a thing." Trik explained.

"Wait, so has there ever been a human Chosen before?" Tony asked with a thoughtful frown.

"I know of only one other but it was with a light elf and it was a long time ago."

"What do you mean *was?*"

"If the human goes to our realm then they will not age, they will stay forever young. She wanted to stay in the human realm and so he stayed with her. He aged with her and died with her."

"Man, that's depressing," Tony said, shaking his head.

Trik laughed. "Some would say it was romantic."

"*Romance* is a lie that gives people an excuse to act like fools and later blame it on the one whom they had bestowed their supposed love upon," Tony sneered.

Trik clucked his tongue at his friend. "My, my, Tony. If I didn't know better I would say that you are a lover scorned."

"Or perhaps I am the fool," Tony told him, his good humor returning. "That's a discussion for another time, or never. You need to go talk to someone you trust who can tell you if it's possible this child is your Chosen."

Trik groaned. "Please do not call her a child, that's just sick. She looks like a grown woman I assure you. There was nothing childlike about her."

"Please man that means nothing. I work in the casino business. I see fifteen year old girls come through here all the time and until they open their mouths and speak you would swear that they were over twenty-one."

"I will find out her age before I pursue this further. You're making me feel like a dirty old man," Trik frowned.

Tony laughed. "Well the old part is correct and I've seen the way women watch you as you walk by, so I would take the bet of you being quite dirty as well."

Trik waved his friend off as he stood to go. "You humans know nothing of pursuing a woman and making her feel like she is the only one who could ever captivate your attention."

Tony lifted his glass in a toast. "Please, by all means, teach me oh wise one. How I long to captivate the beautiful females of this great city."

Trik laughed. "Sorry my friend but you are hopeless. Not even my expertise would work for you."

Tony slapped his hand on his chest. "Ouch, that was harsh Trik."

"The truth hurts. Isn't that what you humans say?" Trik started out of the bar as he called over his shoulder. "I'm borrowing the mirror in your suite."

"Have at it. Oh, and take your girl a balloon and teddy bear, I hear those are things that kids like." Tony chuckled and ducked when the coaster he knew would be coming at his head sailed passed him.

Trik entered Sanctuary through the back door. In the bowels of the large manor that the Dark Elf King and his mate occupied, was what humans might call a club though his kind called it a refuge. It was a place for the dark elves to gather. Food, drink, and other pleasures flowed through the room. Music, seductive to the senses ran across his skin. He cast a shield over himself to keep the hypnotizing notes from drawing him in. He was looking for someone and didn't have time to stay and play. Several of the females vied for his attention but he declined with a smile and kept walking. At the very back of the room in a dark corner he found the man he was looking for.

"Trik, to what do I owe this honor?" Myrin, the wisest of the dark elf elders, asked him.

"I need to speak with you in private," Trik told him, making sure to keep his tone respectful, while trying to impress upon Myrin the urgency of the situation.

Myrin must have seen the earnestness in Trik's eyes because he stood without a word and motioned for him to follow.

He followed the elder out of Sanctuary and down a dark corridor. Finally reaching a door, Myrin pushed it open and stepped back for Trik to enter. Trik, being the suspicious assassin that he was, didn't move. He would never allow a powerful being such as the elder at his back. Myrin rolled his eyes and stepped into the room first.

"What is so urgent that you would pass up the company of the lovely she-elves that so eagerly offer their company?" Myrin asked as he lowered himself onto a very worn overstuffed chair. Trik chose to remain standing.

"What do you know of humans being a Chosen?" Trik asked bluntly.

Myrin's eyes narrowed as he watched the King's greatest assassin and spy.

"I know that it can happen, though it is extremely rare."

"Why?" Trik asked tersely.

"Why can it happen or why is it rare?" Myrin leaned back deeper in the chair and crossed one leg over the other.

"Yes," Trick answered as he began to pace.

"I'm not sure why it happens, or how. However, I believe that it is rare simply because we limit our interactions with the humans. I think that it would probably happen much more often if we spent more time in direct contact with the humans in their realm."

"How do you know if one is your Chosen?"

"There is one thing; and one thing only that determines if a human is a Chosen."

Trik waited for an explanation. When it didn't come, he huffed. "Well, out with it."

Myrin chuckled. "I don't believe that I have ever seen Lorsan's great killer so out of sorts."

Trik's eyes flashed menacingly. "I respect you old one, but my patience is wearing thin."

"Tsk, tsk, Trik. There is no need for idle threats," Myrin sighed. "If she is your Chosen, then she will be able to see you in your true form without your help," he continued, deciding it was unwise to goad the assassin further.

Trik sat down hard on the couch opposite the elder as the words echoed ominously through his mind. A string of profanities in his own language poured from his lips as he considered the consequences.

"Trik," Myrin leaned forward watching him closely. "You've met your Chosen." It wasn't a question.

"She's human, practically a child," Trik ground out through clenched teeth.

Myrin sucked in a breath. "Well that is impossible. A child can never be revealed as a Chosen, even if she were meant to be one. She has to have undergone her maturing."

Trik looked up, his eyes narrowed. "What do you mean maturing?"

"I'm not totally sure what it means for humans, but for our kind she has to be matured to the point of being able to bear a child and be free from the shelter of her sire and mother."

"She still lives with her parents, but I swear by the King that there was nothing childlike about her, other than a certain innocence," Trik added the last as an afterthought.

"You are sure that she is your Chosen?" Myrin asked.

"She saw my natural form while I was in my human guise," Trik answered.

"Have you told Lorsan?"

"No, I needed confirmation," Trik stood and looked down at the elder. "Speak of this to no one."

Myrin nodded and watched as the impenetrable assassin left his apartment.

"I need an audience with you," Trik bowed low before his King.

Lorsan lounged in his personal suite. He knew that something must be seriously wrong as Trik had sought him out in his private quarters. Lorsan motioned for Trik to sit, and since it was the King doing the motioning, Trik obeyed.

"Tell me," Lorsan said without preamble.

Trik let out a slow breath before he met the eyes of his King.

"I've met my Chosen." The words were an ominous declaration in the silence of the room.

Trik waited as he watched Lorsan process the information.

"Triktapic I swear, if this is your way of telling me you are resigning…" Lorsan growled.

"She is human," Trik interrupted the beginning of what he knew was sure to be a grand tirade.

Lorsan snapped his mouth shut as his eyes narrowed. He stared at his assassin intently before he spoke again.

"You are sure?" He asked.

"She saw through my glamour. She saw my true form." Trik went on to explain all that he had told Myrin and watched as Lorsan's eyes widened in surprise and concern.

"She sounds so young."

Trik nodded. "Yes, but it's so hard to tell with humans. As Tony has said, some that are under the human adult age look to be in their twenties, and others that are older look like teens."

Lorsan seemed to ponder Trik's words. After several minutes of silence, he finally spoke again.

"Not that I don't find it very significant that you have found your Chosen, but I still need to know what Tamsin and his elves are up to."

Trik visibly relaxed at being asked a question he felt confident in answering, as it related to a topic with which he was comfortable. "You aren't going to like what I have to say."

Lorsan snorted. "Since when do I ever like what you have to say, and since when do you worry about what I like?"

"Good point," Trik agreed. "Tamsin knows of your new venture."

Lorsan's eyebrows rose and his lips tightened into a thin straight line. "How is it that he came by this knowledge?"

"If you are asking if we have a mole or a traitor, then my answer at this time is, *I have no clue*." Trik held up a hand to hold Lorsan off as he continued. "However, based on what Tamsin said, I would guess that he has made some sort of deal with one of ours."

"Just tell me exactly what was said in this little meeting."

"He said that he wanted his people to look into buying the land that you have had your eye on. He mentioned that he would simply use the excuse of looking for oil in that land if human investors began to ask questions."

"So you believe he knows of Rapture?" Lorsan asked referring to the drink that he had developed.

Trik nodded. "I can think of no other reason that he would have to buy the land where you are planning on putting the store houses."

Lorsan stood and began to pace. "We need to move things forward. If Tamsin is dealing with your human,"

"—Chosen," Trik growled. "My Chosen."

Lorsan waved him off. "Yes, yes, your *Chosen*, then. If he is dealing with *that* little issue, then he won't have had to time to move forward with the land purchase, which means that we should have time to contact Leon and tell him to get it done."

Leon was the human realtor that the dark elves had hired to help them find the land. Trik didn't care for the sleazy little man, but it wasn't up to him who Lorsan employed.

"I'll go see him." Trik stood to go.

"What are you going to do about your Chosen?" Lorsan asked.

"You aren't going to *tell* me what to do?" Trik raised his eyebrows at his King.

"Would you obey me?"

Trik's face spread into a callous smile. "Not when it comes to her."

Lorsan rolled his eyes. "Not when it comes to anything is what you really mean. Do what you must, but at some point you will have to tell her who and what you are. Will she be able to handle it, I wonder?"

Trik shook his head with a low chuckle, "I'm *the* assassin and spy for the Dark Elf King. I kill without remorse. I live for myself and my own pleasure. I come from a dark people with dark hearts. What do you think?"

Cassie spent the next twenty-four hours going through the motions of her day, but her mind was only on Trik. She went from class to class, nodded at the appropriate times, and attempted to look interested when Elora spoke to her.

"You're thinking about him again aren't you?" Elora asked as she nibbled on the carrot she had pulled out of her lunch bag. They sat in their usual spot in the far corner of the cafeteria, giving them a full view of the room. She and Elora were experienced people watchers. They amused themselves by imagining things that people were saying or thinking while they went about their lunch period, unaware of the two girls humoring themselves.

"I can't get him out of my mind. It's like he put a spell on me or something."

"I don't know what sort of magic elves hold," Elora replied.

"Are you still going on about that?" Cassie interrupted exasperatedly.

"What other explanation is there, Cassie?" Elora asked indignantly. "You said that the dude's appearance changed right before your eyes."

"A synapse in my brain must have misfired."

Elora raised an eyebrow at her. "A misfired brain synapse? That's really what you want to go with?"

"As opposed to, *Elves with Magic Abilities for $200,* Alex? Then yes I'm going to go with misfired brain synapse," Cassie smarted off.

"We're going to Lisa's store after school," Elora told her as she took a drink of her soda all the while ignoring Cassie's scowling face. "We can talk to her and see what she thinks."

"Lisa!" Elora hollered as the little bell over the door of Enigma, her mother's store, jingled. Cassie followed her into the new age shop, her eyes never ceasing to widen at the many interesting things that decorated Lisa's store. They walked to the back of the store where the cash register sat and waited for Elora's mom to come up from the backroom.

"What are you girls doing here?" Lisa asked as she drug a large box from the storeroom. Cassie walked around the counter to help her and Lisa smiled. Cassie once again noted to herself that Lisa had one of those disarming smiles that made her feel like everything was going to be okay.

"Cassie saw some elves and then met one who has pretty much put a claim on her," Elora said nonchalantly.

Cassie's mouth dropped open as she listened to her best friend explain the situation to her mom as if she were talking about the weather and not about some mythical species.

Lisa froze and looked from Elora to Cassie, her eyes wide, with disbelief or surprise, Cassie couldn't tell.

Elora shrugged. "I didn't tell her anything, I just gave her an explanation for what she saw."

Lisa took a step towards Cassie. "What exactly did you see?"

Cassie was surprised that Lisa wasn't laughing or telling them that they were absolutely crazy for even considering such an idea.

"Well…" Cassie started. She explained everything she had told Elora and waited for Lisa to finally tell her that she needed some sort of medication for her hallucinations.

Lisa stepped back and leaned against the counter, her arms crossed in front of her chest and a thoughtful look on her face. A face that was nearly identical to her daughter's. Her hair, a dark brown, could have been the same color as Elora's. But Elora had kept hers dyed since before Cassie could remember, so there was no way to be totally certain.

"So what do you think about Elora's ideas about this?" Lisa asked Cassie carefully.

Cassie cocked her head to the side. "What do you mean, *what do I think*? Are you telling me that you believe her?"

Lisa nodded slowly. "I believe her because I know that it's true, as does Elora."

"How?" Cassie practically shrieked.

"We know elves," Elora said in her usual matter of fact tone.

Cassie coughed on her own saliva as she attempted to swallow. "Y-y-you know elves?" She stuttered out her question.

"Have you seen the products I carry in this store? Where do you think I get most of this stuff?" Lisa asked.

Cassie shook her head. "I need to sit down."

"Yeah, you are definitely going to need to sit down before I tell you the really scary part." Lisa walked around the counter and pulled out a chair for Cassie to sit in.

"The *really* scary part?" Cassie's brow rose. "You're telling me that elves being real isn't scary enough?"

"Are you sure that the elf you met said that his name was Trik?" Lisa asked.

Cassie nodded.

"That's not good." Lisa tapped her lips with her forefinger, her eyes unfocused in thought.

"Why exactly is it not good?" Cassie was trying to grasp what Elora and her mother were saying, but it felt like they were making her drag the information out of them.

"Well, if it is *the* Trik, then you met the Dark Elf King's most deadly assassin," Lisa said.

Cassie's head fell forward and landed on the counter with a thud. "You have *got* to be kidding me."

Elora snorted. "Only you would meet the most dangerous elf out there and have him basically tell you that he wanted you to be his woman."

"Thanks Elora, that is really helping," Cassie thudded her head against the counter repeatedly hoping that if she knocked herself out she would wake up and all of this would have been a dream.

"Okay, that's enough," Lisa grabbed Cassie's ponytail to keep her from hitting her head on the counter again. "We have a more serious concern. You said you saw the gentlemen in the conference room in all their Elfin glory. That's not good, Cassie."

Cassie raised a single brow at Lisa. "Really, because the death looks they gave me before chasing after me wasn't a clue at all."

"Well, don't you want to know why they were chasing you," asked Lisa.

"I guess that would be useful information to know."

"It's against Elfin law for a human to ever see an elf in its true form. My family has known of them for generations. I've known of the Elfin my whole life, and even have a close Elfin friend named Syndra. None of us—not one—has ever seen them in their natural form.

"What does that mean, exactly, that I'm not allowed to see them?" Cassie asked nervously.

"Unfortunately, Elfin law states that if a human has seen one in their true form, then the human is marked to die. Even the light elves, who are supposed to be the good guys by the way, stick to that rule. So essentially…"

"Your ass is grass," Elora said absently as she nonchalantly flipped through a magazine as if they weren't discussing her best friend's imminent demise.

"Again, thank you, Elora, for the overflowing empathy," Cassie said matching her friend's dry tone. "Okay so let's say that I believe you, what do I do?"

"I will speak with Syndra and see if there is some loophole that I don't know about. Maybe there is a way to petition the Light Elf King."

"So we are going to basically beg for them to let me live even though I know their little secret?"

"Pretty much," Lisa said nodding her head.

"You two are just little rainbows of positivity, you know it?" Cassie said sarcastically.

Lisa laughed. "Meanwhile, you need to see what Trik wants with you. He is a dark elf, Cassie. No, no, he is *the* dark elf. He isn't one to be trifled with."

"Yes because I make it a habit to trifle with dark elves," Cassie snorted. "Sorry, Lisa. I'm not trying to be a butthead; I'm just a little overwhelmed."

"Understandable," Lisa said as she patted Cassie's shoulder. "We'll figure it out, alright?"

"Did you know my dad's company was owned by the elves?" Cassie asked Lisa.

"Yes, but we aren't allowed to reveal that we know about the Elfin, which is why Elora has never told you that she knew about them."

"Are you going to be in trouble?" Cassie asked her.

Lisa shook her head. "I don't think so. After all, we didn't reveal them to you; it was Tamsin's fault."

"Who is Tamsin?" Cassie asked apprehensively, not sure if she really wanted to know.

"He's the Light Elf King. I imagine he was probably one of the one's you saw in the conference room."

Cassie stood as she blew out a deep breath. "I think I need to head home and stick my head in the ground. Hopefully when I finally emerge maybe the elves will have forgotten about me."

"If you are on Trik or Tamsin's radars, I imagine they aren't likely to forget about you," Elora told her friend.

"Okay, you are not allowed to speak anymore," Cassie pointed a finger at Elora. "Take me home please and keep your happy thoughts to yourself."

Chapter 4

"I'm scared, I won't lie about that. But I can't deny that a part of me—a part way, way, way, waaaayyyy deep down inside is slightly excited about the elves. Okay, and about Trik. Excited about some elves that want to wipe my existence from the face of the earth? Apparently, I'm a glutton for tragic endings. Who knew?" ~ Diary of Cassie Tate

"Should I come back later?"

Cassie jumped when she heard the deep voice behind her, letting out a completely undignified squeal. At the same time, she jerked the shirt back down that she had begun to lift up to pull over her head. Her hand went to the place over her heart as if to hold it in while it tried to beat out of her chest.

"How, what, where…" her words quickly tumbled out as she shook her head and tried to process how the handsome man had suddenly appeared in her room.

"Your mirror," Trik said in explanation to her unasked question as he pointed to the mirror above her dresser.

"What about it?" Cassie asked, finally finding her words.

"It's how I got into your room. That's what you were asking right? How did I get into your room?" Trik crossed his arms as he leaned back against the wall behind him.

Cassie stared at him. She noted to herself that she must be seeing him in his human form at the moment.

"I was trying to be gentlemanly by announcing myself," he said. "Though now that I consider the situation, it would have been much more to my enjoyment to let you finish what you were doing." He continued with a smirk.

"That would have been rude," Cassie told him as she took an unconscious step towards him. She was drawn to him. Something in her longed to be close to him and she could no more turn away from him than she could separate her soul from her body.

"Why are you here?" She asked him.

Trik pushed off the wall and prowled towards her. Her breath quickened as she saw his eyes begin to turn from grey to silver. She watched in awe as his shoulder length hair extended before her very eyes, becoming so dark as to appear tinted purple. His skin became more bronzed and the beauty that was already painful to look at became even more pronounced. She lost her breath as she took him in.

"Wh-wh-what are you?" She stuttered breathlessly.

"I think you know," he told her softly as he came to stand mere inches from her.

He reached up and brushed away a few wispy strands of blonde hair that had escaped her ponytail. Cassie tried to remember to breathe as she looked up into his handsome face.

"How can you be an elf? How is that even possible?"

"How can you be mine? How is that possible?" He leaned forward and placed his forehead against hers.

Cassie's breath caught as she felt something pass between them. It was like her spirit was joining with his. She could feel something deep inside her flowing from her body to his.

"What's happening?" She whispered as her eyes closed giving herself over to the sensation.

"You are my Chosen." Trik answered.

"What does that mean? Chosen what?" She asked breathlessly.

"My mate, the one being in the universe created to be a part of me as I'm a part of you."

"We aren't even of the same species, how can I be a part of you?" Cassie shifted, bringing her body in line with her head so that they were practically brushing against one another.

Trik's hands came up and rested themselves on her hips. She felt his warm breath caress her face. She inhaled deeply, drawing in his smell and finding peace in his presence; peace and comfort that she had no idea that she had even needed.

"I don't understand it, Cassie." Her name on his lips was the most intimate sound that she had ever heard and she found that she longed to hear it again.

"Cassie," Trik said softly.

"Are you reading my mind?" She asked him, still not moving away from him.

"I can see your thoughts when I touch you, remember?"

"That's sort of disturbing," she told him as she opened her eyes and pulled her forehead back from his so that she could look into his eyes.

"I won't invade your most private thoughts; I could never do that to my Chosen."

"How do you know? Have you had a Chosen before?" Cassie asked. Even as the words left her mouth she felt an illogical pang of jealousy and hurt at the idea of him being with someone, anyone else.

Trik's hands tightened on her hips and his eyes narrowed. "We only have one Chosen."

"Ever?" She asked.

"Ever," he confirmed.

"What now?"

She watched in fascination as he licked his lips. She felt her face heat up in a blush when she saw a crooked smile lift his lips. He had noticed what she was staring at.

"Want a taste?" He asked her suggestively.

Cassie's eyes widened. "Are you always this forward?"

"You were the one staring at my lips like they were a succulent feast. Not that I'm complaining."

Cassie tried to pull away but he refused to let go of her. Their eyes met and Cassie felt like she was falling helplessly into those silver orbs. She held perfectly still as his head dropped closer to hers. She knew what was coming and though a part of her thought she should stop him, she made a conscious choice to ignore that part.

"Cassie," his lips were less than an inch from hers.

"Yes?"

"How old are you?"

Cassie started to back away, confused by his question. Again, he refused to let her go.

"Eighteen," she answered.

He grinned, a wicked, wicked grin that sent a shiver through her body.

"I'm going to kiss you now," he whispered.

Before she could protest, if she had wanted to, his lips where pressed to hers.

Cassie's body melted into his and she felt the strong muscles of his arms wrap around her in a firm hold. His chest flexed as he pulled her closer. Cassie let out a breathy moan as she felt his tongue brush against her lips and she opened her mouth without hesitation. She felt one of his hands slide up her back and then to her hair.

Trik grabbed her ponytail holder and slid it out of her hair. He felt the soft strands of her blonde hair flow like water over his hand. He raised both hands and ran them through her now loose hair as he deepened the kiss. In his long life nothing had ever felt so right as kissing the woman before him. If he had doubted before that she was his, he had no doubts now. She was definitely his Chosen and he knew, right then and there, as she ran her hands up his back under his long hair and gripped his shirt in her small hands that he would die for her, and, if necessary, he would kill for her.

He pushed her back until she was pressed against the wall and felt her body tremble against his. The desire that ignited in him was all-consuming and he knew that he would need to be careful and not push her too fast. He pulled back from the kiss and looked into her beautifully flushed face. Her lips glistened with moisture from their kiss and he didn't try to hide the satisfaction in seeing the proof of her desire for him on her lips and in her eyes.

"Whoa," she whispered softly.

Trik didn't back away, but continued to press in closely. He smiled and stroked his fingers through her hair until one hand rested on the curve of her neck, his thumb brushing gently against her throat. He watched as she slowly began to bring her breathing under control and the intense need began to fade from her eyes.

"I think that would be an understatement, *Arwenamin*." The endearment he used was an elfin term and he saw the question in her eyes.

"Is that your language?" She asked, slightly in awe. "It's beautiful. What did you say?"

Trik shook his head. "*That* is for another time." It took every ounce of his control to step away from her and allow her some space. What he wanted, what his very soul was telling him to do, was to wrap her in his arms and take her to his realm where he could protect her from everything and everyone that could hurt her or take her away from him.

Cassie walked over and sat on her bed, pulling her knees up to her chest and wrapped her arms around them. She tilted her head as she watched the inhumanly handsome man walk around her room, inspecting his surroundings.

"So you're an elf?" She asked unnecessarily.

"Yes."

"What kind of elf?"

Trik turned slowly and his eyes met hers. "What do you mean?"

Cassie shivered under is unwavering gaze. "I mean aren't their different kinds?"

"Who have you been talking to *Arwenamin*? Who has been filling your beautiful head with information?" Trik walked closer to the bed as he watched his Chosen closely.

"I know some people who know some people," she answered vaguely.

Trik let out a low chuckle. "You're protecting them. I can respect that. However, you might want to pass on that they need to be very careful what they say and who they speak to."

"Why? Are you going to kill them? Isn't that what you do?" Though her words were honest, her tone wasn't accusatory.

"My, my, you have been busy," Trik circled the bed and came to sit on the opposite side so as not to crowd her and hoping to ease the tension he saw in her shoulders.

"Whatever I tell you Cassie, you need to understand that it changes nothing. You are still my Chosen and I will not give you up," Trik told her with brutal honesty written on his face.

"Is that a threat?" She asked.

"No *Arwenamin*, it's a promise. I have no doubt in my mind that I do not deserve you. I have no right to you based on my actions in my very long life, but those aren't reasons enough for me to walk away from you."

"Well, tell me how you really feel."

"I am of the Dark Elven. I serve the Dark Elf King, Lorsan, as his head spy and assassin." Trik paused and waited to see her reaction to his words. She didn't turn away. He didn't see the expected disgust appear on her sweet face.

"Our enemies are the light elves. We have been enemies with them for as long as I can remember. We live in the Elfin realm, though on separate sides."

"How do you get here, to my realm?" She asked.

It wasn't the question he had expected after having admitted his dark roots, but it was the one she asked and so he would answer.

"We can use any reflective surface to travel between realms. Mirrors, glass, large pools of water, and even some metals and plastics will work. We just think about where we want to go, gaze at our reflection, and step through the material."

"You can go anywhere in the world through a reflective material?" Cassie asked in fascination.

Trik nodded, bewildered by her response. "You did hear the part where I said I'm a dark elf and an assassin right?"

Cassie nodded. "I'm still processing that."

Trik scooted closer to her on the bed. He reached out and tugged one of her legs down and took her bare foot in his hands. He began to rub it slowly and squeezed tighter when she tried to wiggle free.

"That tickles," she said trying not to laugh.

"Try not to think about it."

"Do you always do the stuff you want, even if someone else doesn't want you to?"

"You want me to touch you," Trik said with complete confidence.

Cassie's mouth dropped open. When she tried to respond, nothing would come out. She could feel her face burning up as the blood rushed up her neck and cheeks.

"Now," he started, ignoring her indignation at his comment and the fact that she didn't deny his words. "Are we going to address the fact that I essentially just told you that I am evil?"

Cassie watched his hands as he rubbed her foot. She didn't look into his eyes because she didn't want him to see the fear there because he wouldn't understand the reason for it. She herself didn't understand. She wasn't afraid of him. She wasn't afraid he was evil or of the things he must have done. No, she was afraid for something much more complicated than any of those reasons. Cassie was terrified, because even though Trik had shared with her who and what he was, and made it clear that he was essentially evil, she still wanted him. She still wanted to be his Chosen. Deep inside she knew that she should be appalled at what he had told her. She knew that she should be concerned, but the only thing that she could bother to be concerned about in that moment was her strong desire for this beautiful elf to never stop rubbing her feet. Yep, that's what scared her.

Trik smiled crookedly. "I got all that you know."

Cassie flung her head back as she closed her eyes and let out an embarrassing groan.

"Okay, new rule," she said as she jerked her leg away from his hands. "No touching when talking about my feelings."

Trik's long hair slid forward as his head tilted and a wicked smile spread across his beautiful lips. "So I get to touch you other times?"

Cassie rolled her eyes. "Are you insecure? Cause really you shouldn't be."

"Definitely not," Trik chuckled. He brushed his hair back and somehow managed to not look feminine while doing it. "Something in you calls to me. Your spirit draws me close and my fingers itch to touch you. Tell me you do not feel it," he challenged.

Cassie shook her head. "I can't."

"Can't what? You don't feel it?" Trik growled out.

Cassie scooted back as close to the headboard as possible as she watched those silver eyes bore into her.

"No," she held up a hand trying to placate the dark elf in front of her. "I meant that I can't tell you that I don't feel it because I do. My skin is crawling all over. And as soon as you touch me, it stops. I don't even know if I'm describing it right, but yes I know what you're saying and honestly it's kind of wigging me out."

"Would you like me to go?" Trik asked and stood up from her bed.

"NO!" Cassie jumped up faster than she had ever moved. She wanted to slap herself for her reaction and then she wanted to bang her head into a wall as she watched the self-satisfied expression form on Trik's handsome face.

"I meant, you know, if you don't have anywhere you need to be or anything then you could, ya know, um, you could stay. If you wanted to, I mean it's okay if you don't. I'm cool with that too. It's whatever you want, I mean I have stuff I can be doing, I…"

"Cassie," Trik interrupted his stumbling Chosen. "Hush."

"Okay," Cassie said relieved that he had stopped her from digging her grave any deeper than the necessary six feet.

"I want to stay." Trik pulled out the chair that was tucked under her desk.

"You do?" Cassie asked in honest interest. "Surely there are more exciting things that you could be doing."

Trik let his eyes slide lazily over her form. "I can think of some pretty exciting things," he said with a wink.

Cassie rolled her eyes, but felt the blush all the same.

"When will your parents be home?" Trik asked.

"My dad won't be home until late tonight and my mom…" Cassie pulled her phone from her pocket to look at the time. She was surprised to see that she had been home for over an hour. She hadn't realized how long Trik had been in her room. It was 7:00 p.m. and her mom was usually home around 8:00. "She will be home in about an hour."

"That gives us some time." Trik motioned for her to take a seat back on her bed.

"Time for what?" Cassie asked as she sat down on her bed across from him.

"You have questions. You don't understand how you can want me even though you know I'm not the hero on a white horse. I'm more the forbidden fruit."

Cassie laughed. Trik found himself leaning towards her as he watched her face light up in angelic joy. Her laugh rushed over him and he felt a glowing sensation in his chest more wonderful than any physical pleasure he had ever experienced. He had caused that. He had made her laugh. He realized then that he wanted to do it again. He wanted to be the one to put a smile on her face and to cause her to throw her head back in abandoned playfulness and laugh. He wanted her happiness so badly that it was a physical ache in his chest.

"Forbidden fruit, huh?" Cassie's smile continued to lighten the room even as her laughter faded.

"What are you afraid of, *Arwenamin*?" Trik asked, all playfulness gone.

The smile wiped from Cassie's face as she began to fidget with the comforter on her bed.

"You've killed people?" She asked without looking up from watching her hands pick at the material.

"Yes," Trik answered.

"You've hurt people, good people?"

"Probably." Another short, emotionless remark.

Cassie looked up then. "What do you mean probably?"

Trik saw something in her eyes that he didn't want to see—hope.

"Yes Cassie, I've hurt good people. I won't sugarcoat my past, my present, or my future. I'm a killer, an assassin. I kill who I'm ordered to kill. I've tortured innocents and at this point I don't know if there is any good in me"

"Have you ever killed or hurt a child?" Her voice was a whisper as she spoke and he could hear in her voice that it would be a deal breaker.

"No," Trik let out a deep breath, suddenly feeling very weary. "Children are sacred to our kind; light or dark, a child is never to be touched."

"Have you ever r-r-," Cassie's hands were shaking as she tried to get the question that she knew she had to know the answer to.

"NO! Never," his answer was quick and firm.

Cassie's eyes closed and he saw a single tear slide down her cheek. He was up and by her side from one breath to the next.

"Why do you cry, *A'maelamin*?"

Cassie looked up into his silver eyes as she let him pull her into his arms. She raised her hand and traced a single finger across his forehead and down his chiseled cheek. Silent tears tracked down her face as she spoke.

"You must feel so empty, so alone."

Trik stared into the eyes of his Chosen and saw the compassion that filled her heart. He saw fear, and a hint of anger, but mostly he saw the pain she felt for him. *For him.*

"Why are you letting me touch you?" He whispered as he leaned closer to her and breathed in her scent. "How can you stand it when you know that these hands," he ran the back of his hand across her wet cheek, "have taken more lives than you can fathom."

"Stop," a muffled sound as she pressed her face into his chest. "Why does this hurt?"

"What?" Trik asked as his brow drew together and his chest tightened.

"The thought of not being with you, the thought of telling you to leave and never come back. Why does it feel like my heart is being ripped from my chest and stomped on? What's wrong with me Trik? I should be angry at you or at least disgusted. I should be hitting you, not embracing your touch!" Cassie knew her reaction to him was wrong. The man had just admitted to a life of murder, yet she couldn't walk away. All she could think about was how lonely his existence must be. How cold the darkness must feel, as it consumes him from the inside, and she hurt for him. She ached for the pain his life must bring him.

"Here, holding you, I feel warm. You chase away the darkness, Cassie." Trik had heard her thoughts again. She pulled back and looked up into his face. She saw too much.

"I can't do this," she told him as she stood up and pushed away from him.

"What do you mean?" Trik asked as he too stood.

She looked up and again could see the longing and deep need in him and it scared her.

"You need to go."

"Cassie don't ask me to leave." Trik's voice held the first hint of insecurity she had ever heard from him.

"I need some space, Trik. I need to think. Please, just give me some time." Cassie pleaded. They stared at each other for a long moment and she almost thought he wasn't going to relent. But then he turned and stepped through her window and was gone. Just like that, he was gone and the emptiness that now took his place drove her to her knees.

Cassie curled up in a ball on her side and wrapped herself in the pain of his absence. She felt like she was suffocating as she gasped for breath. She felt the hot tears slide down her cheeks and she bit her lip to keep from calling out his name. Why was she feeling this way? Cassie coughed as she tried to swallow around the sobs. *What's wrong with me?* She thought as she tried desperately to regain control of her emotions, but control would not come.

She didn't know how long she lay in the floor of her room consumed with her misery when suddenly she heard a door slam open and arms wrapped around her pulling her up into an embrace. It wasn't Trik because the emptiness and dread were still there.

"Cassie," the voice spoke quietly, but firmly.

"Cassie, look at me."

Cassie obeyed and looked into purple eyes. Elora, her best friend hugged her tightly. Her brow furrowed as she tried to figure out how her friend had known to come to her.

"Is she going to be alright?" Elora asked someone who was behind Cassie.

"Syndra?" Cassie recognized that voice as Elora's mom, Lisa.

"I knew it wouldn't be pretty, but wow, she looks bad. Once their souls are connected, then being separated is devastating," said a third voice, one that Cassie didn't recognize. "Well, even looking like this, she still looks better than his royal ass-hatness."

"Did you just call the most deadly elf assassin ever, an ass-hat?" Lisa asked slowly.

"Yes, and I'll say it again. I'm a light elf. We're mortal enemies; I get to call him names," the snarky voice quipped.

"Syndra, you worry me." Lisa chuckled.

Out of sheer curiosity, Cassie found the strength to sit up and pull out of Elora's hold. Strangely, as soon as Elora let her go, Cassie felt a little better. She looked up at Lisa who sat on the edge of her bed, her forehead traced with wrinkles as the worry she obviously felt shown through her eyes. Then she turned to the voice she hadn't recognized. A tall woman, who looked nothing like her voice sounded, perched on Cassie's windowsill. Her hair was cut in a short bob and dyed purple. She had large, green eyes and pale flawless skin. Her nose was short and cute and her lips full and red. She was slim, and every movement was graceful and deliberate. She wore tight jeans and a white, long sleeve, V-neck top that shaped to her curves.

"I'm Syndra," the purple haired woman said in a voice that sounded more suited for a little pixie than for a tall she-elf.

"I'm, I…" Cassie tried to speak but her words eluded her.

"You're screwed, love. That's what you are," Syndra said, shaking her head sympathetically.

"Syndra!" Lisa's said exasperatedly.

"What?" Syndra shrugged, "I'm just reiterating what we all see before us. The girl is a mess."

"What's wrong with me?" Cassie asked, finally putting a sentence together.

Syndra stepped down from her perch and walked over to Cassie. She knelt down so that they were eye level and tilted her head to the side. Her eyes traced over Cassie's face.

"He doesn't deserve you. I can see already you have a pure heart." Syndra shook her head and let out a frustrated breath. "You're Triktapic's Chosen."

"Yeah, already got that part." Cassie rolled her eyes, thankful to not be curling in on herself at the sound of his name.

"Yes, well he obviously did a piss-poor job of explaining all that it entails to be a Chosen," Syndra snorted. "But then he is a dark elf so what did we expect, honesty? Like that's going to happen."

"Syndra," Lisa raised a single eyebrow at the elf.

"Right, sorry. Okay so you're his Chosen and at some point in the time you've spent with him, your souls connected. Essentially, they became one. Each link is different and the intensity with which they bind is individualistic, but I would say if you are having this kind of reaction to being physically separated then you and Trik must have one hell of a connection."

"But why? Why does it hurt just because we are apart?" Cassie whispered through a wave of pain.

"It hurts because you are separated against your soul's desire. You are going against nature."

"I asked him to leave," Cassie told her.

"But you didn't really want him to leave. If you and Trik had kissed and said goodnight, mutually agreeing to separate with no ill will between you and knowing that you would be back together in a short while, then you would not be in any pain. But you want him here with you. Your soul is calling out to its mate. Trik didn't want to leave. He desires more than anything to be here by his Chosen's side but you made him leave. You ignored what your soul was telling you; you ignored the call of his soul and so you went against nature. Now you are suffering the effects."

Cassie groaned as another wave of pain wracked her body. "Well that just sucks," she gasped. Elora tried to hold her but Cassie cried out.

"Anyone else's touch will be painful. Her soul wants only one being's touch." Syndra leaned closer to Cassie. "You need to call to him. Say his name; he will come immediately, and the pain will be over."

Cassie shook her head. "He kills people. He's tortured innocent people. He told me he was evil."

Syndra nodded. "Yes, those things are all true—very, very true. But what else is true is that you hold the other part of his soul and you are good and pure, which means that there must be something in Trik worth saving."

"He didn't act like he wanted to be saved," Cassie coughed as she attempted to take a deeper breath.

"He doesn't know that he needs to be saved, but the time will come when he is going to need you. You, Cassie Tate, are his Chosen for a reason. Trik has walked alone for over a thousand years, separated from all because of the job he does for the Dark Elf King, separated from the light elves because of what he is. Destiny has made you his Chosen. You are his and he is yours. Nothing and no one in this realm or the Elfin realm can change that. You can fight it, or you can embrace it. You can doom him to a continued existence alone, or you can bring light to his dark life."

Cassie's eyes narrowed at Syndra. "Who are you?"

Syndra smiled slyly. "I've known Lisa and Elora for the span of their lives and neither has ever really seen me. What do you see Cassie, Chosen of Triktapic?"

The short purple of Syndra's hair faded to dazzling white as it grew, falling past her shoulders to her waist. The green in her eyes flared to life and her pale skin began to glow. Cassie watched as Syndra tucked her long hair behind her ear and that's when Cassie noticed the ear was indeed pointed. She noticed too that a long white robe tied around the waist had replaced the jeans and white shirt she wore. She felt power emanating from the she-elf, a power that kept her on her knees.

"You're old and powerful," Cassie muttered.

Syndra smiled and bowed. "I am Syndra, Queen of the Light Elves, Chosen of Tamsin, the Light Elf King."

"Well what do ya know," Elora said dryly.

Lisa's jaw had dropped open and her eyes were wide with childlike wonder.

Cassie looked from Lisa to Elora and then back to Syndra. The question must have been written on her face.

"No, they do not see what you see," Syndra answered the unasked question.

"You see her in her true form?" Lisa asked Cassie.

Cassie nodded.

"She can see me because she is a Chosen," Syndra explained. "Tamsin had told me that a human had seen us in our true form. He has given orders to hunt you. Now that I know you are a Chosen and that is why you were able to see them that night, he will retract the orders on your life."

"So you all were really going to kill me? Even though you are supposed to be the good guys?" Cassie asked as another jolt of pain erupted. She gasped and tried to steady her breathing.

"We have laws, just as you do. We must protect ourselves. But times have changed in the human realm, and maybe it's time for us to change as well. I will tell you, though, people who have lived for centuries and millennia don't typically take change very well." Syndra watched her closely as Cassie tried to hold herself together.

"You must call him, Cassie. This won't get any better." Syndra told her.

"How did you know?"

"Word travels fast when one of the strongest elves out of dark or light, looks like he has been beaten within an inch of his life. Trik showed up in Sanctuary. I'll let him explain what that is, and word of his appearance spread like wild fire."

"Why did you come?"

Syndra smiled and Cassie could see the genuine concern in her eyes.

"Honestly, I was curious. I sought Trik out and all it took was a light brush against his arm as I walked by to get the information I needed. Normally he would have never allowed such contact, but he's even worse off than you are."

"So you can do the whole touch thing and read minds too?" Cassie asked.

Syndra began to answer, but stopped herself. She turned to look at Lisa.

"You know that nothing said here can leave this room right?"

Lisa nodded. "Of course. I would never share what you say, nor would Elora."

Elora nodded her agreement when the Light Elf Queen turned to look at her. Seemingly satisfied with Lisa's answer, she continued.

"Typically it is something that only occurs between two Chosen, but sometimes we elves gain special gifts as we age. One of my abilities is the power to see into the mind of someone with which I come into physical contact.

The room was quiet after Syndra's response. Lisa continued to stare at the she-elf whom she had called friend for so long, amazed that she was a Queen and Lisa had never known.

Elora watched her best friend struggle to breathe through the pain that she was enduring. Sometimes she didn't understand why Cassie was so stubborn.

"Just say his name already," she whispered fiercely. "There's no reason for you to go through this."

Cassie shook her head. "My mom will be home any minute; he can't be here."

Syndra waved off Cassie's worry. "He can veil himself from humans. You don't need to worry about that. What you need to worry about is your mother seeing you like this. She's going to hall your pathetic looking self to see one of those healers you humans use."

"A doctor," Lisa offered up. She narrowed her eyes at Syndra. "You sure don't sound like a Queen most of the time."

Syndra laughed. "I've had a lot of practice blending in, primarily from hanging out with you and Elora."

"Oh yes, the purple hair totally blends," Elora rolled her eyes.

Syndra smiled at her. "It's less disturbing than the pointy ears I assure you."

Cassie listened to the women around her talk but they were beginning to sound far away, like they were speaking through a tunnel. It was after she nearly passed out that she gave in.

"Trik," she whispered.

She had barely spoken his name when she heard gasps around her and felt strong arms picking her up.

"Leave us." Trik's voice was tight and anger and pain radiated through his words.

"We will talk soon, Triktapic." Syndra narrowed her eyes at the dark elf assassin.

Trik ignored her and the other two humans in the room. He held Cassie tight against his chest as he sat on her bed. He felt the pain subsiding from him and could finally breathe again. He rubbed his face into her hair literally breathing her in.

"I'm sorry," he whispered, his lips brushing against her ear. "I'm so sorry. I should have warned you that this might happen. I shouldn't have left."

"I asked you to," Cassie's voice wavered, but continued to grow stronger as her pain too began to fade. Her face was buried in his chest and once again she felt something inside her reaching for him.

"Do you feel that?" She whispered.

Trik placed a finger under her chin, lifting it so that he could look into her eyes.

"What you feel is our souls reaching for each other."

"I don't understand; how can I feel it? It shouldn't be possible."

"Maybe not, but it is. I won't ever let you go, Cassie. I won't ever let you endure such pain again."

"I'm scared, Trik." Cassie held his gaze as she spoke. She needed him to understand what she was feeling.

"I see inside you, *A'maelamin*. I feel your fear," Trik told her as he brushed her hair back from her face. "I'm afraid as well."

Cassie's eyes widened in surprise. "You? What could you possibly be afraid of?"

Trik leaned forward and pressed his forehead to hers. He closed his eyes. Suddenly images flooded Cassie's mind and emotions pulsed through her like a wild storm. Her breath caught as she realized Trik was sharing his mind with her. Once she realized what was happening, she began to pay closer attention. Her arms wrapped around him and she pressed herself closer as she watched the most dangerous assassin of his kind reveal his deepest fears.

What she saw broke her heart. He was afraid that she couldn't love him knowing what and who he was. He was afraid of losing her and the joy she had brought him, joy that he never imagined could exist. She felt rage unfurl as he pictured her with another guy, felt the pain that quickly followed on the heels of that rage. She saw his existence and the emptiness of it through his eyes and it broke her heart. He also showed her the darkest part of himself. She could tell he didn't want to, but he refused to be less than honest with her. Cassie felt a tear slide down her cheek as she saw the hopelessness in him because he would not stop being what he was, couldn't stop. He was a dark elf; he was an assassin, and that would never change.

Cassie pulled her forehead from his, breaking the connection. She kept her eyes closed as she tried to process all that he had shown her and allowed her to feel. It was so overwhelming, so intimate and all consuming.

"Cassie," her name on his lips was a plea.

She let out a deep breath and opened her eyes. He sat before her in his natural form. She hadn't even paid attention to the fact that he had looked human when he first arrived.

"One day at a time, Trik," she told him softly. "I can only do this one day at a time right now. I don't understand it, but I know that the thought of you leaving and never seeing you again is unacceptable."

Trik moved so quickly that she didn't have a chance. His lips were pressed firmly against hers. She felt the desperation in the kiss and it hurt to know that she had made him feel that way.

He pulled back just enough to speak. "No *A'maelamin,* do not blame yourself. You have handled this better than I could have ever dreamed.

They sat that way, lips nearly touching, breathing in each other's breaths, holding on to the comfort they found in the other's presence. Cassie jumped when she heard the front door open and close.

"My mom," she told him.

Trik nodded but made no motion to move. She started to stand but he held her firm.

"I'm not leaving," his eyes flashed as he dared her to contradict him.

Cassie nearly grinned as she saw the confidence he wore like a second skin slide back in place, all traces of fear gone.

"Syndra said you could keep her from seeing you," Cassie told him.

"That is correct." His head tilted slightly as his eyes narrowed. "I'm curious to know what else the Queen told you."

Cassie raised a single eyebrow at him. "What, you didn't pick that up while channel surfing my mind?"

Trik chuckled. "It wasn't something I was looking for at the moment."

She went to stand again and this time he let her go.

"I have to go down and talk to her. Is it going to hurt when I leave the room?" Cassie shuddered remembering the pain.

Trik stood, closing the distance between them. He gently caressed her cheek and smiled when she leaned into his touch.

"No, *Arwenamin*, as long as our separating is mutual and not of ill will then there will not be pain. I won't allow that ever again."

Cassie rolled her eyes at his overbearing words, but breathed out in relief at knowing she wouldn't hurt once she left her room.

She left him standing in her room, watching her as she closed the door behind her. Cassie walked slowly down the stairs trying to collect herself before she saw her mom. She didn't think she could hold it together if her mom saw something in her and asked if she was okay. She was still raw from the pain and from the things that Trik had shared with her.

She rounded the bottom step and saw her mom going through a stack of mail at the kitchen table.

"Hey," Cassie said as she stopped beside her.

"Hey," her mom smiled. Sylvia Tate was a beautiful woman and always happy, which only made her more beautiful. There were times that Cassie felt like she walked in the shadow of her mother's beauty, but she held no jealousy. Her mom didn't have a clue just how attractive she was.

"Everything going alright tonight?" Sylvia absently flipped through the mail, pausing sporadically to gaze at one envelope or another.

Cassie let out a deep breath, making sure her voice didn't waiver when she answered. No matter how tough she wanted to think she was, she never wanted to go through the pain she had so recently endured.

"I'm good. Tired, so I'm getting ready to call it a night."

Sylvia looked up, her eyes narrowed as she scrutinized Cassie's face. Cassie decided that she must have hid her anxiety well because her mom smiled and gave her a hug.

"Okay then, sleep well," Sylvia told her.

Cassie made her way back up the stairs, trying to gather her thoughts as she prepared to once again face the inhuman beauty in her room.

Chapter 5

"In the very rare instance that a human becomes the Chosen of an Elfin there is only one way that human can be allowed a continued existence. It is a choice not made lightly especially by those of the Elfin race. A bond must be made, unbreakable, eternal and is only possible between a male and his Chosen."

~Laws of the Elfin, Lost Book

"Are you not a teensy bit shocked by everything going on?" Elora asked her mother as they sat at their kitchen table. Lisa had made a pot of herbal tea when they arrived home. Now they both sat, sipping their tea, their minds still struggling to wrap themselves around the events of the evening.

"I've known that Syndra was an elf my whole life, and had no idea that she was royalty. I don't think my mother knew. So yeah, I'm just a tad shocked."

"What does it mean?"

"It means just what Syndra said. We keep our traps shut. We aren't supposed to know about their kind and we sure as heck aren't supposed to know that she is a Royal." Lisa took a sip of her tea as she looked over the rim of her mug at her daughter.

"She said that even knowing who Trik is was dangerous," Elora reminded her mom.

Lisa nodded. "Maybe he'll be honest with her now that he knows Syndra has been in touch with her."

"Yeah, and let's hope that Syndra can talk her elf husband out of trying to significantly shorten Cassie's life span," Elora added.

Lisa snorted. "Knowing how closely they protect their secrets, with our luck they'll probably try hauling her off to Elf land."

"Not funny, Lisa." Elora rolled her eyes at her mother's dark sense of humor, not even realizing how honestly she came by her own pessimistic personality.

Syndra sat while her mate, Tamsin, King of the Light Elves, paced back and forth across their bedroom. She waited while he considered her words and the implications that came with them.

"So you are telling me, Triktapic, famous assassin and continual thorn in my side, has a Chosen and she is human?" Tamsin eyed his Chosen with raised brows.

Syndra gave a slow nod and continued to let him work through the details. She knew how her mate's mind worked and knew that it was best to make subtle suggestions but ultimately let him come up with the decision.

"So she is essentially untouchable," Tamsin thought out loud. "How is it that someone as dark as Trik would possibly be given one so innocent, not to mention young."

"She is young, but not as young as you think. She has what the humans call an old soul. She has an inner strength that I don't even think she is aware of."

Tamsin looked over at his Chosen and wryly smiled. "What of her innocence, my lover?"

Syndra stood and walked slowly to him. She stood inches from him as she looked up into his shimmering eyes. Eyes that never ceased to draw her in and remind her of the love he held for her.

"Trik has held our people, as well as his own, in fear for centuries," said Syndra. "He is Lorsan's pet, but I don't think Lorsan really has control over him, at least not any more. Something is changing; the balance is being tilted in our favor." She brushed a loose hair out of his face and smiled encouragingly. "Whatever Lorsan has planned, it must be something especially evil—evil enough that the Forest Lords are watching. They only take note if either of our sides are doing something that affects the humans. It is my belief that they have chosen Trik to be the instrument of Lorsan's downfall. He is not lost, not yet. His Chosen, this Cassie Tate, already holds a deep place in his heart. She will draw him from the dark."

"And what if he draws her from the light instead?" Tamsin challenged, ever the analytical tactician.

"Then we must beg the Forest Lord's help," she responded. You know that our realm cannot survive without the humans. If Lorsan destroys them, he destroys us all."

Tamsin nodded in acknowledgment. "We must also hope that he does not realize the importance of Cassie's role. If he suspects that she represents a threat to his power, then he will kill her, regardless of whether she is Trik's Chosen."

Tamsin pulled Syndra into his arms pressing his forehead to hers. His love flowed into her. Even after a millennia together his desire and love for her had only grown. He wasn't ready to end their long life; he wasn't ready to give up any time with his Chosen, especially not for a Dark Elf King's selfish desires.

Trik sat surrounded by the darkness of Cassie's room. He smiled as he thought about the appalled look on her face when he suggested that she let him sleep next to her…for her protection of course. Protection from what? She had asked. He had grinned his sly smile and told her protection from any who would take his place in her dreams. She had rolled her eyes at him and he had agreed to sleep on the floor. He had never needed much sleep so he had taken up a seat in the corner of her room, on the chair that had sat in front of her desk.

It had taken Cassie a while to fall asleep. She kept telling him to stop staring at her. But she didn't understand. She didn't understand that when Trik looked at her, he wasn't just looking at her physical beauty. He was seeing all the beauty that she brought into his world, all the beauty that he had never known existed. Cassie held his attention as sure as the sun held the devotion of a flower, seeking out her life-giving rays. Even in the dark, he had seen the blush that had stained her beautiful skin. But eventually, exhaustion had taken over. His thoughts drifted back to the pain they had both felt when they had been separated. He had heard of such a thing happening between Chosen pairs, but never had he ever imagined it would feel like that. It made him sick to think that Cassie had endured such pain. It angered him that he could have prevented it if he had denied her request. He should have stayed and forced her to hear him out. Then again, he didn't imagine his Chosen could be forced to do much.

Trik heard Cassie whimpering softly in her sleep. He went to her and kneeled by her bedside, putting his face level with hers. He gently brushed back the hair that fell like a veil in front of her face. As his fingers brushed her skin she leaned into his touch and she settled. Even in sleep, she knew him.

As he knelt there, captivated by his Chosen, he felt the pull of his King. Lorsan had the ability to call his elves back to him no matter the distance. For the first time in his long life, Trik ignored his Lord's call.

Cassie walked next to Elora through the drab, crowded halls of their high school. Rows and rows of lockers lined the halls, crowding the students as they stopped to retrieve their personal belongings. To any new student, the school might seem interesting, with all the inspirational posters hung on the walls. The posters contained such stirring proverbs as "There is no I in team," and Cassie's personal favorite, "Change is inevitable and life changes as swiftly as the wind blows. It's which direction that you let the wind blow you that matters." Some student, bound to be indispensable to society, had crossed out the word 'the' and then added a 'Y' to the end of 'wind.' Cassie might not get a quality education at Northpointe High, but she would certainly learn the important lessons in life, like how to smut up an inspirational poster.

As they walked, Cassie kept looking over her shoulder to ensure that Trik was still behind her. He leaned casually against a row of lockers, arms crossed over his chest, looking way too edible for his own good. She was the only one who could see him, and that was a good thing since he was in his Elfin form. He had started out the day in his human guise but she had asked him not to use his glamour around her. She didn't know how but she had felt a wave of pleasure emanate from Trik when she had made this request.

"Is he still there?" Elora asked as she bit into the bran muffin Cassie's mom had shoved into Cassie's hand on the way out the door. Cassie didn't have the heart to tell her mom that she hated bran, so she continued to accept them and pass them on to Elora.

"Yep," Cassie answered.

"And he's just going to follow you around all day?"

"So he says."

Elora shrugged. "If you need me to remind you not to pick your nose or dig out a wedgie just let me know."

Cassie rolled her eyes. "Good to know you have my back."

Elora raised a single brow. "Somebody has too. I leave you alone for one night and you go and get yourself tied to a dark elf assassin." She shook her head as she continued to eat her muffin. "Only you, Cassandra. Only you would wind up with the bad boy when really you should be with Mr. All American."

Both girls jumped when Trik appeared next to them back in his human guise, apparently having decided to allow Elora to see him as well.

"Who is Mr. All American?"

Cassie tried not to look at Trik as she answered. "What?"

"You're dark friend here seems to think you would be better off with him." Trik's indignation and possessiveness at her statement were apparent in both his voice and his glower.

Elora made her famous *give me a freaking break* face. "Get a grip man, aren't you some bad ass killer?"

"Yes, please pass that on to this, this All American you are talking about."

Cassie laughed and quickly covered her mouth.

Trik leveled her with a piercing stare.

"It's not a real person Trik. It's a type of guy, you know, like a 'knight in shining armor' type."

"You picked a real winner here, Cass," said Elora. "I think this guy is one arrow short of a full quiver."

Trik's head snapped around to Elora. "How did you know I had a quiver?"

This time Cassie couldn't catch her laughter.

"What are you two laughing at?" Trik growled. "I always keep my quiver full."

The girls roared, Elora losing her usual stoic composure. "That just sounds so wrong," she said when she finally caught her breath.

Trik just shook his head, looking back and forth between the two girls.

"Yep," Elora said as they arrived to their class. "Another day in the life of a typical American teenage girl, walking to class with her dark elf boyfriend, discussing the size of his quiver. What more could a girl want?"

Trik stood looking at them in confusion as Cassie smothered her laughter and Elora glanced back at him with a dismissing wave.

"What the hell just happened," he said to the now empty hall.

Cassie took her seat, trying, but miserably failing to keep her laughter under control. Elora simply had a mildly amused look on her face.

"Quiver?" Cassie murmured from where she sat behind Elora.

Elora turned slightly so that she could see Cassie and the front of the classroom.

"I was taking a guess, but everyone knows that elves use bows and arrows. I thought about the whole wielding a sword thing but really that would have been much worse."

Cassie snorted. "Leave it to you to toss out some sexual innuendos to the dark elf assassin."

"My brother must be wearing off on me," Elora murmured just as Mrs. Davis walked in.

History was one of Cassie's favorite subjects, but even today's lecture about Native Americans couldn't keep her mind from continually drifting back to Trik and the unsettling awareness that she could feel his closeness. She knew that he was just outside the door, waiting on her. She didn't know how to explain it, but that same something that kept drawing her to him, simply knew that he was close. And if she were going to be really honest with herself, she would have to admit that it was comforting knowing he was there.

The class seemed to drag as she fidgeted restlessly. Cassie was beginning to feel anxious as the class wore on. She needed to see Trik. She needed him to tell her that what she was feeling was normal. Just as the bell rang to indicate class was dismissed, she felt a gasp pulled from her chest and an ache take its place. She wasn't in pain exactly; it was more of a feeling of emptiness, as if something essential was missing. She knew then, on the tail end of that thought, that Trik was gone. She snatched up her things and rushed out of the room, not bothering to explain to Elora. She needed to see it for herself.

She stumbled over her feet as she reached the door and caught herself just as she rushed into the hallway. She turned in a circle slowly searching through the throng of students, her eyes moved over every face and every corner, hoping to see him leaning there, but knowing she wouldn't.

"Cassie, could you please explain why you nearly took out three of our classmates in an effort to get into the hall?" Elora asked her, stopping by her side and looking in the same direction she was.

Finally, Cassie made eye contact with Elora. "He's gone," she told her and her face fell as the words left her mouth.

"And how exactly did you know that while we were sitting in History class?"

Cassie shook her head. "I just knew. Somehow, I don't know how to explain it, but I just know when he is close by."

Elora stared at her questioningly. "Are you in pain this time?"

"No, I just feel like something is missing."

"Duh, it's your ass, I mean assassin."

Cassie grinned weakly at her friend's purposely slip of the tongue. "That was weak."

"I'll work on my material. So what are we going to do?"

Cassie shrugged. "What can I do? It's not like I have a cell phone number for him."

"Have you said his name? Isn't that what brought him back the last time?" Elora reminded her.

"Trik?" Cassie said his name and it came out as a question. They both waited, their breaths seemed to freeze in their lungs as the anticipation for a response grew. The halls were beginning to empty as people made their way into their respective classrooms. Cassie hardly noticed. After several minutes, still nothing.

"O-o-okay," Elora said drawing out the word. "So apparently you have to be in unbearable pain for that little trick to work. No pun intended, although that was a pretty good one."

Cassie heard the bell ring and still she didn't move. She knew she needed to get to her next class but she couldn't get her feet to obey her.

"Cassie, you are going to have to suck it up and deal. We need to get to class. Your life does not stop simply because you find yourself painfully and ridiculously attached to Mr. Tall, Dark, and Delicious," Elora said firmly as she took Cassie by the arm and tugged.

Cassie let out a deep breath and looked at her friend. With a single nod of her head, she finally began moving. "You're right, this is silly."

"I didn't say silly. Bizarre, freaky, and quite possibly turning into an unhealthy attachment? Yes, but not silly."

"Thanks for the vote of confidence," Cassie growled.

"I don't sugarcoat things Cass, not for anyone, especially you."

"I know and I usually appreciate it. But could you maybe soften it a little this time?"

"No."

"It was worth a try," Cassie muttered.

Trik glared at his King. The indignation rolled off of him in waves that were palpable.

"You have never forced a summons on me." His words were a knife slicing through the anger that radiated from both of them.

Lorsan met his warrior's fierce stare. "You have never ignored one."

"I have never had a Chosen before. She is human; she needs protection, especially since she has seen Tamsin and his closest men in their natural form. You know the laws they will hold her to."

"You are my spy and assassin first, not her *Sh'mai*," Lorsan snapped.

Trik shook with rage as his fists opened and closed at his sides.

"Is that how you feel of your Chosen?" He asked. "Does your Kingship come before her?"

"That's different and you know it."

"Different how?" Trik challenged.

Lorsan's hand slashed through the air disregarding Trik's words. "Ilyrana and I have been united for more than a millennia. She has held my heart far longer than the existence of the humans, let alone you're little human."

"And that makes your relationship more important than the one between me and Cassandra?"

"I am in the middle of one of the largest endeavors our kind has ever had in the human realm; an endeavor that will bring the humans to their knees before us. Need I remind you of the part you are to play in this?" Lorsan paced restlessly as he struggled with his next words. "I would hate to have to replace you, Triktapic. You have served me longer than most. But do not make the mistake of believing you are irreplaceable."

Laughter that would have caused tremors in a lesser man erupted from Trik. "You honestly think that you have someone amongst your warriors that is even comparable to me? Tell me, Liege," Trik's words dripped with contempt, "do you honestly believe you have a warrior with a tenth of my ability?"

Lorsan's eyes glowed as he held the stare of his assassin. Both refused to admit defeat.

"I have always done what you asked. I have served you faithfully, but in this, I will not bend. She is the most important thing. You know as well as I do that I do not deserve her. I am being entrusted with something pure and good. Do you honestly believe that I would walk away from that?"

Lorsan crossed his arms in front of his chest and raised one hand to stroke his chin. His eyes narrowed as he considered Trik's words. "I admit that I have to wonder why you, of all the dark ones, would be given someone like her. Do you believe that she can honestly care for you? Does she know what you are? What you do?"

Trik growled in frustration. "I have shown her."

Lorsan's hand dropped from his face abruptly. "You connected with her?" His eyes widened as he watched Trik nod.

"I won't keep anything from her."

"And what if she doesn't want you? What if she says that she can't deal with it and won't accept that this is your life? You will not walk away from who and what you are."

Trik chuckled darkly. "Only moments ago you were threatening to replace me. So which is it, Dark King? Are you going to keep me and accept my terms for continuing to be your killer, or are you going to toss me out?"

Lorsan slumped down onto his throne chair. He suddenly looked exhausted.

"You are my right arm, Trik. You are correct when you say that I could not replace you, at least not with someone with your talent. But I need to know that you are going to be reliable. I can't have you distracted. You might get yourself killed."

"I have never let you down. I'm not going to start now. Please do not ask me to choose between you or her. You know that something in our dark nature seems to call deeper to our Chosen. I will give up everything for her. Even if she denies me, I will spend my existence making sure she is safe."

"The reason that I summoned you is because I need you to finalize the deal with the humans. Go sign the documents for the land. Then set up a place for us to cross over there so that we can begin taking the soil that will be needed to grow the plants."

Trik nodded. "I'll check in with you once it's ready."

Lorsan nodded and left the throne room without another word.

Trik looked at the watch he wore that kept human time. He wasn't sure what time Cassie finished with school for the day, but he imagined that it wasn't before their lunchtime which for most of them seemed to be around 12:00 p.m. He pictured a window in her school and stepped up to the reflective wall that ran the length of the throne room. He walked through it and emerged on the other side, standing in the school once again. He was facing a long, empty corridor with the lockers that seemed to line every wall in the building. He began to walk, allowing the soul inside him to search out for its other half. It led him further down the hall and around a corner to a single door on the short hallway. She was behind that door. He knew it as sure as he knew his own name. He opened the door, knowing that everyone but Cassie would think the door was opening on its own. As he stepped through it, his eyes immediately found hers. He watched as she jumped to her feet. A grin crept up on his face as he cocked his head to the side waiting to see what she would do next.

It must have been the amused look and mischievous gleam in his eyes that snapped her back to the here and now. She looked around the room and saw that her classmates were staring at her. She blushed as she sat back down, but her eyes drifted once again to where he stood. Trik glided smoothly through the aisle, making his way towards her. One of the guys was staring at her attempting to get her attention. Trik felt an unfamiliar feeling rush through him, though he knew what it was—jealousy. He instantly loathed the boy looking at his Chosen. As he walked past, Trik swiped his hand across the boy's desk, knocking his things into the floor. Cassie ducked her head to cover her embarrassment. Trik smirked as he watched him skitter to gather his now scattered possessions.

Cassie looked up at Trik as he reached her desk. He knelt down in front of her so that she didn't look like she was staring up into empty air to her classmates. Once he was at eye level, he reached up and grazed her cheek with his fingertips. She fought the desire to close her eyes and lean into his touch.

"You left," she whispered.

Trik nodded and his eyes pleaded for her understanding. "I didn't have a choice."

She figured that he must have seen the confusion on her face when he let out a frustrated sigh. Cassie didn't feel like it was directed at her, but rather his situation. Cassie turned from him and raised her hand. Mr. Singleton motioned for her to speak.

"I need to step out for a moment."

Cassie was glad that it was a male teacher that she was dealing with because they were more inclined to let the female students leave the class without an explanation, always fearful that they would unwittingly expose a 'female issue' to the rest of the class.

"That's fine," he told her.

Trik backed up so that she could stand and then followed her out of the room. Cassie stopped abruptly when Todd put his foot in the aisle to keep her from passing. She looked down at him as her eyebrows rose in question. He discretely handed her a folded piece of paper, a faint smile on his lips, but said nothing. When he moved his leg, Cassie continued forward, confused by his action and beginning to feel the stares of her fellow classmates. She turned back to look at him when she heard him curse and saw that once again his things were scattered on the floor. She glanced up at Trik who shrugged, acting like he had nothing to do with the mess. She shook her head with a small chuckle as she pushed the door of the classroom open.

"Okay," Cassie started before he could speak. "What were the little stunts with Todd about?"

Trik sneered. "If you are speaking of the boy who was drooling over you, then I was simply distracting him from staring at what is mine."

Cassie crossed her arms over her chest and glared at Trik. "Yours?"

Trik nodded. "Of course. I told you already. You are mine and I am yours. Would you be okay with a female eyeing me?"

She huffed and dropped her arms. "Fine, point taken."

"What do you mean you didn't have a choice," she finally asked as they began to walk again and rounded a corner where some water fountains were tucked away from view.

"When my King calls to me I can only resist for so long before he forces my presence."

"Does he do this often?"

"No," Trik shook his head. "In fact he's never done it before."

"So why now?" Cassie asked.

"I've never ignored his summons before." Trik's hair flowed like water, tracking his movements as he paced. Cassie wanted to reach out and touch the dark strands, but refrained.

"What was so important that he had to talk with you?"

Trik stopped and his eyes met hers. He stepped up and cupped her face in his hands. He was so close that she could feel his breath on her face. His scent surrounded her and she fought the urge to seek refuge in his arms. "It's best if you didn't know."

Cassie's lips tensed in a straight line as she tried to step away from him, but he refused to release her.

He shook his head. "I told you I would never let you go."

"Even if I want you to?" She asked quietly.

"You don't want me to," he told her with complete confidence.

"Is it going to harm people? What does your King want to do? Are you going to have to kill someone?" Cassie's eyes implored him to say no; she needed him to say no.

He dropped his hands to her waist and pulled her closer to him. He saw her needs in his mind as he touched her, needs that he didn't know if he could meet.

"Please don't ask this of me Cassie. You know what I am."

Cassie glared at him. She would not let him off that easily.

"I know that you have a choice. Regardless of what you were born into, you have a choice."

"It's not that simple," he pleaded.

"We are the ones who complicate things, Trik. You either choose what's right or what's wrong. What is not simple about that?"

"I have responsibilities that I can't turn from. My loyalty is to my King and my race," Trik's voice was growing into a frustrated growl.

Cassie pushed away from him. His hands dropped to his sides.

"You just met me," she told him. "I don't expect you to suddenly switch your loyalty to me, Trik. I still don't understand all that is going on between us, but I know that I care for you. I care about what happens to you and I'm telling you that if you continue down the dark road you have been on for so long, it's going to destroy you. You may be a dark elf, you may be an assassin, but you aren't evil."

Trik snorted, "Please, *Arwenamin.* Don't romanticize me. Whatever good was in me, if ever there was any, was snuffed out long ago."

"I don't believe that." Her hands fisted at her sides and she challenged him with her stare. "If that were true, then I would feel nothing for you."

"If what you say is true, if there is any light left in me, then how come I am willing to steal you away against your will?" He watched the shock and then fear flash across her face.

"That's who I am, Cassie. Something pure and good has landed in my lap, my Chosen. I never thought I would ever find you, but now that I have nothing will take you from me, not even your desire to leave me."

"I never said that I didn't want to be with you," she said quickly.

"I see the disgust in your eyes when you talk of what I am," he spat at her.

"Not disgust at you, Trik. Disgust at what you have had to do? Yes. Whether you admit it or not, the things you have had to do have left holes in you. It's eating away at you. I'm disgusted at the King who would care so little for you and allow you, even order you, to do such things."

"YOU AREN'T LISTENING!" Trik yelled, causing Cassie to jump.

"I have enjoyed it, Cassandra! I like the kill. I like proving myself better than my adversary. It is in my nature to destroy things." He turned from her, trying to gather his composure, not wanting to scare her any further. "I should let you go. I should leave and never look back. I will wind up destroying you." His words were a whisper on the air, but Cassie heard them and felt the pain of them in her chest.

Cassie started to speak but he cut her off. "I have some things to take care of. I just came back to make sure you were alright. I need you to be okay with me going or else you will be in pain."

"Are you coming back?" She asked him, trying to cover up the desperation she was feeling.

Trik closed the space between them and grabbed her face, pulling her to his own. He kissed her firmly, possessively. Cassie opened her mouth and let him deepen the kiss. His tongue brushed against hers and she felt her knees weaken. Trik wrapped an arm around her waist, supporting her as he continued to kiss her. Cassie once again felt the pull that was becoming all too familiar. She heard Trik groan into her mouth and suddenly felt cold metal behind her. Trik had pushed her back against the lockers and she hadn't even realized they had been moving.

Trik had never felt anything better than his Chosen's lips against his own. He nipped at her bottom lip playfully and pulled back from her mouth only to continue nipping and kissing her across her jaw and down her neck. He heard a gasp from her and felt her breath quicken against his cheek. He needed to stop, but he didn't. He kissed her lower and when his teeth grazed her collarbone; her passionate whimper finally had him pulling back. When a woman makes a sound like that a man can do one of two things; push forward knowing she was beyond the point of saying no, or be a gentleman and step back. Trik had never been a gentleman, but then Cassie brought all sorts of things out of him that he never knew himself to be capable of.

He lifted his head to look at her face. Her lips were swollen and red, glistening from his kiss. Her eyes were half closed, clouded with pleasure and her chest rose and fell quickly as she tried to regulate her breathing. She was breathtaking, Trik thought to himself. Her lips rose into a sultry smile and Trik quickly pushed away from her. He needed some space between them before he threw her on the floor and…

"You look like you're ready to ravish me," Cassie interrupted his thoughts seeming to pluck the very idea from his mind.

"Don't tempt me," he told her with a wicked gleam in his eyes.

"You never answered my questions," she responded.

"Didn't I?" Trik didn't try to hide the smugness on his face.

"You were just as lost as I was, Trik."

"I do not deny it beautiful, which is why I need to go. You test my resolve, Cassandra. I will be back. I will always come back for you." As he started to walk away from her he turned back, continuing to walk backwards. "Oh and if that boy touches you, I'll rip off his arms."

Cassie's mouth dropped open, but he was out of sight before she could respond.

"He threatened to rip Todd's arms off?" Elora asked Cassie as they walked into the backroom of Lisa's shop. Cassie had drifted through the rest of the day unable to think about school or anything that didn't have to do with a certain dark elf.

Cassie nodded.

"Was he serious?"

Cassie looked at her friend, raising a single eyebrow. "Did you really ask me if a dark elf, who kills for a living, was serious about ripping someone's arms off?"

Elora hopped up onto a counter that ran along the back of the room.

"Good point," she conceded as she leaned back and against the cold, concrete wall behind her.

"So he didn't tell you what he had to do that was so important?"

"Nope, he kissed me crazy and then left saying he'd be back," Cassie explained.

"Was the kiss before or after he threatened to dismember Todd?"

"Who's getting dismembered?" Lisa asked as she pushed the door open.

"I don't know what should bother me more," Elora looked at her mom, "the fact that you respond so calmly to us talking about someone being dismembered or that you are wearing that terrible shade of pink." She paused as if to think about it. "I take that back; it's definitely that Pepto pink that bothers me more."

Lisa shook her head. "We can't all pull off the 'dark and mysterious' look as well as you do, Elora."

"This is true," Elora agreed.

"So I ask again," Lisa took a seat across from Cassie and crossed one leg over the other. "Who is being dismembered?"

"No one," Cassie exhaled loudly. "Trik just made a comment that if a boy touched me…".

"Todd," Elora interrupted.

Cassie shot her a glare.

Elora shrugged. "Details are important when you're dealing with a dark elf."

"How would you know?" Cassie shot back.

"Call it instincts," Elora answered.

"Todd…," Lisa spoke trying to get Cassie's attention back.

"Right, Todd. He's this guy that Trik thinks is interested in me because he passed me a note in class."

"What did it say?" Lisa asked curiously.

"Ah, I don't know," Cassie said slapping her back pocket. "I completely forget about it. What the…? The note's gone! That sneaky elf took it somehow when he had me distracted."

"Distracted how?" Lisa narrowed her eyes at Cassie.

"With his charming personality," Elora retorted. "His lips mother, with his lips," she quickly added rolling her eyes.

Lisa made an "o" movement with her mouth as she continued to watch Cassie, who was turning a bright shade of red.

Lisa slapped her thighs as she stood up. "Well, he is something to look at, so I can't say I blame you."

"Lisa!" Elora exclaimed. "Please don't ever say something like that in my presence again. I swear I just threw up in my mouth."

"Oh please, he's older than dirt. It's not like I'm being a pedophile."

"So not the point," Elora muttered.

Lisa shrugged off Elora's sharp tone. "I've got to run, girls. Cassie, I want you to be careful. Hopefully the Light Elf King has called off his dogs by now. But Trik has probably made a lot of enemies over the centuries. Take it slow and watch your back. Don't forget who you are dealing with, no matter how charming he is."

"Don't worry," Cassie answered, her voice mirroring the pain on her face. "I won't."

Chapter 6

"I want to give her the world. I want to fall at her feet and declare all the ways that I love her. I can't. She deserves so much more than me. I should walk away; I should let her go. I can't. I know how to kill a man eight different ways with my bare hands. I have power greater than any human can imagine. I lead an army more powerful than any other in existence, and yet I can't walk away from a mere human girl. But then she isn't just a human, she is my Chosen. She is mine and I refuse to give her up." ~Triktapic

Trik pushed through the revolving glass door of the tall building that housed the realty company Lorsan had chosen to deal with. They had finally found land that would be compatible with the soil from their realm, soil that was needed in order to grow the Almare plants.

Lorsan had asked the realty company to find five hundred acres of the richest and deepest soil in the United States, and so they had—San Joaquin Valley, located in Southern California. The valley is among the richest soil in the world, perfect for what they needed. Very little of the land was actually for sale, but that did not deter Lorsan. When he set his eyes on something, there was nothing that could stand in his way. The agents had found some six hundred acres that was owned by a couple of winemakers, currently being used as a large vineyard. Lorsan had offered a sick amount of money and the owners had finally caved.

Trik stood in the quiet elevator, riding up to the fifteenth floor. He wore his human guise once again, allowing himself to be seen by humans. When the elevator opened a woman was standing, waiting for her turn to get on. She froze as he stepped out, her eyes filling with desire. He was used to the effect that he had on women and usually he would have toyed a bit with her, but he hardly noticed her as he passed. His heart was spoken for, his mind forever captivated by a single thought—Cassie.

He didn't bother to stop at the reception desk, but walked right past her and opened the door to the realtor's office. He stepped in and shut it behind him.

"Trik," a disheveled man in his early forties stood, abruptly dumping the papers that had been in his lap into the floor. His cheeks were flushed, but not for any reason other than it was the way his skin was always colored, as if there was something in his life forever embarrassing him and he was convinced the world knew about it. He was going bald, and not gracefully so. His eyes appeared beady behind his thick, coke bottle glasses. His ears stuck out too far on his large head and his lips stayed in a puckered state as if he was sucking on a lemon.

The man wore a suit that looked as if it had been picked up off the floor and hastily thrown on. As he stepped around his desk, Trik noticed that his pants were an inch too short and he was wearing white socks with his brown, wrinkled suit. The man held his hand out to Trik. Though it was a human tradition to shake hands when meeting,

Trik looked at the man's hand and then back up into his beady eyes. When he realized that Trik had no intention of taking his offered hand, the man quickly dropped it to his side.

"Hello, Leon," Trik said finally after having made the poor man twitch nervously under his scrutinizing stare. "I have come to sign the papers and finalize the sale."

"Yes, yes, of course," Leon seemed to gather himself and rushed around his desk, searching through the mess. He finally found the papers he was looking for and handed them to Trik.

"Just sign wherever the lines are highlighted." Leon told him as he held out a pen.

Trik reluctantly took the pen from the realtor, not bothering to hide his repulsion at having to touch it.

He quickly read through the documents and signed at the appropriate locations. He handed the papers back to Leon.

"So, are we done?" Trik asked.

"Yes, Lorsan has already transferred the money to the sellers. The land is now yours to take possession of," Leon answered.

As Trik turned to leave and his hand reached for the door handle, Leon spoke again.

"You don't seem like the vineyard owning type, Mr. Trik," Leon said nervously. "Why did you want this land so badly, if you don't mind me asking?"

Trik turned the door handle and pushed the door open. "I do mind you asking. Consider yourself warned," he told the realtor. Trik turned towards him as he began to shut the door. Trik narrowed his eyes and let just a little of his power loose. "Do not dig into my business Leon, you will not like the results."

Leon nodded and let out a small whining sound.

Trik smiled to himself as he left the office and then the building. He fed off the power he held over humans like Leon, so easily intimidated. His fear was a stench in the air, his seemingly meaningless existence a waste of air. He frowned at himself and his thoughts as he walked down the sidewalk and rounded a corner to a quieter street. For the first time he could ever remember, he was bothered by how he felt, how he enjoyed causing fear in another. For the first time, he felt guilt over his behavior and he knew why. The idea of Cassie seeing him act in such a way was repulsive. Knowing how disappointed and hurt she would be by his actions and words halted him in his tracks. How was he going to do this? How was he going to be who she needed *and* who his King needed? He turned and found that he was standing in front of a murky window, in a building that was empty and dark. He looked at his reflection, at the human guise he wore, and he was repulsed by what he saw.

He had planned to go back to Cassie but he couldn't see her, not like this. So he headed for a place where he knew that he could lose himself.

He stepped out of one of the many mirrors in Sanctuary. The blaring music assaulted him and he let the darkness and pleasure wrap itself around him. He walked out onto the dance floor and two steps later felt a warm body press itself against his back. Firm arms wrapped around his neck. He knew who it was even before she whispered in his ear.

"Been a long time, lover. Where've you been hiding?" Ziana's voice was a purr against his skin.

There was a time when that would have done something to him, but not anymore, and that pissed him off. With Ziana, he could be who and what he was. He didn't have to change or fight his nature. With Ziana, he could give into the darkness. He lifted his arm and wrapped his hand around the nape of her neck and pulled her around to stand in front of him. He didn't like anyone at his back, especially her. She stepped closer so that their bodies were touching again.

Trik looked down into her yellow eyes. She was breathtakingly beautiful. A human male would fall and worship at her feet if only to receive a tiny morsel from her fingertips. She had a body made for sin and there was a time that Trik had given into that body.

She took his hands and placed them on her hips and he instinctively drew her closer. She pressed her lips to his neck. Just before he closed his eyes to try and enjoy the sensation, they met the piercing gaze of Syndra. If looks could torture, Trik would be writhing in pain in a puddle of his own blood. She made her way towards them as Trik continued to hold Ziana against him, her lips still moving against his neck.

Syndra's eyes narrowed as she walked towards Trik. She had come to Sanctuary simply to observe him, to see if the dark assassin was changing his playboy ways since he had found his Chosen. Though she had originally planned to remain unseen, what she saw made her reveal her presence. She had to remind Triktapic that he was no longer a free elf, even if the other elves saw the Light Elf Queen in the dark elf Sanctuary.

As Syndra stepped up to him, her power rushed through the room as she took the dark she-elf by the hair and ripped her from Trik's grasp. The room came to a standstill and suddenly everyone but Trik, Ziana, and Syndra were on their knees. Syndra held a writhing Ziana in her hand, high enough that her feet did not touch the ground.

"You would defile yourself with this filth after you have found your Chosen?" Syndra's words were knives across his skin.

Ziana stopped struggling instantly and glared at Trik.

Syndra turned to look at the she-elf. "That's right you two-bit hussy, he is no longer his own. He belongs to another and has no business putting his hands on you."

"He makes his own choices," Ziana spat back.

Syndra, in a rare show of anger, threw Ziana across the room, not bothering a second glance at the crashing sound of her body hitting the wall. She turned back to Trik and once again settled that powerful gaze on him.

"What do you think it would do to her if she knew you held another in your arms?"

Trik didn't answer. He knew what it would do. It would destroy the fragile relationship they had built in the short amount of time they had known each other.

"How do you think your Chosen would feel to know another woman's lips had been on your neck? How do you think your Chosen would handle knowing that you CHOSE to hold another?" Syndra was yelling and the air whipped around her as she released her royal power.

"She doesn't need to know," Trik growled.

Syndra laughed and it was so angry that Trik wondered if had really come from the lips of a light elf.

"She has a right to know what or who her *Sh'mai* is doing." Trik stepped back as if she had slapped him.

"A simple dance is not comparable to sharing one's bed." His lips tightened as he met the Light Queen's eyes.

"And if it had been Cassie in another's arms, with his lips pressed to her skin, his body pressed against hers?" Syndra knew she was playing with fire as she taunted the dark elf assassin, but she cared not. She had grown to like his Chosen and she found herself wanting to see Trik happy for once in his long life. She didn't want the idiot to screw it up, and hopefully he hadn't. But Syndra had every intention of telling Cassie what had transpired here. She had a right to know. She needed to know all the facts about Trik before she made a decision to commit to the dark elf, even if those facts were unbelievably painful.

Trik shook with rage as he pictured the words Syndra had spoken. Cassandra in the arms of another, possibly that idiot, Todd. He knew what he would do; he would kill him, and anyone who dared touch her.

Syndra saw the emotions flash across his face, saw him battling the anger.

"You know as well as I do that I am no good for her. She deserves someone who doesn't have the blood of a thousand men on his hands," he snarled at her.

"You are missing the point. It is not about what she deserves or about what you deserve. It is about what *is*. For whatever reason, the Forest Lords have given you a Chosen as pure as fresh fallen snow, untainted by mud, dirt, or the tracks of others. You have been given a gift and gifts are not always deserved, but they should always be accepted. It is not wise Triktapic to throw a gift back in the face of the Forest Lords." Her words were left ringing in the air, and in a rush of wind, the Light Elf Queen was gone.

Trik had heard that the most powerful of elves could travel in their realm without mirrors, but hearing about it and seeing it happen before his eyes were two very different things. The room slowly began to return to life as the music started again and elves stood from their kneeling positions.

He turned to leave, no longer in the mood for the company of others. As he made his way through the crowd, his eyes met Ziana's. She had already moved on and was swaying in the arms of another male. The look she gave him was full of contempt, but he couldn't find it in himself to care.

Cassie stared up at her ceiling as she lay on her bed. She put her phone down after checking the time for at least the hundredth time in the last half hour. She had helped her mom cook dinner, helped with the dishes, and even done a load of laundry in hopes of keeping her mind off of Trik and his whereabouts. Now she had nothing left to do. She picked up her phone again and looked at it, 9:01. One minute later than the last time she had checked. In a fit of frustration, she threw her phone across her room but instead of the thud she expected to hear as the phone hit the wall she heard a voice instead.

"A little upset?"

Cassie shot up out of her bed.

"Syndra?" Her words came out breathless as she tried to calm her beating heart after having been startled by the elf's sudden appearance.

"Last I checked," she told her as she held out her phone. Cassie took it quickly and stepped back just as quickly.

"Are you afraid of me Cassie?" Syndra asked.

"Should I be?"

"No," Syndra shook her head. "I am not your enemy, quite the opposite actually." Syndra made a slow perusal of the room and then turned her stare back on Cassie.

"I need to speak with you."

Cassie heard the ominous tone in the Queen's voice.

"I should sit down, shouldn't I?" Cassie asked as a wave of nervousness rolled through her.

"That might be best," agreed Syndra.

"I-i-is he alive?" Cassie stuttered as she asked a question she feared the answer to as much as she wanted to know.

"Oh he is quite alive," Syndra's words came out dripping with contempt.

"But?" Cassie implored.

"But I'm afraid you might want to kill him once I share this information with you. I hate to be the one to deliver it, but I feel you have a right to know."

Cassie waited in silence. She hoped that everything she was imagining would be much worse than what the Queen was about to tell her.

It wasn't.

"I found him at a place called Sanctuary. It's the equivalent to a club here in your realm, but more than that. It's a place where our kind can gather without fear of assassination attempts or petty skirmishes. It's a peaceful place."

"What was he doing there?" Cassie didn't want to know. But like driving up on a horrible car wreck that she knew she shouldn't look at, she asked despite herself.

"He was dancing," Syndra answered meaningfully.

Cassie's eyes narrowed. "With whom?"

"Another elf."

"Good freaking grief. Syndra. Spit it out already," Cassie growled, unmindful of the fact that the woman before her could squash her like an insignificant bug.

"With a onetime lover from his past," Syndra finally finished.

Cassie didn't know whether she was more angry or hurt. She had spent her day wondering if he was okay, eager to see him again and he had been hooking up with one of his flings. Okay, at the moment, she was more angry. Correction, she was livid.

She stood and began to pace.

"After all his b.s. about me being his Chosen and him never letting me go and kissing me like his freaking, pathetic life depended on it. That lying, fraudulent, piece of, argh!"

Syndra tried not to grin, but couldn't stop herself. Even in anger Trik's Chosen kept a semblance of purity. Her anger was righteous anger. Trik deserved her wrath and her scorn, but even as the words left Cassie's mouth, Syndra watched her deflate like a leaky balloon.

Cassie sunk to the ground, ignoring the sharp pain that radiated up her legs from her knees hitting the floor. She looked up at Syndra, who had genuine compassion shining through her eyes.

"Why? Why would he do that?" Cassie's voice was small and she struggled to keep it from wavering.

"Why does he think it's his choice who *I'm* with? Since when am I not my own person that I can't decide for myself?" Cassie slapped the floor in frustration. "If I want to be with an evil, dark, butthead of an elf, then that is my choice. MINE!" She hit her hand against her chest in emphasis.

"I totally agree, Cassie, which is why I came." Syndra knelt down so that she was eye level with her. "Don't give up on him. I know you are angry and you have every right to be. But try and see things from his point of view. I'm not excusing his behavior, and he will have to answer to you for it. But he is old, and has lived a long time in darkness. It will take time for him to see that not all is lost in him. He needs you just as you need him."

Cassie watched as Syndra stood and walked towards her window.

"It is ultimately your choice, Cassandra. Make sure it is the right one." She stepped through the window as easily as if it were open and was gone.

Cassie didn't know how long she sat on her floor. She was still trying to get her mind around the fact that the same guy who had held her and kissed her so passionately had been in the arms of another hours later. She finally stood and went through the motions of getting ready for bed.

As she lay in the dark in her room, silent tears slipped down her cheeks as she let the pain of loss engulf her.

Days passed and still Cassie heard nothing from Trik. She refused
to talk about it, though Elora continued to ask. Every night she lay in
her bed and her heart seemed to break all over again. She wondered
why she wasn't experiencing the horrific pain that she had that first
time that he had left. When she realized why she began to cry even
harder. If she wasn't hurting, it could only mean one thing, Trik didn't
want to be with her. He wasn't forcing himself to stay away. He really
didn't want to be with her.

It had been exactly one month since the night Syndra had come to
Cassie and told her of Trik's hurtful actions. Four weeks of anger, hurt,
and longing, but still he didn't come.

Trik watched as his brethren brought barrel after barrel of the
powerful soil from his realm into the human world. They spread it out
over the valley, covering the soil where the vineyard had been. They
continually mixed it, so their own soil seeped down into the earth.
Even now as he watched over the wishes of his King, he thought of
her. Pain and anger radiated through him. At times, when her own
anger and pain sought him out, he nearly stumbled under their
oppression. Others avoided him at all costs, recognizing the danger

they put themselves in if they were near him. He didn't care. He didn't care about anything anymore. He was simply doing his duty. Lorsan gave his orders and Trik obeyed. He didn't sleep for fear of seeing her face. He never remained idle, knowing that if he stopped for one second, he would go running back to her, begging her forgiveness. He knew that was the wrong thing to do. She didn't need him. And she surely couldn't want him anymore, not after what he had done.

Trik walked through the fields, inspecting one of the solar panels that he'd had installed throughout the property. The panels were to serve as direct passageways from their realm to the crops, making it easy for the elves to harvest what they needed. As he stood up from his inspection, for the first time in more weeks than he could count, he knew that he heard her voice.

"Trik," she called to him.

Their souls were forever connected and everything in him longed to answer his Chosen. The pain he felt at hearing her say his name drove him to his knees. He clutched his chest as he felt his heart constrict and the breath rush from his lungs. His soul reached out through him, grasping at the voice and Trik realized that it wasn't Cassie speaking his name, it was her soul. Her very soul was crying out to him.

"Why do you call and not her?" His own soul asked earnestly.

"Her heart attempts to move on." Cassie's soul was filled with anguish and disgust at the idea of another.

Trik understood what her soul was saying. Cassie was with someone else. Rage, unbidden, pure, and blinding crashed into and out of him. He felt the fear of those around him but didn't care how his power was affecting them. All he could focus on was Cassie. He thought of her in detail, allowing his soul to reach out even more so that they could find her. He stepped through the solar panel and into a bathroom.

Cassie dressed in what she had deemed the sluttiest butterfly, if butterflies could be sluts, costume she could find. She stood next to Elora, who was wearing the next sluttiest butterfly costume she could find. Elora's costume was only second to Cassie's because Cassie's boobs were bigger. Music pulsed around them and black lights made everything glow eerily.

"I can't believe I let you talk me into this costume," Cassie yelled over the music.

"Give me a break. You look hot. Todd can't keep his eyes off you," Elora yelled back.

"Or his hands," Cassie muttered. She glanced around the room, looking between the swaying bodies and past the make out sessions to see if she could find the host of this year's anticipated Halloween bash, and to her chagrin, her date.

"Where did octopus arms run off to anyways?" Cassie leaned in close to Elora's ear this time so she didn't have to yell.

"I think he and Sam went to get us drinks," Elora answered.

Elora had talked her into being Todd's date to the party, after giving her a lecture that a month with no word from the *cowardice, feeble excuse for a dark elf assassin, emphasis on the ass,* was long enough to mope over and to get her ass up, Elora's words.

So here Cassie stood in a room full of blaring music and scantily clad Halloween costumes, waiting for a guy she didn't like to bring her a drink she didn't want. "Happy freaking Halloween to me," Cassie muttered under her breath just as she felt an arm slip around from behind her.

"Got my girl a drink." Cassie felt Todd's breath against her neck and tried not to cringe at the unwanted sensation. He smelled of sweat and beer. She took the drink from him and slyly slid from his arm as she turned to look at him.

"Great party," Cassie yelled over the music.

Todd nodded. "It's even bigger than the one I had last year."

Cassie smiled over the rim of her cup as she took a small sip. She tried not to cough as the burn of the alcohol hit her throat. She had told herself that after that one sip she wouldn't take another, especially after she tasted just how much alcohol Todd had poured into it, but the more Todd talked the more her hand seemed to raise the cup to her mouth. Cassie hoped that she was nodding in all the right places as she tried to listen to him, but found it increasingly difficult as her brain began to get foggy. Finally someone yelled Todd's name and he excused himself.

Cassie's shoulders slumped in exhaustion. Who knew how tiring it would be to fake interest in a conversation?

Elora nudged her as Todd walked away. "You awake?"

"Am I that obvious?" Cassie asked.

"An unbiased observer might say that you would rather watch paint dry than spend time with your date."

Cassie groaned, "His voice is just so, so…".

"Not Trik's?" Elora finished.

"Exactly," Cassie paused. "What? No, no, that's not what I was going to say." She frowned at Elora. "He's just not someone that I'm attracted to. He's so Todd-ish," she finished lamely.

"Todd-ish?" Elora raised her eyebrows at her friend. "How much alcohol did he put in that drink?"

"Not enough," Cassie grumbled.

Elora laughed. "I've never seen you plastered Cassie. This might be exactly what I need."

"What you need? What about what I need?" Cassie whined.

Elora was looking over Cassie's shoulder when she finally responded.

"Oh you're about to get what you need." She shot back the rest of the contents of her cup and then grabbed Cassie by the shoulders and turned her around.

Cassie's mouth dropped open when she saw what Elora had been watching.

Trik, in all his tall, pitch black hair, Elfin glory, had Todd by the throat. The room was frozen, though the music continued to rip through the air. Cassie felt like she was moving in slow motion as she moved across the room. It felt like an eternity before she finally reached them.

"Trik?" Cassie blinked at him, confused at his sudden appearance, and the fact that he was holding Todd by the throat.

"Or treat?" Elora asked as she stepped up next to Cassie.

Cassie realized then just how much she had had to drink because she snorted at Elora's comment. Elora's lips twitched at her friend but Trik's eyes narrowed.

"Are you intoxicated?" He asked, his scowl deepening.

Cassie scowled back. "No. Maybe." She paused, thinking, and then finally nodded, "definitely."

They continued to glare at each other. Elora finally cleared her throat.

"So, hate to interrupt the death stare, but your victim is turning blue." She motioned with a nod of her head towards Todd. "I didn't know if you were intending to kill him in front of all these witnesses or not."

Trik broke the stare with Cassie and turned back to Todd.

"Stay away from her," he growled

Todd made a small nodding motion with his head. Trik finally let go of him and Todd stumbled back. Cassie moved to help him but Trik intercepted her and the intensity of his silver eyes made her freeze. Trik looked away from her to the rest of the room. Suddenly it was quiet. Somehow, the music just stopped. She heard the room gasp and Cassie realized for the first time that she saw him in his natural form and, judging by the reactions around her, so did everyone else. He looked around the room and, in a voice as cold as the air had become, he spoke.

"Get. Out."

No one had to be told twice. They were up and moving, a stampede of humans, all trying to stay as far from Trik as possible.

Trik looked at Elora when she made no motion to leave and Elora folded her arms across her chest, a clear challenge that if he wanted her to leave then he would have to physically remove her. Cassie, even in her inebriated state, knew that she needed to intervene. She stepped in between Trik and Elora just as Trik took a step towards her best friend.

"What do you want?" Cassie met his stare and though she wanted to back away from the fury she saw there, she held her ground. She felt Elora standing at her back.

Trik laughed and it was so evil that her skin crawled.

"What do I want?" He snarled. "I want to know why my Chosen is drunk, half-dressed, and with another male?"

Cassie looked down, remembering her skimpy Halloween outfit. She turned to look back at Elora who shrugged. "How the hell was I supposed to know he was going to show up?"

Cassie's head swung back around to Trik. She mimicked Elora's shrug. "Too bad."

Trik gestured impatiently. "Too bad what?"

"Too bad, so sad," Cassie snorted out laughter at her words.

Elora patted her on the back trying to cover her own laughter. "Hold it together a little longer lightweight."

Trik still looked confused and that made Cassie laugh harder. She wiped her eyes as she began to calm down.

"Too bad, we don't always get what we want Trik," Cassie felt herself begin to sober just a little at the memory of what Syndra had told her. "I didn't want to hear about you touching another woman but you know what, Trik, I didn't get what I wanted. I didn't want to hear about another woman putting her lips on your neck or about how you let her, but that's exactly what I heard, so you don't get to know why I'm dressed like a slutty butterfly or why I'm smashed or why I let Todd put his arms around my waist." She paused, she could practically see the steam rising from Trik's head. "And you don't get to know if I would have stopped him from shoving his tongue down my throat."

Cassie felt Elora lean close behind her. "You were doing great 'til that last part."

"Too much?" Cassie whispered.

"A teensie bit," Elora told her, holding her hand up to indicate with her fingers the small amount.

Cassie folded her arms across her chest as she glared at a very pissed off dark elf assassin.

"I think you need to leave," Cassie motioned toward the door.

"I'm leaving," he started to walk past her, but then grabbed her hand at the last minute, "but not without you." He didn't break stride as he pulled her behind him and right through the living room window. Cassie heard Elora's voice behind her and then silence.

They emerged on the other side in a dark, lush bedroom. Candles lit the room and bathed it in a soft glow. She jerked her arm from his grasp and ignored his glare as she looked around at her surroundings.

"Where are we?" She asked as she looked at the large, ornate wood bed with a black comforter and a ridiculous amount of pillows strewn across it. Her eyes continued to roam the room. There was a large fireplace along one wall. A fire suddenly flickered to life in it. Her eyes widened but she refused to be impressed. Along another wall was a large desk and built in above and around the desk was a bookshelf that lined the entire wall and around the rest of the room. The floor was hardwood and a white, fluffy rug lay in front of the large bed. Finally, having no other place to look she met his eyes.

"What do you want Trik?" She asked trying hard not to slur her words.

"You. And you want me." He told her in his usual confidence unbothered by her anger.

"No I don't. Did you not just see that I was on a date, and it wasn't with you?"

He took a menacing step towards her but Cassie knew that he would never hurt her.

"It would be wise, if you wish for Todd to live, to not bring him up again."

Cassie rolled her eyes. "Fine, whatever. Can I go now?"

"We are far from done, Cassie. You called for me."

She laughed. "In your dreams."

Trik smiled. She could tell that he knew something that she didn't. Something about his smile told her that she wasn't going to like it.

"Your soul did not like you touching another. It called to me. It called so loudly and with so much pain that it brought me to my knees." Trik didn't gloat, he simply stated the facts. Somehow that made Cassie even angrier.

"Well my soul is a dumbass who loves to be tortured." Cassie decided to chalk that off as the alcohol talking but went ahead and went with it.

Trik moved slowly towards her and Cassie began to back away. She was being stalked by a predator, a very patient predator that was used to catching his prey.

Her butt hit something and she turned, only to realize that he had backed her against his bed. She closed her eyes and chanted to herself, *stupid, stupid, stupid.* When she opened her eyes, Trik stood mere inches from her. She felt his warm breath on her face. When he took another step closer, their bodies were touching. She could feel his heart beating against hers. He raised a hand and stroked her cheek gently. Though she tried not to, she leaned into his touch and nearly whimpered when his lips touched her ear.

"I'm sorry," he whispered. The warm breath brought goose bumps to her skin. She shivered.

"I'm so, so sorry," he whispered again. The sincerity in his voice pounded against the floodgates she had so carefully barricaded inside. Like a damn bursting open, a sob wrenched from her chest and the tears began to flow freely. She hit his chest over and over. She knew that the alcohol was probably making her even more emotional but she was beyond caring.

"Why? Why would you do that to me? How could you touch her? How could you let her kiss you?"

"Because I'm an idiot, *A'maelamin*. Please, I beg of you. Forgive me." Trik pulled back so that he could look into her tear stained face. The pain and betrayal that he saw there tore a hole inside him. He fell to his knees in front of her.

"Please Cassie. Please forgive me."

"How do I ever trust you again?" She wiped tears from her face, smearing her black mascara while trying to regain her composure. She stared down into his silver eyes and gave in to the urge to touch him. She traced a finger across his forehead and down his cheek. Trik closed his eyes and let out a desperate breath.

"*Arwenamin,* I've missed you," he told her but she only understood the last part.

"You hurt me Trik."

"I know, baby. I know I did." He wrapped his arms around her and pressed his face to her stomach. He breathed in her scent and pulled her closer. He had tried to do what he thought was right. He had tried to let her go, but he knew now that it was impossible. Neither could live without the other. Their souls would slowly begin to die until they were empty shells, like the leftover skin of a locust.

"I thought I was doing what you needed," he told her, his voice muffled in her clothes.

She pulled his face back and looked at him. "You don't make my decisions for me. It's my choice if I want to be with you."

Trik nodded once. "And do you? Want to be with me?"

Another tear escaped as he stood and looked down at her. He took her face in his large hands. As he looked into the face of her broken heart, he felt the first tear he'd shed in over a millennia slide down his own face.

"Yes," she whispered. That simple word made Trik's soul sing.

He pulled her to him and took her lips in a kiss that was nearly violent. He swept his tongue against her lips and she whimpered as she opened her mouth. Their tongues met and Trik slowed the kiss, enjoying the way she tasted. He walked her back and continued pressing until she lay on his bed. Cassie felt her fake wings crushed beneath her, but quickly pushed them from her mind as he climbed over her and slowly laid his body on top of hers. He felt her tremble underneath him and he smiled when his soul answered her own. The connection that drew them became so powerful that Trik wasn't sure where one began and the other ended.

Cassie felt Trik wrap an arm around her, pulling her body closer to his. She wrapped her arms around his neck and held on with everything she had, afraid that at any moment she would wake up and discover this had all been a dream. She gasped as his other hand slid down her hip to the back of her thigh and he pulled her leg up, bending it at the knee as he wrapped it around him. Cassie tilted her head back when he pulled away from her lips and began to kiss her jaw and then her neck. She moaned without shame as his tongue traced her collarbone. He nipped it with his teeth and she jumped beneath him drawing a chuckle from Trik. She leaned forward and bit his shoulder in retaliation and smiled to herself when he groaned. He pulled back and looked down at her. His hair falling over his shoulder created a dark curtain around them, closing them into their own private world.

"I don't deserve a second chance," he told her as he traced her brow.

"No, you don't," she agreed. "But I'm giving you one. Don't screw it up."

Trik grinned and Cassie's heart jumped at the innocence that she saw there, an innocence she'd not seen in Trik before.

When he spoke again his words were in his own tongue and the beauty of it took her breath away.

"What did you just say?"

Trik blushed. He actually blushed. "You are my everything, the very breath I breathe, the water I drink, the food I eat; you are all that I need, all that I want and all that I am is yours."

Cassie's heart constricted in her chest and she felt something deep inside her burst forward and she knew what it was—her soul.

"I feel like I want to crawl inside of you, Trik, like I can't get close enough," she confessed.

Trik stroked her face, unable to keep from touching her. "I know the feeling," he murmured.

"Will it always be like this, so intense?"

Trik's eyes continued to roam over her face as his fingers ran through her hair. He leaned down and pressed a gentle kiss to her lips and whispered against them. "Hmmm, some of that might be the liquor." Cassie slapped his arm and he chuckled but then sobered and added. "From what I understand it grows deeper and stronger."

Cassie groaned. "I can't imagine feeling any stronger than I do now."

Trik smiled. "I can."

Cassie saw a wicked gleam in his silver eyes. "Do I want to know?"

He chuckled. "Well I imagine it's something that we are going to have to talk about at some point."

Cassie's brow furrowed, "What are you talking about?"

He leaned forward until his lips were against her ear. He let out a slow breath and the warmth caressed her skin. She trembled and Trik pulled her closer to him.

"A bed is not made only for sleeping, Cassandra," he whispered and then she felt his tongue dart out and flick across her ear.

She was dazed for a moment and the meaning behind his words hit her. She couldn't breathe as she considered what he was saying.

Trik pulled back so that he could look at her face. He had to admit he was enjoying the fact that he had shocked her, probably a little more than he should be enjoying it.

"Breathe Cassie," he told her gently. "We don't have to go there until you are ready and sober."

"I um, well that is that, you see it's like," she stumbled over her words, as she tried not to be embarrassed by the topic.

"I never intended to go *there* until I was married," she finally told him with only a moderate amount of blushing.

The smile that spread across his lips was dazzling and made her momentarily lose her train of thought.

"So you've never lain with another male?"

"If by *lain* you are speaking in the Biblical sense, then no, I have not."

Trik watched her carefully. Relief he hadn't realized he would feel at the information bloomed in his chest.

"Just to be clear," he began again. "You've never...".

Cassie groaned. "Good grief Trik, do I need to spell it out?"

He nodded.

"I've never had sex. Are you happy now?"

"Unbelievably so," he told her as he nuzzled her neck.

She pushed at his shoulder. "What about you?" She asked as his eyes met hers. She saw them darken and was surprised to see shame in them. Her heart fell, though she didn't know why she had been expecting a different answer. The guy was possibly so old that he had a dinosaur for a pet.

She looked away and tried not to be hurt.

"I'm sorry, baby." Trik gently took her chin and turned her face back towards him. "I never even considered that I would ever have a Chosen."

"It's fine, really. I don't know why I expected any other answer."

"They meant nothing," Trik told her desperately imploring her to understand. He didn't want to hurt her but he could see that he had.

Cassie wondered as she looked up at him, the worry in his eyes, if maybe she was rushing into something that she would later regret. Maybe she should date more before she committed to something so permanent. Maybe she needed to have other experiences with other guys. Trik's fingers brushed her skin and when his face darkened, she knew he had seen what she had been thinking.

"I will give you any experience you are curious about." His words were harsh but his hands continued to be gentle. His voice softened as he continued. "Besides, I assure you that any experience with another would never hold a candle to what I can give you."

Cassie blushed again knowing what he was talking about—
pleasure.

"Awe my sweet lótë, you are correct. I will one day, when we are, what did you say? Married? Yes, when we are married I will give you such pleasure that you will never want to leave our bed."

Cassie gasped as she slapped his shoulder. "You can't say things like that."

"Why, I speak only truth," he told her matter of fact like. He rolled over quickly, pulling her with him so that she was on top of him. "So when do we get married? Soon I hope."

Cassie laughed. "Hold on there, tiger. I haven't even graduated from high school."

"What does that have to do with us getting married?" He asked genuinely confused.

"Well, most girls don't get married in high school unless they get knocked up, and to get knocked up you have to do the deed, which we are not."

"Knocked up?" Trik trailed his fingertips across her back causing her to arch into them. "What does that mean?"

Cassie had closed her eyes as she enjoyed the sensation of his touch.

"Cassie."

"Hmm," she answered as she continued to relish his fingers. Her eyes flew open when his hands pulled the back of her shirt up and began to trail his fingers over her again, only this time they were against her flesh.

"What does knocked up mean?" He asked again. Trik grinned as he watched his Chosen respond to his touch; a response that only he could pull from her.

"You have to stop touching me if you want me to be able to talk like a semi-intelligent person."

"Then I suppose you will just have to be unintelligent because I can never stop touching you."

Cassie groaned, but finally gathered her thoughts into a coherent sentence. "It means to get pregnant."

The idea of Cassie pregnant with his child flashed through his mind and he was surprised to find that it was a very welcome idea.

Cassie's eye's met his and widened.

"You caught that?" He asked her.

She nodded. "Trik, I'm not going to be ready for children for a while."

Trik took one of his hands from her back and pushed her hair way from her face and then rested his hand on the nape of her neck. "That is fine, we have plenty of time for that. Besides we will need lots of practice."

Cassie laughed. "You are such a guy." She rolled off of him, needing to put some space between their bodies.

"What does that mean?" He asked her as he moved to his side and propped himself up on his hand.

"It means you are like all guys," she told him as heat rose on her skin.

Trik cocked his head to the side. "Meaning?"

Cassie groaned as she looked up at his ceiling. "Meaning you like sex, a lot."

Trik laughed. "What male doesn't and if he doesn't it's because he's doing it wrong."

Cassie grabbed a pillow and hit him in the head with it. "Not a smart thing to say to your, your…" Cassie wasn't sure what to call herself.

"My Chosen Cassandra, you are my Chosen."

"Fine, Chosen. You should not admit to enjoying sex when it isn't with me."

"We need to get off of this bed and out of this room if you are going to start talking about us making love." Trik jumped up and grabbed Cassie's hand pulling her with him.

"Where are we going?"

"Don't you need to be home soon?" He asked her.

Cassie pulled her phone from her back pocket and looked at the time.

"Crap," she muttered. "I'm ten minutes late."

He began to pull her towards the mirror but she stopped.

"We can't just show up in my room."

Trik rolled his eyes. "I'm not an amateur at sneaking around, Cassie. We will go into your room and then I will get us down to your front door."

"Oh, right. I knew that." He began to pull her again and this time she allowed him to.

Elora stood in the kitchen with her mom. She had left the party as soon as Trik and Cassie had disappeared through Todd's window. She had called Cassie's phone twenty times trying to make sure that she was alright and still she had heard nothing from her best friend.

"What the hell, Lisa, why isn't she answering her phone?"

Her mom replied. "He won't hurt her."

"You did not see how angry he was. He nearly killed Todd." Elora slammed her hand down on the counter. "You need to call the Queen Bee and tell her to do something."

Lisa laughed. "Yeah, like she would just do something because I told her so."

"Do you have a way to get in touch with her?" Elora asked.

"Yes, she has a cell phone, believe it or not."

"So what are you waiting for, the elf apocalypse caused by the ass himself?"

"Elora, please quit being so dramatic. It's so unlike you." Lisa shook her head at her daughter.

"Dramatic? Seriously mother," Lisa's head snapped around, she knew Elora was upset because she only called her that when she was livid, "my best friend was abducted by a crazy ass, quiver carrying, too good looking for the health of women everywhere, dark elf assassin and you think I'm being dramatic."

Lisa's brow rose as her eyes widened. "He carries a quiver?"

"UGH!" Elora groaned. "That's all you have to say?"

"Well you have to admit that is an interesting tidbit."

"Why are you so calm about this?"

"Because I know that he won't hurt her," Lisa said again for the hundredth time.

"Okay, I hear that you are saying that you do not think he will hurt her. However, the evidence against his ability to stay in control is quite damning. So I would like to just lay out there, just as a suggestion, that maybe we should not trust the dark elf assassin who nearly killed my friend's date."

Lisa stared at her daughter as she picked up her cell phone and dialed a number.

"Syndra, I'm sorry to bother you but I have a little problem." Lisa held up her hand when Elora started to speak.

"Would I be correct in assuming that this problem has to do with a certain dark elf and your daughter's best friend?" Syndra asked.

"You would be correct," Lisa agreed. "Elora has told me that Trik showed up at a party where she, Cassie, and their dates were."

"Cassie was out on a date with a male?" Syndra's voice was full of concern.

"Is that a bad thing?" Lisa asked.

"The males of our race are very possessive of their Chosen. And because of the nature of the dark elf, they take that possessiveness to a whole new level. Did he kill the boy?"

"No, but according to Elora it was a close call."

There was a pause and Lisa waited for the Elf Queen to speak. When she finally did the voice came from behind her.

"Well."

Lisa and Elora jumped in surprise. Elora glared at Syndra. "Could you somehow announce your presence before you just walk through our window?"

Syndra clucked her tongue at her. "Testy aren't we? Nice outfit." She motioned to the costume Elora still hadn't taken off.

Lisa stepped in before Elora could respond.

"Do you think that Cassie is safe with Trik?"

Syndra leaned against the counter and tapped her chin with a long fingernail.

"Trik won't hurt her. She's his Chosen and he is, therefore, incapable of hurting her. Now, anyone that comes between them is fair game." She gave Elora a pointed look.

Elora held up her hands. "I'm not trying to go toe to toe with Mr. Bad Ass; I just want to know that my friend is ok."

"She's ok," Syndra responded.

Elora rolled her eyes and threw her hands in up in the air. "Well now that that is all cleared up."

"Why don't we all just go over to Cassie's house and see for ourselves if she is alright?" Syndra said with a wave as she walked through the same window she had arrived in.

Lisa was shaking her head at the Queen as she watched her go. "Can you imagine how much time we could save if we could do that?"

"Can you imagine how much easier it would be to sneak out of the house?" Elora responded with a smirk.

"Good point."

"I'm home," Cassie hollered into the house as she closed the door behind her and Trik.

"I don't know why you insist on meeting them now," she muttered to him.

Trik twirled a strand of her hair around his finger and Cassie slapped it away when she heard her mom coming down the stairs.

"Isn't it customary for the boy to meet the girl's parents?" He whispered in return.

Cassie started to respond but her mom came into the entryway. "Where have you…," she started to speak but then stopped midsentence as her eyes fell on Trik. Cassie watched as her mom took in the incredible masculine beauty that was Trik in his human guise.

When it was apparent that her mom wasn't going to stop any time soon, she snapped her fingers in front of her face.

"Mom, hey, I'm over here. Remember me, your daughter?"

Her mom blinked several times and finally looked over at Cassie. She cleared her throat as she tried to remember what she had been going to say.

"Yes, Cassie."

"Well, at least you remember my name," Cassie mumbled.

"You're late and who is this, this," Sylvia looked Trik over again as she tried to find the right word.

"This is Trik," Cassie interrupted. "He's…"

"I'm the boyfriend." Trik took Sylvia's hand and brought it to his lips, kissing it chastely and then quickly releasing it. "I can see where Cassie gets her beauty."

Sylvia colored. "Oh you're good, but not good enough for me to forget that my daughter is late and actually left with a different boy than she has arrived home with."

Cassie grimaced at her mother's tone. She turned to Trik and smiled. "So I'll talk to you later?"

"Is that a not so subtle hint of telling me to get lost?" Trik raised a single brow at her.

"Pretty much."

Trik leaned down and gave Cassie a quick kiss on the cheek and then a slight bow to her mother.

"It was very nice to meet you."

"Uh-huh," Sylvia was once again struck by his inhuman beauty and didn't snap out of it until the door finally blocked him from her view.

Sylvia's head snapped back around to Cassie.

"Who on earth was that?"

Cassie smiled nervously. "That was Trik."

"I got that much, Cassandra. But *who* is he, and where did you meet him, and how old is he, and how on earth is he that good looking?"

"Slow down mom," Cassie told her mom as she headed for the kitchen. She needed some caffeine to help clear more of the alcohol from her brain before she dove into this whopper of a lie she was about to have to get her mom to swallow.

"As I was saying," Cassie began again as she pulled a Coke from the refrigerator. "His name is Trik and I met him over a month ago at dad's work."

"Does he work in your dad's building?" Her mom asked.

Cassie took a quick sip of her drink as she tried desperately to come up with a plausible explanation for Trik being at her dad's work. "He's a courier for one of the offices in the building."

"How old is he?"

"He's 18, but he graduated last year. He was homeschooled," Cassie added.

Sylvia crossed her arms over her chest and stared at her daughter. Cassie could tell that her mom was deciding on whether to call her on her load of crap story or just let it go for now. Thankfully, it was the latter.

"Next time please call if you are going to be late and your father needs to meet Trik before you go out on a date with him again, or return from a date with him." Sylvia laughed at her words.

"Ha, ha, very funny," Cassie said dryly as she tossed her empty Coke can into the trash.

"I still don't understand how you left with Todd, but then came home with…"

"Hotty Mctotty?" Cassie grinned.

"Yes, I will agree, he is quite good looking."

"Mom, who would you come home with? Todd or that?" Cassie pointed in the direction Trik had exited and gave her mom a deadpan look.

"Well, despite how attractive Trik is, it wasn't nice of you to leave Todd out to dry," Sylvia chided.

"Oh I think Todd was quite glad that we left him," Cassie mumbled as she walked past her mom. "I'm calling it a night."

"Sleep well, honey," Sylvia grabbed Cassie in a quick hug. Cassie patted her mom's back. "Sorry I was late." She told her again, really meaning it.

"Just get some rest Cass," Sylvia told her with a final pat. "And don't think I didn't smell the alcohol on your breath. We'll talk about that later."

Chapter 7

Long ago, deep in the forest of Aldeon, the Forest Lords created a race full of magic, strength, intelligence, and cunning. This race divided itself into two factions. And so the light and dark elves came to be. The Forest Lords were not pleased by the division of their creation, and so they removed themselves, watching as they fought and destroyed one another. But the time has come for the Forest Lords to once again bring order and peace to their children, the time of the light and dark elves is over. The time of the Elfin is just beginning.

Lorsan felt his anger rising as he listened to the report from his second in command. He felt his Chosen's hand rest on his arm, an attempt to calm him. It wasn't working.

"You're telling me he left a week ago, you haven't heard from him since, and you are just now making me aware of this?" Lorsan gritted his teeth in frustration.

"My Liege," Alok said as he knelt before the Dark Elf King. "I thought he must be handling something for you and I didn't feel it my place to question. Trik has always come and gone as he pleased."

Lorsan paced the throne room as his mind raced. He had always allowed Trik more freedom than any in his army, but then Trik had never given him cause to question his loyalty. Trik had always done what he'd asked, always followed through, even if he did give Lorsan grief over just about everything; he still did as he was told. But that was before he had found his Chosen.

"Alok, how are the crops coming along?" Lorsan asked.

"They are growing well. The human soil seems to be mixing well with our own," Alok answered quickly, which irritated Lorsan further because he knew that Trik would have purposely dragged out the explanation, adding a few smart-ass comments of his own. Oddly enough he found that he preferred a contrary assassin to a cooperative one.

"When will the first batch be ready to harvest?"

"By the end of this week," he answered again with a no non-sense tone.

"That will be all," Lorsan dismissed the warrior.

"What of Triktapic, Liege?"

Lorsan's head snapped around and the look in his eyes made Alok step back.

"I will deal with Triktapic and you will make sure the first batch of Rapture is successful." Alok bowed and quickly made his way through one of the mirrors in the throne room.

"What is your plan?" Ilyrana asked once she and Lorsan were alone again.

Lorsan threw his hands in the air. "Of all my warriors, he was the one I would have bet my life would remain loyal."

"You don't know that he has defected yet," Ilyrana argued. "This *is* Trik we are speaking about, my King. He has always come and gone as he pleased but he has always returned."

"He has never gone so long without checking in with me or one of his warriors. Nor would he ever allow a project of this magnitude to go unsupervised for so long." Lorsan's eyes narrowed as he continued. "He is being distracted by his human at a time when I don't need him distracted."

"She is his Chosen."

"So he says," Lorsan cut his own Chosen off.

"So bring her here," Ilyrana challenged. "Let us see for ourselves that she really is his Chosen."

"What will that change?" Lorsan growled. "I still expect him to do his duty; I still expect his loyalty to be to me first."

"I agree with you, love. But maybe if Trik feels that we are welcoming her into our race, then he will not feel the need to stray."

Lorsan looked at his Chosen and was, once again, struck by her aptitude in forethought. He, more often than not, let his temper get the best of him while she remained cool and logical. He had decided long ago that this was why the Forest Lords had given her to him.

"So we shall have a banquet in honor of Triktapic's Chosen," Ilyrana told him with a smile.

"I can't decide if this plan in ingenious, or just your way of getting to throw a party," Lorsan chuckled, but felt his anger diminishing as he watched his Chosen.

"Maybe a little of both," she teased.

Trik sat in Cassie's room, waiting on her to come back upstairs. He thought about the past week that he had spent with her. They had only been apart when she was in class, with her parents, or in the bathroom. They had talked about anything and everything. His mind drifted off to one particular conversation that still troubled him.

They had been lying on her bed, her head on his stomach as he weaved his fingers in and out of her hair. She had looked up at him and asked him what his childhood had been like, what he had been like. It had been so very long since Trik had thought about his childhood, and the longer he had sat there trying to think of something to tell her, the harder it had been for him to even get a picture in his mind of what his childhood had been like.

"Very different from your childhood I think," he had told her.

"What do you mean *think*?" She had asked him.

Trik had pushed as hard as he could in his mind to form some thought of his childhood, but no memories came.

"I don't remember it," he had told her, his voice flat and devoid of emotion though inside he had felt like something was beginning to weaken, some wall that had been erected was beginning to falter in its hold.

"You don't remember anything about your childhood." Cassie's voice had been full of disbelief and sorrow.

"It's been a long time, Cassie. I am ancient, remember?"

He had teased her, trying to keep her from feeling bad for him, all the while, trying to shake off the uneasy feeling growing inside of him.

Trik sat up abruptly as the unwelcome pulling sensation drew him from his memories. He knew that sensation and it was one that he was beginning to dread. Lorsan was calling to him. He wasn't forcing him, but he was definitely summoning him.

Cassie's bedroom door opened and Trik stood quickly, closing the distance between them.

"What's wrong?" Cassie saw the frustration written across Trik's handsome features as he pulled her into his arms.

"Lorsan summons me; I must go."

"When will you be back?" She asked him calmly, pushing out any of the possibilities for which his King would be calling him.

"As soon as I can." Trik pulled back and looked down at her. "I don't suppose you can stay in your room until I come back for you?"

Cassie stifled her laughter into his shirt. When she looked up into his silver eyes, she saw worry there. "Trik, I can't just stay in my room when you aren't with me."

"Why not?" His brow furrowed in frustration. "I can't keep you safe when I'm not with you Cassie."

"There is nothing you need to keep me safe from."

"*A'maelamin,* I am the most feared assassin in the history of my race."

Cassie was surprised to hear no vanity in his tone. He was just stating the facts.

"I have taken more lives than you have probably met and pissed off double that amount. Believe me, there is plenty to keep you safe from. The news that I have found my Chosen is spreading quickly. You will soon become a target to anyone who wants to get to me."

Cassie started to speak but he cut her off with a firm kiss.

"Look, it's Saturday," he smoothed her hair back from her face as he looked down at her. "Just stay in your home until I get back. I won't be gone long."

"Fine," she said in exasperation as she stepped away from him and flopped onto her bed. "I'll wait for you here like a good little girl."

Trik grinned down at her and her heart nearly stopped at his Adonis look. The elf really was too good looking for his own good.

"I shall reward you accordingly." He leaned down over her, his hands on the mattress on either side of her head and pressed his lips to hers. Trik lingered over her, breathing in her scent and memorizing her taste.

"See you soon beautiful," he whispered against her lips. Cassie's eyes closed as she relished his closeness, but they opened as soon as she felt a soft breeze caress her face. She sat up and blinked as she looked around her room. Trik was gone.

She flung herself back on her bed with a groan. A whole Saturday stuck at home. "This is crap," she muttered to herself.

Her cell phone beeped. She grabbed it from her bedside table. It was a text from Elora.

E: U up?

C: Yep. Cassie texted back.

E: Quiver boy there?

C: Nope

E: Bored?

C: Yep

E: Go out?

C: QB says it's dangerous

E: So is breathing in the noxious fumes we call air. Point?

C: Well, when u put it that way

E: Can't argue with my logic

C: Uh, u mean can't argue with you period?

E: That too. So- u in?

C: Bring it.

E: That's my girl

Cassie grinned as she tossed her phone onto her bed. Elora to the rescue. It was good to have a friend who liked to stick it to the man, or to anyone for that matter.

"It's been a while, Triktapic." Lorsan waited for him in the large garden located behind the King's palace. Trik looked around as he entered the large garden and thought that it must look much like what humans described in their enchanted tales. Lush grass carpeted the ground. Tall trees with strong trunks and long branches covered in ornate leaves shaded the garden. Flowers in every color imaginable bloomed around them, tall, short, small, and large.

Trik smirked to himself, thinking that Cassie would ask why the dark elf castle was not actually dark, at least not on the outside. Regardless of the heart that lurked in Lorsan's chest, he still liked beautiful things and his garden was indeed beautiful.

"It's been a week, my Liege, hardly any time at all." Trik knelt before Lorsan knowing that it would both please and irk the King.

"A week since you have bothered to check on your duties," Lorsan's words were clipped and tight.

Trik continued to kneel. "Alok has it under control."

"How would you know? You haven't checked in with him in a week."

After a long pause, Trik stood, tired of playing the part. "I do not answer to Alok, and if he thinks that I am not keeping an eye on what is going on, then he is not the Second in Command that I thought he was." Trik's head snapped around to look at Lorsan.

"You know that I would not let such a project go unchecked. You honestly believe that in a week I have not laid eyes on the crops myself?" Trik didn't hide the contempt in his voice.

Lorsan stood, staring at Trik. After several moments of silence he let out a long breath.

"I don't know what to think, Trik."

"Lorsan, I have found my Chosen, not lost my mind."

"They are one in the same if I remember correctly," Lorsan chuckled nostalgically.

A slow smile spread on Trik's face as his temper faded. "So you remember?"

Lorsan walked over to a chair that had been placed beneath the largest shade tree and sat. He motioned for Trik to take the seat beside him.

"I remember," Lorsan agreed tiredly, truly remembering what it was like when he had first laid eyes on his Ilyrana. "I have been wrong to question you Trik. But in my defense, this is a very important and dangerous time."

Trik nodded and said with a sly smile. "I can agree to all of that."

"Why don't you bring her here, let us meet her?" Lorsan offered.

Trik leaned back in his chair as he considered his King's words and kept his face carefully blank. It wouldn't do to let Lorsan know that the last thing he wanted to do was to taint Cassie, his pure Cassie, with the darkness of his realm.

"Ilyrana wishes to throw a ball in your honor," Lorsan continued when Trik didn't speak.

Trik groaned inwardly at this news. "She's knows how I hate balls, besides humans don't throw balls."

"Sure they do," Lorsan's Chosen walked gracefully into the garden. "They call them parties."

Trik smiled at his Queen and bowed his head.

"Really Trik, all this formality from you is going to begin to go to my head and I might actually think I am the Queen of an Elfin race."

Trik laughed. He always had liked Lorsan's Chosen.

"We wouldn't want that."

"So will you bring her?" Lorsan interrupted their banter.

Trik stared at his King boldly. He searched his eyes, looking for any ill intent. Though he could see that Lorsan had an agenda, he couldn't seem to see that there was any threat to Cassie.

Trik nodded. "When shall I bring her?"

"Give me three days," Ilyrana announced. "It is all planned. Now I just need to put it all together."

"That quickly?" Lorsan asked his Chosen.

"It will be very small. There's no need to frighten her."

Trik stood and took Ilyrana's hand. He bowed over it and brought it to his lips. He kissed her hand gently and then looked up into her eyes. "Thank you my Queen, you honor my Chosen."

The formality of his actions caught both Lorsan and Ilyrana by surprise. He was asking her blessing over his union.

Ilyrana nodded once and answered formally. "As all will honor her."

Lorsan stood and echoed his Queen's words. "As all will honor her."

Trik cleared his throat. Emotion from their acknowledgement of his Chosen welled up in his chest.

"We shall see you in a few days then," he told them.

Lorsan nodded and Ilyrana smiled. Trik turned and left quickly before his emotions overwhelmed him.

Lorsan looked to Ilyrana after Trik had gone. "He asked our blessing." Surprise laced Lorsan's voice. Trik never asked for anything, but in that moment when he had knelt before his Queen and spoke the formal words, he had been asking the blessing of his King and Queen on his union with his Chosen.

"I told you that his loyalty hadn't wavered," his Chosen chided him.

"I was wrong to have questioned him," Lorsan admitted again.

"Triktapic is his own creature Lorsan, you can't control him. But he has just proven again his loyalty to you, his fealty to you. You would do well not to forget it."

Lorsan chuckled. "You would make a fine King my love."

"Yes, yes I would." Ilyrana teased.

"So where are we off to?" Cassie asked Elora as she climbed into her beat up Neon.

"On my way out the door Lisa asked if we could come up to the store and help with some inventory. She's gotten behind."

Cassie smiled "You know I'm all about hanging with your mom, she's cool."

Elora rolled her eyes, "You just think that because she isn't your mom."

"Your mom knows an Elf Queen, owns a new age shop, and dresses like she's twenty," Cassie stated as she raised her eyebrows at Elora.

Elora shrugged. "Okay so she's kind of cool."

Cassie laughed. "I am so going to tell her you said that."

"I'll deny every word."

Cassie turned on the radio, thankful at least that it still worked. She clapped her hands when she heard her favorite song, *Just Give Me a Reason* by Pink, coming through the speakers. She turned up the volume and started to sing along at the top of her lungs. Elora laughed at her friend and, to Cassie's delighted surprise, joined in.

"Lisa!" Elora yelled as they entered Enigma.

Lisa came out of the backroom carrying several boxes in her arms.

"Thank goodness. The cavalry has arrived. Thank you girls for helping me out."

"It's no big thing," Cassie told her. "So, put us to work."

"Go to the back room and grab some boxes," Lisa motioned towards the door she had just emerged from.

Cassie and Elora both headed through the door. They both froze as they entered the storeroom. The door closed ominously behind them as they saw three very intimidating elves standing before them.

"Uh, hi." Cassie gave a meek wave.

Trik, in his Elfin form, stood across from two other figures. Apparently Trik wasn't bothering to hide himself from Elora. He leaned lazily against the back wall, but he wasn't fooling Cassie with the relaxed pose. She could tell that he was ticked off and knew that it was because she hadn't stayed at her house like he had asked.

Across the room from him, stood Syndra and another male elf. Syndra smiled at Cassie warmly.

"Hello Cassie, Elora," Syndra's smile didn't quite meet her eyes.

Elora crossed her arms. She looked over at Trik. "Okay I know why you are here. You're pouting because Cassie didn't obey your orders." She looked over at Syndra and the male elf. "I don't have a clue why you are here and who is the tall dude?"

"This is Tamsin, King of the Light Elves, and my *Sh'mai*," Syndra explained.

Tamsin bowed his head slightly as he watched Cassie closely. He seemed to be ignoring Trik's presence.

"Cassie, could you please come here?" Trik asked. His voice could have cut through tempered steel.

Cassie cringed.

"Now probably isn't the best time," she told him.

"Now is the perfect time. Come here." She saw that his eyes were glowing.

Elora clucked her tongue. "Why don't you just put a collar on her if you're going to treat her like she's your pet?"

Trik's eyes snapped to Elora, who had the intelligence to not back away from the stalking predator.

Cassie looked over at Elora, nervous for her friend for being so blunt with an obviously ticked off dark elf assassin.

Cassie gave up and walked over to him.

He reached for her as soon as she was within his grasp. He took her hand and placed it on his chest. He didn't bother to speak out loud but instead shared his frustration and fear at finding her room empty.

"I was bored," she tried to implore him with her eyes.

"I explained to you why it was so important for you to stay at home. Cassie, I can't lose you. I won't. If something happens to you I would destroy the world, no one would be safe from my wrath."

Cassie could see that he was not bluffing or exaggerating, could feel the resolve in his mind.

"You would lose what good is left in you if you allowed yourself to act on those words."

"I keep telling you there is no good in me, never was."

"I don't believe that."

"Nor do I," Syndra interrupted.

Cassie turned to look at her, having forgotten that others were in the room with them. Trik had that effect on her, when he was with her he took over her world.

Tamsin stepped forward and Trik pushed away from the wall and pulled Cassie behind him.

"I mean her no harm," Tamsin told him.

"What do you want Tamsin, King of my enemies?" Trik asked and it sounded strangely formal.

"I've come to implore you to seek out the Forest Lords."

Trik's eyes glowed even more and his face turned to stone.

"Why would I do that?" He asked sharply.

"Because you know that something is changing. Something is causing this change and I think you know what it is. What does your King have planned that the Forest Lords have emerged from their long absence from our people?"

"I know not of what you speak," Trik lied smoothly.

Cassie leaned around him and glared daggers up at him.

"Really? That's your answer?" She folded her arms across her chest.

Elora snorted out a laugh. "Man you sure know how to dig your own grave rather impressively."

Trik ignored her, his eyes still locked with his Chosen's.

"Cassandra," his lips were drawn tight. "You do not know what you ask of me."

"Please." It was Syndra who snorted this time. She rolled her eyes. "You are your King's most trusted warrior. You know that whatever he has planned, it is not good."

"Has he figured out just how important your Chosen is?" Tamsin asked.

Trik and Cassie both blurted out questions at the same time.

"Excuse me?"

"What are you talking about?"

"She will be Lorsan's downfall," Syndra answered.

"How? How do you know this?" Trik's voice was full of concern and more than a hint of skepticism.

"Seek out the Forest Lords. They are waiting to hear from you, and take your Chosen with you." Tamsin repeated.

Trik thought of something then. "You know of the land and the plant. Why are you acting as if you have no knowledge of it?"

Tamsin folded his arms across his chest and leaned back against the wall behind him, taking the same nonchalant air as Trik.

"So you were at the meeting?" Tamsin's eyes narrowed.

"You suspected me?" Trik asked surprised.

"Something felt off. I didn't detect your presence, but I knew that something wasn't right."

"Are you going to answer my question?"

"I know of the plant and the land," Tamsin agreed. "However, I do not know why he wants to grow the plant in the human realm, or for what purpose he intends to use it."

"Is all that true?" Cassie asked Trik, her arms still folded across her chest and growing anger marring her face.

"We will speak in private," Trik told her and then turned back to the King and Queen.

"Triktapic, dark elf, assassin, spy, right hand of Lorsan the King of the Dark Elves," Syndra's voice was quiet, but it dripped with power.

Cassie watched in awe and a little bit of fear as the Light Elf Queen stepped forward, her human form faded away and she stood there in all her royal glory. A light seemed to glow around her and the room suddenly felt small and dingier next to her glorious presence. Cassie glanced at Trik to see his reaction and to her surprise she saw rage written in every line of his face. His body shook with it as he stared daggers at Syndra.

"Though I am not your Queen, I am an ancient bloodline—royal. A bloodline that at one time coursed through almost all of our kind. I do not use my power lightly. I do not control my race by fear and I have never forced compliance from anyone."

"But?" Trik interrupted. His voice barely controlled.

"You and your Chosen are too important. I tell you now that if you choose loyalty to Lorsan over the wellbeing of your Chosen, she will be taken from you."

There was no warning, not even the slightest movement, but suddenly Trik lunged at the Light Elf Queen.

"NO TRIK," Cassie yelled and rushed to reach forward and grab him, but she needn't have bothered. Before Trik could reach the Queen, he had come to an abrupt halt, jerked to a stop almost as if a rope was tied around his neck and he had reached the end of it. Cassie could feel the power pulsing off of the Queen, repelling Trik's advance.

"How dare you threaten me! How dare you threaten to take what is mine!" Trik snarled. His voice dropped and the controlled rage was even scarier than the yelling. "No one will ever take her from me and should it happen, I will rip through your kingdom and destroy any in my way to find her. You know what I am capable of; do not think that you and yours will be safe from my wrath, not when it comes to my Chosen."

Cassie had only thought she had been afraid of Trik before. Now, as she saw the look of pure, undiluted fury on Trik's face, she could imagine the fear that his victims must feel.

"I am not threatening to harm her," Syndra's voice was just as firm as before and still very calm, as if she was speaking to a disobedient child.

"I am telling you that we will take her to protect her. She will never be safe again in the human realm. You know how many enemies you have, Trik, and until now there was nothing they could do to hurt you; not physically or emotionally. But now they can. They can destroy you. All they have to do is get their hands on Cassie."

"I would never let that happen."

Tamsin, who had not moved a muscle since Trik's outburst, pushed off the wall and stepped before Trik's unmoving form.

"You are not flawless, despite what others may think. You are not omnipotent or omniscient. You will not be able to protect her at all times and still remain Lorsan's lap dog."

"Ouch," Elora murmured. "That has got to sting."

Cassie's eyes snapped over to her friend but Elora simply shrugged.

"I am not now, nor have I ever been, his lap dog," Trik's dagger-like stare had turned on Tamsin.

"You have to go to him when he calls, do you not? No matter where you are or what you are doing."

"Or who," Elora's fake cough she used to veil her words echoed ominously.

Cassie rolled her eyes in frustration. "Elora, really?"

Once again the famous Elora "whatever" shrug accompanied her retort. "Just calling it like I see it."

When Cassie looked back at Tamsin she was surprised to find a hint of amusement on his face.

Trik's eyes never left Tamsin. He didn't respond to the question, he didn't need to. Tamsin was right. Trik would always have to go when Lorsan summoned him, no matter what he was doing.

"You will not take her from me," Trik's voice was low and brought a shiver to Cassie's body, and not the good kind.

"Then do what you know is right, Trik." The power that had pulsed around Syndra had diminished now and she was once again in her human appearance.

"Why do you care?" Trik stepped back, the invisible hold no longer keeping him in place. He once again attempted to shield Cassie with his body but she was having none of it and moved to stand beside him, which earned her an irritated glance.

"She is not a light elf; she does not belong to your court."

"That may be, but she is an innocent. She has been thrust into a world and battle that is not her own and to which she has no defenses. We will not allow her to suffer because of the ill will between the light and dark elves. If you will not protect her from our race, then we will. Besides," Syndra smiled, "I like her."

Cassie smiled back, surprised by the admission.

"You will not take her from me," Trik repeated for the third time.

"So you have said," Syndra gestured. "Do not put me in a position to have to."

Just then the door to the storeroom opened and Lisa froze, her jaw dropping.

"Oh," she said surprised. "I didn't realize there was um," she didn't know quite what to say.

"The Elfin mafia hanging out in your store room?" Elora filled in.

"Something like that," Lisa said as the door closed behind her. "Is everything alright, Syndra?"

Syndra smiled at Lisa. She looked like she was there for a friendly visit, not the intense meeting they had been having.

"Everything is fine, Lisa," Syndra assured her. "We were just on our way out."

Cassie stepped towards Syndra but didn't make it far before Trik wrapped an arm around her waist and pulled her back towards his chest. Cassie didn't bother to acknowledge the possessive gesture.

"Um, I have a question," she told the Light Elf Queen.

Syndra motioned for her to continue.

"Is Elora on your hit list since she has seen you and Trik in your true form?"

Lisa's eyes widened at that question.

Syndra shook her head. "We have made an exception for Lisa and her daughter. Things are changing. You are going to need your friends to support you, Cassie, and I will not take from you what you are going to so desperately need very soon."

Cassie stared at Syndra in shock. She felt a tightening in her chest and a feeling of inevitably set in. Syndra's words were not an exaggeration. She was not trying to induce unfounded fear. Cassie could see in her eyes the knowledge that haunted the Queen.

Tamsin took his Chosen's hand and together they walked to a large mirror that stood in the far back corner. Cassie had never noticed it before, but it now made sense as to why Lisa had it there.

"We will see you soon, Trik," Syndra announced just before they stepped into the mirror.

"So, what's it going to be lover boy?" Elora's arms were folded across her chest and her foot tapped impatiently. Her eyes were narrowed at Trik.

Cassie pulled out of Trik's hold and he reluctantly let her go. She turned to look up at him. She saw so many emotions warring in his eyes and her heart ached for him. He reached for her hand and pulled it to his chest laying it over his heart.

"I need to speak with you," his voice was soft but Cassie still heard the edge of his anger that lurked beneath the surface. He looked over to Elora then.

"Elora can you please take Cassie home?"

Elora cocked her head to the side. "Is that what you want Cass?" She asked ignoring Trik.

With her hand on his chest, Cassie could see into Trik's mind, confirming that he needed to speak with her privately and that it was important.

"Yeah, we obviously have some things to discuss."

"Fine, let's go," she motioned towards the door.

"I will meet you there," Trik told Cassie as he tucked her hair behind her ear. He leaned down and gently, though possessively, kissed her. Cassie felt light headed as he pulled back. She felt the warmth of his lips all the way to her toes and thought disappointedly that it was entirely too short of a kiss. Her hand still lay against his chest and he chuckled at her thoughts.

"Later," he whispered in her ear as he walked past her and dropped her hand at the last possible moment. He looked back and his silver eyes met hers. For a moment she wanted to run to him, wrap her arms around him and tell him it would be okay. But she couldn't. She couldn't because she didn't know if it was going to be okay.

They pulled into Cassie's driveway and just sat in silence. Cassie made no move to get out of the car. She just needed a moment. She needed to gather her thoughts and prepare herself to be alone with Trik. He was just too much at times. His confident, devil may care attitude was alluring, and the way he looked at her was disarming.

"How's your brother Elora?" Cassie's voice shook, though her question was simple and totally unrelated to the mess she was in.

Elora shook her head with a small laugh. "He's good. He's actually enjoying the whole college experience."

Cassie nodded with a small smile. "That's good." She paused. "How do you think you did on the English paper?"

Elora tilted her head at her friend and empathy filled her purple contact colored eyes. "You're stalling."

"Pretty much."

"You don't have to go up there."

"Yes, yes I do." Cassie grabbed the door handle and pushed the door open.

"Cassie." The worry in Elora's voice made Cassie pause as she placed both feet on the pavement. She looked back over her shoulder.

"They will protect you, Syndra and Tamsin. You will be safe."

Cassie's face softened as she let out a weary sigh. "Yeah, but who will protect Trik?" She climbed out of the car and shut the door behind her. Taking a page from Elora's book she didn't say goodbye, but simply headed for the front door of her house.

"Mom, I'm home," Cassie announced.

"Okay, I'm in the dining room."

Cassie found her mom sitting at their dining room table, stacks of paper surrounded her. She had a pencil tucked behind her ear and her shoulder length hair had been pulled up haphazardly in a ponytail. Her mom was a lawyer and a good one. She practiced family law and she worked nonstop for her clients, oftentimes it seemed she was more a therapist than a lawyer.

"I'm going to head up to my room to work on some homework," Cassie told her mom as way of an excuse for her to spend a Saturday in her room.

Her mom nodded at her, waving her understanding, never taking her eyes from her work.

Chapter 8

"Once an elf has found his Chosen, the union must be bound in blood by the King. Once the binding has been completed, the elf's loyalty and devotion will always be to his Chosen first and foremost. This is to preserve the future of our race. The ambition of Kings could keep their warriors allegiance to the point of failing to protect, cherish, and love their Chosen as the Forest Lords originally intended. The unions of our race must not be taken lightly, for it is by strong unions that we flourish as a people. It is by the example of the devotion in our unions that our offspring learn integrity and commitment. Woe be it to us if we should ever forget that. ~ Myrin, advisor to Lorsan.

Cassie opened her bedroom door and stopped at the sight of Trik, in all his Elven glory, lying on her bed. He was so graceful and masculine at the same time. His hands were tucked behind his head, his legs were crossed at the ankle and stretched out in front of him as he reclined on her pillows. His head turned and their eyes met. Her breath caught at the devotion she saw blazing from them; devotion that was aimed at her.

"Come here," he told her as he sat up, his movements so fluid that it was mesmerizing to watch. And mesmerized, she was.

"Cassandra," his firm voice shook her out of her stupor.

She walked towards him slowly, not out of fear but out of a strong
need to just look at him, to not blink for fear that he wasn't real and
when she opened her eyes he'd be gone.

He sat on the edge of her bed and when she reached him she was
once again struck by his confidence and passion. He reached up and
his hand traced her neck until it was under her hair and holding her
possessively. His other hand gripped her hip and pulled her closer.
They were eye level with one another because he was seated and that
meant their mouths were in perfect position for doing what Trik was
pulling her in for. His lips connected with hers and she was lost. The
world faded away. Syndra and her ominous words, Tamsin and his
imploring about the Forest Lords, the Dark Elf King and his evil plan,
it was all gone in the wake of Trik's incredible mouth. Cassie was no
longer tentative in her kissing with Trik and so there was no hesitation
when he encouraged her to open her mouth. Their tongues danced to
an intimate rhythm and Cassie could feel it pulsing in her chest. And as
before, she could feel deep inside, her soul reaching for his. Trik pulled
her closer and she knew that he felt it too because the intensity
wrenched up another notch. He groaned into her mouth and it brought
a gasp from Cassie's lungs. Her hands lifted of their own accord and
she ran her fingers through his long, dark hair. Trik pulled back from
her lips and began to kiss her jaw line, down to her ear, behind her ear
and down her neck. Cassie's head fell back and she heard Trik chuckle.
She felt his tongue swirl against her skin and the desire that ran
through her body was so intense it jerked her up.

Trik felt her body stiffen and let her take a step back from him.

They both stared at the other, their breathing fast and uneven. Trik's eyes glowed and Cassie watched as his hands flexed open and closed as if he were fighting to keep from touching her. She knew the feeling. She wanted nothing more than to run back to his arms, but they had to stop. She refused to toss aside her morals because she couldn't control herself, no matter how amazing Trik felt.

"Are you alright?" He asked her softly.

Cassie nodded. "What about you?"

Trik chuckled. "I'll be okay, beautiful. You are a temptation like I have never known. Everything inside me screams, *she's yours, take her, bring her into your world, bind her to you.* It's ingrained into my DNA, it's written on my soul. You are a part of me and I long to be complete, I long to complete you. Physical intimacy is incredibly intense."

"Ya think?" Cassie snorted.

"I will never try and push you Cassie. We will wait until we do your human ritual, and until we are bound before the King."

Cassie's brow furrowed. "Uh, what do you mean bound?"

"Please tell me you don't have some kinky ritual where they tie us together naked under the moonlight."

Trik laughed. "As intriguing as that sounds, no. That is not what being bound means. In order for the binding of our souls to be complete we must go before the King and he will perform the binding ceremony. It is something the Forest Lords implemented, a sacrifice of blood in order for our souls to join. Once we consummate our union it will be done. You will be bound to me for eternity and me to you."

Cassie stared at Trik, unsure of how to respond.

"Cassie?" Trik leaned forward and tugged her by the hand. He pulled her down onto the bed to sit next him. "Talk to me, *A'maelamin*."

"I'm not really sure what to say. That seems, so, permanent."

"Is your marriage not permanent? Are you not bound to that man for life?"

Cassie snorted. "Hardly. Not very many people stay married for life. We aren't bound soul to soul. It's a choice."

"You have a choice Cassie. I won't force you to bind to me."

Cassie looked up at him. "What happened to, *I will never let you go, you are stuck with me* blah, blah, blah?"

Trik grinned. "Oh you are stuck with me. Even if you don't choose me, I'm not going anywhere. I will be your constant shadow."

Cassie rolled her eyes. "So my options are possessive dark elf mate, or freaky stalker dude?"

"That about sums it up," Trik confirmed.

Cassie smacked his chest playfully.

Trik took her hand in his and pulled it to his lips. He kissed her palm and looked into her eyes.

"We need to talk," he murmured against her skin, all playfulness gone.

Cassie nodded and let out a deep breath. "I know."

She turned, pulling one leg up on the bed while the other dangled off the side so that she could look at him. "You said you wouldn't keep secrets from me."

Trik nodded his head once.

"What is your King planning, Trik?"

Trik let go of her hand and stood up. She watched his graceful movements as he paced her room. She waited patiently.

"The dark elves own more than half of the Casinos in your country, and many throughout the world."

Cassie's mouth dropped open. "More than half?" She asked.

Trik nodded. "We use the income from the casinos to finance our lavish lifestyles in this realm."

"Meanwhile, the light elves own almost all of the U.S. energy companies. Oil, natural gas, wind, nuclear, they own it all. They use these companies to help keep your earth safe and clean. The dark elves are more about pleasure, gratification, and anything that pertains to self."

Trik continued to pace as he tried to gather his thoughts. He had never felt ashamed of himself or his actions—until now. A part of him didn't want to have to justify himself to her, another part of him didn't want to see the look in her eyes that said she finally understood who and what he was.

"Lorsan wants our income to increase from the Casinos. Your economy is struggling and so people aren't spending money frivolously like they used to. Income has dropped across the board. To combat this problem, Lorsan has created a drink from the small fruit of one of our plants that creates a euphoric sensation in humans. It loosens inhibitions."

"He's going to drug people?" Cassie couldn't believe what he was telling her.

"It's not a drug; it's natural, made from a plant."

"So is heroin and marijuana! That doesn't make them safe." Cassie had to control her temper, so her mom wouldn't hear her.

"It's not harmful, Cassie. It doesn't cause any health issues. It's really no different than the alcohol humans consume so freely and with such exuberance."

Cassie snorted. "Yea and some people don't handle that alcohol well and there are horrible consequences." She gestured in frustration. "What about driving? Can they drive safely under the influence of this *oh so natural* fruit drink?"

Trik stopped pacing and leaned back against the wall. His arms were folded across his chest and he appeared relaxed. Cassie knew better than to believe that pose.

"How about this?" He responded. "We can put a regulation on each of the Casinos. If a person has had too much Rapture then they aren't permitted to leave and will be put up in one of the hotel rooms." Trik spoke as if that would fix it all, like he had just solved the only dilemma to his King's plan.

"*Rapture,*" Cassie said the word and it was a bitter taste in her mouth. "That's what it's called? Oh, that's rich."

Trik didn't flinch under her hard glower. He didn't appear to be affected at all by her reaction and that only angered her more. She held his stare, not the least bit intimidated. She knew that he would never hurt her, no matter how angry he became. He let out a growl worthy of a pissed off lion.

"Shh, my mom will hear you," she admonished.

"I've taken care of that, no noise can leave this room while I am in it," he barked.

Oh well, thanks for sharing, Cassie thought sarcastically.

"I told you who I was, who I am. I told you, showed you that it is what I will always be. Nothing has changed." Trik's body was tense, his lips narrowed into a thin line. The soft, sexy lips that had been pressed to hers only moments ago were gone.

"I know what you told me. I know what you think you are, but you do have a choice, Trik. There is always a choice."

"NO! There isn't Cassandra. You are so young, so naive to the responsibilities of someone in my position."

"Do not," her eyes narrowed, her voice an angry whisper, "do not make the mistake of thinking that because I am not a thousand years old that I don't know anything, that I am clueless."

"I bear the protection of an entire race, Cassie. I have served my King for hundreds of years. There is not any way that you can possibly understand."

"I know the difference between RIGHT AND WRONG!" She yelled, now knowing that her mom wouldn't hear them.

"What is so wrong with making people feel good? What is so wrong with giving them the choice to take something that allows them to let loose? It's not like we are going to force it down their throats. It will be a *choice* that they will make. Isn't that what you keep saying to me?"

Cassie scoffed at him. "Are you kidding me? Trik there are all kinds of drugs that humans have concocted to make them feel better, to make them let go of their worries for a time, and guess what, they cause more problems than they solve and they are illegal! Do you know why they are illegal, *even though it is a choice*? They are illegal because the innocent, the weak, and the ones who can't stand up for themselves need to be protected. You are willing to make available something that will probably cause addiction, drive people to spend money they don't have and who knows what else, all because your King wants more money. Why? What does he need money for?"

"Even for us, we must have money to be a part of your society, to have nice things, to enjoy all that being in this realm means."

"So that is what it always comes back to, pleasure, enjoyment?"

"What is so wrong with that?" Trik snapped back. "What is wrong with wanting to enjoy life as much as possible?"

"When it's at the expense of other people, it's wrong." Cassie closed her eyes and brought her hands up and framed her face, shaking her head in anger and pain. How could he think it was okay to drug people? How do you justify such behavior?

Several moments of frustrated silence passed.

Trik knelt down in front of his Chosen. He took in the slump of her shoulders, the anger etched on her face and knew that she would never get past this.

"What would you have me do?" He whispered.

Cassie lifted her head to look at him. He was too beautiful, too handsome for words. In the few months that she had known him, she had come to see the light in Trik. She knew there was hope. They spent six weeks apart because he thought she would be better off without him. That proves that he isn't completely lost. He just needs a road map to point him in the right direction.

"I can't stop him Cassie."

"Then take the next best, first step."

"Tell me," he implored. "Please, I can't stand to see you like this because of me."

"Quit," she said plainly.

Trik's head tilted to the side as he tried to understand her meaning. "Quit?"

She nodded. "Turn in your resignation. Tell Lorsan that you are done being his killer."

Trik's mouth dropped open and then closed. Deep down he knew that it would eventually come to this, but somehow he had hoped to still be a part of the people he had known for over a thousand years and still have Cassie.

"You want me to walk away from everything I've ever known?"

"Is that not what you were going to ask me to do? To go to your realm to live with you," she countered.

"Touché"

They sat staring at one another, not touching, not speaking, just searching for something in each other's eyes.

"Alright," Trik said wearily. "Alright, if that's what it will take to keep you."

Cassie's smile could have lit a stadium. His heart skipped as he watched her climb off of her bed and into his arms. He pulled her close and buried his nose in her neck. He could never give her up. He knew that as sure as he knew that Lorsan would never let him go alive.

"Thank you," Cassie whispered against his chest and the heart that he was sure could not break, fell apart. He hadn't lied to her. He would leave Lorsan, but it would have to be strategically done. He didn't think she would understand that sometimes you have to bide your time. You can't run head first into a battle that you know will be a massacre.

"I have a question for you." He stood up from his position on the floor never letting go of her and sat back down on the bed.

"You look a little nervous," she grinned clearly enjoying an uneasy Trik.

"Lorsan and his Chosen would like to meet you. They are having a party in honor of our union. It's a great honor."

Cassie cleared her throat as she considered going before a man willing to enslave humans so that he could line his pockets.

"Why?" She asked.

"If an elf has high enough standing in the kingdom, such as I have, then it is tradition to throw a ball in honor of him finding his Chosen. It signifies an acceptance of the Chosen to her rightful place by his side in the kingdom."

"But I don't want to be part of that kingdom?"

"I know, but it will cause many problems if we don't attend," Trik responded.

"This is important to you?"

"Not just me, us," he responded honestly.

"And we just go and eat, talk, and that's all?"

"That's all," Trik concurred.

"Okay," she reached up with her hand to smooth away the worry lines that had formed on his forehead. "If it's that important to you, then we will go."

It was Trik's turn to smile. "Thank you."

"So when is this party?"

"In three days."

Cassie absentmindedly played with a strand of his long, dark hair as she thought.

"So am I going to need to wear a dress?"

"Yes, but I will bring you an Elfin dress suitable for the occasion. You are my Chosen and you will wear my crest and my colors."

Cassie raised a single eyebrow. "Let me guess, your crest has a quiver in it and your colors are black?"

Trik growled playfully at her and tickled her sides until she relented.

"Okay, okay I give," she laughed.

"What will you give, beautiful? Will you give me your heart? Will you give me your soul? Will you give me your body? " Trik asked as he paused in his tickle assault.

Cassie's breathing became shallow as she took in the possessiveness, need, and want dancing in his silver eyes. His words repeated themselves in her mind as she tried to focus on what he was asking. Trik leaned down and his nose brushed against her cheek.

"Cassandra," he whispered softly.

"Yes," Cassie's breath and the word came out at the same time.

Trik closed his eyes on that one little word. He reveled and rejoiced in it.

"Say it. Say what you will give me." He was looking into her eyes, his stare penetrating to her very soul. Though they could look into each other's minds, Trik wanted to hear the words out loud.

Cassie reached up and traced the features of his face as she spoke. "I give you my heart, I give you my soul, and I will give you my body."

Trik's eyes filled with mischief. "Will?"

Cassie blushed as she spoke. "Eventually."

Trik leaned down and kissed her lips, a slow kiss meant to write the words she had spoken onto his heart.

He pulled back abruptly and stood. Cassie looked at him, confused by his sudden change in mood.

"I have to go take care of some things," he told her as he reached for her hand to pull her to her feet.

"Things?"

Trik nodded, not bothering to clarify. He would let her draw her own conclusions. It would be better that way. With one last kiss he turned away from her and in a blink he was through her window and gone as if he'd never been there.

Cassie suddenly felt alone without Trik's overwhelming presence. He didn't say what he was doing, but she guessed that he must be going to talk to Lorsan. She shivered as she thought about how that conversation would play out. Would they still want them to come to their party? Would they still want to honor Trik for having found his Chosen?

She shook her head, trying to clear all of the thoughts from her mind. She suddenly felt very tired. She lay back down on her bed and she had barely hit the pillow before she fell asleep.

Chapter 9

"The Forest Lords have spoken for the first time in a millennia. They have sent out a plea to our people to unite. They have said that a dark one's Chosen will tip the balance, but they worry that his darkness is greater than the light in her. We must guide them as much as we can. They belong together, were made for each other, and will either destroy each other, or destroy the evil that has leaked into the human realm. It is a choice, their choice. Let us hope that they choose wisely." Tamsin, Light Elf King

"Do you think she can save him?" Tamsin asked his Queen as they lay in their bed.

"Yes," Syndra answered, "but he has to want to be saved. She can't force him and she can't make his decisions for him."

Tamsin rubbed his face in frustration. He pushed himself up and leaned against the headboard.

"I don't understand why he is so blind to what Lorsan is, and what he is doing."

"You forget, my love, he comes from darkness. He has lived in that darkness for more than a thousand years. That's a lot to overcome."

"That's what scares me. Can he overcome it in time to save the human race from becoming mindless slaves?"

Syndra sat up and took his hand in hers. She looked into the face of her mate, framed by striking dark blue hair; his eyes, shimmering like diamonds met hers. She gazed into the face of the man who had held her heart and the other half of her soul for over a thousand years. "We will do all we can to help him overcome. We will protect Cassie and we will defeat Lorsan."

Tamsin leaned forward and pressed a kiss to her forehead. "The Forest Lords blessed me beyond all measure when they gave me you."

Syndra smiled at him and pulled him back down. She snuggled in close to his side as he wrapped her in his strong arms. She wanted this for Cassie and Trik. She wanted them to find comfort and peace with each other. She knew they couldn't see it now, but the time was coming when they would need each other more than any other, a time where they'd be the only ones who could keep the other safe.

Trik stood in the field overlooking the crops that would become Rapture. At one time he would have stared out over this land and felt a sense of accomplishment. Now, now he just felt sick. Cassie had looked at him as if he had handed her the moon when he told her he would walk away from Lorsan and, though he meant it, he knew that they weren't talking about the same time frame. He hadn't bothered to clarify. He couldn't stand being in the room with her one minute more, couldn't stand seeing her adoration when he didn't deserve it.

Something inside him pushed at him to go back and tell her the truth, but he couldn't. Lorsan would destroy everything Trik cared about if he walked away. Since the only thing he cared about was Cassie, then she would bear the entirety of Lorsan's wrath.

"The first plants will be ready to harvest by tomorrow," Alok said as he walked up to stand next to Trik.

"Is the lab ready for them?" Lorsan had his most trusted potions masters working on getting the plant into a liquid form. They had converted one of the large buildings on the land into a lab and it was there that the drug would be manufactured.

"It will be finished tonight," Alok answered.

Trik nodded at him but said nothing more. He didn't want to speak with anyone in his race. He didn't want to look into their eyes for fear that they would see that something in him had changed. Something in him had suddenly burst forth to life like a new born babe taking its first breath. Cassie. Cassie's soul, so pure, so caring had connected with his and now his dark soul would never be the same.

The other elven voices surrounding him began to intrude on his thoughts, annoyingly loud, interrupting his self-loathing. He needed to think. He needed to be alone. That wasn't the truth, though. He needed to be with Cassie. His soul was beginning to ache at the distance he had put between them and he knew that he would need to return to her soon because she would begin to feel the pain of their forced separation; forced by him.

He turned and walked toward the large building that had become the lab. He walked around to the back side where there were several glass windows. With the pain becoming more and more noticeable, he stepped quickly through the window and emerged in a small cabin. He stepped out of the cabin into the lush land of his people. The trees were tall, older than even he. Canopies of bright green vines lovingly draped the trees. The ground was clothed in soft, thick, green grass with moss covered rocks scattered here and there. All around, foliage and flowers shot forth, reaching for the light that helped them grow.

He took a familiar path that led to a river, which ran through the Elfin realm. A waterfall towered over the river and the rush of the crashing water pulled Trik closer. He stood on the edge of the river and looked down at his reflection. He didn't recognize the man who stood before him. His usual cocky smirk gone, replaced by worry, fear, and pain, three things he was not familiar with and didn't know how to handle. He knelt down and looked into the eyes of his reflection, searching for the good that Cassie saw in him, but he saw nothing there. Trik knew each and every life that he had taken over the past thousand years. He had spilled enough blood to fill the river before him and all the rivers of the earth. She was so young, so innocent. She couldn't possibly understand the depth of Trik's sedition. Because she didn't understand it was his job to protect her. He had to do this his way, and if she found out he would have to convince her that it was because he loved her.

Trik's head fell forward and he felt his soul screaming for its mate. Did he love her? He knew that he cared deeply for her, he knew he couldn't lose her, and that he would be nothing without her. Is that love? Whatever it was, Cassie was his, his Chosen and he had waited too long to give her up now.

It was for those reasons that he had to bide his time with Lorsan. He prayed to the Forest Lords that Cassie would understand.

Elora sat in her mom's store flipping through a book she had found while helping her mom clean the storeroom. It was a book about the elves.

"Where'd you get this?" Elora asked as she turned another page.

Lisa stopped in mid-step as she saw what Elora was holding. Her eyes widened slightly but she schooled her expression quickly.

"Just a book that Syndra loaned me."

"Syndra loaned you a book that holds the history of their race?" Elora raised a brow at her mom.

Lisa shrugged. "She said she trusts me."

"Uh-huh," Elora grunted as she watched Lisa's tense, jerky movements.

"We really should put that away. Syndra doesn't want others knowing that it's here."

Elora closed the book and handed it to her mother's outstretched hand.

"Lisa, are you okay?" Elora asked, "You have been weird ever since the elves let themselves out."

Lisa took a deep breath and seemed to gather herself. "I know we don't talk about your father very much."

Elora interrupted. "He died, what more is there to say?"

Lisa chuckled. "You are a lot like him. He was so matter of fact about everything."

"So why the sudden nostalgia?"

"Because, to—" she choked on her words as she tried to hold back the tears, "tomorrow is the anniversary of his death."

Elora's face fell and she regretted having been so uncompassionate. She knew that her mom had loved her father immensely. Elora didn't remember him. He died before she could even walk.

"He adored you. I don't know if I've ever told you that." Lisa looked at Elora and her eyes seemed to glaze over as she remembered a time long ago. "He used to sing to you and you would laugh and smile. He thought you were the most incredible blessing. I know you don't remember him and you don't feel much towards him, but I just want you to know that you were his world."

Elora tried to discreetly wipe the tear from her eye before it made its appearance on her face. She didn't like to cry. She didn't like to feel something for someone she'd never known or would ever know.

"Thanks," she whispered not trusting her voice to not waver.

Lisa smiled. "It's getting late. You ready to call it a night and get something to eat?"

Elora nodded. She followed her mom out of the store and waited while she locked up. Elora pulled her phone out of her pocket to see if Cassie had responded to any of her texts. She hadn't. She was very tempted to go over and check on her but what explanation would she give Cassie's parents? *Hi, just checking on Cassie because she has a dark elf quiver carrying assassin in her room.* Yeah, that would not go over very well.

She climbed into the car and looked out into the dark night. She let her thoughts take over as she replayed her mother's words about her dad. She thought it odd that her mom had never said that the man was Oakley's dad, but she had never asked why and neither had Oakley.

Cassie felt her bed dip down as she tried to clear her head from the deep sleep that had claimed her. She tried to turn over but an arm, or what she figured was an arm, snaked around her and pulled her close.

"Shh, beautiful, it's just me." She felt Trik's lips on her neck before he whispered again. "Go back to sleep. I will stay with you."

Cassie woke up Sunday morning feeling light and refreshed. She turned to find Trik sound asleep. She took the opportunity to study him. He was so handsome, from his shiny, dark hair, to his silver eyes that saw into her soul, to his strong jaw and straight nose. He was perfect, and he was hers.

Suddenly his eyes snapped open as they met hers. A wide grin spread across his lips.

"So, I'm yours?"

Cassie's face turned bright red as she hadn't even realized that she had reached out to touch him while she took him and all his glory in. He had seen that thought in her mind.

He pulled her down next to him and pressed her head to his chest.

"Do you hear that?" His fingers ran through her hair as he spoke. "My heart beats only for you. I may be yours, but you are every bit mine. So do not be embarrassed to feel that way. I like knowing that you are possessive of me." He sounded so smug.

Cassie rolled her eyes. "Could your ego get any larger?"

"Maybe. Want to try stroking it?"

Though Cassie heard the playfulness in his voice she choked as she tried to swallow a laugh with her embarrassed gasp.

He clucked his tongue at her. "I was talking about my ego, Cassandra. Teenage minds always jump to the wrong conclusion."

"You knew what you were saying and how it would sound."

Though she couldn't see his face, she knew that he had a smile plastered across it and his eyes danced with mischief.

"Maybe, maybe I'm as innocent as freshly fallen snow."

"Well that's not very innocent because by the time snow has fallen it's full of all the crap that is floating around in the air from our pollution."

Trik leaned down and kissed her hair, and she felt it all the way to her toes.

"You always have a retort."

"Not always," she said pushing away from him. She watched as he raised an eyebrow at her.

She realized that she had just proven him right by once again taking the bait he had so temptingly dangled before her.

"So, what are we doing today?" Trik pushed himself up and leaned back against her bed.

Cassie shrugged. "What do you want to do?"

Suddenly his face lit up like a child on Christmas morning seeing the presents piled under the tree.

"To show you my realm."

Cassie froze. "I've been in your room."

He nodded. "Yes, but I want to show you the beauty and glory of the Elven realm."

He looked so excited. Cassie had never seen him with such boyish enthusiasm. She didn't want to squelch it or hurt his feelings. "Okay," she finally said.

He leaned forward and took her face in both of his hands and pressed his lips to hers. He pulled back much too soon and jumped up out of the bed. "I'll be back for you in an hour. Be ready."

She watched as he disappeared through her mirror.

"Well okay then," she muttered to herself as she climbed out of bed.

She grabbed her phone and checked her texts. Elora had texted her five times while she had been in her coma like sleep.

She dialed Elora's number listening to the rings as she waited.

"So did you dump quiver boy?" Elora said with no preamble.

Cassie laughed. "No. We talked and he finally relented. He's going to tell Lorsan that he will no longer be his assassin or spy."

Elora was quiet.

"You there?" Cassie asked.

"Yeah. Do you really believe it will be that easy, that Lorsan will just let his most powerful weapon go?"

"What choice does he have? By the way everyone makes it sound, Trik could wipe the floor with him."

"Lorsan is a Royal. They have all kinds of sneaky tricks up their sleeves."

Cassie's eyes narrowed at Elora's words.

"How do you suddenly know so much about the Royal Elves?"

"I found a book. It contains the entire history of the elves. Not only does it detail their history, but it also discusses their bloodlines, listing the strengths and weaknesses of each one. I didn't get very far in it before Lisa took it from me. This book in the wrong hands could destroy them."

"How on earth did your mother end up with it? Surely she didn't buy it on eBay like she does a lot of her stuff." Cassie was deep in thought. She realized just how dangerous it was for Lisa to have something so important to the elves.

"She says Syndra gave it to her, but I'm not buying it," Elora grumbled.

Cassie agreed. Syndra didn't seem the type to leave something so detrimental to their race in the hands of a single mother who owned a new age shop. But then again, maybe Syndra thought nobody would ever think to look there.

"I need a favor," Cassie started.

"Let me guess. It has something to do with a mysterious figure that is tall, dark, and pointy eared?" Elora said dryly.

Cassie rolled her eyes though Elora couldn't see her.

"He wants to take me to his realm."

"Hmm, so what I hear you saying is a that dark elf assassin, who is helping his Dark Elf King make a drug that will make all the humans that take it become pleasure seeking morons wants to take you, by yourself, to the world where all that is going down?"

Cassie nodded her head slowly then remembered that Elora couldn't see her so she added, "Uh-yeah."

She heard Elora let out a sigh. "I swear Cassie, I can't decide if you have a unique sense of adventure or are just looking for the most original way to get yourself killed."

"So can you cover for me? If you will come pick me up I can tell my mom that we are going to hang out and then you can drop me off somewhere Trik can meet us."

"Fine, but if you get yourself killed I reserve the right to flush your ashes down the toilet while I sing the theme from Titanic."

"Elora you don't sing."

"Not the point."

"So, you in?"

"Fine. What time is QB going to be ready?" Elora asked.

"He said in an hour or so," Cassie pulled the phone away and looked at the time then returned the phone to her ear. "We've got about thirty-five minutes until he's back."

"Okay, I'll be there in twenty."

Cassie grabbed her clothes and headed for the bathroom. She showered in record time and then blow-dried her hair until it was just a tad damp. She pulled it back into a messy bun, looked herself over and decided that that was as good as it was going to get.

Downstairs, Cassie found her mom pouring a cup of coffee. Her dad was sitting at the dining room table, trying to make a spot for his plate amongst her mom's mess of papers.

"Hey mom, dad," Cassie headed for the fridge and pulled out the milk. She grabbed a bowl from the cabinet and placed it on the counter. She turned to get the Lucky Charms cereal from the pantry but her mom already had it in her hand. Cassie took it and smiled at her.

"Sleep alright?" Sylvia asked.

"Yep. Hey Elora called and she wants to hang out. Is that alright?"

Sylvia lifted the cup of coffee as she answered. "That's fine." She took a sip and then pinned Cassie with the stare. "So when are we going to get to meet Trik again?"

Cassie's head whipped around to see if her dad was paying attention. He wasn't.

"Have you told dad about him?" Cassie's eyes were wide.

Sylvia grinned mischievously. "Why don't you ask him?"

Cassie groaned. "Come on, you know how he is. He will drill Trik for an hour and want to know everything right down to his blood type."

"Well that could be important information. What if you needed blood and he was the only donor and your dad was the only person who was there to tell the doctors his blood type?" Her mom gestured to her. "See, then you would be glad that your dad was so thorough."

"Seriously, mom?" Cassie threw her hands in the air and marched into the dining room.

"So dad," she fidgeted with her shirt. "I met this guy, and we've sort of been seeing each other and I really like him."

Her dad smiled up at her and it was a smile that said the cat has caught the canary.

"By all means, invite him for dinner. I would love to meet him."

"Dad, promise you won't make him fill out a form with all his information like you did with Cory."

"That information was important. I needed to know his parents' names and numbers. What if you two had been in an accident and we found out first?"

"You asked him his sexual orientation and if he had ever been sexually active," Cassie folded her arms across her chest and tapped her foot.

Her dad frowned. "I still say he was lying."

"What, like it's impossible for a seventeen year old guy to be a virgin?"

"I believed that part. I was talking about the sexual orientation," he told her. "I didn't think I had anything to worry about with him."

"Promise me." Cassie stomped her foot. Her dad started laughing and when her face continued to stay contorted in anger he held his hands up in surrender.

"Okay, okay, I won't make him fill out a form."

"Or give him any *what if scenarios.*"

"Those are important, he needs to be prepared."

"Dad," Cassie groaned. "You asked the last guy what he would do if he was intimate with me and realized he didn't have a condom."

"And he got it wrong. The correct answer was I wouldn't be intimate with your daughter, sir. The dummy said, *uh, not go any further.*"

"Dad," Cassie growled.

"Fine, no scenarios," he finally relented.

Cassie stared at him for another minute. A knock at the door finally had her turning away.

She opened the door to Elora's scowling face.

"Hi sunshine!" Cassie plastered a huge smile on her face.

Elora stomped past her. "Stuff it."

"Oookay then," Cassie muttered as she closed the door.

"So where is lover boy?" Elora asked as Cassie closed her bedroom door.

Before Cassie could answer, Trik stepped out of her bedroom mirror.

He walked straight over to Cassie not even bothering to look at Elora.

"Well hello to you too," she smirked at him.

But Trik's eyes were on his Chosen.

"Everything okay?" She asked him when he was standing inches from her.

He smiled, but Cassie noticed it didn't meet his eyes.

"Everything's fine." He stood there staring at her. He didn't try to kiss her or touch her and Cassie was suddenly unsure if she should touch him.

Elora clearing her throat finally breaking through their senses.

Cassie turned to look at her friend. She stepped away from Trik and for the first time he didn't attempt to keep her close to him.

"Elora has agreed to be my reason for leaving today. I'm going to leave with her and meet you somewhere," Cassie explained.

Trik nodded, "I'll meet you at the park downtown." He stepped up to her and kissed her on the forehead and then he was gone, moving quickly through her window and away from her.

"Did something seem off to you?" Elora asked her.

Cassie nodded. "Maybe Lorsan took it harder than he thought." Cassie said as way of explanation but not believing a word of it.

Chapter 10

"I've given you my heart; I've given you my soul. What else can I give? I'm asking you to stay with me. I'm asking you to pick us. I see in you the man you don't think you can be, but I know you can. The man who has held me in his arms like I was the most precious thing in his world, *that* man cares, *that* man is who I need, who we all need. I've given you everything, what are you willing to give me?" ~Diary of Cassie Tate

Trik watched from the shadows as Cassie climbed out of Elora's car. She waved at her friend and made her way into the park. Elora's car didn't budge and he knew that she wouldn't leave until she saw him with Cassie. He watched as she looked around for him. The words *for him* ricocheted off his mind. She was here *for him*. He took a deep breath and let it out. He wanted this day with her. He wanted to show her what he could give her.

He stepped out of the darkness moving quietly towards her. He could have made his entire approach silent, she would have never known he was there until he touched her, but he didn't want to scare her so he purposely snapped a twig with his foot. She turned at the sound and her eyes locked with his. He saw the apprehension there, the insecurity because of the distance he had kept between them in her room. His heart ached because he had put that look in her eyes.

"Hey," she said in a small voice.

He shook his head as he reached her. "Don't."

Cassie looked confused. "Don't what?"

"Don't look at me like you are unsure of how I feel for you."

Cassie looked down at the ground not wanting to meet his eyes.

He placed a finger under her chin and raised her head. He waited until her eyes finally met his.

"You are mine, my everything. Never doubt that or the fact that I want you, I will always want you."

He wanted to tell her he loved her, it was on the tip of his tongue, but he held himself back. He felt the struggle inside him. His soul demanded he give her everything, but the darkness demanded as well and he had been doing what the darkness commanded for a very long time. Regardless of his soul's cry he didn't feel he had the right to say those words to her; not until he had dealt with Lorsan.

He stared into her eyes a minute longer. When he was satisfied that she had heard him he took her hand and began leading her to the small building that housed the park bathrooms. They slipped into the door marked for families and Trik walked straight at the mirror pulling Cassie with him.

Cassie's breath caught as they emerged through another mirror, this one led into a small cabin.

"Is this your place?" She asked as she spun around looking at the small but clean space. There was a small kitchen with a sink, refrigerator and stove. A small table with two chairs stood in the center of the kitchen. Just past it was a living area with a fire place against the back wall and just past the fireplace was a door that she assumed led to the bedroom.

"It's one of the places I like to come to when I need a break," he told her.

"It's cozy."

Trik laughed "That's your way of saying it's small."

Cassie smiled, relieved to see this side of Trik. This is the Trik she knew, the one no one else saw.

"Come on," he tugged on her hand and pulled her to the front door.

They stepped out onto a small porch and then walked down the steps into the most beautiful forest that Cassie had ever seen.

Trik smiled at the look on his Chosen's face. Though he had been there recently without her, and though it was peaceful, it was nothing compared to the peace he found with her standing in his place with him, where she belonged.

"It's beautiful, Trik," her words were breathy as she took in the tall trees, deep green grass, and beautiful flowers.

"I've never brought anyone here." He didn't know why he told her that, but he felt it was important that she know.

"Never?" She asked without looking at him.

He stepped up behind her and brushed her hair from her neck. He leaned down and kissed her neck before whispering. "Never."

Cassie stopped breathing as she felt his lips on her skin. She closed her eyes and soaked up the sensation, the feeling of having him close. She felt him slip his hand into hers and she opened her eyes.

"I want to show you something," he told her with a grin.

She loved that grin.

She let him tug her forward and enjoyed the carefree way he moved. Usually he was deliberate in his every move, constantly watching for an attack. But here, here he was relaxed and open. Suddenly the trees cleared and opened up to a river and a beautiful high water fall. Her mouth dropped open at the site. The light of the sun shined off the water cascading towards the river. A rainbow reached out from the spray of the water fall, dazzling the surrounding trees. It was picture perfect. She was sure she had never seen anything so breathtaking.

"What do you think?" Trik smiled at her.

"It's amazing," Cassie didn't try to hide the awe she felt.

Trik walked over to a large rock that sat over the river. He sat down and stretched his legs out in front of him. Cassie followed suit. She looked up into the sky and saw a sun, bright and warm on her skin.

"You have a sun?" She asked.

Trik chuckled. "Of course we have a sun. Our realm isn't much different than yours."

"Is it all like this?"

"For the most part. There are some dark forests that few will go into."

"Why, what's in them?" She asked as she pulled her legs up and wrapped her arms around them.

"The Forest Lords," he said with narrowed eyes.

"I thought they were good guys."

"It's not because they are bad that no one goes into the forest. It's because being in their presence is," Trik paused trying to find the right word, "unsettling. They can see inside you. They know what is to come and what has already been."

Cassie shuddered at the thought of someone knowing her future, knowing her past, and knowing what was deep inside her.

"Those are the Forest Lords that Tamsin and Syndra want you to see?"

"Yep," Trik tells her, popping the P.

"Are you going to?" Cassie looked out over the water as she waited for his answer.

Trik didn't know what to tell her. He didn't want to go to the Forest Lords for fear of what they would tell him. But at the same time, he wanted to go because he needed to know what they would tell him.

So he was honest. "I don't know."

They sat in companionable silence, each lost in their own thoughts. Cassie was careful not to touch Trik because she didn't want him to see the worry or fear in her. No matter how he tried to act, she could tell he was pulling away.

Trik watched Cassie out of the corner of his eye. She was incredible sitting there with sun shining on her blonde hair and smooth skin. He had never been so attracted to someone and it was all he could do to keep from pulling her into his arms and kissing that worried look off her face. He wanted to see her smile, to see the sparkle in her eyes. He stood up and reached for her hand. She looked up at him, the confusion of his actions written clearly on her face.

"I have a surprise for you." He smiled at her as he waited for her to put her hand in his.

Finally she did and allowed him to pull her to her feet. She followed him through the lush forest, her eyes constantly roving over the life that was so apparent. A cool breeze blew across her face and raised the tendrils of hair that fell from her bun onto her neck. Trik stopped just before a small clearing appeared.

She started to speak but stopped when he raised a finger to his lips. Trik cupped his hands around his face and made a sound that Cassie could only describe as a cat growling. She cocked her head to the side as she watched him.

"Just wait," he whispered as he pointed in the direction of the clearing.

Cassie tried to breathe as quietly as possible, but felt like the harder she tried to be quiet, the louder she became. After several minutes she began to see the leaves and grass on the other side of the clearing move. Her breathing stopped as she waited in rapt attention to see what was going to emerge from the lush foliage.

She let out a gasp and clamped her hand over her mouth as she watched two large white tigers walk smoothly into the clearing. They were looking around as if they were expecting someone. Without any word to her, Trik stood up and began to walk towards them. The tigers tensed. When Trik came into their view, they relaxed. Her mouth dropped open when one of the tigers playfully bounded up to him as if it were only a ten pound kitten rather than a two hundred pound tiger. Trik reached his hand out and the beast rubbed his head against it. Trik turned back to where she still knelt watching him. He motioned for her to come over.

She stood slowly and began moving forward, when the two tigers' eyes finally noticed her she froze.

"They won't hurt you, Cassie," Trik told her.

After a moment's hesitation she got her feet to continue on towards Trik and the beautiful cats. When they had first walked into the clearing, Cassie had thought their stripes were white, but the closer she came, the more she realized that their stripes were actually dark silver; and slightly shimmered when they moved. Their eyes were large, gold and lined in black as if they were wearing eye liner. She stopped when she made it to Trik's side. The tigers where less than three feet from her and she stilled, waiting for what would happen next.

"Tyndril," Trik spoke to the tiger closest to her, "come say hello."

The tiger he had called Tyndril took slow steps towards Cassie, as if she understood her fear. She sat down on her haunches directly in front of Cassie and stared at her. Cassie reached her hand out and couldn't stop the grin that spread across her face as the large cat pressed her head into it. She looked over at Trik who was smiling at her.

"What are they?"

"They are called *tiriths*. They are the equivalent of your tiger species, only they are a little special."

"Special how?" Cassie asked as Tyndril moved closer so she could rub her body against Cassie's. She laughed as the large cat nearly pushed her over trying to snuggle closer.

"For one, they understand us."

Cassie's eyes snapped up. "What do you mean they understand us?"

"I mean they have a superior intellect and understand our language, and I have taught these two English."

Cassie looked at Tyndril closely. "Can you understand me?" The large cat nodded its large head. Cassie's eyes widened and her grin grew impossibly large.

"That is so cool!"

Trik laughed at her enthusiasm.

"This affectionate girl is Tyndril, and this guy is Tao."

"They are beautiful," Cassie walked around Tyndril towards Tao and reached her hand out to him. He stepped forward and bowed to her before pressing his head into her hand.

"What else makes them special?"

"They have a healing ability which makes them dangerous in battle. Their wounds restore almost instantly."

"Wow, that's impressive."

"Their noses are about four times stronger than that of your tigers and once they have your scent it's committed to memory, they will never forget you and would be able to track you to the ends of any realm."

"They are really amazing. Thank you so much for introducing me to them."

"Tyndril, Tao," Trik addressed them and the two large tigers both looked at him. "What do you think of my Chosen." He gestured to Cassie.

Cassie didn't know what to expect but when both tigers stood, placed one leg out in front of them and bowed their heads to her, she knew that was not it.

Cassie looked up at Trik, her eyes wide in question.

"They honor you and are pleased that the Forest Lords have chosen you to be mine. It also means that they will always protect you against any threat."

Cassie bowed her head in return. "Thank you. I treasure your friendship."

Trik watched as the woman who held the other half of his soul, the woman not of his realm, accepted a part of his world. She took joy in the two cats. He hadn't expected to be so affected by her presence in his realm, or by her reaction to it.

They spent the day walking through the forest, sometimes talking, sometimes not. Tyndril and Tao, their constant sentries, were never far away. They finally ended up back in front of Trik's small cabin and he pulled her to a halt before she could reach the door. Cassie turned to look up at him and her breath caught in her throat at the emotion that shone through his silver eyes. His hair blew gently in the breeze and his full lips caught her attention.

Trik reached out and pulled her to him. One hand at the base of her neck the other gripped her hip. He pressed his forehead to hers and closed his eyes.

"This has been the best day of my life," he whispered to her.

Cassie smiled. "I can't decide if I should be flattered or feel sad that hanging out with a girl in a field is the highlight of your thousand plus years."

Trik chuckled. His fingers traced up her arm and across her neck to her jaw line.

"What's sad is that I've been waiting a thousand years for you, and now I no longer deserve you—if I ever did."

Cassie heard the sadness in his voice and it broke her heart.

"It doesn't matter what's in the past, or what's in the future, Trik. What matters is this moment, now, and what we choose to do with it." Cassie opened her mind to him as his fingers traced her collarbone. She wanted him to see exactly how much she meant those words. She didn't care about his past, and all the ugly things. All she cared about was now.

Trik pulled her into his arms and held her close. He kept back the part of him that would show her the love that had grown painfully strong in his heart for her. While he kept this back, he couldn't stop his soul from reaching for hers. He heard her gasp at the sensation that was so hard to describe to anyone who had never felt it. She tilted her head back to look up at him and to his surprise she grabbed his face and pulled him to her. She kissed him with an intensity he had never before felt. He felt her soul reach into him and wrap him in warmth and love. In that moment he felt protected and cherished.

He deepened the kiss and pulled her body closer. His hand reached up and pulled her messy bun free from its confines. Her hair flowed down over his hand and he ran his fingers through it and felt her shudder. His other hand moved from her hip slipping to her lower back bunching her shirt in his fist. His fingers grazed the soft skin of her back drawing a hiss from her lips as she pulled back. Her lips glistened from their kiss, swollen and red. He smiled down at her and she blushed.

"Beautiful," he whispered as he stroked her cheek. "My beautiful Cassie."

Cassie didn't know what to say. She had tried to show him through her kiss that she wanted him, all of him.

"I know *A'maelamin*, and I believe you."

"Then why the sad face?" She asked him.

He shook his head. "Not sad, just trying to memorize everything about you so that while I'm gone tomorrow, I can remember. Remember your smell, your taste, the way you feel in my arms."

"Oh," Cassie said as she tried to breathe around the lump in her throat.

"I think it's time for me to take you back." He stepped back and took her hand in his.

Cassie smiled and nodded, though she didn't want the day to end.

He followed her out of the park to where Cassie had told Elora to meet her through a text message.

"So you aren't coming back tonight?" Cassie asked remembering that her parents had wanted her to invite him for dinner.

"I've got some things to take care of. I'll be by in the morning before you leave to give you the dress to wear for the party."

Cassie nodded, not wanting to think about going to the party that the Dark Elf King and Queen were throwing in honor of Trik finding his Chosen.

"When you come to get me tomorrow evening you are going to have to meet my dad."

Trik noticed the worry in her eyes.

He laughed. "You act like I will be going before a firing squad."

"Oh, he won't try to kill you. He will simply pry into your life seeking out your deepest, darkest secrets. So just be prepared."

Just then Elora's car pulled up. Trik leaned down and placed a sweet kiss to her lips and then waved at Elora, who gave him the finger.

"I don't think she's happy with me." Trik smirked.

Cassie simply shrugged and backed away towards Elora's car.

"Oh," she called out as she opened the car door, "and remember. Any question that he asks about sex, your answer is that you never plan to have sex with me."

Trik's brow furrowed. "You want me to lie?"

"Through your ever-loving teeth," she said with a smile and a wink.

Trik watched as Elora backed up and then drove away with his heart. He would check on her later that night, after…

"You're glowing," Elora said to Cassie as they drove to her house.

"Am I?" Cassie asked nonchalantly.

Elora let out a disgusted groan. "I have a feeling that I should get used to the taste of vomit because I'm going to be throwing up in my mouth a lot around you two."

Cassie laughed.

"That wasn't meant to be funny," Elora said dryly. But Cassie wasn't listening. She was lost in the memories of the most incredible day of her life.

They pulled into Cassie's driveway and Elora turned the engine off. She turned in her seat so that she could face her friend.

"Okay, wipe that googly eyed look off your face long enough to think clearly."

Cassie smiled but quickly sobered under the single raised brow stare of her gothic friend.

"Are you sure you should be going to see the spawn of Satan Elfin style? Do you think it's safe?"

"You know Trik won't let anything happen to me," Cassie assured her.

"I hate to burst your bubble," said Elora.

"No you don't," Cassie quipped.

"Okay you're right; I don't give a damn if I burst your bubble. I know Trik may be the best assassin to ever grace any realm, but even he can be killed."

Cassie frowned. "I know that, but Lorsan isn't going to kill him."

"How do you know that?"

"I don't know, but something tells me he won't."

Elora rolled her eyes. "Fine, but if quiver boy gets put out of commission, don't come crying to me. I won't be offering you a comforting shoulder."

Cassie snorted. "Yeah right. You'd be the first one on your knees to hold me together."

Elora waved her out of her car. "That may be true but once you had pulled yourself together I wouldn't hesitate to point out that we sat in this very car and I told you it could happen."

Cassie pushed the door open and climbed out of the car. "Now *that* I believe." She closed the door and with a wave headed towards her house.

"Mom, Dad, I'm home!" Cassie yelled into the quiet house. The smell of food wafted to her from the kitchen and she followed the smell.

Her mom stood at the stove stirring something in a pot.

"Hey," Cassie said to her.

Sylvia turned her head. "Hey," she said back with a smile. "Where is Trik?"

"Oh, he can't make it tonight. His parents needed him."

"I hope everything is alright."

"Hope what is alright?" Her dad asked as he walked in behind Cassie.

"Trik can't make it tonight because his parents needed him," Sylvia explained.

"Well that's too bad," her dad said as he tucked some papers quickly behind his back.

Cassie's head fell back as she let out a groan. "Dad, tell me that isn't what I think it is."

"I don't know what you're talking about," he replied innocently.

She snapped out her hand to him. "Hand it over."

It was hard not to laugh when her dad's face took on the *I've been caught with my hand in the cookie jar* look as he handed the papers to her.

Cassie smoothed the papers out on the counter in front of her and began to read. Her mouth dropped open and the more she read, the more she was sure that it would hit the floor at any moment.

"Are you kidding me?" She cried out indignantly.

"Those are all very important details," her dad defended.

"Number 1," she began reading, "date of last drug screening and results." She paused, waiting for his justification.

"Don't you think it's important to know if he is using illegal drugs?"

Cassie skipped down a few lines. "Number four, Date of last sexual interaction and did you use protection; if so what kind?"

Cassie ignored her mom who was standing at the stove trying, but failing to hide her laughter.

"Wouldn't it bother you to know that only a week ago he might have been crawling out…". Cassie held her hand up to stop her dad from continuing that statement.

"Number twenty five? Really dad, twenty five?" Cassie gestured to the papers. Her dad simply looked at her innocently. "Number twenty five," she continued. "How many children have you fathered, are they all with the same woman?"

"Okay, maybe that one wasn't necessary considering if any of his answers led him to that one I would have already kicked him out," her dad admitted.

"I thought we decided that you weren't going to do the papers."

"Technically, yes we did."

"Technically, what does that even mean?" Cassie tore the papers up and threw them in the trash can. "You are not asking him those questions."

He shrugged as if he could care less. Cassie knew that meant he would just print another one. Apparently he had a database.

They sat down to eat and Cassie tried to decide the best moment to drop the news about tomorrow night.

There was a pause in the conversation and she decided that it was as good a time as any.

"So, Trik is taking me on a date tomorrow night."

Her dad raised an eyebrow at her, while her mom smiled with a nod. She figured that smile was just because her mom was happy to get to see his beautiful face again. Cassie totally understood.

"He will come in and talk to both of us before you leave," her dad told her.

Cassie nodded. "I told him that."

"Good," her dad said to no one in particular and Cassie swore that she saw the shadow of a smile cross his face.

Trik stepped into the court of the Light Elves. He had been surprised that he was able to get through. His kind was usually blocked from entry. He stared into the large throne room. The soft light glowed off of the pearl stone that fashioned the room. The lights seemed to come from the stone, illuminating everything, removing all shadows. Trik looked down and noticed his shadow was very light, but it was still a black spot in the room of white.

"What brings you to my court, Triktapic?" Tamsin walked out of one of the side walls. Trik realized that the pearl walls put off reflections allowing them to be used as openings to other realms.

"I have come to seek your council." Trik knelt down on one knee and bowed his head before the Light Elf King, something that he would not normally do if he hadn't been there to ask him for a favor.

"The world must be coming to an end if the Great Triktapic kneels before us," a feminine voice spoke across the room, her voice carried as it bounced off the high walls.

"He comes with a request," Tamsin told his Chosen as she came to stand next to him.

Syndra made an impatient noise as she looked down at the usually proud assassin. "Good grief Trik, stand up. What situation have you gotten yourself into that you would come to your enemies?"

Trik stood slowly and lifted his head. His eyes swam with emotion, emotion so deep it was like looking into a deep well and not being able to see the bottom.

Syndra took a step towards him. "What has happened?"

"Nothing. Not yet anyway." Trik took a deep breath and exhaled slowly before speaking again. "I have come to ask an oath of protection on my Chosen."

Tamsin and Syndra both frowned. "We already told you we would protect her."

"If I chose not to," Trik qualified. "You said that you would protect her if I chose not to. Now I need you to protect her in the case that I fail to."

"Why would you fail? When have you ever failed to protect your target or to take it out?"

Just then Trik made a decision, one that he'd always feared that he would eventually have to make. Trik's presence seemed to swell and suddenly he was bathed in a bright light and his radiance. His power filled the room making it feel small and inconsequential. His hair shimmered, black as night, and the silver of his eyes nearly became metallic with the intensity of their gleam. Tamsin and Syndra both took a step back, their mouths dropping open.

"You're a Royal," Syndra spoke quietly as she stared at Trik's Royal form.

He nodded once.

"Does Lorsan know?" Tamsin asked.

"No. He would have killed me long ago."

"You are right about that." Syndra snorted.

"I don't want to lead. I have never wanted to be King."

"How did you wind up as the King's right hand man?"

"That is a story for another time. I need to keep my secret from Lorsan for as long as possible. It is the only chance I have at defeating him."

"You are going to attack Lorsan?" Tamsin's voice was skeptical.

"If it comes to that. Cassie has asked me to walk away from him. I told her I would. She is under the impression that I've already done just that."

"You haven't?" Syndra frowned in disapproval.

"I have to do this strategically. I can't just walk into his court and tell him that I'm leaving. Cassie won't understand that. I have to appear to still be on board with his plan in order to protect her."

"If he thinks that she is the reason that you are leaving then she will be the first thing he goes after," Tamsin reasoned.

"Exactly."

"So you want us to protect Cassie if Lorsan decides to take you out?"

"I know she is not of your court."

Syndra held up a hand to stop him. "She is a pure one. She belongs here more than in your court. We will protect her, I give you my word." Syndra bowed to Trik.

"Thank you," Trik nodded and reached out to take her hand. Syndra placed it in his and her eyes widened as she felt him push pure, royal power into her.

"How?" She whispered to him.

He stepped away and without another word walked towards the pearl walls.

"What was that about?" Tamsin asked.

Syndra's eyes stayed on the wall where Trik had just disappeared through. Her mind was still trying to wrap around the revelation that Trik had just shared. Finally she turned to her *Sh'mai*, "He is the King."

"Yes, he is supposed to be the Dark King."

"No, Tamsin, my love. Triktapic is THE King."

Tamsin's mouth dropped just as Syndra's had. "Of the entire race?"

She nodded.

"How?"

"I have no idea."

He stood in the shadow of her room and watched as she slept. The gentle rise and fall of her chest reassuring him that she was safe, alive, and whole.

He hadn't planned to reveal his secret to Tamsin and Syndra, but he needed them to understand just how far he was willing to go to keep Cassie safe. If he had to destroy the entire dark elf race then he wouldn't hesitate, not even for a second. He knew that there would be consequences for his actions and he would deal with them, but he had to deal with each battle as it came. He stepped out of the darkness and the moon basked him in its soft glow. He approached her bed soundlessly, his motions so smooth that he hardly disturbed the air around him. He rarely used his Royal powers, but he was going to need them soon and he was out of practice.

He looked down at the woman who had slipped into his heart and taken over. Her soul was so pure that it chased all the shadows from his own. He reached down and stroked her cheek, barely a whisper against her soft skin. He leaned down and pressed a kiss to her hair and whispered.

"Dream of me, *arwenamin*, always dream of me." Using a subtle push he placed the idea in her mind so that he would be what she saw every time she closed her eyes.

He decided to stay and watch over her while she slept. In all honesty he couldn't leave. Knowing that she would be in danger the very next night in Lorsan's court, he didn't want to miss this time to be close to her. He stretched out beside her and pulled her into his arms. She would think she was dreaming. He smiled to himself as he looked into her mind, the benefits of being who and what he was, and thought that as long as she was dreaming of him, he could make it a good one.

Chapter 11

"I've figured out why it's better that the elves keep themselves hidden from humans. Because they're crazy, plain and simple. They are as whacked as they come. I wear black from head to toe; I decorate myself in morbid jewelry and pierce myself in places that should never be pierced, so if I am saying they are whacked then we have to accept that we are *royally* screwed. Pun intended." ~Elora

"Do I even want to know why you have that dreamy look on your face?" Elora asked dryly.

Cassie shook her head. "Probably not, unless you need to vomit this morning."

They walked into their first class and took their usual seats. Elora turned back to Cassie and gestured for her to talk. "Let's have it quiver lover."

Cassie blushed as she thought about why she had the smile plastered on her face that morning.

"I had the best dream."

Elora raised her eyes suggestively. "As in *the* best?"

Cassie grinned even bigger.

"Oh man, you're right I'm going to puke." Elora grumbled. "So are you going to be this annoying all day?"

"Probably."

"Damn."

Cassie laughed as she pulled out her History book and tried with all her might to appear interested in the things that were discussed. She was sure that she wasn't doing a good job based on the frowns she kept getting from Mrs. Davis.

By lunch time Elora was ready to punch her best friend in her dreamy face.

"Seriously, this can't be healthy," Elora ripped open her sack lunch as Cassie sat across from her.

"I'm telling you Elora, I've never had a dream that was so real."

"You have got to be kidding me, still with the dream. Okay now I have to know. If this dream was an all-day orgasm-inducing experience, then you are obligated by the Girlfriend Code Book to share."

Elora was sure Cassie's face invented some new shades of red as her eyes widened.

"Wow," was all Elora got out before Cassie's head jerked around, her embarrassment forgotten.

"Let me guess, your quiver radar has detected the quiver carrying bandit."

Cassie looked back at Elora and rolled her eyes. "Are you trying to come up with as many nick names as possible?"

"I'm writing a book."

"Really, what's it called?"

"The Quivers Among Us," Elora announced without missing a beat.

Cassie shook her head in exasperation at her friend.

She felt the familiar tug again and scanned the lunchroom for her Chosen. And then she saw him, and so did everyone else.

He was in his human guise, which was nearly as beautiful as his Elven one. He was tall and his gate was regal and bold. He held the attention of the entire room and all he was doing was walking. He was wearing faded denim jeans, his black boots, and a black t-shirt that said *I'm kina of a big deal.* She had never seen him in regular human clothes, and she had to admit he rocked a pair of jeans and novelty T-shirt like nobody's business.

When he finally reached their table he pulled out a chair next to Cassie and sat down. He leaned back and laid his arm on the back of her chair and nonchalantly played with a strand of her hair. The lunchroom was still quiet as they all watched Trik. His shirt was being proved right as they stared at him, doing absolutely nothing.

Elora saw his shirt and let out a snort of laughter as she shook her head at him.

"So does that mean you like me now?" Trik asked her.

"About as much as I'd like to throw up in my mouth all day."

"So that's a no?" Trik grinned, not bothered by Elora's jab in the least.

Cassie looked around the room as gasps ricocheted off the walls. His voice was a caress and she wasn't the only one affected by it. She felt a wave of possessiveness rush over her and knew that he had felt it too. He leaned in close to her ear and whispered. "You're hot when you're jealous."

Cassie stuck her tongue out at him and he laughed at her. She swore some of the girls were on the verge of passing out.

Elora looked around and then back at Trik. "Hey I bet we could make some money if we let them touch you, and charged for it."

This brought another burst of laughter from Trik. Cassie slapped his arm and whispered, "Stop laughing or some poor girl is going to die of a heart attack. What are you doing here anyways?" She asked him.

"I wanted to let you know that I have your dress for tonight."

"Is it weird?"

Trik scrunched up his face at her. "Explain weird."

"I think she's asking if it's some virginal, see through, sacrifice dress." Elora smiled at Cassie. "You can thank me later."

"That has some serious possibilities. Maybe I've gone too conservative in my choice." Trik teased Cassie as he watched her face flush.

"Can you leave now and take her with you so that I can eat my food without constantly regurgitating it?"

"I like you Elora."

"So not what I was going for," she told him, her voice dripped with sarcasm.

Trik stood and grabbed Cassie's hand. "Walk me out?" He asked.

She nodded at him and let him pull her up to her feet. Cassie gave a small wave to Elora who rolled her eyes and shook her head.

Trik watched as Cassie walked in front of him. The sway of her hips was natural and her every move was made with a subtle sensuality that she wasn't even aware of. Cassie was oblivious to how desirable she was and based on the number of eyes following her progress, she filled more than a few of their thoughts. The idea of them thinking about his Chosen in such a way filled him with rage. Cassie stumbled as she felt his fury through their hands that were clasped together. Trik's eyes roamed the room landing on stare after stare and their faces paled at what they saw in him. He knew they felt it. When he met their eyes they knew they were staring at the face of death.

Cassie tried to walk faster but Trik didn't let her pull him. He wanted every male to know that she was his and to pursue her would be their demise. Was he overreacting? Probably. Did he care? Nope.

Once they were outside Cassie folded her arms across her chest trying to fight off the crisp, cool, fall air.

"I put the dress in your car," Trik told her as he wrapped an arm around her waist and pulled her to him.

Cassie looked around to see if anyone was watching. She was pretty sure that guys that weren't students weren't supposed to be hanging out at the high school. She had been so caught up in him being there that she hadn't thought of it in the lunchroom.

"Nervous?" he asked her.

"I just don't want to get caught standing out here in the arms of an older guy who isn't a student."

"You'd rather get caught standing out here in the arms of an older guy who is a student?" Trik teased, but she saw the underlying tension in the narrowing of his eyes.

"Why were you flipping out in the lunchroom?"

He looked down at her, taking in her beauty that wasn't only skin deep. Cassie was beautiful from the inside out. She was the furthest person from vain that he had ever come across and she was oblivious to her effect on the opposite sex.

"Cassie, every guy in that cafeteria was drooling on themselves as you walked past. I don't go to school here so they don't see me with you. For all they know you are available. I wanted them to know that you were the complete opposite of available."

Cassie laughed. "*You*, tough guy assassin are insecure?"

Trik frowned, "I'm not insecure. You don't realize how possessive the males in my race are of their Chosen. Cassie, I have waited over a thousand years for you. You are beyond precious to me and so yes, I'm possessive and overprotective. But I'm not insecure. The males in that room," he motioned towards the lunchroom, "could never give you what I can, care for you the way I do, make you feel the way I do. You would always feel empty with another male."

"What about you?" Cassie leaned back so she could see his face clearly. "Am I the only girl who can give you what you want, what you need? Do you think that no other could care for you the way I do?"

"There are no others. There is only you. No other could be what I need and want. No other could love me as you will. No other will ever make me feel the way you do. My soul would cry out in betrayal if I tried to be with another, just as your soul would cry out."

Cassie didn't realize that she had been holding her breath. She had been waiting for him to bust out the L word but he had yet to tell her that he loved her. She couldn't decide if it was because he wasn't there yet or if maybe he couldn't love her. Maybe his dark nature would keep him from ever loving her. Her heart broke at the thought and she quickly pushed it away not wanting him to see it.

"I'll see you tonight," Trik told her as he released her and stepped back. She smiled at him and blew him a kiss as he walked backward towards the parking lot.

"I'll take that as a promise," he called out to her with his wicked grin.

Cassie laughed and gestured for him to go. She turned and went back inside the school. Lunch had just ended and students filled the hall, making their way to their next class. Cassie stood watching as they went about their normal, daily activities. She realized then that this normal life would never be enough again, not since Trik. She had tasted what it would be like to be with him in his world and it was decadent. Going back to her life would be like trading the finest chocolate for the generic brand at the Dollar General.

"Earth to lover girl," Elora snapped her fingers in front of Cassie's face.

Cassie blinked several times clearing her mind. She looked at Elora, who was frowning at her and said, "Hey!"

Elora raised a single brow at her friend's perky demeanor. She had decided that as soon as she and Trik had left the lunchroom that she would not be asking Cassie about her midday interlude with the dark one. "You ready?"

Cassie nodded and a slow smile crept across her face. "Definitely."

"Is everything ready for tonight?" Lorsan asked Ilyrana.

She smiled and nodded. "It's going to be perfect."

"I agree," he said with a wicked smile.

"What plan do you have up your sleeve King of mine?"

Lorsan's eyes narrowed as he spoke. "Tonight, my love, I will find out if Triktapic really is as loyal to me as he says."

"How?"

"Simple, I'm going to have a chat with his Chosen, and see how much he has told her; if he really has been as honest with her as he claims to be."

"You think she will be honest?" She asked.

"If she's as good and pure as Trik makes her out to be, then yes, she will be honest."

Ilyrana let out a deep sigh. "I hope, for Trik's sake, that he really is still your warrior in heart and action."

Tamsin sifted through page after page of archives and letters of centuries long past. He was searching. The Forest Lords had told him that a great change was coming and that one that was lost would be restored. Was it Trik they were talking about? If he is the King of the Elven race and he has been lost, in a manner of speaking, would he not be who they were talking about being restored? If so, Tamsin knew that something would need to take place to be the catalyst for that change. Something in Tamsin told him that he needed to find out what that catalyst would be.

He had been at it for hours when he came across the oldest record thus far. It was written by the first scribes of the Elfin people, the scribes to the King, before they were divided.

I, Cyntree, scribe to the King of the Elves so write this account of the last record of his reign. Our people are fighting amongst themselves. They have forgotten the Forest Lords and the love for their creation. They no longer honor their creator or the King put in place by them. Triktapic,

Tamsin paused over the name, he couldn't breathe, couldn't move. Trik was indeed the King of all the elves; it was him.

The King of the Elves has petitioned the Forest Lords. He asks that they relieve him of his duty for he is tired of his people ignoring his council, refusing to obey his commands. He has tried to show them mercy, tried to understand what it was that was tearing them apart, but he has grown weary. The Forest Lords were not happy with the King's request, but they granted it. Written here is a summary of the terms by which they allowed Triktapic to abdicate his throne.

He would give up his Royal powers endowed to him by the Lords. He would become like the other elves.

His abdication would cause a split in the elves, dark and light, and his place would be with the dark.

He would serve the new Dark Elf King as an assassin, merciless and fierce. For if he was tired of being a loving King then he would know no love.

His appearance would be altered so that none would recognize him and his reign would fade into history.

Only one thing would restore him as the rightful King, only one thing will unite the dark and light elves and once again make them the Elfin race. The King's Chosen. Trik would have to love his Chosen above himself, above his desires, wants, and needs. He must do for his Chosen what he did not do for his people. He must love her unconditionally through the peaceful times and the times of strife and war, no matter how difficult it became. He must recognize this love and choose it. Choose to love her for she will not always be loveable, just as his people were not always loveable. Once his heart has been restored to its once selfless state, then he will be King once more.

The Forest Lords gave him one last warning before they completed the request. Because of the life he would soon lead, darkness would begin to seep into his once

pure heart. He would kill, torture, and destroy many lives before he would meet his
Chosen. Their warning was this—if the darkness consumes you fully before you
meet your Chosen, you will have lost your ability to love selflessly. For love brings
life, life is brought forth in light, and if darkness seeps into every cavern, crevice and
secret place inside you there will be no room for light to shine and no way for love to
grow.

Tamsin sat in stunned silence as he read the last paragraph over
and over. His Chosen. Trik must love his Chosen. Did he love Cassie?
Tamsin could tell that he felt strongly for her, he was certainly
possessive and protective of her, but did he love her? He was willing to
walk away from Lorsan. Was that an act of love? But he wasn't being
honest with Cassie about how he would be walking away. Would the
love for your Chosen allow you to lie to her or would it pierce your
heart so strongly that you kept nothing from her.

No, Tamsin wasn't sure if Trik loved her. And if he did he might
not even realize it. He needed to speak with the Forest Lords again. He
needed their guidance on how to move forward. Tamsin wondered
then if Trik remembered the decree given him by the Lords, or if it was
too late and he no longer had enough light left in him to remember.

Cassie stood in her room staring at the bag sitting on her bed. The
bag Trik had left in the back of her car because it was supposed to have
her dress in it. She shook her head at it as she thought that there could

be no way a dress could fit in that bag, and if there was a dress in that bag then it was for a Barbie doll. She was actually a little nervous about opening it and found herself stalling. She took a shower, blow-dried her hair, then put on some makeup. But now there was nothing else she could do other than open the cursed bag and get it over with. Her mom had asked her what it was and she did not want to see her mom's expression when she told her that Trik had bought her a dress to wear. So she just told her it was a surprise from Trik and she hadn't opened it yet. And that was the truth. It would be a surprise to find out how he stuffed a dress for a grown woman in that tiny, blasted bag.

"Okay," she muttered as she stepped towards the bed, "moment of truth."

She grabbed the handles and held them like they were covered in flesh eating mucus as she pulled the bag open. She reached down into it and felt her fingers touch a handful of fabric. She bunched it up in her hand and pulled her arm out. She held out a piece of material and watched as it seemed to grow in her hand. She dropped most of it, only holding on to a small piece and the fabric continued to magically grow. Finally it stopped.

Cassie grasped it in both hands and spread it out and saw that it was a beautiful, black dress with a black lace shell over the fabric. It had long lace sleeves that allowed the skin to be seen and a V neck that plunged a little lower than she would have normally picked. She held it up to her and stood in front of her mirror. The dress hit just below mid-thigh, short enough to be sexy, long enough to not have to pull it down constantly.

She grabbed the bag off of her bed intending to lay the dress out while she got undressed and realized that the bag was not empty. She was sure there hadn't been anything else in the bag when she had pulled out the dress. Peeking over the edge of the side she looked back into it and grinned. She reached in and pulled out black heels, the strappy kind that accentuate small ankles. She hadn't thought about having shoes to match. Well Trik was good for one thing at least. She smiled to herself knowing that Trik was good for much more than one thing.

She undressed and quickly slipped the black dress on, eager to see if it looked as good on as it did lying on her bed. It slipped over her head and down her body caressing her too sensitive skin. She shuddered at the sensation of the cool material against her. Once the dress was completely on she felt the fabric shift and move, stretching here and shrinking there. She stood in front of the mirror watching in fascination as the dress fit itself to her very form, every curve and straight line. It was molding itself to her body. Finally all movement ceased and she stood their wearing the most elegant dress she had ever laid eyes on and couldn't believe how amazing it made her look. She turned in the mirror looking at the back only then realizing there was an even more daring V cut than had been there previously. Apparently Elven clothes had more magical properties than even a Victoria's Secret bra and she had to admit that it was pretty freaking cool.

She strapped on the heels, fluffed out her hair, took one last look in the mirror and froze. There was a soft knock on her door.

"Come in," she said softly as that was all she could manage as she took in the woman who stared back at her from the mirror.

Cassie's mom inhaled sharply as she entered the room and saw Cassie standing there.

"Is that what was in that little bag?" She asked.

Cassie nodded still unable to speak.

"You look grown, no longer my little girl." Sylvia looked into the mirror with Cassie and she met her daughter's eyes. "You look astonishing."

Cassie cleared her throat and smiled. "Thank you."

"Where is he taking you that you have to be dressed so fancy?"

Cassie was momentarily caught off guard by the question and stumbled before she finally got out an answer. "He wouldn't tell me."

Sylvia nodded slowly, a hint of skepticism in her eyes.

The doorbell rang and Cassie rolled her eyes at herself when she thought, *Saved by the Bell.*

She followed her mom out of the room and down the stairs just as her dad was opening the door. Cassie stopped in her tracks, her mom stopped, time stopped. Trik stood at her door in a sleek black tuxedo. And just as she had thought many other times, she didn't know how a man could look sexy in a suit with a bowtie, but he pulled it off magnificently. He was, of course, in his human guise so his hair was shorter than normal, but just as black. His silver eyes met hers and she shivered as those intense eyes traveled down her body, not bothering to hide his intensity or possessiveness in that look.

He held his hand out to her father introducing himself but his eyes never left her. She realized her dad was speaking and finally tore her eyes from Trik's penetrating stare.

"What dad?" Cassie asked.

"I said why don't we have a seat in the living room?" William Tate motioned in the direction of the living room.

Trik waited for Cassie to descend the rest of the stairs and met her at the bottom. He held his hand out to her as she hit the last step. She stepped down and Trik pulled her close as they followed her dad.

He leaned down as they walked and put his mouth next to her ear. "There are not words that could describe how you look tonight."

Cassie felt her face heat as the blood rushed into her skin. She looked up at him and he winked at her, which did not help her already dazed condition.

Her dad sat on the couch next to her mom, making it painfully obvious that he did not want her and Trik sitting close, as the only chairs left were a rocking chair and a winged back chair. Trik smiled at her as he took the chair directly across from her dad. Cassie sat down and she was stiff with nervousness at what her father might do. She immediately buried her face in her hands when her dad handed Trik a piece of paper and a pen.

"Trik, this is just a questionnaire on things that I feel are important for me to know. Your phone number, address, emergency contact info, that sort of thing."

Trik looked down at the paper in his hand and scanned over it. The first five questions were indeed generic information questions. Question six was a tad more personal and asked if Trik had ever consumed alcohol or smoked cigarettes. Question seven asked if he had ever tried or was currently using recreational drugs. It wasn't until question ten that Cassie's father hit his famous stride.

Under the pretense of trying to concentrate on the paper before him, Trik began to read aloud, knowing that it would only cause Cassie to cringe. "Number ten, have you ever participated in a sexual encounter."

Right on cue, Cassie groaned.

Trik smiled to himself and continued reading silently. He frowned at one question in particular and began to read out loud again. "If your mom asked you to buy her a bra and she said to get her a 34 C, would you know what that meant? If so what does the number 34 represent and what does the letter C represent?"

Cassie groaned when Trik stopped. She couldn't look up for fear that he would tell her to have a nice life and walk as quickly away from her crazy father as he could.

Trik looked up at William Tate after reading the question and chuckled. "Mr. Tate, I think the better question would be what kind of weird relationship do I have with my mother that I would be buying her a bra?"

Cassie peeked through her fingers, first at Trik, and then at her dad. To her surprise her dad was chuckling right along with Trik.

William held his hand out for the paper and Trik handed it over without having written down a single thing.

"Maybe I go a little over board in my protectiveness of Cassie," he admitted.

Trik shook his head. "I can understand why," he turned to look at her and she had finally dropped her hands from her face. He smiled at her as he spoke. "I feel very protective of her as well." He looked back at her dad and the smile was gone and his face was serious. "I assure you Mr. Tate, I will treat her with respect and I will keep her safe."

Cassie's dad stood and everyone followed suit. He held his hand out to once again shake Trik's hand.

"Thank you. It was very nice to meet you, Trik. Have a good time and please be safe."

Cassie took Trik by the hand and pulled him out of the door before her dad decided to ask Trik to pull out his wallet to see if there was a condom in it.

"What did you think?" Sylvia asked William after shutting the door as Trik and Cassie drove off.

He narrowed his eyes in thought and rubbed his chin. "He seems a lot older than eighteen, but doesn't look older. I think he was telling me the truth about respecting her. He won't touch her without her permission."

"I have to agree. The way he looks at her, like she is the only thing in his world and more precious than the most beautiful diamond."

"The question is, is that a good thing or not?" He asked her.

"They are young," Sylvia agreed.

"We'll see how tonight goes," William said. "Heck, she might have a horrible time and hate him by the end of the night."

She shook her head at her husband, "I don't think Cassie could hate anyone."

"Everyone has their breaking point Sylvia, you know that."

"That wasn't too bad," Trik told Cassie as they drove, to where Cassie didn't have a clue.

"Trik, he asked you about your sex life."

"Or the lack thereof," he interjected, which earned him a fist in the side.

"He asked you if you understood bra sizing. What exactly would you consider too bad?" She asked, obviously still very embarrassed by her father's actions.

"Well it could have been worse."

"No I don't think so," she said shaking her head.

"What if he had asked me to label pictures of sexual positions?"

Cassie slapped her hands over her ears. "You did not just say that. I am going to totally ignore that it even came from your mouth."

Trik laughed and pulled one of her hands away. "Okay I'll conduct myself in a more gentlemanly manner."

She lowered her other hand cautiously.

"Or what if he would have asked…."

"STOP! Not another word."

"Okay, okay," he relented.

"So where'd you get the fancy car?" Cassie asked, changing the subject, as she sunk into the rich leather seats of the BMW.

"I'm not without my resources," Trik winked.

Her eyes widened as she asked. "You didn't steal it did you?"

Trik looked at her from the corner of his eye and then back to the road. "Cassie, I've been around for quite a while, surely you don't think I haven't the money to purchase a car."

Cassie shrugged. "Dude, you work for an evil elf King hell bent on taking over the world. I don't think it's a stretch for me to consider that you might have illegally procured a vehicle."

"Okay I concede your point." He glanced at her then a crooked smile appeared. "What's with the big vocabulary? Procured?"

"I'm just trying to keep up," she told him, "one minute you are throwing out slang with the best of them and the next you sound like Wilfred."

"Who's Wilfred?"

"You know, Batman's butler."

Trik laughed and butterflies danced in her stomach at the joy that shone on his face.

"You mean Alfred?"

Cassie's mouth dropped open. "How do you know that?"

"I'm seriously beginning to be insulted, beautiful. You think that just because I'm old…"

"Ancient," she interrupted.

He frowned at her. "Fine, ancient, and from another race, you think that I don't know anything about your world."

"Do you watch a lot of movies?"

"I have a human friend that I've spent time with and he often wants to sit and watch movies. He calls it male bonding."

Cassie smiled. "Do you like movies?"

Trik thought about it. "I guess some of them. I'm amazed that they create such worlds in their movies but can't fathom that they might actually exist."

"We are often scared of what we don't understand and what we don't understand we often chalk up to imagination, not reality," she said.

Trik reached over for her hand and brought it to his lips. He placed a kiss tenderly in the center of her palm. "Sometimes you seem so very young, and then you go and say something like that and I wonder if you too have been waiting for me as long as I have for you."

They drove in silence, lights from the other cars shined into theirs and Cassie watched as each car illuminated Trik's face for brief moments in time and each time she was caught breathless by him. She finally tore her eyes from him and began to pay attention to where they were. Her eyes widened as they pulled into the parking lot of her dad's building.

"What are we doing here?" She asked.

Trik got out of the car without a word and came around to her side. He opened the door and helped her out, quickly wrapping an arm around her, blocking the cold night air from her exposed skin as he pulled her into the protection of his body.

"I have something for you," he said as they began walking.

Cassie's brow rose. "And it's in my dad's building?"

He nodded but didn't say anything more. He led her to one of the large glass windows and pictured the conference room he had been standing in when the Forest Lords had brought his Chosen to him. He stepped through the glass pulling Cassie with him.

They emerged into the conference room and Cassie's mouth dropped open.

She turned in a circle as she took the room in. Candles lined the walls on shelves, that hadn't been there the last time she was there. The long table that had been in the middle of the room was gone and in its place a small round table that held a single, small black box. Light from the candles fell down across the box and though it was the smallest thing in the room it seemed to take up the most space. Soft music played, though she didn't know where it was coming from.

She finally looked over at Trik who was watching her with eyes full of passion. He reached for her and pulled her into his arms. He wrapped one arm around her and his hand found the bare skin from the V in her dress. He took her other hand in his and held it to his chest and began to move with her.

"I wanted some time with you alone. And I thought what better place to go than where we first met. Once we arrive at Lorsan's I will get little time to hold you," he told her as he pulled her tighter against him. Cassie laid her head on his chest and immersed her senses in Trik. His scent, the feel of his body, the touch of his hand on her back, the breath pouring over her hair as he laid his cheek against her head. Cassie didn't think it could get any better than this. Trik chuckled as he caught the thought.

He leaned down and whispered into her ear, as his lips grazed her skin. "It gets better beautiful, much, much better."

Cassie's breath caught and they stopped dancing as she looked up at him. He took her face gently in his hands and his traveled over it. She was sure that he was going to say it, but she locked that thought away. She wouldn't ruin this moment by worrying about what hadn't been said. She would focus on all he had said to her. He trailed his thumb across her lips as he spoke.

"*Arwenamin, a'maelamin, lle amin ar amin naa lle nai. Amin mela lle.*"

Cassie listened as the language of his people rolled off his tongue and poured over her heart.

"What did you say?"

He moved his thumb from her lips and caressed her jaw as he brought his lips to hers. As he spoke, his lips brushed hers with every word. First in Elvesh, and then in her language.

"*Arwenamin* means my lady, *A'maelamin*, my beloved, *lle amin*, you are mine, *ar*, and, *amin naa lle nai*, I am yours to command."

Cassie felt each word in the very deepest part of her soul. She felt her soul reaching out to him, wrapping her in the promise of them. She pulled back from his lips and her head tipped to the side as she examined his eyes. "What about that last part? What did that mean?"

Instead of answering her he pulled her over to the table that held the little black box. Cassie felt her heart begin to race as she watched Trik pick up the box, opened the lid and pulled out a ring. It didn't look like an engagement ring and she couldn't decide if she was glad or disappointed. He took her left hand and as he slipped the ring on her finger she felt him tremble. That's when she realized that this was extremely significant.

He stared at the ring on her hand. His eyes were intense and she watched as he dropped his human guise and his Elfin form took over. Her eyes widened as a halo of light bathed them both in warmth and as suddenly as it had come it was gone.

"Trik?" Cassie said hesitantly.

He looked up at her as his thumb stroked across the ring. She didn't look at it. She couldn't, not yet, not until she knew for sure that his heart belonged to her.

"I cannot tell you what it means right now. What I can tell you is that I am yours; I will follow you to the ends of any realm. Never has there been and never will there be anyone who holds my heart as you do." He pulled her into his arms and pressed his lips to hers. His hands followed the contour of her body drawing her closer to him. He deepened the kiss as she opened her mouth to him and he drank her in as a dying man who had gone a lifetime without water. Trik walked her backwards until her back was pressed against the wall. His lips left her mouth and she groaned in protest. He smiled against her skin as he kissed her jaw, behind her ear, down her neck, and across her collar bone.

Cassie gasped when Trik suddenly turned her around so that her back was pressed to him. He gently brushed her hair aside leaving her neck bare and the complete V of her dress visible. He kissed the back of her neck and up to her ear nipping her before he whispered. "I'm not sure I approve of how deep this plunge is my love." He punctuated his words with a finger trailing down the opening from her neck to her lower back where the V ended.

Cassie hissed at his touch and arched her back. "You don't get to complain, you picked out the dress," she told him breathlessly.

Trik chuckled against her soft skin, "Touché, *Arwenamin.*"

Cassie looked over her shoulder at him. "Am I," she paused as the emotions she had been holding together began to crumble, "am I your lady?"

"Shh, my beautiful one." His words only made Cassie's tears fall faster. "Of course you are mine. Have I not shown you, told you, possessed you body and soul?"

"Yes," she whispered through the tears and though he had done all those things, one thing still remained and she tried to stop the thought before it came but she knew that he had seen it when he tensed. It took only one heartbeat for him to relax again.

The tears stained her face as she began to compose herself. She was being ridiculous. Trik had shown her how he felt about her; she didn't need to hear it to know it was true.

He held her face and kissed each tear away and then pressed one gentler kiss to her lips.

"We should go," he told her as he stepped back and helped her straighten her dress.

He smiled and considered her slightly tousled look. "You are breathtaking after I have loved on you."

Cassie rolled her eyes. "Is that a compliment for me or you?"

He took her hand and laughed as he pulled her back towards the windows. "A little of both I suppose."

"Of course it is," she mumbled as they once again stepped into the glass.

Chapter 12

"I feel it deep inside me. Something pushes, a memory, but I do not know if I want to learn what that memory is. The realms are restless, as dark skies overtake the light. I know everything is about to change. I'm going to have to make a choice. What if I choose wrongly? What if I choose her? I don't know if I can be what she needs. I know I don't deserve her. I know that I have done something in my past that has made me unworthy of her love. What is it? What did I do? I know who I was, but I don't know how I became who I am." ~Triktapic

Cassie and Trik walked down a long corridor, with cathedral ceilings and pristine, black onyx walls. It was a breathtaking sight. Spaced evenly along the length of the corridor were torches hanging on the walls. The flickering flames cast shadows across the floor appearing as if caught in a timeless dance.

When they had stepped into the glass of the conference room window and out of a mirror into one of Trik's suites in the Dark King's castle, Cassie was convinced that she had to be dreaming. Everything she laid her eyes on was beautiful, made of the highest quality and most precise technique. It was clear that Lorsan spared no expense.

Even now as she walked through the castle and down the corridor gradually growing closer to the main room, the evidence of his greed was all around her.

"Why does he have so many nice things?" Cassie asked Trik.

Trik looked down at her as his brow furrowed. "Because he can." His answer was so clipped that Cassie realized that Trik had thought her question ridiculous.

"We shouldn't always do something just because we can, Trik."

Trik let out a deep breath and lowered his eyes. "I know," his words were barely above a whisper.

They finally stood before the large doors of what Trik had called the main hall. Cassie never understood why they called a large room the main hall, when it wasn't a hall at all. She shrugged off the thought and brought her mind back to the matter at hand. She was about to enter the room where the Evil King and his Queen were waiting for them. They had put together this Happy Chosen party and she was the guest of honor. *Yippee*, she thought to herself. She felt Trik squeeze her and saw a smirk on his face. He was looking into her mind and catching her little sarcastic tidbits.

She let out a deep breath and plastered a smile on her face, though all she felt like doing was throwing up.

"Please don't," Trik whispered to her.

"Would you please mind your own business?"

"You are my business, beautiful," Trik told her never missing a beat.

He pulled her hand up to his mouth and kissed it. His eye caught on the ring and he touched it lightly. "Better take that off for now. Can you put it somewhere?"

Cassie quirked an eyebrow at him. "I'm wearing a dress that fits like a second skin and you ask me if I have some place to stick a ring?"

Trik grinned and it was a wicked, wicked grin. "That dress is no doubt incredible, but it's what's underneath that is stunning."

Cassie blushed as she slipped the ring off. She looked down at herself and thought nothing could be done for it. So she looked up at Trik with her own wicked grin and stuck the ring down in her ample bosom. Her grin spread even wider when Trik's eyes nearly bugged out of his glorious face.

"If you," Trik started to speak but Cassie held up a hand to stop him and whispered. "Not a word."

The doors to the main hall began to open and Cassie held her breath as she waited.

"Breathe love," Trik whispered.

When the doors were finally opened all the way Cassie was able to see that the black onyx theme carried into the hall. The only difference was the subtle red accents added to this room. The tables along the side of the room, which held every food under the sun, had a black table covering with vases of red flowers spaced throughout.

Huge chandeliers with silver candles hung from the cathedral ceiling. In-between each chandelier was a banner with a different picture depicted on them. There were a total of four banners alternating in color from red to black holding a picture that was the opposite of the banner. So the first banner was black and had a red snake, or what looked like a snake on it. The second banner was red with a black tree on it, the third black with a red dragon on it and the fourth was red with black stars on it. Cassie stared at the banners and for a moment she swore she saw the great red dragon move.

Trik looked over at her and saw that she was staring at the banners.

"Those are the pictures depicted in the dark elf crest," he explained.

"Do you all have a team cheer too?" Cassie asked dryly.

Trik simply stared at her and she looked slightly ashamed.

"Sorry, I'm just a little tense."

He gave her hand a squeeze. "It will be over before you know it."

Before Cassie could respond a tall man with gold eyes walked up to them. Cassie had to blink several times as she took in the male before her. He was every bit as handsome as Trik, but he made her skin crawl. His eyes were gold and they stared into her making her wish she could crawl into the deepest, darkest hole she could find. He too wore a tux, which surprised her. She expected them to be in some sort of medieval clothes like she often saw Trik wear when he was in his Elfin form.

He smiled at her and reached out his hand to her. She remembered the first time that Trik had made the same motion to her. Her emotions then had been screaming at her not to take his hand, but she had felt like it was because something in her would be changed forever. Now as she stood before the Dark Elf King and his out stretched hand, again her emotions screamed at her to run, but this time it was for her life. They told her to run as far and as fast as she could because this man could easily take her life. She knew that if she denied his hand that it would be rude and embarrass Trik and she didn't want that. So she reached out her own hand and placed it in his. He brought it to his lips and pressed a cool kiss there, his eyes never leaving hers. It wasn't the type of eye contact that would be considered flirting; more like the way a snake would look at a mouse. Cassie shivered and politely pulled her hand away.

"I am honored to meet Triktapic's Chosen," Lorsan told her.

Cassie smiled and tried very hard to make it convincing.

"Thank you," she responded. "It's very nice to meet you as well."

A woman stepped up next to Lorsan and Cassie guessed that she must be his Queen though Trik had never really spoken of her. She was beautiful, of course. Cassie had yet to see an elf that wasn't. She had long dark hair that shimmered when she moved. Her eyes were a dark purple and made Cassie think of the contacts that Elora wore. She wore a dress that was similar to Cassie's, only the elf's dress was long and had a short train that trailed behind her.

"I am Ilyrana, Queen of the dark elves." The woman stepped forward and smiled at Cassie. Cassie was surprised to see the warmth behind her purple eyes.

"Hello," Cassie smiled. "I'm Cassie."

"I know," Ilyrana let out a small laugh, "you have caused quite the stir."

Cassie wasn't sure what to say to that so she simply smiled. Trik took her hand and pulled her close to his side as the Dark King and Queen continued to stare at her. Finally after a few moments of awkward silence, Lorsan spoke up.

"Come let me introduce you to my court. He took her hand and placed it in the crook of his arm and started walking before she or Trik could argue. Cassie looked over her shoulder at Trik who was being pulled to the dance floor by the Queen.

Lorsan introduced her to all sorts of elves. Most were warriors, but some were gardeners and some were cooks. She met a weapons crafter and a weapons master, a grounds keeper, a seamstress, a decorator and a librarian. It was all so very medieval. She hadn't realized that she had spoken out loud until Lorsan answered.

"You can't expect us to have the same things that are in your realm; we are not human. We do not need the same things; our magic takes care of much that you would need a machine to do."

"Why do you still have gardeners and not grocery stores?" she asked him.

Lorsan shook his head. "My people rely on me for their needs, and that is the way it should be."

"So you keep them dependent on you by controlling all of the goods they receive," Cassie challenged.

Lorsan frowned. "No, they are not dependent. They can have their own gardens and learn their own trades. But why should they when I provide it for them?"

Cassie shrugged. "I come from a democracy. A dictatorship just seems selfish to me."

"It is my job to maintain order in my kingdom. I am the King of a dark race with dark ambitions and desires. You cannot compare us to your people."

"You might be surprised," Cassie muttered.

Lorsan chuckled. "True enough. Come," he told her as he began walking again, "let's have a dance."

Cassie groaned inwardly. She was not the dancing type, but again, she did not want to embarrass Trik. She allowed Lorsan to pull her onto the dance floor and lead her into a dance that seemed old and oddly symbolic of something.

"Why did you introduce me to all of those people?" Cassie finally asked the King.

Lorsan raised a brow at her question.

"I thought you would want to know the people that you will soon be living with."

Cassie's movements slowed as she looked up at the King.

"Living with?"

Lorsan nodded, "Surely Trik told you that you cannot stay in the human realm."

Cassie recalled Trik mentioning this, but they had yet to discuss it since he had told her he would walk away from being Lorsan's killer.

"You would be willing to let Trik live here even though he is no longer your assassin?" Cassie asked cautiously. Not that she had any intention of living with the Dark King and his little dark minions.

Lorsan stopped abruptly causing Cassie to stumble. He stepped back from her and she had to lean forward with her arms out to keep from falling on her face. She stood up once her balance was restored and looked up into a face filled with mistrust and disbelief.

"What are you saying Chosen of Triktapic?" His voice was a menacing whisper.

Cassie's eyes shifted around the room as people began to stop and stare.

"Didn't Trik tell you that he was quitting?" She asked slowly.

Lorsan's frame began to shake with anger. "Quitting?" He growled.

Suddenly Trik was at her side pulling her behind him. Lorsan's eyes met Trik's and Cassie was sure that if looks could kill then Trik would be a dead dark assassin.

"What lies does she spew, Trik?"

Trik looked back at Cassie and it was then that she saw it. Guilt. She took a step back as her mouth dropped open. Her eyes widened and when he took a step towards her she held a hand up to stop him from coming any closer.

"You didn't tell him," Cassie's voice was hoarse as her throat threatened to close off. She tried to take in gasps of air but her lungs seemed to be constricting, not allowing any life giving air to pass through.

"Cassie," her name was a plea on his lips.

"Why? Why did you lie to me?" Cassie continued to back away from the man she loved, the man who had now broken her heart.

"You never intended to leave him did you? You were just going to keep on doing what you do best, killing and lying."

"Cassie you don't understand," Trik tried again to move towards her.

"NO! YOU DON'T UNDERSTAND," she yelled. "I trusted you, I believed in you, I gave my heart to you and what did you do? You lied to me."

Cassie didn't see him move and he was standing directly in front of her.

"Cassie I lo…." Cassie slapped him across the face before he could finish his sentence.

"Don't you dare say those words to me. You have no right. I told you what I could handle and I told you what was a deal breaker." Tears began to form in her eyes as the anger began to turn into pain.

"I just wanted you to choose me, to choose us, Trik." She looked up into his silver eyes one last time. She took in the beautiful dark hair and full red lips. This would be the last time she saw him and she wanted to remember. Trik must have seen the intent in her eyes because as she turned and ran for the mirrors along the walls he lunged for her calling out her name. She didn't look back and didn't stop to think that she might just crash into the mirror instead of going through it. But she needn't have worried. She reached the mirror and her foot slipped right through. She felt a hand on her arm but ripped it out of the grasp. She emerged in the store room of Enigma and crumpled to the cold ground. Sobs ripped from her chest as she curled into a ball and let the pain of their separation sweep over her and drag her under.

"GRAB HIM," Lorsan bellowed as he watched Trik reach for his Chosen as she disappeared through the mirror.

Trik felt hands grasp his arms and pull him away from the mirror where his love had vanished.

Trik fought their hold as he roared into the great hall. The pain in his chest ripped through his body and he flung those who attempted to hold him away, their bodies crashing into mirrors and walls. He knew that he needed to get control of himself. He would need to fool Lorsan now or he would be locked up and never be able to get to Cassie. His body shook as he tried to regain his composure. His head slowly rose as he looked at his King.

"You were going to leave me?" Lorsan's face was shrouded in darkness as his eyes bore into Trik.

"Did you not just hear my Chosen yelling that I had lied to her? I obviously had no intention of leaving you. I had hoped that she wouldn't find out," Trik lied smoothly. He needed Lorsan to believe that he was loyal, that he had no intention of defecting. Lorsan continued to stare at him, searching for any deceit in his words.

The room was still and everyone held their breath as the Dark King deliberated over his dark assassin.

Finally Lorsan spoke.

"You are not to see her again." He paused waiting to see Trik's response.

"She is my Chosen," Trik growled.

"And she has made her choice. She cannot accept you as you are. What more is there to discuss with her.?"

Trik glared at his King but did not say anything more about it.

"Are we done?" He asked.

"Do you have somewhere to be?" Lorsan asked.

"If I remember correctly, there is a crop of Rapture being bottled tonight. Am I not still in charge of this venture?"

"Yes, you are. Fine go and take care of it." Lorsan motioned. "Trik I meant what I said. Stay away from the human."

Trik turned and walked to the mirrors. Without looking back or acknowledging the King's words, he stepped through.

Lorsan turned and caught Alok's eye. "Keep an eye on him."

Alok nodded and headed to a mirror to follow Trik to California where the crops and labs were.

Ilyrana walked over to her mate and lifted her hand to his face. He closed his eyes at her touch.

"Leave us," he announced to the hall and a few moments later they were alone.

"Do you believe him?" He asked her.

"No," Ilyrana answered. "She is his Chosen, and I saw the way he looked at her. He was going to leave you, but it was going to be in his time, not hers."

"What should I do?" Lorsan's eyes opened and met his Queen's.

"Keep an eye on him. If he seeks her out, then we take her. She is his weakness. If you have her, then you control Trik."

Lorsan nodded and pulled her to him. He wrapped his arms around her and buried his face in her neck.

He grieved. He was a Dark King. He held power over a great Kingdom, and yet for the loss of one assassin, he grieved.

"He was more than your assassin," Ilyrana picked up on his thoughts. "He had become a friend."

"You are the only one that I can trust," he pulled back and looked down into her face and ran his thumb across her cheek. "Through all of these years still only you remain faithful."

"And I always will."

"No matter what?" He asked.

She nodded.

"Things might get ugly before all is said and done."

Ilyrana kissed him gently and then looked into his eyes. "You will always come first."

Lorsan pulled her close and laid his head on top of hers. He thought of what had happened that night and of Trik's deception. He knew it would come down to him taking Cassie. He would have to take her to break Trik. And he would. He would break Trik and have him humbled on his knees before him begging for mercy.

"Cassie?" Elora stepped into the storeroom cautiously. Cassie had finally pulled herself together enough to call her best friend. Though she was unable to get out anything coherent, Elora finally deciphered that she was at her mom's store. It was after eleven o'clock when Elora arrived.

Cassie sat curled up in the far corner across from the mirror that she had emerged from. She eyed it wearily, expecting at any moment for Trik to come crashing through it.

"Cassie?"

She turned at the sound of her name being called a second time. When Elora saw the broken look in her friend's eyes, she rushed forward. She pulled Cassie into her arms and held her close.

"I'll kill him," she growled. "I told him that if he hurt you that he was a dead dark elf."

Cassie began to cry again as the pain continued to wrack her body. She wanted to go to him, to beg him to hold her and make the pain go away. She needed to hear the words that she didn't let him finish and she needed him to tell her it was alright, that everything would be alright. But it wasn't and it never would be. As long as Trik was out there, without her, it would never be alright. She cried for the loss, she cried for the hurt and the lies, she cried as her soul mourned its mate as if he had died. Her eyes burned and her throat felt dry as her sobs poured out. She knew that she was scaring Elora but she didn't care. She was dying. She was dying and Trik didn't care.

He had stood there and not denied her words. When she had slapped him he had looked like a whipped puppy, the confident, cocky Trik gone. Part of her had hoped he would have thrown himself at her feet and begged her forgiveness, part of her wished he had been the barbarian he had claimed and thrown her over his shoulder and hauled her off to be with him, and then part of her hoped that he would never contact her again. When that thought crossed her mind she wailed and shook.

"Cassie, please," Elora patted her friend and rocked her. "Please tell me what happened. Are you hurt?"

Cassie nodded.

"Physically, Cass, are you hurt physically?" Elora clarified.

Cassie pulled back to look at her friend. Tears streaked her face. Her eyes, swollen and bloodshot, were devoid of any life.

"What did he do to you?" Elora snarled.

"He killed me," Cassie whispered. "He ripped out my heart and threw it in my face."

Elora watched as Cassie scooted back from her hold and looked up at her.

"He lied. He told me he was leaving Lorsan, but he never told Lorsan."

Elora shook her head and bit her tongue. Now was not the time to point out that she had said this would probably happen.

Elora pulled her phone from her back pocket and dialed her mom's number.

"Hey, you need to get the Queen and her man to your store a.s.a.p.," she said when she heard her mom's voice.

Elora hung up without waiting for a response.

"Where is he?" Elora asked.

Cassie let out a snort that was filled with indignation. "Who knows, who cares? I told him to stay away from me."

"You think he will listen?"

"Don't know, don't care."

Just then a leg followed by the rest of Tamsin's body emerged from the mirror with Syndra hot on his heels. Cassie scampered back quickly, her eyes glazing over with pain.

Tamsin and Syndra stopped short as they looked down at the broken person before them.

Syndra looked over at Elora. "What has happened?"

Elora stood up and folded her arms across her chest. "Trik lied to her. He said he would leave the Dark King, but apparently the Dark

King had no knowledge of it. And from what Cassie says Trik didn't argue with her when she told him that he had lied to her."

"Where is the assassin now?" Tamsin asked.

Elora shrugged. "Cassie doesn't know. He didn't follow her here."

Syndra knelt down before Cassie and brushed her hair away from her face.

"Cassie," Syndra's voice was soft and melodic. "We need to keep you safe. We told Trik that we would protect you if he failed."

Cassie looked up at the Light Queen. Her eyes were vacant. "What does it matter? He doesn't care what happens to me."

"That is not true," Syndra told her. "Whatever his reasons for doing what he did, he cares for you."

"It's not enough," Cassie whimpered as another tear fell.

"No, you are right, it isn't. He needs to love you."

Cassie's eyes snapped up at Tamsin who had spoken.

"We have much to discuss. We need you to come with us."

"What about my parents?" Cassie asked as she let Syndra pull her to her feet.

"Syndra will deal with your parents. You are vulnerable and if Lorsan's entire court watched you run from Trik then they will not wait long to pursue you in order to get back at him for centuries of being the right arm of the Dark King."

Cassie took Syndra's hand and then reached for Elora.

"Please let her come with me."

Elora rolled her eyes. "Like they could stop me."

Cassie let Syndra pull her towards the mirror and Elora followed, her hand holding tight to her best friend.

When they emerged on the other side, Cassie's eyes widened as she looked around. Elora openly gaped and shook her head. "We aren't in Kansas anymore, Toto."

Syndra laughed at the girls' expressions.

"What did you expect? We are royalty, you know?"

Tamsin emerged behind them. He watched as Cassie and Elora took in everything around them.

Cassie had never seen such elegant beauty. The room looked as if it had been carved from ice. It shimmered as pillars rose high to the tall cathedral ceiling. Sitting all around, sculptures of animals and people, also looking as if carved from ice, stood proud watching over the great hall. Large, long windows lined the walls, allowing light to pour into the room creating a wonderland of crystals and rainbows. It was breathtaking.

Syndra motioned for them to follow her and Tamsin. They walked through the great hall and out of a large pair of silver double doors containing a beautiful crest carved into them. The crest was of a large tree surrounded by all manner of creatures, both foreign and familiar to Cassie.

They continued on down a long hall as light shined in through windows along the hall and lit their way. Finally Tamsin turned right into another room. As Cassie and Elora made their way in, they saw what they might call a den, or family room.

Large couches formed a circle around a table that held drinks and food. Shelves full of books and odd looking knickknacks lined the walls. The room was painted a light periwinkle blue and candle light white.

"Please have a seat," Tamsin instructed.

Both girls took a seat on a large white couch and sunk into the softness. Cassie gasped as once again pain tore through her chest.

"Cass, what's wrong?" Elora asked.

"She is feeling the pain of the separation from Trik," Syndra explained.

"She's going to go through what happened in her room?" Elora referred to the first time Trik had left Cassie and she had watched her friend writhe in pain on the floor.

"The pain will come and go because a part of Cassie truly does want to be away from him, but then her soul longs for him."

Syndra whispered something to Tamsin and then left the room quickly.

Elora looked up at Tamsin waiting for an explanation.

"She is going to deal with Cassie's parents."

"Deal with them how?" Elora's eyes narrowed."

"Calm yourself, human. She isn't going to kill them. She will simply suggest to them that Cassie is going to be staying with you for a while because you are going through a difficult time. Lisa will be informed so that she can corroborate the story if they call her."

"At some point they are going to want to see her," Elora pointed out.

"Once we have sufficient protection on her she can periodically go back to her realm."

Cassie took slow deep breaths and then sat up, unfolding herself from the fetal position the pain had caused.

"Am I to stay here for the rest of my life?" She asked Tamsin.

Tamsin sat on the couch across from them and looked at her. His eyes softened as he saw the fear and worry that marred her young face.

"You will never be safe again in your world. I am sorry for that. You were supposed to be bound to Trik and he would protect you and you would…"

"Live happily ever after?" Cassie interrupted. Her words dripped with sarcasm. "I don't believe in happily ever after, not anymore."

"I understand your anger Cassie, but I think you need to learn some things about Trik before you judge him too harshly."

"What things could lessen my anger? What could you possibly tell me that would shed light on why he lied to me?"

"Things that even I had forgotten. I am going to tell you about Triktapic, who he was, who he is, and who he is meant to be."

"Queue *the ena is coming* music," Elora said dryly.

"You might want to get comfortable," he told them. "This could take a while."

Chapter 13

"Love isn't supposed to be easy, I know that. Nothing worth having is ever easy. But it *is* supposed to be honest; it is supposed to be true and unconditional. Love is messy and painful and joyous and not without sacrifice. Love is supposed to conquer all. Is it enough if the love only comes from one side? Is the love of one person enough to conquer the hurt of two?"

~Cassie Tate

Trik stood at the door to the lab. It was taking everything in him not to go after Cassie. He could find her. He would always be able to find her as long as her soul was in her body. Something told him the time wasn't right. He didn't know what it was but there was a feeling deep inside him that was directing him to a path he never intended to follow.

He pushed the door open and walked into what looked like a scene from a movie. Tables lined the walls and beakers and tubes and bubbling liquid topped them. A sweet aroma filled the air as smoke wafted from a large suspended basin where a red liquid was being continually stirred. From the bottom of the basin a tube protruded and periodically one of the elves would turn the dial on it and the red liquid would pour into the vial they held.

The production of Rapture had begun. The next step would be the trials. Lorsan would need to test it on humans to make sure it didn't have a negative effect on them, too negative effect that is. He also needed to know how much they would have to drink to achieve the desired effects.

Trik walked over to a thin, dark haired elf with eyes black as coal and hair the color of chrome, Tarron, Lorsan's top chemist.

"How is everything going?"

Tarron took a vile of Rapture in his hand and held it up to the light. He swirled the liquid around and around in the tube. Trik didn't know what he was looking for but he must have found it because Tarron smiled and placed the tube back in the holder with the others.

"So far everything is as it should be," Tarron finally answered.

"When will he be testing the first batch?"

Tarron didn't look at Trik as he answered. "From what I understand, he is in the process of securing the humans he will be testing on."

Trik nodded and started to walk away but was stopped by Tarron's words.

"Is everything as it should be with you Triktapic?"

Trik turned to look at the chemist.

"Speak plainly Tarron. I do not have time for your riddles," Trik snapped.

"There are rumblings that your Chosen is human and that she has fled your protection," Tarron watched Trik closely, a spy for Lorsan no doubt told to keep an eye on Trik.

"She has left." That was all Trik said as he turned and walked quickly for the door.

"I will be back tomorrow to check on your progress," Trik called over his shoulder.

The door closed behind him and he let out a deep breath. Pain was beginning to pulse through his muscles and he knew the pain of the separation was only going to get worse. He closed his eyes and wrestled with himself. He needed to protect her, but she didn't want him anywhere near her and Lorsan had forbid him to go near her. He had to see her, just one more time he had to see her.

If Lorsan thought he could keep tabs on his most accomplished spy, then he didn't fully understand the depth of Trik's talents. Trik was only seen when he wanted to be and right then he was done being seen. He stepped into the shadows and followed the line of the building until he was moving into the forest beyond. He moved quickly and soundlessly through the forest until he found a small lake. Trik walked up to the edge of the lake and looked down into it. He saw himself staring back at him. He took a step and his leg sunk into the water but instead of getting wet it emerged dry in another forest.

As he slipped into the realm of the light elves, he crouched down low and looked around the forest. He was deep in their lands and would have to travel on foot the rest of the way to their castle. Tamsin had wisely enchanted his kingdom so that anyone entering their realm that wasn't a light elf, or welcomed by the light elves, would be traveling quite a distance to get to them.

He moved swiftly through trees, careful not to disturb the plants around him. He felt eyes on him everywhere and knew that Tamsin would have the forest watched. He didn't know the light elves land like he did his own, but he was a very good tracker and would have no problems finding the light elves' stronghold.

Tamsin watched Cassie's face as the enormity of what he had just shared sunk in. He hadn't told her everything; she wasn't ready for that. She wasn't ready to know that if Trik didn't choose her, if he didn't choose to love her, then all would be lost. Not only was she not ready to know but she didn't deserve that kind of burden either. Cassie would feel responsible if Trik made the wrong choice and she would blame herself. Tamsin didn't want that for her. She was so young, so full of love and compassion.

"Trik is a King?" Cassie asked for the fifth time.

Tamsin nodded.

"And then he chose not to be a King anymore because…," Cassie drew the word out as she waited for Tamsin to fill in the explanation.

"Our people were fighting amongst themselves. We were once all pure and good. The Forest Lords showed their favor over us, their creation, and we flourished as a whole species. Then," he paused and looked away from her, his eyes losing focus as he remembered the long buried past, "then something inside us changed. Selfish desires began to take over and some elves grew vain and conceited. They thought themselves above the Forest Lords, and above the one who had been appointed King. It was a difficult time. We each struggled with our own darkness, however great or small. Some gave in and some fought and are still fighting. The final straw was…"

"Trik," Cassie whispered.

Tamsin nodded. "He was tired. And instead of seeking the help of the Forest Lords, he walked away. He had the weight of a race on his shoulders, a race that was dividing itself more and more every day and it just became too much."

Cassie sat silent. She didn't know what to say. Who was she to judge? She'd never ruled a nation, never had the wellbeing of a race dependent on her.

"So the Forest Lords just let him walk away?" Cassie finally asked.

"There were consequences. Trik became the man he is now."

"Wait, he wasn't always the way he is now?"

"He wasn't full of darkness, he wasn't a killer. But he was always powerful and still just as sure of himself."

"You mean to say that he was just as much of a cocky ass back then as he is now?" Elora interrupted.

A low chuckle came from Tamsin. "Yes, I suppose that is a good way to put it."

"So he walked away from his responsibility knowing that he would become an assassin, knowing that he would be evil?" Cassie's eyes brimmed with tears as she pictured a broken King, a broken Trik.

Tamsin didn't answer, he didn't have to.

Elora looked from her friend back to Tamsin.

"What does it mean?" She asked him.

"What does what mean?"

Elora rolled her eyes. "Okay we may be human and not old as dirt, but we do still have active brain cells. You can't tell me that you figuring this all out now isn't significant, that there isn't some purpose in this information."

Elora and Cassie watched Tamsin as his lips tightened into a thin line.

"I knew it," Elora said as she shook her head. "What is it with you pointy eared leaf huggers that you can't just spit out the truth all in one sitting?"

Tamsin let out a deep breath and in a very human gesture rubbed his forehead where wrinkles of stress were currently marring his flawless face.

"There is more, much more, but this isn't the time." He raised his hand when Cassie started to object. "Later, let me at least show you to the room you will be staying in." He stood and waited for the girls to do the same. Seeing that they weren't going to get any more information from the Light Elf King, they stood up and followed him out of the room and back into the hallway. They walked from the throne room down a long twisty corridor, brilliantly illuminated by the same crystal-like walls. After several turns they arrived before a large shimmering door. It carried the same theme of the ice sculpture and diamonds and, though it should have appeared cold and uninviting, seemed to welcome them in. There was peacefulness about the castle that neither Cassie nor Elora had ever experienced. The door opened on its own accord as they approached and they followed Tamsin inside.

"I take it that whatever it is you do, it is lucrative," Elora mumbled as she looked around the large bedroom.

Cassie's eyes roamed the room as she winced against the pain that still attempted to overwhelm her. There was a large four-poster bed made of rich wood on the far right wall of the room. The posts and headboard were intricately carved with scenes of the forest so lifelike that Cassie half expected them to come to life at any moment. The silver blankets that lay across the bed beckoned to her, tempting her to curl up under them and push the pain and worry away. The walls were silver and shimmered as the candle light danced across them. There was a beautiful desk made of the same wood as the bed on the opposite wall. The carvings in the wood appeared to match the ones in the bed. In the center of the room was a large white couch with pillows stacked around it, clearly made for serious lounging. There was a fireplace across from the couch and a blue flame flickered to life as Cassie stared at it. Under different circumstances she would have been impressed, but currently she just couldn't bring herself to care.

"I will leave you to get settled. There are clothes in the wardrobe," Tamsin pointed at a tall cabinet that stood to the right of the desk, "and you should find that they will all fit." As he opened the door he looked back at Cassie. "Please don't give up on him. We will figure all of this out."

Cassie stood frozen as she watched him close the door behind him. Elora sunk down onto the large couch and laid her head back. Cassie walked over to the wardrobe and pulled out a tee shirt and shorts. Syndra must have stocked it if there were such human clothes. She pulled the dress off and her heart fell as she saw the ring Trik had given her fall to the floor. She had forgotten it. She picked it up and stared at it. She wanted to throw it out the window, she wanted to hold it close, she wanted so much at that moment. In the end, she couldn't part with it. Call her crazy but it was the only thing she had of him. She slipped it on her finger but turned it so that the top of the ring was facing her palm so that if someone saw her hand it would look like all she wore was a plain band. She walked over to where Elora sat and collapsed next to her friend. She was so tired and she hurt all the way to the marrow of her bones. Her arms felt like lead and her brain was having a hard time processing all of the information that Tamsin had given her. She laid back and closed her eyes thinking she would just rest for a moment, and before she knew it she had slipped off into darkness.

The leaves flew past his face and the warm breeze brushed his skin as he ran. The pain continued to course through him and it was becoming a part of him. He was running as fast as he could, running from a darkness that was determined to keep him cold and alone. He was tired of being alone. He was tired of feeling empty. Cassie had changed him. She had made him feel. She had filled him up and now he couldn't go back to what he had been before, without her. He ran and ran, his footing was sure and his movements swift and lithe as is common of his race. He had been running for hours and it wasn't until he saw the tree with the same missing bark, in the same place as the last one that he realized he was running in circles. He hadn't made any progress, hadn't gotten any closer to his goal.

He stopped. Trik's breath was slow and even and he looked like a man who had simply just walked down a hallway, rather than sprinted for hours. He walked over to the tree with the missing bark. He felt like he should know it, like he had been there before.

"Triktapic."

Trik stepped back from the tree his head whipping around. He'd heard his name, a whisper on the wind, but it had been his name.

"Triktapic."

Stronger that time as the wind began to pick up speed. The limbs of the trees swayed and the leaves rustled, sounding as if they were speaking a language only they understood.

"Show yourself," Trik called out into the forest. The wind continued to blow, growing stronger as he stood in the forest of the light elves. Suddenly, the sky darkened and thunder boomed overhead. He showed no fear, as nature around him began to unravel. Lightening cascaded from the dark sky, striking the ground as the sky opened and rain began pouring down. Trik leaned his face back and closed his eyes.

He felt the first drop hit his face and suddenly he was covered. The rain pelted him relentlessly and Trik knew this storm was for him. He felt the water washing away the dark places, carving through them like a river carves through a mountain with its overwhelming force. The thunder and lightning continued their dance in the sky as the rain continued to drench everything below. Trik fell to his knees, driven there by the weight of the memories being unlocked one at a time. Each door was forced open as the water pushed its way into every unclean place in him. Every life he had taken, every lie he told, every deed done in the shadows. He was stripped bare, his very soul exposed and he saw what he was, he remembered what he had been, who he had been. And he wept. The storm raged around him, the trees reached up with their braches to the life giving water, all of the realm cried out for it, cried out for restoration. And Trik knelt on the soaked ground, an assassin, once a King, now humbled by the memories that had been covered in the darkness of his selfishness.

He wept for his race. He wept for the destruction he had caused when he left the throne. He wept for the hurt and pain that he had caused and that he had allowed. He tilted his head back and threw his arms out and wailed with everything in him. He yelled until he had no more air left in his lungs to do so. And when his voice was silenced, the rain stopped. The wind died down and the thunder and lightning were gone. Everything was still, waiting. All of nature seemed to hold its breath as the wounded King sat broken before them. And then in the stillness Trik heard it again, his name.

"Triktapic," the voice boomed through the stillness. "The greatest of our creation, the appointed King of the Elves, the one in whose care was entrusted all that we love, we are calling you back."

Trik felt warmth on his skin and opened his eyes, only to have to shield them against the radiance before him. The Forest Lords stood before him. There were three men, tall as the trees around them. They had long hair like the race they created; only theirs was the color of the earth below their feet. Their eyes shown emerald green, bright and rich like the leaves that covered the branches. They wore robes of white that billowed around them, though the wind was calm and still. They looked down at Trik and he felt not their condemnation, but their hurt, and sadness at the life he had chosen. He felt their love, their longing to see him be the great King they had destined him for. He felt their forgiveness, if only he was willing to accept it and to walk away from the life that he had lived for so long.

"My lords," he said as he bowed his head. "I am sorry. I have failed you for so long." Trik felt the darkness in him stirring, the rebellious nature in him trying to rear its ugly head.

"Triktapic, such a time has come that you are to be humbled. We have allowed your rebellion for long enough. We love you. We created you for a purpose and it is time for you to fulfill that purpose. Let us heal the brokenness inside you. Let us be the strength you need. Let us bear the burden that falls on your shoulders."

Trik took a shaky breath in as he allowed their words to wash over him. He wasn't alone in his walk as King; he never had been. And now his people needed him, the human realm needed him, and the Forest Lords would stand with him and guide him.

"We have given you a Chosen worthy of her station. She will be Queen to your race. She will need your strength and you will need her compassion. It will not be an easy union for love is a choice. True, abiding, unconditional love is always a choice. Though you will struggle, it is through that love that you will become the King that you need to be—the King that you must be. Hear us now Triktapic, King of the Elves, you will crush the evil one who desires to enslave the humans. You will tear him down until he is but a crumb at your feet and through his destruction you will unite your people. There will no longer be light and dark elves, but only the Elfin."

Warmth flowed over him again and he felt loving arms wrap around him and he was enveloped in the love of his creators.

"You were created for a purpose. It is your choice; it always has been and always will be, but we will never let you go, for you are our child and we love you."

He sat still in that knowledge. Suddenly he was released and his eyes snapped open. The Forest Lords were no longer standing before him, and yet he still felt them. He pushed himself up from the ground and stood. Everything around him looked brighter, as if a film had been wiped away from his eyes and for the first time in a very long time, he felt peace. The pain was still there, but he welcomed it because it proved to him that she was real, his Queen, his love, the other half of his soul. She was real.

"Run Trik, run through our forest. Listen to the wind and the leaves. See with new eyes what has been given to you and yours; the beauty in the land, the joy in the animals and the hope that comes after the storm. Run, she needs you." The words danced in the air around him and he did, he ran. He didn't think, he just ran. Out of the corner of his eye he saw Tyndril and Tao running with him. He felt their urgency and knew something wasn't right. Cassie was in trouble and that thought spurred him on even harder. He pushed himself until the trees were but a blur and his feet scarcely touched the ground and still he didn't know if he would make it in time.

Lorsan was sitting in his throne room when the rumbling began. The room began to shake and the walls of his great castle shook.

"What is going on Lorsan?" Ilyrana asked as she came rushing in to the throne room wide-eyed and nervous.

Lorsan didn't answer. His head snapped up as a booming voice rolled through the air.

"He is coming. Your time has reached its end and the true King shall be restored. He is coming."

Lorsan lunged to his feet as a feeling crept inside. It took a moment for him to realize what the feeling was—fear.

"Lorsan!" Ilyrana shouted.

His eyes met hers and he knew that she saw that fear and that made him angry. He would not be made to look weak, not in front of his Queen, not in front of anyone. Anger, sharp as a blade and hot as the flames that burned on the sun, raged inside of him.

"Get me Vashti!" Lorsan roared.

"Lorsan tell me what is going on now!"

"Triktapic knows."

Ilyrana's hand flew to her mouth as she gasped.

"He remembers?"

Lorsan nodded. "He remembers and the Forest Lords are backing the dried up King. I need to speak with Myrin. I need to know Trik's history. I need to know what the Forest Lords have up their sleeves and my gut tells me it has something to do with that human. Get me Vashti."

"You're going to lure the girl out?" Ilyrana asked.

"From what I understand she has been in the protection of Tamsin and his Queen. It would be impossible to get to her there; I need her back in the human realm."

Ilyrana hurried from the room only to return a few moments later with the elf Lorsan had asked for.

"My King," the elf named Vashti bowed her head. Her eyes were black and she wore her black hair in a long braided rope that ran the length of her back. She wore the black uniform of a dark elf warrior. She carried a sword on her back and various weapons strapped to her thighs.

"I need you to bring me a human girl," Lorsan told her. "She is the Chosen of Triktapic."

Vashti's face paled. Lorsan raised a single brow at her, daring her to defy him. She schooled her features and lowered her eyes.

"What is her name?" She asked him.

"Cassie Tate. You will need to be her best friend, however, that is how you will get close to her."

"I need to know what this best friend looks like," Vashti explained. "I can't take the form without first seeing the image."

"Alok has been following Trik, he can take you to Elora, that is the friend's name."

Vashti nodded once, bowed and then ran towards the mirrors along the throne room walls.

Lorsan watched as the last transmuting elf in their race exited the building.

"What are you going to do to her once you have her?" Ilyrana asked.

"I'm going to kill her, slowly."

Chapter 14

My name is Triktapic. I was King of the Elven race long, long ago. I walked away; I deserted my people to become a killer. The time has come for me to be the King my people need me to be, but to be that King I must be the killer I have become. I must be as ruthless as my advisary; for if I am not, the world as the human race knows it will be gone. Cassie will be gone and that is not acceptable. I am Triktapic, King of the Elfin. My wrath is great and though I once was tolerant of the evil ways that some in my race chose, that tolerance has been burned away by the light of the Forest Lords. I am Triktapic and I am coming.

Cassie wandered through the garden located at the front of the light elves' castle. It had been several weeks since she had been brought there by the Queen and King. She was beginning to become stir crazy. Syndra kept telling her how unsafe it was for her to go back to her realm but she was ready to take that risk, if for no other reason than to feel human again.

Elora had gone back because she had to go to school and keep the rumors that Cassie had fallen off the face of the earth at bay, not to mention keep Cassie's mother from freaking out. Cassie was able to call her every day and had gone home one time to keep up the appearance that she was only at Elora's house, helping Elora get through the difficult time of dealing with memories of her father. Yeah, it was a pretty lame excuse but Sylvia Tate was a very compassionate person and so she was very willing to allow Cassie to be there for her friend as long as her grades didn't suffer. Elora was bringing her the homework so that she could stay up with her classes but even that wasn't enough. Cassie wanted to go back. She was in constant pain from being separated from Trik and her heart hurt over the fact that he hadn't tried to contact her. She had decided that he must not have felt the way she felt. He had never told her that he loved her and maybe he didn't.

Cassie felt her back pocket vibrate and pulled her phone out. Elora had texted her.

E: Coffee?

C: Def.

E: Come there?

C: Nope, I need out of here. I'm coming to you. Meet you at the coffee shop.

E: See you there. Bye

Cassie stared at her phone in shock. Elora had said bye. That was completely out of character. For a heartbeat she paused, her gut telling her that something wasn't right, but then what was right? Cassie was living in a castle in a world not of her own. Things were stressful and maybe Elora was feeling sentimental; yeah and that man in hell who wanted ice water had finally gotten it. Cassie pushed the apprehension from her mind and went in search of a mirror to take her back to her own realm, her own life.

Cassie smiled at the chime as she walked into the coffee shop. She took in a deep breath of the rich aroma and closed her eyes. Familiar, that's what she was feeling, and it was a pleasant break from all the unfamiliar things in her life. She opened her eyes and looked around for Elora. She found her sitting at the back of the coffee shop. Once again, Cassie was assaulted with the apprehension that something wasn't right. She pushed it away again and headed towards her best friend.

"Hey," she smiled as she pulled out a chair across from her.

"Hey," Elora mimicked.

"It feels so good to be back in the land of the humans," Cassie joked lightly. She felt a familiar wave of pain pulsing through her veins and took slow breaths, attempting to get through it without cringing.

"How are things at school?" She asked trying to distract herself from the pain.

Elora shrugged. "You know, same old, same old."

Cassie noticed that Elora seemed uncharacteristically restless. Usually her friend was unflappable, steady, and completely subdued.

"Everything okay?" She asked her.

Elora shrugged again. "I don't know. Let's get out of here."

"Oh, um, okay." Cassie's eyes narrowed slightly as she watched Elora stand and begin to walk off, not bothering to wait for her. That was more like her friend so she followed, deciding that maybe she was just having an off day. Everyone had off days…right?

"Elora, where are you going?" Cassie hollered as she watched Elora disappear around the corner of the shop. She quickened her pace and just as she rounded the edge of the building she felt a sharp pain at the back of her neck and then blackness engulfed her.

Trik knew that Tamsin was doing something to slow his progress as he made his way across the light elf realm. He had been running for weeks, which didn't really surprise him. Their land was vast and you could run for miles about miles without seeing a single elf. He stopped at the top of a hill and in a loud voice he yelled.

"Tamsin! I come in peace. I need to see my Chosen please stop hindering me."

He waited and the silence was deafening. Finally, after several minutes, he got his response.

"She needs to heal, let her be Triktapic." Tamsin's voice traveled on the wind and seemed to surround him.

"You know that I can't do that. I need her and she needs me. Even now I can feel her pain."

"And whose fault is that?" Tamsin asked.

Trik growled a completely inhuman sound. "We all make mistakes, King. You know this."

"Some greater than others," the Light Elf King mocked.

"Do not test my patience, Tamsin. I do not want to force your submission but I will. If you do not let me see my Chosen, my Queen, I will make you bow before me, before your true King."

Trik felt the surprise and the momentary fear that quickly morphed into hope and suddenly Tamsin was standing before him.

"You spoke with the Forest Lords?"

Trik smiled weakly. "They found me."

Tamsin laughed. "They have a way of getting your attention when you refuse them an audience."

Trik nodded. "Yeah, well they definitely got my attention." Trik's eyes narrowed and he cocked his head to the side. "You knew?"

"I've been doing some research. I wasn't supposed to tell you. The Forest Lords were adamant that it all must be your choice. Even now you have many choices before you."

Trik crouched down as he let out a deep breath. More pain, more agony at the separation.

"I have to see her Tamsin," Trik confessed with heart breaking honesty. "I'm dying without her and I know she has to be hurting. I need her to know how I feel. I need her to know that," he tried to finish but the words choked up in his throat. He loved her. He loved her so much that he was drowning in the emotions that were so unfamiliar to him. He couldn't remember if he had ever loved this deeply before. His mother, a friend? He didn't think so and he understood why he hadn't. There was no one else in his life who had ever met the need that Cassie did. She made him a better man. She brought out the good in him and without her he was lost. Without her life was meaningless and the world might as well burn up because Trik would give in to the darkness. He would rip the world apart one piece at a time if he lost his Chosen.

"I have work to do Tamsin, and I cannot do it without her. She is my everything and she will restore me."

Tamsin knelt slowly and his eyes met Trik's.

"She is already restoring you. I pledge my fealty to you King Triktapic of the elven race." Tamsin placed his hand across his heart and bowed his head.

Trik stood and for the first time in a long time he felt right, like he was where he belonged.

"Stand King Tamsin, you will not bow to me. You, who never turned from your people, can teach me much."

Tamsin stood and nodded, then motioned for Trik to follow him.

"Come with me." And then they were running.

Within a matter of minutes they were before the light elf castle. Tamsin lead Trik into the castle and to the throne room. He sent one of his warriors to get Cassie.

"Do you think she will see me?" Trik asked in a very rare show of vulnerability.

"I think that she is hurt and confused, but yes I think she will see you."

The warrior Tamsin had sent came rushing back into the throne room and Syndra was on his heels.

"Tamsin," Syndra was breathless as she approached her mate. The worry in her eyes put both Trik and Tamsin on edge.

"Where is Cassandra?" Trik asked briskly.

The warrior looked from Trik to Tamsin and it was apparent that he did not want to be the one to reveal the news, so Syndra took over.

"She's gone."

"What do you mean gone?" Trik's voice was a very soft whisper and the power that had been buried deep began to pulse around him.

Syndra took a step back, and her mouth dropped open. She immediately dropped to her knee and bowed her head.

"My King," she said "It is good to have you back."

"Rise Syndra, Queen of the Light Elves, we do not have time for formalities. Where is my Chosen?"

"She's gone back to the human realm. We didn't realize she had left," Syndra explained. One of the female elves saw her leaving through the mirrors in the bathing rooms.

"And she did not think that this was information you might need to know?" Trik's voice began to deepen as his anger surfaced. "Where is the she-elf?"

Syndra reached out for her subject.

Ava, the female elf who had seen Cassie leave came rushing into the throne room.

"You called," she spoke to Syndra.

"Ava, how long ago did Cassie leave?" Syndra asked.

"It's been four or five days now," she told them.

Trik cursed in their language and headed for the reflective walls of the throne room.

"Where will you go?" Tamsin asked.

"Enigma," Trik called over his shoulder.

Syndra and Tamsin hurried after him, both hoping that Cassie was indeed there with her best friend.

As Trik passed through the wall he pictured Lisa's store in his mind and emerged into her storeroom. Instantly he knew that Cassie was not there. He closed his eyes and searched for her in the human realm, seeking out her soul. Nothing, he felt nothing and he knew that she was in trouble. Something was blocking her, keeping him from feeling her soul.

He roared into the small room and Syndra who had emerged behind him reached out to touch his arm gently.

"We will get her back Trik."

"He has her," Trik growled. "That slime of a King has my Chosen!"

Tamsin reached out for the leader of his warriors. Within a minute Taegan was coming through the mirror.

"Liege," he bowed his head at Tamsin and then to Trik, "My King." Trik simply shook his head. He was leaking Royal power all over the place and the other elves could feel it. He would worry about the implications of that later

Tamsin looked at Trik, his mouth tightened into a thin line. "Who would Lorsan use as his spy now that you are not at his disposal?"

"Alok," Trik answered without hesitation.

"Find him," Tamsin told Taegan. The warrior nodded and was gone in a flash.

"I could track him more quickly," Trik told the King.

Tamsin shook his head. "You need to visit Lorsan. He needs to know who he is dealing with."

Trik laughed. "Oh I imagine he knows already. That is probably what had him move against me."

Syndra was quiet and it brought the two King's attention to her because of her uncharacteristic silence.

"What is it my love?" Tamsin asked her.

"I'm trying to reach into the magic of our realm. You know that sometimes the wind will speak. Maybe it can tell us why Cassie left."

They waited as Syndra sought out her answers.

Several minutes later Syndra was rushing towards the storeroom door. She called out for Lisa as she walked into the store.

"LISA!"

Lisa came around the counter to see the three elves standing there. The two males looked fierce and angry while Syndra appeared frantic, very un-Syndra like.

"Syndra what's going on?" Lisa asked with worried eyes and a shaky voice, knowing that it couldn't be good.

"Where is Elora? Has she seen Cassie lately?"

Just then the store's front door opened and Elora came walking in. Her eyes widened at the sight of the elves.

"What's happened," she asked immediately registering that something was definitely wrong.

"Have you seen Cassie?" Trik asked before Syndra could.

Elora's lips tightened and her eyes narrowed. "What has happened? Where is she?"

"So you haven't seen her?" Trik asked without bothering to acknowledge her questions.

"No, I've been at school, why would I have seen her?" Elora looked over at her mom. "What's going on Lisa?"

Lisa shook her head, obviously not knowing anything more than her.

Syndra closed her eyes and her brow scrounged in frustration. "Cassie received a text from you about a week ago, and agreed to meet you in this realm at a coffee shop," she told Elora.

"A week ago?" Elora asked outraged. "She's been missing for a freaking week?" Elora shook her head. "I can't believe we are just now realizing she's not here. I haven't been able to make it to see her and she hasn't returned my text, but I figured she was just pining over *him*," she said pointing at Trik. "The best thing to do when Cassie is in a mood is to just leave her alone. Damn if I'll ever do the best thing again. If I had just checked on her we would have known sooner. I wouldn't have let her come here."

"It's not your fault, Elora," Syndra stepped towards her. "We all had been giving her space. She's been hurting and we all thought it best to let her grieve in her own way. If anyone is at fault it is Tamsin and I. We promised to protect her and we failed."

Elora's eyes had begun to tear up and she wiped at them angrily. She hated to show emotion, especially in front of other people. Without another word, Elora turned to leave.

"Where are you going?" Trik asked after her.

"To the coffee shop, I want to know who she met."

They all followed after Elora and Lisa turned the 'open' sign in the window to 'closed' and locked the door behind her. They hurried after Elora who was walking at a pace that would rival the speed of an elf.

They arrived at the coffee shop and as they walked in, heads turned and eyes stared. Though the elves had put on their human guises, they were beautiful and their presence commanded the attention of the room.

Elora headed for the counter and saw that one of the girls who Cassie and she saw on a regular basis was working.

"Megan," she called out to the girl.

Megan smiled and waved. "Hey Elora, how's it going?"

Elora ignored the question and asked one of her own. "Has Cassie been in recently?

"Uh," she thought for a second. "Not since you both were here about a week ago, but I haven't seen her since then," Megan told her with confusion written across her face. She looked past Elora and saw the elves and her eyes widened.

"Who are the tall, too beautiful for words, people who came in with you?"

Elora rolled her eyes. "Distant relatives," she said dryly. Trik stepped around Elora blocking her from Megan.

"Did Cassie look alright when she was in here?" He asked the girl.

Megan took a step back as the intensity and power from Trik's worry and anger reached out to her. Trik tried to leash it and managed to tamp it down slightly.

"She um, she," Megan stumbled. "She looked fine."

Trik nodded and turned, walking quickly through the door not bothering to walk around people just heading straight for them and not worrying if they got out of his way, which they did.

The others followed Trik as he headed back for Lisa's store. He opened the door without Lisa having to unlock it and she decided now wasn't the time to ask how in the world he managed it. He walked back to the storeroom and began to pace.

"What now?" Elora asked.

Before Trik could respond a body crashed into the wall, having been flung through the mirror and Taegan emerged behind it. He looked over at Trik and smiled.

"He wasn't too hard to find; he's been following you."

Trik moved swiftly as his anger flared. He grabbed the slumped form that was Alok and threw him in a chair. The dark elf was unconscious and Trik slapped him hard across the face immediately bringing him around. Trik's eyes began to glow intense silver and the glory that was his kingship, his blessing from the Forest Lords began to radiate from him. He wrapped a hand around the elf's neck and began to squeeze.

"Where is my Chosen?" He growled menacingly.

Lisa gasped. "Trik!" She had never seen someone so angry with a look so cruel on his face. She was sure that he was going to murder the man sitting before him.

Trik's head whipped around at the call of his name and his eyes narrowed. A soft glow began to hum around him and he took a step towards her.

Trik watched as Syndra placed a hand on Lisa's shoulder to prevent her from moving any closer to him. He looked around the room at the shocked faces. To his surprise, Elora had sat in a chair; her usually indifferent stare was gone as tears streaked her cheeks. Lisa too had begun to cry as tears streamed down her face and they suddenly both looked exhausted, as if they had gone days without sleep.

His eyes snapped back to Alok.

"Where. Is. She." Trik's words were clipped and vibrated with rage.

Alok started to speak but there was a commotion behind Trik. He turned to see one of Tamsin's light elves step through the mirror, dragging a woman behind him. Trik realized quickly that it was Vashti, Lorsan's trans-muter. He turned back to Tamsin.

"What the hell is going on, Tamsin?"

"Elora, Lisa, I think it would be best if you left the room," Tamsin told them in a calm voice though his eyes never left Trik.

Elora rolled her eyes. "I'm not going anywhere, not until Cassie is back."

Tamsin told Vesperr, the elf who had dragged in Vashti, to put her in the chair next to Alok. Trik slapped her across the face just as hard as he had Alok and watched in growing anger as she awoke. He held them in their chairs by his will alone. Their eyes widened as they took in Trik and then they both began to struggle against his hold.

"I'm going to ask one more time. Where is my Chosen?"

At his words of claiming, Elora felt the shock and pain and anger bubble up to the top and she could no longer contain herself. She jumped up and ran towards Trik. Her fist slammed into his chest and she let loose of all of it.

"THIS IS YOUR FAULT! IF YOU WOULD HAVE JUST CHOSEN HER, SHE WOULD BE HERE WITH US! YOU SELFISH JACKASS! SHE'S GONE! THAT PSYCHO OF A KING THAT YOU WORSHIP HAS HER!" Elora collapsed at his feet, her breathing was ragged and the tears poured freely down her face. "You could have kept her safe," her voice was barely a whisper. "You could have protected her. Nobody dares to mess with Mr. Bad Ass assassin, huh? Well you can't protect her if you are not with her." Elora rose back to her feet. "So this is on YOU!" She jabbed a finger at him.

Lisa stepped forward and pulled Elora into a hug. The fact that she allowed the physical contact was a testament to the amount of pain Elora was feeling at losing her best friend.

Trik stared at the human. She was so small, so breakable, and for a moment he was tempted to remind her that he was not one to be trifled with. But he knew that she was hurting for her friend and that hurt brought about anger and anger caused people to often do things they would not normally do, so he would let her insolence slide. Not to mention, she was exactly right.

He looked back to the two prisoners.

"Alok," Trik said his name softly.

"It's been a while Trik," Alok said as he composed himself and tried to tamp down his fear. His words were conversational though his voice shook.

"I've been busy."

Alok seemed to gather his courage. "Busy being a deserter? A traitor to your people?" He spat at his former leader.

Trik simply stared at him. Alok's eyes shifted nervously.

"I'm going to ask you some questions," Trik said calmly, too calmly. "You have one chance to answer them."

Alok simply stared back.

"Where is Cassie being kept?"

No answer.

"That's one," Trik told him. "Has she been hurt?"

No answer.

"That's two." Trik's voice never raised, his composure never wavered. "What does Lorsan want with her?"

No answer.

"That's three." Trik stepped back.

"Just get it over with and kill me, Triktapic," Alok snarled.

Trik ignored him. He looked over to Lisa. "Do you have a tool box?"

Lisa slowly nodded her head.

"Could you please bring it to me?"

"Trik," Tamsin warned.

Trik looked up at the King. "She is my Chosen, what would you have me do? What would you do to find Syndra if she had been taken?"

"Anything," Tamsin answered without hesitation.

Lisa returned with the tool box and handed it to Trik. Trik set it down on the floor next to his feet. He then looked over at Lisa, Elora and Syndra. "It would be best if you closed your store and left."

Syndra rolled her eyes. "I'm not leaving Trik. I've seen it all. But I agree Elora and Lisa should not see this."

Lisa started to pull Elora from the room but Elora pulled away and walked over to the chair where Alok sat. She looked into his eyes, her mind registering that this elf knew where Cassie was, knew what was being done to her. Before she had even made the decision she slapped him hard across the face. She then turned to the female.

"Who is she?" She asked the room.

"She is one of Lorsan's warriors. She's a transmuter; she can mimic the appearance and voice of another. That is who lured Cassie away," Trik explained his voice deceptively calm as he watched Elora.

Elora looked deep into the she-elf's eyes and it took everything in her not to punch the woman in the face.

"If we don't get Cassie back I will personally beat the ever loving crap out of you. I don't care who you are or how black your soul is. If my best friend comes to harm because of you, you will know what evil is because I will rip you apart myself and smile while I do it." She turned to look at Trik. "Get her back."

Everyone in the room was silent and their mouths had dropped open at the sight of the human girl threatening to do unspeakable things to a dark elf, and she meant it. There was not a doubt in their minds that Elora was not bluffing.

Trik bowed his head to her as a show of submission to her wishes.

Elora turned and left the storeroom without another word, Lisa following behind her, the shocked look still plastered on her face.

Trik knelt down and opened the tool box. He found what he was looking for and stood back up.

"I told you that you had one chance to answer my questions. I never said I was going to kill you." As he spoke he took Alok's hand and held it steady. The needle nose pliers he held, guided by his experienced hand, latched onto the first fingernail. They were short so he had to push the nose of the pliers under the nail to be able to grab it. Without any warning he ripped the nail from his finger.

Alok screamed in pain. Trik didn't appear to hear him as he moved to the next nail and then the next. He stopped after the third nail had been torn away. Alok was writhing in pain, breathing heavily. His face was red, his brow damp with sweat.

"Three questions not answered. Three nails ripped from your hand." Trik set the pliers down on the counter and stood before Alok, just as calm as before he had tortured the elf.

"I am going to ask you some questions. You have one chance to answer them." Trik repeated his earlier words.

Alok groaned and gritted his teeth. "I won't betray my race as you did, Trik. I won't betray my King."

Trik smiled, and it was not the smile of a sane man. The temperature in the room seemed to drop several degrees.

"Then you will suffer," Trik responded smoothly.

Trik once again picked up the pliers.

"Where is Cassie being held?"

No answer.

Two more questions and two more silence responses later, Trik, just as emotionless as before, ripped three more nails from Alok's hands. Alok's screams reverberated off the walls.

Vashti sat in stunned silence as she continued to struggle against the invisible hold from Trik's power. She was sweating and though nothing had been done to her yet, she felt Alok's pain and dreaded what was to come.

Trik waited for Alok to compose himself. "I'm going to ask you some questions."

"It's not going to work, Trik, can't you see that," Alok blurted out interrupting the assassin. "I will scream but I will not become a traitor to my people."

"You have one chance to answer." Trik continued as if Alok hadn't spoken at all.

Trik didn't notice the look Syndra gave Tamsin, or the slight shake of his head that Tamsin responded to his Chosen. Syndra let out a deep breath but didn't say anything.

It was much later when he broke. After all of his nails had been removed from his body, each finger broken individually by a hammer that Trik had found in the tool box, each toe broken individually by the same hammer, it was the screws that finally got him. Trik had found a Philips-head screwdriver and a handful of screws. Alok began begging him to stop after the first one had been screwed into his foot.

"Talk," Trik told him.

"Lorsan has her. She's staying in the castle. He, he has her on Rapture." He stumbled over his words as the pain from his inflictions began to catch up with his mind.

Trik showed the first sign of emotion since he had begun to torture his former comrade. His lips tightened and his eyes narrowed.

"He is testing it on her, to observe the long-term effects on humans."

"How long has she been on it?" Trik asked.

"A week."

"Have there been any side effects so far?" Trik's anger and fear began to increase as he watched Alok blanch at his question.

"Lorsan didn't know what would happen," he stammered. "He had only tried it on a few humans before and only in small doses."

Trik took a step towards the man who he had worked with for so long. "He didn't know what would happen?"

"It's addictive; to some more than others. She's addicted to it." Alok watched as Trik's face morphed from anger to rage. His speech increased as he tried to get out everything before Trik began to torture him again. "It took one time, one drink, and as soon as it began to wear off she was begging for more. If you haven't noticed Lorsan has managed to block all the entry points into Sanctuary except for the one that comes directly from his throne room. He has her dancing at Sanctuary."

Trik lunged for the dark elf but Tamsin was there in an instant. "Wait!"

Alok let out a sardonic laugh. "You needn't bother rescuing her, Trik. She is not the girl you knew. She would not leave with you, not unless you promised her Rapture. The girl you knew was good and pure and innocent. You knew Cassie. But it's like the drug draws out a side of the humans that is buried deep. They lose inhibitions, but that's not all, they begin to give into that part of them that they keep buried, the part of them that wants all the pleasures life can bring and damn the consequences. Your Chosen is sultry, sexy, and more than one elf has petitioned Lorsan to have her."

Trik roared and Tamsin lost his grip on him. Power pulsed through the room driving the other elves to their knees. Alok and Vashti cowered in their chairs as Triktapic, King of the Elves lost his cool façade. He grabbed Alok from the chair and threw him across the room. The dark elf hit the brick wall with such force that shards of debris broke off the wall and scattered across the floor. Trik moved towards Vashti and had her by the throat in a matter of seconds.

"You are the reason she is gone. You are responsible for what is being done to her and I, Triktapic, King of the Elven race, chosen by the Forest Lords, sentence you to death.

Vashti's face morphed into a look of contempt as she looked down at Trik.

"You sentence me to death? You have killed thousands, you have tortured thousands upon thousands and you think you have the right to sentence me to death because your little human is addicted to a plant?"

"Careful she-elf, I hold your fate in my hands. I can kill you quickly and it will be over, or I can drag it out for decades and the pain will be so atrocious that you will beg for me to break your pathetic neck," Trik snarled. He used his power to put pressure on her mind and her organs. She would feel like she was being crushed from the inside. He watched as she struggled to breathe and panic began to settle in.

"I have killed, I have tortured, and I will suffer the consequences of my choices. That life is over for me. I am your King; you will not speak to me with such insolence." Trik eased up on his power and Vashti took in a deep ragged breath.

"Lorsan will kill her and you," Vashti told him. "No matter what you do to me she is already dead, and that is no more than you deserve. You should suffer as those you made suffer." And before he could stop her Vashti produced a knife out of thin air and stabbed herself in the heart.

Trik dropped her body to the floor and it hit with a sickening thud. He looked down in disgust at the one responsible for his Chosen's capture and knew that her words were true. He deserved to suffer. He deserved to die, but Cassie did not and he would not leave her in the hands of the Dark Elf King.

"Tamsin," Trik turned to address the Light Elf King.

"My lord," Tamsin bowed his head and waited.

"I will not ask you or any of your warriors to assist me. I do not deserve your loyalty. I would ask that if I get Cassie out, that you would care for her and protect her."

Syndra stepped forward and met Trik's eyes. "We will always care for our Queen, but you must return, Trik. Do not let the words of a mad she-elf turn you from your fate. The Forest Lords have called to you and want to see you fulfill your purpose, don't let the judgment of those who do not matter keep you from your path."

A slight smile appeared on Trik's face, though it was brief. "Tamsin, I do believe your Chosen is wise."

Tamsin smiled and looked at Syndra. "She is more than wise, Triktapic, and you would do well to hear her words."

"I hear them. I will not fail my people a second time." Trik turned back to where Alok's body lay. The elf still breathed but he was unconscious.

"Put him in a prison. I will not grant him the mercy of death just yet," Trik told Tamsin. "I will meet you at your castle in a few days. I imagine that I will have to make my way through Lorsan's land and he will not make it easy on me, though I have some old tricks up my sleeves that he will not expect."

"Before you go, I have some things that belong to you," Tamsin told him. "Come back with me to the castle and then you can depart from there."

Trik's head cocked to the side. "Things?"

Tamsin smiled slyly. "The Forest Lords did not leave you unarmed and defenseless."

Chapter 15

Darkness is all around me. I'm at the bottom of a pit and no matter how hard I try to climb up the walls I cannot get to the top. My nails bleed from the clawing and my face and body are covered in dirt. I writhe in pain and misery and I cry out for more; more of the red liquid that brings me happiness, fleeting though it may be. My body hums in remembrance of the warm liquid sliding silkily down my throat. I dance and those around me sing and laugh. Some whistle and call out my name and I dance faster. Then the feeling is gone and I'm sinking into the pit again and I cry out for more; more pleasure, more warmth, more feeling, more anything but the emptiness I feel when the high is gone. ~ Cassandra Tate

"Cassandra," a female voice pushes through the haze that fills Cassie's mind. She tries to sit up but her body won't cooperate. Her breathing is labored and pain courses through her veins.

"More," her voice is hoarse from the hours of screaming.

"I know you want more, but first we must get you ready," the female voice tells her as she helps her stand. It's painful. Her legs are weak and don't want to support her body, but she is thinner now and so she is able to force them.

"Ready?" She asks wearily.

"You must dance tonight. Dance for a suitor. King Lorsan is growing tired of the endless requests for you and so he is going to give you to a male tonight."

Cassie frowned, or at least she thought it was a frown. Give her to a male. What did that mean? So she asked.

"It means you are going to be Bound in Union," the woman answered.

"Bound?" Cassie whispered.

"Yes, but you must try to stop saying his name at night. You call it out endlessly and I imagine your mate will not take kindly to his woman calling the name of another."

Cassie's breath caught in her throat and she felt jolts of pain sear through her. She yelped in pain and fell to the floor. Whose name? Who did she cry out for in the darkness of night, in the dreams that swirled in her mind as she slept? She could see his face but his identity eluded her. She reached for him in her dreams and no matter how fast she ran she could not catch him. When she got close to him she would hear the words that repeatedly ripped out her heart.

"I don't want you," his deep, smooth voice carried to her ears.

"Please," she would whisper as she fell to the ground. "I love you."

Always he would shake his head, his beautiful black hair so dark that it appeared to have a purple tint and pity would fill his silver eyes. "I don't love you." His red, full lips moved and yet the words that came out were words that she never wanted to hear.

"Who is he?" she asked the woman. She could never remember her name, but she came every day and helped bathe her and dress her.

"You don't need to worry about that; it's best if you simply forget him." She held out a glass to her and Cassie's eyes glazed over. She grabbed for the glass greedily and guzzled the liquid down. The warmth hit her mouth and trailed down her throat and she moaned. She knelt there as the full effects of Rapture coursed through her body and when she was numb and consumed in the glorious high she stood, her movements like a languid cat.

"That's more like it," the woman crooned. "Now off to the bath with you." She ushered Cassie through a door that led into a lavish bathroom. A tub was filled with steaming hot water and Cassie could smell the perfume that had been poured into the bath. She stripped off her night gown and climbed slowly into the tub and let out a soft sigh as the hot water surrounded her. Her skin tingled everywhere that it touched and she giggled at the sensation.

The woman clucked her tongue at her. "You really are much too young to be married off." She hurried around the bathroom, setting out clothes and a towel. She placed a brush on the counter and various lotions and oils, all of which were designed to make Cassie's skin softer and shiny and her hair silky. She had to admit that she enjoyed being pampered. She didn't think that it had always been this way. She couldn't help but think that in another life she had not had all the luxury that she had now. But as Rapture continued to haze her brain with pleasure, she pushed the thoughts away and focused on the sensations and the here and now.

The woman had been talking but Cassie hadn't been listening to a word she was saying. She looked over at her and saw that she was very young, though her demeanor seemed so much older, more like a mother hen than the young chick she appeared to be.

"What is your name?" Cassie asked.

"Tsk, tsk," the woman frowned. "You ask me that every day and I tell you every day. Why don't you just make one up and try to remember it?"

Cassie smiled. She liked this woman with her spunky attitude and sparkling eyes.

"Okay then, I will call you Flora," she told her with a decisive nod.

"Why Flora?"

"Because she's a fairy godmother, and you remind me of one, always flitting about and taking care of me."

Flora smiled. "Well that's nice. It's better than calling me a mother hen so I will go with it."

Cassie smiled and it was a dreamy look. Flora looked at her and Cassie saw the sympathy that filled them. Why did Flora feel that way towards her? It's not like her life was hard. She just slept, ate, drank her wonderful red drink and danced. What was so bad about that? But there at the back of her mind, something lay just out of her reach, something important discarded and forgotten.

"Why do you look at me that way?" Cassie finally asked.

Flora quickly pushed her features back into a motherly smile. "You just seem tired and I wish that Lorsan would give you more time to rest."

Cassie didn't feel tired, well at least not then. She knew that eventually the red liquid would wear off and she would crash. She didn't like the crash and she pushed the memory of it away as quickly as it had come.

"I'm fine, Flora," Cassie assured her. "Really, I like to dance."

Flora shook her head. "You shouldn't be dancing for those elves with their greedy stares and goofy grins."

Cassie stood up in the tub and the water cascaded off her body. She glistened from the oils that had been added to the water. She smiled as she spoke. "They can't help it; they are enamored with my beauty."

Flora smiled as she helped Cassie from the tub, but Cassie could see the hesitation in the smile.

She dressed in silence and Flora hummed as she fixed her hair. When she was finally ready she stood in front of the full length mirror and, as she did every time that she looked at herself, she wondered who the girl in the mirror was. She didn't think that she had always looked this way. Her clothes were more revealing than she thought she would ever choose for herself. Her makeup was heavy and accentuated her eyes and lips. Her hair was done in elaborate twists with tendrils hanging down to frame her face. There was no doubt that she was beautiful, but her eyes were empty and so she avoided looking at them.

She turned to follow Flora out of the room and she staggered against the door frame. She squeezed her eyes shut against the first onslaught of the crash. She heard Flora muttering under her breath about needing more and more and something not lasting. She couldn't understand what the woman was saying because of the sound of her own blood pumping in her ears. Her heartbeat was fast and hard in her chest and her palms grew sweaty. She drew in a ragged breath as she moaned. "More Flora, I need more."

"I know child, I'm moving as quickly as I can."

She heard the splash of liquid into a cup and groped blindly for it. The cup was pushed into her hands and she guzzled the liquid as a thirsty man parched from the desert would guzzle water. *No*, she thought. *Not a thirsty man for water, a desperate one for his next fix, a user for the next high that he lives for.* That's what she had become and as the warmth brought on by Rapture flooded her system she pushed the thought far from her mind because she didn't care. She felt good again, she felt invisible and it was time for her to dance, and dance she would.

Lorsan sat at the long table in the throne room. The room was loud with talking and laughing. Warriors had come from all over his land wishing to see the human girl, the woman that was enthralled with Rapture and danced so uninhibitedly. Lorsan reasoned that he wasn't totally depraved as he never requested that she remove her clothes. She stayed fully covered and yet her dancing enthralled all who saw her. Many of the male elves had come to him seeking to have her and he was growing tired of it. He thought to kill her, but now he had decided that an even more painful fate for Trik was for him to see his Chosen in the arms, in the bed, of another man. Lorsan knew what it would do to him if he were to ever see Ilyrana in the arms of another, the thought alone put him in a murdering rage, and because of that he knew that Trik would quite possibly go mad when he saw Cassandra held by another. He had to plan it just right so that when Trik came for her, as he knew he would, he would find her in the throes of passion with another. *Okay,* he thought. *Maybe I am more depraved than I thought.*

The room was plunged into silence as the doors to the throne room opened and Cassandra walked through them. She was dressed in a deep blue gown with split sleeves that left her shoulders bare. When she walked, the slits on either side of her legs gave teasing glimpses of her calves. The back of the dress was see-through lace encrusted with blue sapphires that shimmered as they caught the light. The silk of the fabric moved with her as she walked further into the room and she held her audience captive.

She walked to the end of the table and bowed her head.

"Warriors," Lorsan stood and the other elves followed his lead. He held up his hand gesturing to Cassie. "I present Cassandra. She will be dancing for us and one of you will be chosen to take over her care." A rumble rippled through the room as the males voiced their approval.

Cassie walked over to the platform that had been placed in the room. She took slow measured steps as she kept trying to shake off the wrongness of what she was doing, but she couldn't stop. The Rapture flowing in her pushed her forward and as the music began, she was lost. She stepped onto the platform and her body took over. She moved with the beat and though she did not understand the words that the elves sang, she knew that it was a song of love and loss. Her hips swayed. Her arms flowed around her as they rose above her and her head fell back. She didn't know where she had learned to dance in such a way but she did. She danced until sweat pearled on her skin and trailed down her spine. She danced until the pain returned and she fell to the floor. She tried to remain calm. Lorsan had had her beaten the last time that she had lost control in the presence of others. She heard his voice over the pounding of her heart.

"Get her Rapture," he snapped over the concerned voices of the others.

Flora was suddenly kneeling beside her. "Cassie," she whispered. "Cassie here, take this."

Something in Cassie cried out. She tried to push the cup away; she didn't want anymore. She didn't want to be drunk on it, to not feel, to not remember.

"Please Flora, no," she groaned quietly. "Don't make me." The plea was thick on her tongue as she swallowed back a scream.

"You must," Flora insisted. "You must or he will hurt you."

"Then let him hurt me," Cassie growled and she knew her eyes must be wild with the withdrawals from the Rapture.

"You don't want that," Flora told her. "Just drink this and it will be better."

Cassie slapped the cup away and red liquid splashed all over Flora. "I DON'T WANT IT!" She yelled. She tried to get up but her arms and legs were too weak. So she crawled. She crawled to the edge of the platform and booted feet met her. Suddenly she was in strong arms and being carried out of the throne room.

"I will take her to her room. She just needs some rest my liege," Cassie heard the deep voice rumble in the man's chest as she lay her head against him. Pain wracked her body.

"Shh," he crooned. "You will be fine little one."

The words stirred something deep in her. *Little one?* Hadn't someone else called her that?

A door opened and then closed and then she was being laid softly on a bed.

"Open your eyes for me, beautiful," the deep voice told her. But she couldn't. He had called her beautiful and that too was familiar. Why?

"I need to know that when I leave this room that you are going to be alright. So please Cassie, open your eyes."

Cassie? He had called her Cassie. She had only been Cassandra since she had been here. Where was here and when had she gotten here? She was so confused, her mind so jumbled. She opened her eyes and for some reason she expected to see silver eyes, but green ones stared back at her.

He smiled at her and she had to admit that he was breathtaking, but he did not stir her heart.

"There you are," he murmured.

She cringed in pain and felt her breathing increase. She needed the drink, the red liquid that made everything better.

"Please," she whispered, "I need…"

"No," he told her sternly. "I intend for you to be mine, and I will not have some mindless addict. You will be sober when you come to me."

Her eyes narrowed as she stared into his handsome face.

"Yours?" she asked.

He nodded once. "You are to be my Bound, or I suppose you would better understand if I was to call you my bride, my wife. Lorsan has already agreed, though the others do not know."

"Wife?" For some reason her ability to speak had suddenly been reduced to one word sentences.

His lips turned up in a slow smile. "You are something to behold and soon you will dance only for me."

Cassie felt herself recoil at the thought. She didn't want to dance, not for anyone. She didn't want to do anything but crawl into a hole and die. She must have spoken out loud for he growled at her.

"You will not die. I will make you happy. You will be fine and I will love you and you will love me."

Love? Didn't she already love someone? Didn't someone love her? *No*, she remembered the dream. *He said he didn't love me.* Who needed love? Love simply expanded your heart so that when it was ripped from your chest there was more to crush.

She closed her eyes and tried to sink into the darkness, away from the pain, away from the elf who laid claim to her, away from everything.

"Where is Alok?" Lorsan asked Tarron as he stood in the lab. He had left the throne room in a fit of anger after Cassie had collapsed. She was growing tolerant of the level of Rapture and was requiring more and more in order to maintain the euphoric state.

"Is there no way to maintain the potency for longer?" He asked his lead chemist. "She is requiring the drink more and more often in order to keep from having withdrawals."

Tarron continued to mixing and pouring and studying the color of the mixture in the beaker. He finally looked up at Lorsan. "It will affect each human differently. Some will not require more to keep the feeling, others will, it just depends."

"So nothing can be done?"

Tarron shook his head. "You need to try it on more humans, not just the girl."

Lorsan sighed in frustration. "Fine, get some sent to Sereg; it's the largest of my casinos. Have our people there choose some lucky winners and give away a couple of free nights at the hotel. Make sure they have plenty of spending money so they hang around. Begin by giving the drug to these people first. Tell them that the hotel is trying out some new drink "specials." Watch them closely as you give them the Rapture and let me know how it goes. I will let Dorien know that you are coming; he has been acting as the CEO of Sereg."

Tarron continued to watch the red liquid, staring at it as a parent stares at a child.

"It's beautiful, and powerful," he told Lorsan. "It will bring the humans to their knees."

Lorsan watched as his lead chemist's face morphed into one of greed and malice."

"What did the humans do to you to make you hate them so?" Lorsan asked.

Tarron's face went blank as he began to pack up some of his things.

"They mean nothing to me," he grumbled. "I am simply doing what you asked. You want the humans to spend more money so that you may have your luxuries and power in their realm and I am delivering that to you. They are mere puppets, a means to an end."

Lorsan heard his words, but believed none of them. Tarron hated humans, hated them with a fierceness that he didn't understand and he didn't know what had brought the dark elf to feel that way. He would need to keep his eye on Tarron to make sure that his own personal desires did not interfere with his plans.

Trik, that was his name. Cassie remembered as she stared at the elf before her, his long dark hair, his silver eyes, his tall, lithe body and his graceful movements. Triktapic, the one she loved, the one who held her, kissed her, filled her with things she'd never experienced and then broke her.

"Why are you here?" She asked him.

"I'm not, this is your dream," he answered.

Cassie took a step towards him. He held his ground. She took another step and her heartbeat picked up. She could even smell his masculine scent. He seemed so real, not like a dream, but real flesh and blood before her.

"A dream, or a nightmare?" Cassie frowned at him. He continued to watch her, his eyes steady and his stance relaxed. He was leaning against a tree, his usual indifferent pose and for once she couldn't tell if it was a front, or if he really was indifferent to her presence. She certainly wasn't indifferent to him. Even now as she stood there remembering how he had lied to her, she wanted to run to him. She wanted him to hold her, to tell her that he was sorry and that he had made a mistake.

"Come here," he told her as he held out a hand to her. She stared at his hand and then looked back to his face. She was torn. She wanted, more than anything to go to him, but why? So he could stomp on her some more? She shook her head.

"Cassie," her name on his lips made her tremble and she saw the familiar cocky smirk. "Come. Here." His tone was clipped and she could tell that he was getting impatient.

It was just a dream, she told herself. What would it hurt to go to him, to feel his comfort for just a breath in time? So she did. She walked slowly to him. Her eyes never left his as she approached and as soon as she was in his reach he grabbed her around the waist and pulled her tight. His other hand came up and tilted her face up to his. He stared deep into her eyes as he spoke.

"My beautiful Cassie." He brushed wisps of hair from her face and his hand slid around to the nape of her neck. He fisted her hair in his hand and gripped it tight pulling a gasp from her and then he kissed her. If this was a dream, it was the most realistic dream she had had in all her life. He kissed her with a ferocity that she had only seen in his eyes once before and she kissed him back. Her hands slid up his chest and around his neck pulling him tighter to her. She moaned as his tongue slipped into her mouth and she felt him smile as she bit his bottom lip. In a swift movement Trik had spun them around and had Cassie's back pressed against the tree. He pulled back from the kiss and his eyes ran over her face. She felt like he was memorizing her every nuance.

"You're sure this is a dream?" She asked again.

"I love you, Cassie," Trik whispered instead of answering her question. That was when she knew without a doubt that it was a dream because Trik had never told her he loved her. She was desperate to hear it, to believe it.

She closed her eyes and willed herself to wake up, or at least to push this dream away, no matter how amazing it felt to be in his arms again.

"Cassie, open your eyes." She heard Trik's voice. But she didn't comply.

"Wake up," she told herself.

"Don't Cassie, don't go," Trik pleaded with her and she knew that this was only because it was what she wanted to hear.

She felt tears begin to run down her face and she once again felt the soul piercing pain building inside.

"I'm coming for you Cassie," Trik's voice sounded further away but his words are what caused her to open her eyes. "I'm coming for you," he told her again and for a moment she let herself believe it.

Chapter 16

I dreamt. I dreamt of you. I dreamt of your skin, your hair,
your eyes, your lips, all perfection to me. I dreamt of your smell,
your touch, your voice, your words and then you were gone. My
soul was ripped in two as you melted away. I saw the doubt in
your eyes as I bore my heart to you, doubt that I put there. I
dreamt. I dreamt of you and you were safe in my arms but when I
awoke my arms were empty, you were still gone and I was more
alone than ever. My love did not believe me, my love was
convinced that I did not want her, need her or love her. I did that
to her. I did that to my Chosen. ~Triktapic

Trik woke with a start. His heart was pounding in his chest, sweat
drenched his body and his clothes stuck to his skin. She had been so
real. He had felt her, tasted her. It couldn't have just been a dream. He
had told her at first that it was a dream, for what else could it be? He
had told her that he loved her. Even though it was just a dream he had
needed to say the words to her. And the Cassie in his dream had
looked at him with such doubt that it pierced his heart and soul. He
pressed a hand to his heart and squeezed his eyes shut as he tried to
keep the pain at bay.

Tamsin had convinced him to take just a couple hours of rest and
Trik had finally relented. But now he was even more desperate to get
her back, to convince her of his love. He was afraid that he had lost
her, not just to Lorsan, but to her own doubt and anger. He couldn't

lose her, it was a fate worse than anything he could imagine and not one he was willing to accept. He rose quickly and gathered his weapons, his bow and quiver, and his knives that were concealed in his clothes.

In the throne room of the light elf castle he found Tamsin, Syndra, Elora, and Lisa sitting around a table. They all stood when they saw him walk in. They all looked at him warily. He must not have realized how crazed he had seemed before he laid down. He raised his hand motioning for them to sit back down and they did so cautiously.

"Relax, I'm not going to…" he paused not sure what he was going to reassure them of.

"Go bat shit crazy up in here?" Elora asked in her usual dry tone, though her eyes were flat and emotionless.

"Yes, that," he agreed.

"Are you ready?" Tamsin asked.

Trik nodded. "Show me what it is the Tree Lords have left me."

Trik followed Tamsin from the room and noticed that the others did not attempt to join them.

They entered a large room that appeared to be an armory. Weapons lined the walls, a warriors dream. Tamsin walked over to a cabinet that was heavily padlocked. He waved his hand over it and the lock clinked and the doors opened slowly. The inside was illuminated by an unseen light and Trik took a step back when he saw what the cabinet held.

"My sword," he whispered in awe. The sword forged for him by the Forest Lords bestowed upon him when he became King.

"They also left you this," Tamsin pulled out a small box from a shelf in the cabinet and held it out to Trik. He took it and his hands shook as he opened the hinged top. Inside sat one ring, though there were places for two. The ring in the box was his, the ring of the King, his signet. The other was meant for his Queen. The ring he had given Cassie, though he didn't remember the significance of it at the time. He wondered what she had done with it. Had Lorsan found it? Had she thrown it away in a fit of anger?

He felt the power emanating from the ring and he pulled it from the box. He slipped it on his left ring finger and felt it warm around his skin as it sized itself perfectly to his hand. The air shifted around Trik and suddenly three Beings stood in their presence. Both he and Tamsin dropped to their knees before the Forest Lords.

"Lorsan has begun using Rapture in the human realm. It is time, Triktapic, to take back your people. Lorsan has to be stopped."

Trik bowed his head. "I need to get her back."

"And if she is lost to you?" The Forest Lords asked. "Will you still do what is necessary?"

Trik's shoulders shook with anger but he knew what his answer had to be.

"If she is lost to me, then I will do what I must, but," Trik looked up at the lords, "I ask that you have mercy on me and end this long life."

"You would rather die than lead your people?"

"Tamsin can lead. He deserves it and is worthy to be called your child."

The Forest Lords stared down at him and he felt like his soul was bare before them. *So be it*, he thought. *See into the darkness I have let rule me, see that without her there is nothing good left.*

Then he heard in his mind. *"You choose goodness, you choose right and wrong. She is a constant reminder of that goodness, that choice. She does not make you good, nor does the absence of her make you bad."*

"Maybe not, but she makes me want to be a better man. I won't live without her." Trik stood and pulled the sword from the cabinet. He strapped it on his back and then turned back to the Forest Lords. "Tell me it's not too late. Tell me there is still hope for her, for us." Trik's voice was soft but urgent.

"There is always hope, Triktapic. She lives, she is fading, but she lives. It will take much patience and love from you to get through what is to come. She needs you. You need to hurry, be swift, be strong and do not give up."

Trik bowed his head to the lords and then to Tamsin.

"Light Elf King," he said respectfully and then he turned and ran straight at the mirrored wall. He pictured his once homeland in his mind, pictured the small cabin that he had spent many lonely nights, worn out from a mission Lorsan had sent him on and emerged in the small kitchen. He wasted no time as he gathered food for the journey that Lorsan was bound to make difficult. He was out the door and sprinting in a matter of minutes. He knew exactly where he was going, knew how long it would normally take him to get there and yet he also knew that Lorsan could make it take days instead of minutes.

He stopped suddenly and turned in a circle looking at the trees, grass, and foliage around him. This was his land but he no longer felt welcome.

"I'm coming Lorsan!" He yelled into the empty air. "I'm coming to take back that which is mine!" He started running again and, had he not been expecting Lorsan's attacks, he would have been bowled over by the large wolf-like animal that charged at him from the trees. Trik pushed hard with his legs and jumped over the beast. In one fluid motion he pulled his sword from its sheath on his back and turned so that when he landed on the ground he was facing his adversary.

The draug, as they were called in Elvesh, had a similar appearance to the wolves in the human realm, only they were much larger. Like Tao and Tyndril, the draug were more intelligent and could understand the elves.

The draug snarled at Trik and Trik snarled back. He lunged at the animal but pulled up short and quickly faked to the right and then reversed left. The draug tried to keep up, but swiftness wasn't its strong suit. Trik hated to kill the beast as he knew it was just doing what it had been told, but he knew that the draug wouldn't stop until Trik was dead. The draug headed at him again in a dead run and Trik ran forward rushing him. He yelled a battle cry and as he jumped he spun so that his sword met the draug's neck and slit it open. The large animal's front legs gave way and he slid to a halt, the rest of its body crashing down behind it. Blood poured from the mortal wound at its throat and Trik watched as the life faded from the great beast's eyes.

He walked over to where the draug lay, defeated and lifeless. Trik shook his head at the loss, sheathed his sword and continued his journey. Once again he ran, fast and hard, he pushed himself and when Cassie's face appeared in his mind he pushed even harder.

A day passed before Trik fell under attack again. This time Lorsan sent a lindir. One might look at the small birdlike creature and think it harmless, but its name meant singer and they did indeed sing. A lindir would sing you right off a cliff. They had the power to enthrall a person with their song and the person would follow the lindir anywhere it lead.

As soon as Trik saw the small creature he tore off a strip from the bottom of his shirt, quickly tore the strip in two and stuffed the pieces in his ears. He watched as the lindir flew closer, its bird-like bodies flapping up and down. The lindir watched Trik with faces resembling a feline animal. They waited, and when he did not follow, they flew even closer. Trik slowly shrugged off his bow from his shoulder and pulled an arrow from his quiver. He notched the arrow and released it at one of the lindir. It hit the creature before it could react and fell dead to the ground. The other lindir looked at each other and then back at Trik. He notched another arrow but didn't have to even raise his bow. The lindir were flying away leaving him once again alone in a land no longer his own.

On the fourth night Trik sat on the ground, his back propped up against a tree and closed his eyes. He felt the pain in his soul, the constant ache that was his ever present company and he sent the call out to his mate.

"I'm coming," his soul cried out. "My Chosen, my love, I'm coming, do not give up on me, do not cast me aside."

Trik waited. He held his breath as all of time seemed to stand still. Even the trees stopped swaying and the scurrying of animals ceased as they waited for the answering call of the soul of the King's Chosen.

One, two, three. Trik's heart beat in his chest, a drum counting down the time. He opened his eyes as he felt his heart sink. His head dropped forward and he grasped his head in his hands and gritted his teeth to keep from crying out in anger, in pain, in loneliness.

"Triktapic," so softly was his name that he nearly missed it and had he given into the impulse to scream his indignation he definitely would have missed the soft voice. He recognized it instantly. It was the same voice that had called out to him when Cassie had been at the party with another male. Her soul. Her soul was answering his call.

"Triktapic," he heard again.

"I'm here," his own soul answered back and it was as natural as breathing to have the very core of him reaching out for its other half.

"Something is wrong," he heard the distress and fear in her and his own fear perked up.

"Is she hurt?" Trik asked her.

"Not today."

Trik snarled. "What do you mean not today, my love?" He softened his tone as he felt her pull away at his anger.

"She has been beaten, but not today. Something is wrong, she drinks a liquid and it makes me fuzzy and I cannot control her. She does things that she would not normally do."

Trik closed his eyes. He steeled himself for the answer of his next question knowing that it could possibly make him go mad.

"Has anyone touched her?" Trik felt the confusion in Cassie's soul, so he clarified.

"Has she lain with an elf?"

He felt the repulsion from her at the idea of being with anyone other than her soul mate and it eased something inside him.

"No, but there is one. An elf to whom she has been promised. He told her that she was to be his Bound. I keep trying to remind her of who you are, her mind does not remember, her heart is so broken, so fragmented that she runs from the very memory of you. You must get here, Trik, you must, before the Dark King gives us to the elf. He looks at her as only you should. He has danced with her and held her and I screamed but the drink holds her captive."

Trik shook with murderous rage. He wanted a name, the name of the one who dared to touch his Cassie, who dared to lay claim to her, to look upon her with lust and greed.

"Who is he?"

"He has given her no name and the Dark King has not used it in her presence."

Trik's soul battled within him as he fought to control his rage and to keep his head clear. But then his love spoke again, and all control was gone.

"He's coming," he felt her fear and it shook him to his core. "The elf, he's here. Triktapic, please, he's going to take her. Hurry my love you must hurry."

Then she was gone. Trik never knew that silence could have a sound but it did, and it was screaming at him as he felt Cassie's soul be ripped from him. His own soul cried out and raged inside. He jumped to his feet. He cried out to the Forest Lords imploring them for their help and felt power and strength pour into him.

"I'm coming beautiful Cassie and I will kill everyone in my way until you are in my arms." Trik ran and not even the wind could keep up with the Elfin King in pursuit of his Chosen.

Tarron watched as the humans tossed back the Rapture handed to them in the small glasses. They laughed in carefree merriment and continued to gamble more money than he had given them and more than they probably had in their bank accounts. It had been four days since they had begun giving Rapture to the humans and it was more effective than he could have hoped on the weak, selfish humans, seeking out pleasure with no regard to consequences.

So far the only thing that he had noticed was when Rapture began to wear off, the humans instinctively sought out more. It was like their bodies knew exactly what it craved. Though the addiction varied, the response to the drink was universal. Inhibitions flew out the window. Doubt, worry, stress, was all gone and all that remained was the pursuit of pleasure and what could bring that pleasure.

Tarron walked over to the bar and motioned for the elf who was acting as the bartender.

"Release it to the masses," Tarron told him. The elf's eyes widened.

"Is that direct from Lorsan?" He asked Tarron.

"Why else would I give an order? Now do as you're told and offer it to every human who comes to the bar. Reveal the name of it and get them to talk about it so that it spreads like wildfire."

Tarron turned to go, leaving the stunned elf to introduce the humans to Rapture and a smile crept up his cruel mouth as he thought about the one thing he had not reported to Lorsan. When Rapture wore off on the males they did not simply seek it out, they hunted for it. They became predators and violence poured off of them in waves. The first night they had had two males nearly kill each other when one received the Rapture before the other. It didn't seem to affect the females in the same way. Tarron had yet to isolate the distinction, but he imagined that it must have something to do with the Y chromosome they carried.

Security had called the police and had the males arrested. When Tarron called one of their contacts at the police department, he found out that the males had to be placed in cells by themselves because they were so violent. Since then Tarron had made sure to have waitresses following the males who were drinking the Rapture ready to refill their glass when the effects wore off. But tonight there would not be enough waitresses to follow every male who would consume the addicting drink. Tonight the humans would begin their self-destruction, one drink at a time.

"We have to do something," Elora stomped into the storeroom of Enigma.

"What can we possibly do?" Lisa asked. "Tamsin and Syndra said to give him time. They will act when they feel the time is right."

"It's been five days Lisa, five days and he hasn't come back. That tells me that something is wrong. Trik needs help."

"I suppose that you are the one to aide him?" Elora's head snapped around as the saw Syndra step from the mirror into the storeroom.

"Well if you yahoo's aren't going to go get my best friend then yes, I am the one who will go and help him."

"You do not know your way, or even where to begin," Syndra pointed out.

Elora rolled her eyes. "Yeah well Rome wasn't built in a day, but it *was* built so don't count me out just yet."

"What is your plan?" Syndra asked as she pulled a chair over and sat down.

"Storm the castle, kill the evil psycho elf, save the damsel, and get the hell out of dodge before it all comes crashing down." Elora folded her arms across her chest and tapped her foot. "What do you think?"

"It has potential," Syndra smiled. "I've been to see Cassie's parents."

"What did you tell them?" Lisa asked.

"I convinced them that they had seen Cassie today and had a pleasant chat. They think she is fine and going away for the weekend with you two."

"How exactly did you convince them of that?" Elora's eyes narrowed at the Light Elf Queen.

"Elora dear, you already have seen, and heard more than any human should. Let's keep things on a need-to-know basis, shall we?"

Elora snorted. "Does that include my demise? You will be a dear and make my death a need-to-know issue right?"

Syndra's smile widened. "I assure you, you will be the first to know when the time comes for your last breath."

"How kind of you," Elora said deadpan.

"Now," Syndra stood up and clapped her hands together. "If you are ready, I do believe we have a King to help and a friend to save."

"Finally, someone says something worth listening to," Elora breathed out a sigh of relief.

Syndra headed towards the mirror and as she began to walk through it she called out over her shoulder.

"You probably won't live through this Elora dear."

Elora rolled her eyes. "I changed my mind, I don't need to know anything, just keep your big mouth shut." Elora heard Syndra's laugh as she was engulfed by the mirror. She looked over at her mom and shrugged. "You ready for this?"

Lisa nodded without hesitation. "Cassie is family. We will get her back and if anyone isn't going to make it through this it's me. You had better live, Elora, or I will be very ticked off."

"Don't die," Elora nodded as she put one foot through the mirror, "maimed, crippled, grotesquely disfigured, okay, but dead is a no go. Got it."

Lisa groaned. "You are really instilling confidence in my choices as a mother you know?"

"Oh lighten up, Lisa, you're a great mom. What other mother would let their daughter walk through a mirror following a Royal elf to go after a King, once the greatest assassin ever, to kill another King who desires to rule the world and save her best friend, all while trying to keep from being slaughtered like little sheep?"

Chapter 17

I can't breathe. I feel like I'm drowning and no matter how I try I can't get enough air. Someone is calling my name. I ask who it is and the voice says she's my soul. I tell her that I don't want a soul. A soul makes you feel and I don't want to feel. I don't want to hurt, I don't want to remember. Remember what? My name. The voice is saying my name but I am no longer Cassie. I am Cassandra, and I want to forget.

Cassie threw the brush across the room and Flora had to duck in order to keep from being hit in the head. It had been that way since Cassie woke up. She had become violent, screaming and throwing things.

"Cassandra calm down, everything is going to be,"

"DO NOT TELL ME IT IS FINE!" Cassie bellowed. "IT WILL NOT BE FINE UNTIL YOU BRING ME MY DRINK."

Flora cringed under the hateful stare that came through those empty eyes. This was not the girl who had been brought here weeks ago. That girl had kindness in her. The one that stood before Flora now was only the leftover shell.

"Your betrothed has ordered that you not be given anything," Flora explained for the tenth time.

"If he wants to basically marry me then he had better give me Rapture or I will claw his eyes out."

Flora grimaced. "Well, at least you're honest," she muttered.

Flora realized it was the final straw when Cassie broke the mirror and then held a shard of the glass to her throat.

"I swear I will slit my own throat where I stand, Flora."

"Cassie," Flora spoke softly, attempting to calm the wild animal inside the girl. "You don't want to die, not for a drug."

"And what do I have to live for if not for a drug, Flora?" Tears welled up in her eyes and her hand slipped. The mirror shard cut her skin and Cassie felt the warm blood flow onto her skin. It wasn't a bad cut, but it hurt, and Cassie reveled in that pain. It was pain that she had caused. She could control it, unlike the pain that struck her when the Rapture had worn off, the pain she could not control and didn't understand.

Flora rushed into the bathroom and brought out a towel. She pressed it to the cut, all the while clucking her tongue and chastising Cassie.

"Please," Cassie whispered as the she-elf cleaned her wound. Flora let out a tired breath and slowly pulled out a small bottle from her dress pocket. Cassie recognized the color immediately and snatched the bottle away from her. She unscrewed the lid and guzzled the liquid. Her eyes closed and she felt the warmth of the drug seep into her. She let out a breath and took in another. In and out, in and out, finally she could breathe.

The rest of the morning went smoothly with Flora fluttering around dressing Cassie, fixing her hair, talking about stuff that Cassie didn't care about and thus ignored. As soon as Cassie would begin to get agitated Flora would produce another little bottle of Rapture, Cassie would down it, and all would be well again.

Night came and Cassie noticed that it was Flora who was becoming agitated.

"Flora, what's wrong?" Cassie asked and for a moment the sweet girl who had come to Flora, was back.

She walked over to Cassie and took her hand. "You are to enter into a Union."

Cassie shrugged. "What's the big deal about that?"

Flora once again became agitated as she waved her hands in the air, gesturing wildly as she spoke. "What's the big deal? Cassandra you are to be Bound to an elf, a warrior, one you don't know and who isn't Triktapic."

"At least he's handsome," Cassie pointed out. "I could be marrying an ogre, so see, you just have to look at the bright side."

Flora threw her hands in the air. "Did you not hear me? Triktapic, your love, he's not who you will be crawling into bed with tonight."

Cassie groaned. "You just had to go there didn't you? Well for your information I know all about what happens between a man and wife so feel free to keep that little speech to yourself."

Flora watched Cassie closely and then it hit her. "You don't remember him do you?"

Cassie shook her head. "Remember who?"

"Trik, the King's assassin."

Cassie's eyes narrowed as she thought. She felt something pushing inside her and heard the whisper of her name again. Her soul.

"Damn why won't she just give up?" Cassie growled. "I don't want to remember; I don't want to feel. Leave me alone."

"Who are you talking to?" Flora asked anxiously.

Cassie's head snapped around to look at the elf. "No one and I don't know who this Trik guy is, and what is up with that name? Seriously, they call him Trik?"

Flora stood in shock at Triktapic's Chosen. She knew of the connection between two Chosen. Her parents had been soul mates and her mother had often told her about the bond between the souls, that it was almost a separate part of them. Cassie was talking about her soul.

"Cassie what is your soul saying to you?"

Cassie shook her head. "I don't know what you're talking about."

"Yes you do," Flora challenged. "You do know and you need to listen to her. She's calling for him isn't she?"

Cassie was walking around the room in jerky, agitated movements. "I don't know what you're talking about Flora, just stop. Stop talking."

"NO!" Flora snapped. "Listen to your soul, Cassie Tate."

Cassie met Flora's eyes and Flora, though she wanted to take a step back under the furious glare, held her ground.

"Why do you care all of a sudden?" Cassie nearly snarled.

Flora paused and thought for a moment. "Because I've grown to care for you and no one should give up their soul mate. You will hate yourself and the elf waiting for you if you do this."

There was a knock at the door and both of their heads whipped around to stare at it. Cassie moved first. She walked over to the door and put her hand on the handle.

"Cassie, wait," Flora's voice was urgent. "Listen to her, if only for a second."

"No," Cassie told her firmly.

"Why? Just tell me why?"

"IT HURTS!" Cassie yelled. "It hurts to listen to her. I don't remember him, but he hurt me, he didn't want me and I don't want to hurt anymore."

"You would rather feel nothing?" Flora asked.

"Nothing can't hurt me, nothing can't break me." Cassie answered coldly.

"It can't love you either."

Cassie ignored her words and pulled the door open.

"It's time." The tall elf who had carried her to her room stood at the threshold. He was handsome. He was strong and tall and *he* wanted her. He held out his hand to her and she placed her small one in it. His fingers wrapped around hers and she fought not to pull her hand away and recoil at his touch.

He led her to a small room. It was lit in soft candlelight and a large bed took up over half of the space. She quickly darted her eyes from the bed, not wanting to even consider what might happen there. She turned to the opposite wall and saw Lorsan standing there with his Chosen next to him. They were the only ones in the room with them.

"Andaer," Lorsan motioned for them to come stand in front of him.

Cassie shivered as she walked beside the elf who she now knew was named Andaer. She wasn't sure how it was spelled but it sounded like *and-dire* and in that moment it struck her as slightly funny that she hadn't known the name of the man that she was about to essentially marry. She tried to stifle a hysterical giggle and turned it into a cough. Three sets of eyes landed on her and she blushed.

"Sorry," she whispered. "Just a little nervous."

Andaer squeezed her hand in what she was sure was supposed to be a comforting gesture but it made her skin crawl and again she felt the pushing, the warring soul inside her.

"My King," Andaer spoke. "This is the woman I've chosen for my Union and I ask your blessing."

Lorsan nodded and held out his hand to his Queen. She placed a shiny, very sharp dagger in his hand. Cassie took an involuntary step back but Andaer wrapped an arm around her waist and pulled her close to him.

"A blood sacrifice must be made," Lorsan told her holding out his hand. Andaer took Cassie's hand and held it out to Lorsan. She didn't want to watch but like a bad car wreck she couldn't tear her eyes away. She sucked in a breath as Lorsan ran the dagger across her palm. Blood welled up from the wound and Cassie fought to keep her hand open. Lorsan made the same cut across Andaer's palm and then he turned their palms so that they would meet.

"I, Lorsan, King of the Dark Elves, bless this Union. A sacrifice of blood has been made and the Union will be complete once consummated." He pressed Andaer's hand to hers and her first thought was that it could not be sanitary to be swapping blood with an elf she didn't know. Again that made her laugh but she swallowed it down when Lorsan frowned at her and Andaer's frown matched that of the King's.

It seemed like they were waiting for something and when nothing happen Lorsan finally released their hands. She pulled her palm away from the elf—her now, what? Mate, husband? She stared down at the blood smeared there. Whether it was the sight of the blood or the screaming in her head that she could no longer pacify, she didn't know but she felt darkness engulf her as she fell.

Andaer caught Cassandra as her body crumbled. She was pale and her skin felt clammy. He picked her up and took her to the large bed and laid her down.

"What is wrong?" He asked Lorsan, though his eyes did not leave Cassandra's still form.

"Perhaps she doesn't like the sight of blood," Ilyrana suggested.

Andaer nodded, but his gut told him that that was not why his Bound had fallen. He heard the door close behind him and knew that the King and Queen had left him to be with his mate. There was a knock at the door and he called out gruffly. "Enter."

There was a squeak behind him and he turned to find the she-elf who had been Cassandra's handmaiden staring wide-eyed at the human.

"What happened?" She rushed over to the side of the bed and placed a cool towel on Cassandra's forehead.

"She passed out after the Union," he explained.

The she-elf tsked at him. She muttered under her breath as she wiped Cassandra's face and positioned her hands on her stomach.

"Will she be alright?" Andaer asked her.

She glared up at him. "Yes," she snapped, "she will be fine. But when she wakes you will want to give her this." She held out a small bottle of Rapture.

Andaer snarled. "NO! I will not have her drunk on that any longer."

"Then you will lose her."

"What? What are you saying?"

"She threatened to kill herself if she did not get the Rapture. She needs it; you have your King to thank for that."

Andaer stared down at the human girl who had claimed his heart the moment he had seen her dance for the first time. She was so graceful, so uninhibited. He knew that she was Triktapic's Chosen, but he had heard that Trik had discarded her and would not claim her. Andaer counted the assassin a fool to give up such a creature. So he had gone to Lorsan and petitioned the King for the girl. Lorsan had made him swear a blood oath to protect him should Triktapic come for him. Andaer had known Trik a very long time, knew of his fighting ability, his cruelty, and power to bring others to their knees. Still he couldn't say no because he wanted Cassandra, at any cost.

"Will she always need it?" He asked.

"You have taken that which is not yours. Her soul cries out for another and the only thing that quiets that voice inside her is the red devil—Rapture. She will always need it if you don't want her to crawl into a hole and wither away, which will still happen, only more slowly if she is smashed on the drink and dead inside."

"This is not my fault!" Andaer shouted. "Triktapic, the fool, left her. He did not protect her, claim her. He is to blame for this. I only want to care for her."

"Then take her to him. That would be truly caring for her."

Andaer shook his head. "I can't do that," his voice was a whisper as he brushed Cassandra's hair from her beautiful face. "I can't give her up."

"Then you are just as much as a fool as Trik and you both are causing the girl's death. You both have stuck a knife in her and are slowly turning it ripping her insides to shreds until her organs will no longer work."

Cassandra began to stir and Andaer moved closer to her. "Leave us," he told the she-elf.

She looked one last time at the human before she hurried from the room. Andaer heard stifled weeping as the door closed behind her.

He leaned down closer to Cassandra as her eyes fluttered open.

"Hi beautiful," he whispered to her.

"Please don't call me that."

"What would you like me to call you?" Andaer couldn't stop touching her. She was here, in his bed, Bound to him.

"Anything but that." Cassie tried hard not to shrink from his touch. She began to shake as his hands roamed and though he didn't touch her anywhere that she hadn't been touched before, she felt naked before him.

He leaned down and buried his face in her neck. She squeezed her eyes closed and bit back a whimper.

His hand slid up to the tie that held the dress she wore on either shoulder and she felt him pull the strings loose. Cassie tasted blood as she bit harder into her lip. He began to pull the dress down and she could not stop herself any longer. Her hand grabbed the dress and held it in place.

Andaer pulled back and looked down at her. He didn't look angry, but his brow furrowed at her.

"You are mine and I will have all of you."

Cassie swallowed hard. "Um, I've never, uh, I haven't been with a man before, or been touched anywhere that would normally cause me to knee a guy in the jewels." She shivered nervously and watched a slow smile slide across his lips.

"You are pure?" He asked.

"Of course I'm pure, what did you think I was, dirty snow?" She snapped at him, her fear slipping just a little at the surprise in his eyes.

"You dance as one with much more experience," he told her as he traced her lips with a finger.

"I watch Dancing with the Stars, and I'm a quick study," she told him as she stalled for time. She looked around the room and saw the small bottle on the table beside the bed. *Jackpot,* she thought.

"Can I have some of that?" She nodded towards the bottle.

Andaer looked from the bottle to her and the she-elf's words echoed in his mind. He reached for the bottle and opened it for her. He helped hold her head up so that she could drink the liquid and his eyes were drawn to her throat as he watched it move with each swallow. He leaned down and traced her throat with the tip of his tongue and he heard her moan. He smiled against her skin and took the sound as submission. His hand wondered up to the dress and just as it would have exposed her smooth, untouched skin he heard a voice and he froze.

Trik knew that only the protection of the Forest Lords had gotten him inside the Dark King's castle. Once inside he had opened himself and allowed his soul to seek out their Chosen. He made it to the room where he had heard her voice. He tried the door handle and it was locked. Just as he was about to kick it in, a little she-elf came around the corner. She squeaked in surprise and then her face lit up.

"Praise the Forest Lords, you're here," she told him as she hurried to the door. She pulled out a key and slipped it into the lock and turned it quietly.

"You must get in there. Lorsan has already bound her to him with a blood sacrifice and now he plans to consummate it."

Trik felt his blood begin to boil but he knew that he had to keep his calm. He had centuries of experience masking his true emotions. He drew on this experience and cloaked himself in the cold sensation.

"Thank you," he told the woman.

She clucked her tongue at him and pushed him forward. "Quit thanking me and go save your Chosen."

He didn't have to be told twice. He pushed the door open silently and stepped into the room.

Chapter 18

Don't ever tell yourself that you aren't capable of murder. Under the right circumstances, anyone can become a killer. Under the wrong circumstances, the killer becomes the one capable of torture, anguish, cruelty, and all manner of unspeakable things. I am one such killer and the wrong circumstances have happened to my beloved. Death will be a mercy to those who have earned my wrath; it will be a mercy they will not receive.

~ Triktapic, King of the Elves

Trik bit back a growl as he saw his mate, his love, lying on a bed with Andaer, a warrior he had fought beside many times, leaning over her body, pulling her dress down.

He leaned casually back against the wall and pulled out the dagger from his sheath on his thigh. He flipped it in the air nonchalantly as he spoke.

"If you pull that material any lower I will cut your hands off."

Andaer froze and then in a rush of movement was on his feet blocking Cassie from his view.

"Trik," Andaer growled, "how kind of you to come and wish me blessings on my Union."

Trik laughed humorlessly. "I've come to bless you brother, but it will be over your cold corpse as I push you over the cliff and into the oblivion." Trik continued to flip the dagger up and catch it, blade, then handle, blade then handle, never losing his rhythm as he spoke.

"You knew she was my Chosen, and yet you dared to touch her." Slowly the boiling anger began to rise to the top and the calm façade slipped. "You put your hands on my mate and for that your life is forfeit."

"Not only my hands Triktapic?" Andaer wished immediately that he could take those words back.

Trik pulled on his power, the Royal power in his blood, bestowed upon him by the Forest Lords and he dropped the cloak that kept his kingship hidden. He stood before Andaer in his true form, the King of the Elven race. His radiance filled the room and Andaer fought to stay on his feet. His eyes widened as he looked at Trik and swallowing became difficult.

"You shouldn't be, you are gone, you left," he stuttered.

"I have returned," Trik's voice rumbled in the room. "I am no longer the King I once was, tolerant of your selfishness. We are a people of many blessings, magic being chief among them and we have wielded it with wicked intent. I am tired of living in that darkness. Cassie, my Chosen, has broken the hold that it had over me. I am your King, your *rightful* King, and I have spoken your sentence."

"I didn't know it was you," Andaer argued. "I would have never claimed her."

"Does it matter who I am? She is the Chosen of another. You know what that means, you know how sacred that is and yet you attempted to defile and seduce her. You attempted to take that which was made for me, that which completes my soul. You acted out of lust and selfish desire without thought to what it would do to her."

"It is not only his fault," a small voice came from behind Andaer. Trik moved like lightening as her grabbed Andaer and slammed him to the wall. He pulled on his authority and held the elf there by his will. Turning away from him he walked slowly over to Cassie. His movements were calculated and cautious as if approaching a frightened animal.

"Cassie, love," his voice was soft and she felt the caress of it to her soul. The voice inside of her was screaming and reaching for him.

Trik felt it, felt his soul answer hers. He sat down on the bed next to her and reached down very slowly, pausing to see if she would stop him. When she didn't he continued his pursuit and tied both sides of her dress back together. She let out a breath that she had been holding as she stared up at Trik.

She felt fuzzy, but she opened herself to the urgency of her soul and let the memories out that she had hidden from for so long. Tears formed in her eyes as she saw Trik's face when she had called him a liar, when she had slapped him, and when she had told him never to come near her again. A sob broke free and she tried to curl up on her side away from him.

"Oh no you don't, beautiful," he gathered her in his arms and held her close. "Never hide from me, *A'maelamin*. I'm here, though you told me never to come near you. Surely you know by now that I go where I want and do what I want."

Trik felt her shudder against him. He pulled back and cradled her face so that he could look at her.

"I know I hurt you, but will you let me explain?" He waited and when she finally nodded he sighed a breath of relief.

"I was going to leave him, Cassie. I was going to walk away from Lorsan, but I felt I had to do it strategically and I should have explained that to you. I was afraid that you wouldn't understand and so I thought that as long as you didn't know then it wouldn't hurt you. I was a fool. I need you to know that I want you, I need you." He switched to his native tongue as he spoke to her soul, *"Amin mela lle".*

"I still don't speak Elven," she told him with a shy smile.

Trik's eyes twinkled mischievously. "I know many languages beautiful, which would you have me speak?"

Cassie bit her lip as she tried to hold herself together but her control was slipping. Tears began to slip from her eyes as she stared into the silver eyes of the only man she could ever love. "I need to hear it Trik, please, don't make me beg."

Trik's eyes widened in disbelief and then it was replaced by shame. "Cassie, *Arwenamin, A'maelamin,* you will never have to beg me for anything. I love you with everything inside me, I love you."

Cassie's hands gripped Trik's shirt as she fought to keep from collapsing under his declaration. He loved her. She could feel it flowing off of him, feel it in his touch, his stare, his soul.

Trik saw the memories, the hurt, and the pain in Cassie's mind as he held her face and shame crashed into him again. How could he have made her feel so worthless, so unwanted, his beloved? He didn't deserve her, but he wouldn't give her up. She would be lucky if he ever let her out of his sight.

Trik buried his face in her neck as words of love in his native tongue poured from him. He wanted to kiss her, to have her feel everything inside him but he would not share their intimacy with anyone. He stood and placed her on her feet. He looked down at her and smiled gently.

"Can you stand?" He asked.

Cassie nodded her head and Trik saw a glimpse of shame in her but she shut it off from him. He frowned at her. He didn't want any secrets between them.

"Later, Trik. Let's just get out of here and we can deal with everything else," Cassie told him but she took his hand and squeezed it, reassuring him that she was with him; she wasn't going anywhere.

Trik walked over to where Andaer was still being held to the wall. His eyes narrowed at the elf.

"You will apologize to your Queen," he told him.

Andaer looked at Trik and then at Cassie. She started to duck her head but Trik reached out and gently raised her chin.

"You bow to no one; you hide from no one. You are my Queen, my beloved, and you will hold your head high." Cassie felt his words give her strength, but still she felt the shame of what she'd done. She knew she was still addicted to Rapture, even now as she stood there she was beginning to shake with withdrawals. She knew that she couldn't think about it just then; she had to get out of there. She pulled her shoulders back and remembered who she had been before. She had been confident and not with the help of a drug. She met Andaer's stare and waited.

"I apologize, my lady. I only wanted to care for you." Andaer was sincere. Though he had still been seeking to fulfill his own desires, she had never felt threatened by him.

Trik was satisfied with the apology but that did not mean he had granted the elf mercy. He began to squeeze Andaer's throat with his will and knew that it would only take a little more pressure to crush his windpipe, but her voice stopped him.

"Trik, no." Cassie stepped up beside him and placed a hand on his arm. She looked up at him and shook her head. "Don't do this. He didn't hurt me."

Trik growled. "Do you think what he had planned wouldn't have hurt? Do you think you would have enjoyed his touch, his kiss?"

She recoiled as if he had slapped her. "Of course not. I couldn't enjoy anything, I was dead inside!"

Trik stepped towards her and he softened his voice. "Cassie it would have been rape. You weren't consensual. You weren't yourself. You were…"

"High as a kite," Cassie finished for him and her voice dripped with disgust at herself.

"It wasn't your fault, Cassie. But he *knew* what he was doing."

"Don't kill him. You are not a murderer any longer. Please."
Though her words pleaded for Andaer, her voice was emotionless.

Trik turned back to Andaer and with a snarl freed the man. He
dropped to the floor gasping for air and rubbing his throat.

"Thank you, my King, for mercy."

"Do not thank me just yet. I won't kill you today but you will
spend the rest of your miserable life looking over your shoulder. You
will lie in bed at night and hear whispers on the wind and you will
shake in fear wondering if your time has come. You will always wonder
if that day is your last because I am coming for you. I grant no mercy
for one who would take advantage of the helpless, and I sure as hell
won't grant mercy to one who dares to touch my Chosen."

Trik stepped back, giving Andaer room and gestured towards the
reflective walls that were in every room. "Leave now before I forget
what Cassie has requested and give in to my desire to cut your fingers
off one at a time."

Andaer blanched and was up and through the wall in the span of a
heartbeat.

Cassie was beginning to shake and her palms were sweating. She
gritted her teeth against the withdrawals from Rapture and refused to
beg Trik to get her some. She couldn't stand the thought of seeing him
look at her in revulsion if he saw the desperation in her eyes and the
pleading in her voice when she needed more. Cassie thought of the life
that she had been living less than a month ago and she snorted in

disgust at what she had become. Cassie Tate, wall flower, rule follower, innocent to the ways of the world, was a drug addict. How's that for irony?

"Cassie." Trik was watching her and when he reached for her she pulled back. She didn't want him to see what was warring inside her, how she couldn't stand the feel of her own skin.

"Are you afraid of my touch?" Trik took another step towards her and she took a step back, a dance of love and fear, doubt and shame. "You know I would never hurt you, don't you?"

"Yes," she answered honestly.

"Then why do you pull away from me?"

Cassie looked up into his face, his amazing, perfect, beautiful face. He was searching her own face for truth, for a sign something to tell him that she was still his. She wanted to run to him, she wanted to let him be the hero and let him carry her, if only for a little while. But instead of telling him that, she lied through her teeth.

"It's just too soon since," her words faded away as she looked over to the bed and Trik jumped to the conclusion that she had wanted him to.

"Okay, okay," he told her as he raised his hands and stepped back, "you need time and space, I can do that. But I can't live without you, so if you have any grand ideas of running from me you can just kiss them goodbye. I'm done living without you. I need you and you need me."

"Triktapic, King of the Elves," Cassie's eyes narrowed as she spoke. "You speak so boldly, so sure of yourself. After everything, how can you be so sure?"

Before Trik could answer, the door flew off its hinges and crashed into the opposite wall. Trik barely had time to pull Cassie out of the line of its path. He pushed her behind him and pulled his sword from its sheath.

Lorsan walked slowly into the room and though there was a moment of fear that flashed through his eyes it was gone just as quickly.

"So you remember where you came from, who you were."

"Who I am, not who I was." Trik's voice was calm, even though his stance was sure and ready to respond to the slightest threat.

"Your time has come and gone, Triktapic. Who will follow a broken King?" Lorsan sneered.

"I'm hardly broken. My soul is complete. The Forest Lords have restored me as they said they would when I found my Chosen. So you see, I am far from broken."

Trik reached back and touched Cassie's hand and pushed his thoughts into her mind.

"I want you to walk slowly back and push yourself through the wall. Picture my cabin. Go there and wait for me."

He saw Cassie roll her eyes in her mind before he heard her words. *"I'm not leaving you. You don't want me out of your sight. Let's just say the feeling is mutual."*

Trik growled. *"Cassie, this isn't time for defiance. You are my love and I need you safe. Please go."*

"No."

He shook his head at her stubbornness. He felt her suddenly slam down the walls in her mind and push him out. He started to turn to look at her and just as he moved Lorsan attacked. Trik pushed Cassie hard behind him to get her as far from Lorsan's blade.

Lorsan brought his sword down and Trik pulled his up at the last second. Sparks flew as metal met metal. He pushed Lorsan back and separated the swords, dancing on the balls of his feet. Finally he could kill someone. He had been itching to rip someone apart since he learned Cassie had been taken and who better than the one who had stolen her.

"What do you hope to accomplish by fighting me?" Trik taunted. "You can't possibly think you will win."

Lorsan lunged again but Trik was already spinning away, deflecting the Dark King's blade. As he did, he pulled his dagger from the thigh sheath and bent low, slicing across Lorsan's thigh. He growled in pain and swung back around quickly. Once again, Trik barely pulled his sword around in time to block the strike.

"Even if you defeat me here, I have already won." Lorsan stepped back from the battle and held his sword at the ready. "I've already put Rapture in the casinos. Already humans are falling under its power. I have discovered one small problem with it." Lorsan watched as his words began to catch Trik's attention. "You see, I underestimated the human's chemical makeup and how quickly their bodies grow dependent on foreign substances. Rapture is extremely addicting, but that isn't really the problem. The problem is that the withdrawals are so intense that it's driving them mad if they can't get more. Already there have been five suicides. But really it saves me the problem of having too many addicted at one time. Population control and all that."

Trik heard Lorsan's words. He understood what he was saying but all he could see was blood; the blood of the King before him as he writhed in pain at his feet. He lunged at Lorsan so quickly that the dark elf didn't have time to prepare and Trik's sword met the flesh of Lorsan's sword arm. It wasn't a fatal blow, but it was painful and would slow Lorsan down. Lorsan switched his sword quickly to the other hand and he had to jump out of the way to keep from being impaled by Trik. They parried and clashed, dancing an ancient war dance between enemies constantly moving, their lithe muscular bodies built for fast combat. Trik cornered Lorsan and held his sword out in front of him. His eyes narrowed and he felt power pulsing through him.

"She is going to die, Trik. No matter if I live or not. You cannot save her. She has been on the Rapture for weeks. She cries out for it in her sleep. At first it was your name that she cried out, but now…" Lorsan looked passed Trik to where Cassie stood pressed against the wall, attempting to stay out of Trik's way. "Now there is only one thing that she craves, only one thing that she wants and needs," he looked back at Trik and with a wicked smile he added, "and it's not you." And then he was gone. While he'd been speaking, he'd slowly been inching backwards. When he finally felt the wall behind him, he had pushed himself through.

"Damn these mirrored walls!" Trik growled. He could follow him, but that would leave Cassie alone and he would never do that again.

He turned back to Cassie and held out his hand. "Come, we need to get out of here." Cassie walked over to him but she didn't take his hand. Trik shook his head in frustration but didn't push her. She followed him to the wall and grasped a small piece of his shirt to keep from being separated from him as they passed through the mirror.

They stepped out of the mirror into Trik's cabin and Cassie nearly wept at the feeling of freedom, but it was fleeting as the pain from the withdrawals began again. She grabbed for the chair at the small table to steady herself. Trik wasn't looking at her. Instead he was standing with his eyes closed as if deep in thought. She remained as quiet as she could as her hands shook and sweat trailed down her back.

Just as Trik opened his eyes, another body came out of the mirror and then Syndra's arms were wrapped around her.

She tried not to cry out in pain but there was no holding it back. Syndra pulled back. She looked into Cassie's face and Cassie felt the Light Queen probing her mind.

"NO!" Cassie yelled and pushed herself from her. She fell to the ground and scrambled backwards, putting space between her and the two elves.

Trik watched in horror as his Chosen shook all over, her face was white as snow and the pupils in her beautiful eyes had nearly covered all of the color. He took a step towards her and she screamed out again and held up a shaking arm to keep him from coming closer. Trik fought every instinct he had to keep from denying her wish and pulling her into his arms.

"Cassie love, let me help you." He spoke softly and knelt down so that his face was level with hers.

She shook her head and her eyes were wild and unfocused. "Th-th-there is n-n-n-no help f-for me. You heard what Lorsan said." Her words came out in a string of stuttering and she growled in frustration.

"Trik," Syndra pulled his attention from Cassie. The Light Elf Queen's eye shined with unshed tears. "It's the Rapture?"

Trik nodded.

"What does she mean there is no help?"

Trik bowed his head as he thought of the King's words. "He said the addiction to it was too much for the humans, and the withdrawals were more than their bodies and minds could endure. Already some have killed themselves because they couldn't get any more of the drug."

Syndra's hand came up to her mouth as a small gasp escaped. She looked over at the once full of life, fiery human and saw that the withdrawals were killing her.

"Syndra, I must ask you to leave us and do not allow anyone to come here. She would not want anyone to see her like this."

"What will you do?" She asked him cautiously.

"Whatever is necessary."

"Trik," Syndra knew what he meant and she also knew that there was nothing she could say that would sway him from his decision.

She knelt down and looked at Cassie. Cassie saw no judgment, no pity in the Queen's eyes and it made the tears she had held onto fall.

"Cassie, fight! You are loved, you are needed. You will fight this and you will win." Syndra stood and left without another word. She had total confidence in her commands, as if Cassie had a choice in the matter.

Trik sat down on the floor as close to her as he could without her going into a fit of hysterics. He watched her tremble and longed to hold her.

"What can I do *A'maelamin?* Tell me what to do." Trik felt like his heart was being ripped out all over again as he sat helpless to comfort his mate.

Cassie hadn't spoken in so long that he thought she might have fallen asleep but then she looked up at him. He had never seen Cassie look at him like that, a predator hunting its prey. Under different circumstances it might have made him feel differently, but seeing that look in her eyes now made his stomach clench.

"Get me what I need, Trik." Her voice was a purr as she unfolded herself from her sitting position and began to move towards him in a sultry crawl. "If you will get me the Rapture, everything will be fine, I will be fine."

Trik knew this wasn't his Cassie speaking. He knew that it was the drug in her, the addiction. But to see her like this, attempting to seduce him into doing her will, it broke something in him.

"I can't do that, Cassie, you don't need it," Trik told her firmly. "I'm here. We can get through this, beautiful."

Once she was within touching distance, she ran a finger up his stretched out leg and Trik caught it before she could go higher than his thigh.

"If you will just get me my drink, then we can do a whole lot more than just get through this." Cassie reached up to untie one side of her dress and Trik stopped her.

Her eyes snapped up to his. "You don't want me?" Outrage and hurt quickly distorted her face but then the sultry smile was back.

"I can make you want me, Trik. I can dance for you. The others liked it when I danced for them, but for you it will be special."

Trik bit the inside of his mouth so hard that he tasted blood. *It's the drug,* he told himself over and over again. He pushed the image of men leering at her perfect body while she danced for them from his mind and focused on reaching his Cassie. But he had no idea what he was in for and he prayed to the Forest Lords that they both would make it through the battle for Cassie's soul.

Chapter 19

Rescue mission advice #1: Have a plan. Rescue mission advice #2: Have a plan…Rescue mission advice #142: Have a plan.

You would think that would be a no-brainer, right? Tell that to the two humans and five elves that went traipsing off into the dark elf realm hell bent on rescuing the King and Queen, dispensing justice where it was needed. Ask them how that worked out for them once they get their own asses rescued. ~ Elora

"Lisa, if you ask me if we're there yet one more time, I swear I'm shoving you through some reflective surface and back to the human realm," Elora growled as they walked through the dark forest. Tamsin, Beleg, Nedhudir, Rincavornon and Sidhion, which were four of Tamsin's strongest warriors, along with Lisa, and Elora had all set out together. Syndra had stayed behind at the command of the King to keep an eye out for Trik should he return. They had been walking for two days and Tamsin had finally seen fit to tell them that Lorsan could hinder their progress by shifting the realm so that they were literally going in circles.

Since then they had been marking the trees with strips of fabric as they walked, hoping that if they passed the same tree again they would know for sure that Lorsan was at work.

The night of the second day they were all sitting around a campfire. Tamsin, Beleg and Sidhion had gotten them dinner in the form of some strange birds. Elora had made it a point to step away from the camp while they prepared the meal and was trying to keep from picturing the birds strung up while she ate.

"So can I ask something that I've been dying to ask?" Elora looked at Tamsin and then at each of the elves. They all nodded. "I don't promise an answer," Tamsin added before she asked.

She waved him off as she swallowed her last bite. "It's not anything top secret." She cocked her head to the side as she looked at the five male elves. "Then again, as strange as you guys are it may very well be a matter of life and death."

Tamsin and his elves waited patiently.

"Is there a competition amongst your parents to see who can give you all the most difficult name to say and spell? Or do your parents just hate you?"

There was silence as the five elven men stared at Elora. Lisa's mouth dropped open and she started to stand, thinking she just might have to protect her from the good guys when the five men erupted into laughter.

It was several minutes, while Elora stared at the beautiful elves with weird names, until they found their composure.

"Our names have meaning," Tamsin told her as he wiped his watery eyes. "They are not just picked for how they sound. They are chosen based on their meaning."

"Huh," Elora nodded. "Okay, let's hear'em."

Beleg was the first to answer. "My name means *strong*. No hidden meaning for why my sire and mother named me that. It's what they wanted for me; to be strong."

Rincavornon spoke next. "My name means *quick moving*."

"Did they think you were going to be chased a lot?" Elora asked with a straight face.

The other elves laughed and nudged him.

"Like you have room to laugh," Rincavornon gestured to Nedhudir.

Nedhudir made some of his own hand gestures, all the while spitting out what Elora guessed was elvish profanity.

"Wait, wait," Elora held up her hands. She looked at Nedhudir and a wicked grin spread across her face. "Come on, pretty boy, what are they ragging you so hard about? What does your name mean?"

Nedhudir glared at the four elves who were failing miserably to stifle their laughter. He looked over at Elora and she had to lean forward to hear his muttered answer.

Her mouth dropped open as she sat back and stared at him wide-eyed. "Shut-up! You're parents gave you a name that means cushion? As in a place to set your butt after a long, hard day?"

Nedhudir stood and walked over to a tree away from the fire. After several minutes, Elora composed herself and looked over at Nedhudir. She felt slightly bad for teasing him, sort of. Okay who was she kidding, his name was freaking *cushion*, how could she possibly feel sorry for laughing about that.

She watched him as he stood there, quietly looking out into the forest. He didn't look mad, just thoughtful. It was then, as she stared at him, that she realized that he was every bit as beautiful as Trik, only different. The elves no longer bothered to hide their true form from her so she saw them all now in their Elfin form and she had gotten used to the odd eyes, and out of a box colored hair. Nedhudir's hair was long and he wore it in a braid down his back. He was blonde, not dirty blonde, but truly blonde and it shimmered like golden threads had been weaved into the strands. He wore a band around his forehead that should have looked odd, but somehow looked right on him.

His eyes were light blue and shined like glass. He had a straight nose, high cheek bones and a square, strong jaw. Typical of his race, he had pointed ears. Elora didn't know how he didn't look feminine with pointy ears, but Ned was anything but feminine. *Ned,* she thought. *Oh hell, I'm giving him a nickname.*

He was tall, and a little wider than others of the Elfin who tended to be leaner. Where they were more swimmer builds, he was closer to a linebacker. He wore a green vest, leaving his arms bare. He was muscular, and very, very intimidating.

Elora walked up to him and he slowly turned his head. He looked down at her, and with a small nod said, "Elora." And then went back to staring at the forest.

"Okay, so maybe I shouldn't have laughed at your name, but you have to admit being named after a butt pillow is just a tad hilarious." Elora waited for his response but he didn't even acknowledge her words. "I feel like I should disclose to you that I intend to call you Ned, or Cush, haven't fully decided, but in your case a nickname is a necessary evil." Still no reaction. Elora rolled her eyes and turned to walk away. "Glad we got that cleared up," she called over her shoulder. She swore she heard a chuckle and quickly turned, but he stood, stoic as ever, without even the slightest smile.

The next day was as uneventful as the first two, until after their third break. Tamsin and the other four elves suddenly all unsheathed swords, some of which Elora had no idea that they even had. Tamsin pushed Lisa to the center of the circle that the elves were making. Nedhudir grabbed Elora's arm and pulled her behind him. Elora tried to quiet her breathing as she looked out into the foliage and forest around them. Tall trees towered above them and rich greens of all shades covered the leaves, the blades of grass, and the shrubs. She looked for anything that didn't fit with the green and still she saw nothing.

Then Tamsin made a motion with his hand and spoke words that Elora didn't understand. Slowly they began to move, Lisa and Elora in the center of their elven shields, being herded to the cover of the trees. They didn't make it.

"Well the day wasn't a total loss."

Elora's head swung around as a deep voice resonated behind her.

"Lorsan," Tamsin growled and it was a sound worthy of a pissed off lion.

"It's been a while, Tamsin." Lorsan stood casually, his shoulder leaned up against a tree. He didn't seem worried over the very sharp swords pointed at him, or the very fierce elves that held them. "I've lost a prisoner and a dethroned King today, and thought that it would end without anything being accomplished and then this little gift is dropped in my lap."

Elora looked around Cush. That's what she finally settled on for the name that most suited him. She looked at Lorsan and threw her hands up in the air. "Are you kidding me? We've been going in circles for days, trying to get to your jacked up castle to rescue the two love birds and you're telling me they escaped? And now instead of rescuing them, *we* are being captured?"

"Elora when did you get so snarky?" Lisa asked.

"When elves invaded our lives and drug us into their centuries old useless battle. That tends to make a person a tad snarky."

"A tad?" Cush asked her as he looked at her from the corner of his eye, his sword still held high and at the ready.

"Oh, now you decide to talk to me? Really?" She crossed her arms over her chest and turned back to glare at Lorsan. "Let's get this over with already. I'm tired, I stink, and I'm sick of the bad guys winning."

Elora felt Cush nudge her with his shoulder and felt something at her side. She looked down and saw he was handing her a dagger. She smiled wickedly.

"Do not hesitate," he told her firmly.

"You don't have to worry about me, Cush. I have about as much sympathy as a rabid dog on crack."

"What?" He asked, clearly unsure of what Elora had meant.

"I'm mean; that's all you need to know."

"Noted," he replied.

Tamsin turned to look at his warriors. Something he did must have been a signal because his warriors roared in unison and rushed the Dark King. Elora looked over at her mom.

"We can go down fighting or crying? What's your vote?"

Lisa pulled a dagger from under her shirt where a sheath had been tied.

"You had to ask?" She snorted at her daughter. They both turned to see that Lorsan was no longer alone. Warriors dressed in black had joined him and were fighting Tamsin and his elves. Elora felt a battle cry well up inside her and, though she didn't understand why, it felt right. She ran with her dagger held high, her mother beside her, both yelling at the top of their lungs and plunged into the fray.

Life or death, they had decided they would fight. They would fight for the good left in the world, in theirs and in the Elfin. They would fight for Cassie and all she had been through. They would fight for Trik, the King who had found his Chosen and found love again. They would fight because sometimes a few must make sacrifices to save many.

Chapter 20

I told Tamsin that I didn't believe in happily ever after anymore. I believed my heart was broken beyond repair and that anyone this broken could not possibly be happy and, therefore, never have a happy ending. I believed Trik was gone, that he had chosen a life of darkness over me. Turns out I was wrong, not about the happy part, but about Trik. He had chosen me. He saved me, or what was left of me. But I have not chosen him. I can't. He is not what I crave and what I crave I cannot have. So I can't choose Trik, and all that is left for me to choose is existence or death. Flip the coin, tails stares back at me. Death it is.

~ Cassie Tate

Trik ducked as a lamp flew past his head. He heard it crash into the wall behind him but he didn't dare take his eyes off of Cassie. They had been through the attempt at seduction, and bargaining, and now she had moved on to anger.

"If you cared for me at all you would do this for me!" She yelled at him. "You see that I'm hurting, you see what it's doing to me and yet you do nothing."

More objects flew at him. *Collateral damage*, Trik thought.

"Cassie, I do care for you, more than anything and that is why I cannot give you what you want. I love you." Trik told her for the umpteenth time. And still she raged.

Finally, after more than an hour, she collapsed. Her breathing was labored and he saw her shoulders shake as she wept.

"Trik," he heard the small voice and felt the pull. Her soul was reaching out to him. It had pushed through the raging addict. He rushed to her side and pulled her to him as he had been longing to do.

"I'm here, beautiful, I'm here."

"Trik, please." He thought that she was going to beg again for the Rapture but what she asked for was worse. "Please kill me."

Trik closed his eyes and fought to keep his own composure. A world without Cassie was not an option and never would be.

"I can't do that, my love," Trik smoothed her hair back from her face and kissed her forehead gently.

She looked up into his eyes and he saw his Cassie staring back at him. She was afraid and lost. She didn't understand who the person was that screamed at him, that threatened him, and she didn't want to be that person.

"It's not you, Cassie. It's the drug."

He saw her thoughts, uncensored because she was so weak. He saw that she was ashamed and that she didn't want him to see her this way. She felt like she should have been able to fight Lorsan and keep from drinking the Rapture. She should have been stronger. He saw deep into her soul, the light that still shined there, the hope that was Cassie. The hope gave him strength.

"You never have to feel ashamed with me. You cannot comprehend all of the atrocities I have committed in my long life, and they were my choice. This, Cassie, this was beyond your control. It was not your choice, nor your fault. The fault lies with me and me alone."

Cassie was shaking her head as tears fell down her face.

"I should have listened to you. I threw a fit like a spoiled child and, oh god," she groaned at the memory. "I hit you." She looked up at Trik as horror filled her eyes. "I've never hit anyone in my life and I hit the man I love. What kind of person does that?"

"The kind whose heart has been broken. I do not blame you, my love. I should have gone after you. I should have made you listen to me. Of all the times for me to not do what I wanted to, I picked a very stupid one."

Cassie shook in his arms as the pain continued. She didn't know how much more she could take. She hurt all over. Breathing felt like work and with every breath she was tempted to just not take the next. She was beginning to sweat again, a cold sweat that chilled her to the bone. As Trik held her, she shivered as her clothes became drenched. Trik pulled back and looked down at her, taking in her appearance. Her lips had a blue tinge to them and she had grown paler.

"You need to be in dry clothes, Cassie." He stood up and placed her back on the bed. Before he walked away to find something else for her to wear he took her face in his hands and stared into her eyes. "Stay with me." He pushed power into his voice and reached for the bond that had begun so early on in their meeting. "Fight, Cassie. Let your soul reach for mine and please hold on."

All she could manage was a single nod. He stared a moment longer and then released her. He was gone and then back in a matter of seconds. He had a towel, a wet cloth, and a large tunic that he laid on the bed.

He took the wet cloth and wiped her forehead and then her neck. She closed her eyes and found some small measure of comfort in his care of her.

"Cassie, I need to change your clothes. Can you look at me?"

She opened her eyes with great effort and met his stare.

"Don't take your eyes from mine, alright?" She nodded her agreement.

Trik undressed her quickly. He used the towel to dry as much of her skin as he could and then he slipped the tunic over her head and helped her get her arms into the sleeves. His eyes never left hers and his hands moved with clinical efficiency. The tunic was much too large for her but that worked out well as it covered her completely.

"Why don't you lay back and rest," he told her as he helped her under the blankets. She still shook from the pain that continued to beat at her small body. Finally, mercifully, she passed out.

Trik checked to make sure that she was still breathing and then he sunk down to his knees beside the bed. He took her cold, clammy hand in his and he held it to his lips. He kissed the back of it and then the palm. He leaned his head against her side and closed his eyes.

He was exhausted and for the first time in his long, long memory he was terrified. Not scared, not worried, the feeling went beyond those small emotions. The King of the Elves, the greatest assassin his people had ever known, was utterly and completely terrified. He felt a tear slide down his cheek and he didn't care that maybe it made him weak to cry. He had been holding on by a thin strand, wanting to give Cassie strength. But now, as she lay still before him, her body thin and the luster gone from her young skin, he let go.

He wept. Despair shrouded him and he pulled the familiar darkness around him like a comforting blanket. His shoulders shook, and he didn't attempt to choke back the sobs.

"I petitioned you once long ago," he spoke into the quiet room, as he swallowed hard against the pain. "I came before you then, weary of the world I lived in, worn out from the constant battle of light and dark, good and evil. I walked away. You told me the consequences of my actions and told me my fate, but you did not tell me this." His jaw tensed as he continued to speak. "You did not tell me that I would find her only to lose her. Is this my punishment and, if so, why her? She is an innocent, young with so much life to live, why take that from her to punish me?"

Trik felt them before he saw them. The Forest Lords stepped into his cabin and filled the space until it felt barely large enough to stand in.

"You are needed by your people. You have a duty to them, and to the human race. You have been given great power, Triktapic. That power brings great responsibility. Even now Light King and his warriors and the humans give of themselves to save many. So too must other sacrifices be made for the greater good."

"Not HER!" His voice filled the room as he stood from his kneeling position. "Her life is not comprisable. I offer mine for hers. I am not so unique that you can't find another worthy to lead. Please, let me take her place. Let her live. Let her find love and happiness and give hope as she so freely does."

"You are willing to die right there where you stand to spare her?"

"There is nothing that I am not willing to do for her. Nothing." Trik waited and held his breath for their decision.

"Would you live for her, if she were to pass from this world to the next? Would you stay and do what you must?"

Trik wanted to shout at the top of his lungs, that 'no, he would not live, he would not go on in a world without his beloved.' But he knew that Cassie would not want that, would expect more from him. Could he live without her? No, he couldn't. But he could exist to fulfill his duty and then, once his people were safe and the humans were safe, then he would join her.

"I would do what was needed," he told them honestly.

"So be it." The words shuddered ominously in the small cabin as Trik watched the Forest Lords vanish.

He was in shock. He couldn't move though he wanted to lunge after them. They were going to take her from him. After all he had said, all he had begged for, they were going to let her die. He turned to look down at her and then sat beside her. He stared at her face, the face he had fallen in love with the moment he saw her come running into that conference room. He smiled at the memory of her brief moment of relief, only to watch her face morph into shock at the sight of him, then curiosity and attraction and stubbornness. His stubborn mate, with a soul more beautiful than he could fathom.

He leaned forward and laid his head on her chest, feeling it rise and fall and listening to her weak heartbeat. He held his breath, waiting for the moment when she would breathe her last and her heart give way to the abuse her body had taken from the drug.

Minutes ticked by and still she breathed. And then there were fingers in his hair. His head jerked up and his eyes met clear, bright, un-dilated green eyes. His hand reached up to her face and traced her pink skin, no longer pale and sweaty. She was warm to his touch, warm and healthy.

"Trik," she said his name and it was with a strong voice. "Why are you crying?"

Trik hadn't even realized he was and he didn't care. She was alive! She was breathing and healthy and here with him.

"Are you in pain?" He asked her nervously.

She shook her head. "I feel fine." Cassie's brow furrowed as she wiped his cheeks. "What happened? Why am I no longer writhing in pain, begging for you to end it?"

Trik pulled her up into his arms. "The Forest Lords, they spared you."

Cassie let out a deep breath and wrapped her arms around him. "Tell them thank you for me."

"I have a feeling that you will have the chance to tell them yourself, love."

She pulled back and looked at him and without warning, she kissed him. Trik didn't move at first but when the surprise wore off, he took over.

"I'm sorry," she told him in between kisses. "I'm so sorry."

"Stop saying that Cassie or I'm going to stop."

"If you stop kissing me, Trik, then you have a death wish."

He chuckled as he laid her down on the bed. His body covered hers as he whispered words of love to her and then showed her just how much he meant them.

It wasn't until much, much later that Cassie pulled her lips from his and came up for air. She sat up suddenly and Trik followed her movement.

"What's wrong, beautiful? Are you hurting again?"

Cassie shook her head. "Trik, where is Elora? Where are Tamsin and Syndra?"

Trik looked away from her eyes as he berated himself for not mentioning it earlier. "They're volunteering for the greater good."

"Volunteering?" Cassie's eyes narrowed. "Where? At the Goodwill?"

"Picture a little less second hand clothes and a lot more danger and mayhem."

"My best friend has been fighting for her life while we laid here making out?"

"It seemed like a really, really good idea at the time."

Cassie growled her frustration at him. She jumped up from the bed and headed straight for the mirror.

"Where are you going my love?" Trik asked, still sitting on the bed, in all his shirtless glory.

"We have to help them, Trik. You're a king; surely you have some sort of kingly powers."

He nodded and stood, unfolding his body slowly, knowing that she would be watching. She rolled her eyes at him impatiently.

"Cassie, love," Trik purred her name and she wanted to kick herself for the warmth it flooded her body with.

"What Trik?" She snapped.

"I know you want to help them, and so do I."

"Good, let's go," she interrupted and once again turned and headed for the mirror.

"I want to help them," Trik continued. "And as effective at distracting the enemy might be with you marching into battle in absolutely nothing but a thin, pale, tunic, I would much prefer my eyes be the only ones who see you in such splendor."

Cassie looked down at her bare legs, and as she felt Trik's eyes roaming over her, she realized just how unclothed she was.

"I totally knew that I needed clothes."

"Of course you did, love."

"It's not like I would have just ran headlong into a battle with my butt on full display."

"I didn't doubt you for a second."

"You are never going to let me live this down are you?"

"Not in this life or the next."

"Will you at least please get me some clothes so that I can rescue my friends and kick Lorsan in the head?"

"I will do better than that beautiful. I will get you some clothes, a sword, and your very own assassin to join you on your quest."

"Oooh, just what I've always wanted. A man whose job title had the word ass in it not once, but two times."

Trik tossed her some clothes as he muttered under his breath.

Once she was dressed Trik took her hand and led her to the mirror. He looked down at the ring still on her finger, the ring he had given her and smiled. "You kept it."

Cassie frowned. "Of course I kept it."

"Because you love me," he grinned triumphantly.

She held her hand up with her forefinger and thumb separated slightly. "Just a little."

This time he rolled his eyes at her. "Whatever, you are totally in love with me."

He heard her snort as she turned and stepped through the mirror and he used his mind to push her where she needed to go. He was right behind her. When they emerged in the light elf castle Trik wrapped an arm around Cassie and pulled her close. His face lost its playfulness as he looked into her eyes.

"You are not allowed to get yourself killed," he told her sternly.

She let out an exasperated breath but a smile played on her lips and her eyes, so bright and full of life, sparkled. "I'm getting orders from the guy whose job title is essentially *ass* squared. How seriously am I supposed to take that?"

Trik growled at her and pulled her into a firm kiss. She pulled back, breathless. Even under the circumstances she wanted to shout from the highest mountain the joy that she felt in her heart.

"No worries, love," she winked at him. "I can't die. Then who would remind you that you're too cocky for your own good?"

"You're right; I have nothing to worry about. You would never allow me to live in such ignorant bliss, nor rob me of the opportunity to spend eternity being called *ass squared.*"

Cassie laughed for the first time in a very long, dark time. "Damn straight," she murmured just as she saw Syndra come around the corner.

The Light Elf Queen stopped and put her hands on her hips. She narrowed her eyes and met Cassie's.

"Took you long enough."

Cassie shook her head at the snarky she-elf. "I do apologize, your majesty, for not getting over the whole dying from adrug addiction thing a little more quickly."

"I'll think about accepting your apology. In the meantime, get your butts in gear. We have friends to rescue, an enemy to crush, and the human population to save."

"Oh, is that all?" Cassie retorted nonchalantly.

"Piece of cake, babe. Piece. Of. Cake."

"I'm going to tell you where you can shove that piece of cake if you don't get a move on," Syndra growled over her shoulder.

"Take notes my love," Trik pointed at Syndra's retreating form. "That is why she is Queen."

Cassie nodded. "Got it. Note to self: Successful Queen equals bitch."

"I heard that," Syndra yelled.

Cassie gave Trik a high five. "You're well on your way, beautiful," he told her with a wink.

From Quinn:

Thank you so much for taking your time to read Elfin, Book 1 in my new series. I hope that it met your expectations and maybe even exceeded them.

Books by Author Quinn Loftis:

The Grey Wolves Series

Prince of Wolves

Blood Rites

Just One Drop

Out of the Dark

Beyond the Veil

The Elfin Series

Elfin

Now check out this sneak peak of Tiffany King's *Jordyn*

<u>**Sneak Peak Tiffany King**</u>

Jordyn

A Daemon Hunter Novel

Book One

By

Tiffany King

www.authortiffanyjking.blogspot.com

Chapter One

I loved the tickling feeling of the sand eroding from underneath my feet as the ocean waves continued to roll in and then back out to sea. I'd stood in this spot so many times over the past year. It was beautiful here, the way the ocean looked like it went on forever in the distance. Still, as significant as this beach was to my new family, the way their entire existence seemed to gravitate around this spot, it didn't hold any significance for me. I'd never dreamt of this place or met some soul mate hottie in my dreams in this spot. It was just a beach where I hung out with friends and family, nothing more. *God, self-pity much?* I thought. This wasn't why I'd come to the beach. I came here to think about the anger-filled blowup during dinner earlier. Coming here always helped me chill out, and I had hoped that for once this spot would finally unlock the memories that were lost to me. The fight I'd had earlier with my supposed aunt and uncle, who were practically my age, by the way, was typical. I was over their evasive answers about my past. They didn't seem to understand how frustrating it is to know nothing about who you are, where you come from, or even worse, why you have no memories of anything like any normal person. At times like this, I missed my best friend, Lynn. I needed someone to vent to, but she had left two weeks ago to join her Protector in Utah on an extended mission. It sucked not having her around. Sure, we texted and Facebooked each other twenty-four/seven, but it wasn't the same. Truthfully, I didn't see why Robert couldn't handle the mission on his own. Of course, I knew how the whole "link" thing worked, which made how I was feeling totally irrational, I realized, but I didn't care. I missed my only friend, damn it.

My errant thoughts were interrupted when my pulse quickened and the hair on the back of my neck felt like it was standing on end. I wasn't the only mystical being on the beach tonight.

Sweeping my eyes over the boardwalk behind me, I spotted the source of my "freak alarm"—Daemons. Two of them by the looks of it. They were using human hosts they'd obviously hijacked from the mortuary, judging by the gaping bullet hole in one of them. They both had waxy complexions courtesy of a mortician's hand. The sky around us was dark enough that the other occupants of the boardwalk paid no attention to the Daemons' odd appearances. It showed how oblivious humans could be.

I walked casually toward them, knowing they couldn't sense me. I didn't emit the same vibe that a Guide or Protector or even an Arch Angel would. I was like the shadow you couldn't see until the sun decided to cast its rays. I watched them for a moment, creeping along the shadow from the wall that separated the boardwalk from the beach. I wouldn't be detected until I was ready. Typical Daemons. Steal human hosts and prey on the weak. They're nothing but cowards themselves. I knew I should have called Haniel the moment I'd sensed them, but I was still pissed off enough at the world right now and decided to throw caution to the wind. I could take them out. I may be an anomaly, but at least I was a badass one.

It wasn't until I was within three yards of them that I spotted their source of entertainment. Homeless Joe was leaning back against the wall in a drunken stupor. One of the body snatchers proceeded to pour tequila down Joe's throat while the other held Joe's head in place.

"Two on one seems a little unfair, don't you think?" I asked as they dropped the bottle to the sand in surprise.

"What the hell are you?" the bullet-holed Daemon mumbled, breaking through the wire the mortician had used to sew his lips closed. It was obvious they sensed I wasn't ordinary.

"Are you two dipshits normally this stupid, or did you leave your brains at the mortuary?" I taunted them, placing my hands on my hips. They hesitated to make a move, no doubt thrown off by the fact that they were unable to get a read on me. I rapidly calculated how I would take them out in my head. "Surely you know this area has angelic protection?" I mocked.

"You're no angel," the second Daemon slurred through the dead mouth of his host. He dropped Homeless Joe back to the ground and turned his hulking body toward me.

He was right, but what a dick thing to say. I wasn't an angel, and I never would be. It wasn't in my genetic makeup, but hearing a soul sucker remind me of that fact only pissed me off more.

"Wow, you're a sharp one," I answered, stepping closer. My nose wrinkled from a sudden whiff of embalming fluid the mortician had used on the bodies.

"You're awful cocky for such a small little treat," Bullet Hole taunted, taking a menacing step forward.

His words struck my hilarity button and I burst out laughing, which I could tell confused them both as they studied me like I'd lost my marbles.

"All I can say is talk about being in the wrong place at the wrong time," I said through my laughter. "Let me guess. Your boss has no idea you're here. You thought you'd win brownie points by bringing back a soul, right?"

My knowledge of their origins seemed to unsettle them.

"What are you?" Bullet Hole demanded again.

"Your worst nightmare," I snickered before turning deadly serious. Cheesy, I know, but I heard it in some old movie I'd watched over the weekend.

This time they both laughed, which came across distorted and eerie around the wires that poked out of their lips on both sides.

"You're one crazy little bitch," the Daemon slurred, taking a bounding jump toward me.

Anticipating his movement, I used my momentum and his forward motion against him by slamming my small but effective fist into his esophagus. While he was reeling from the blow, I twisted him around and thrusted my foot against his spinal cord, snapping it in half. Without a backbone to hold its host upright, the Daemon dropped to the sand at my feet like a sack of bricks.

"So, pretty girl can fight," Bullet Hole snarled, no longer playing as he slowly circled me.

"Dude, you have no idea," I mocked, keeping my eyes on his.

He smiled crookedly before sweeping in to wrap his massive arms around me.

Jerk off, I thought as I threw my head back. The force of the blow broke the bones in his face, causing him to drop his arms. With lightning-quick reflexes, I scraped my fingers across his face, grimacing as my sharp fingernails dug through the soft waxy skin.

I maneuvered toward my next strike when the body of the host dropped at my feet. The Daemon stood in front of me, no longer using the cadaver as a shield.

"What's the matter, can't handle the excess baggage?" I teased. He was ugly as sin. Large grotesque boils covered his body and crooked horns stuck out on either side of his head. I sighed when he jumped forward. He laughed darkly, naively believing he held the upper hand as he reached out to grab my arm. This time it was my turn to laugh as the skin of his clawed hand ignited in flames which slowly danced their way up his forearm, past his elbow and toward his shoulder.

"What are you?" he yelped one last time as the flames moved across his shoulder, engulfing his head.

"I'm an aberration," I finally answered as he landed in a pile of ash at my feet.

I turned to the remaining Daemon who studied me, puzzled over what had transpired. I took a step toward him. He glared at me before bursting into a ball of flames, leaving me with another pile of ash.

I kicked at the pile of ash, frustrated. I was pissed that the fight had ended before it really started. Kicking Daemon ass would have at least taken my mind off my woes from home.

The sound of applause behind me made me stop in my tracks. I felt no human pull, which meant the unwanted visitor behind me was not human. I used my gifts to access which side of the earthly realm he came from, but came up empty.

"What are you?" I asked, turning around to glare at my unwelcome audience that stood in the shadows. The irony that I had repeated the Daemons' question wasn't lost on me.

"I think the more important question is: What are you?" he asked, letting out a low whistle of appraisal at the piles of ash at my feet.

"I asked first," I demanded. I wasn't used to being in the dark in a situation. I felt no threatening vibe from him, but the fact that I couldn't tell where he came from unsettled me.

My wayward thoughts were interrupted when he finally stepped out of the shadows. A glaring ray of light from the boardwalk shone down on him and I was startled to see he was roughly my age, although he looked nothing like the boys I went to school with. His dark hair was longer than what I was normally attracted to, falling just below the collar of his jacket, but for some reason it worked for him. Human or not, he looked the part. His jeans had a distressed worn-in look and a plain red t-shirt and black leather jacket covered his torso, completing his simple but cool ensemble. I'm sure he picked his clothing, thinking he would blend in, but it had the opposite effect. He looked like he belonged up on a stage holding a guitar. The guy was hot.

There was something magnetic about him, and I curiously stepped closer, hoping to figure out what the strange vibe was. His eyes glistened in the light and a small smirk turned up at the corners of his lips.

"Jordyn, that's close enough," a stern familiar voice bellowed behind me.

"Haniel," I acknowledged my mentor without turning around.

"Jordyn, back away from the Soul Trader," Haniel commanded loudly when it appeared I wouldn't listen.

"Soul Trader?" I asked, more than intrigued.

"Haniel, good to see you, buddy," the stranger mocked, ignoring my question. "I thought you were banished to the heavenly realm a few years back," he added.

"I was not banished," Haniel bristled. Something about the dark stranger seemed to be rubbing the Arch Angel the wrong way.

"That's not the way I heard it, but hey, at least you got the girl, right."

"Jordyn, come with me, now," Haniel insisted.

"Haniel, what is a Soul Trader?" I asked, not taking me eyes off the guy in front of me.

"Soul Trader sounds so harsh," the stranger taunted. "I'm just a negotiator."

"What does that mean, you take souls?" I asked breathlessly, feeling lightheaded from his words. Any kind of Soul Taker was scum in my book. They went against everything we believed in.

Everything we fought against. They repulsed my kind and yet, he didn't repulse me.

"Someone has to do it, sweetheart," he mocked, answering my question.

"Yes, but it should be Angels," I answered, confused about the conflicting emotions racing through me. My DNA should have put me on the defensive. I should be plotting how to take him down, not wondering where the tattoo ended that I has just discovered on his neck that disappeared beneath his collar.

"And what about the rotten-as-sin souls?" he questioned, raising an eyebrow at me.

I cringed at his words. I didn't like to think about the Daemons that claimed those souls.

"Or what about the questionable souls? The ones your Light hasn't decided what to do with. Should they be forsaken?"

"The Guides save them," I defended, thinking of my friends and family who were created for that purpose.

"So, you're telling me that Guides manage to save every questionable soul?" he chided me like I was a naive child.

"Well, no, but they do the best they can," I retorted, aggravated at what he was insinuating.

"Ah, well, that's where I come in, right, Haniel?" he asked.

385

"Correct," Haniel bit out, still clearly bothered. "Jordyn, we must go. Humans are approaching. It would not bode well for you to be found with cadavers from the mortuary and an unconscious human," he added, latching his fingers around my wrist to drag me away.

I dug my heels in to the sand, not quite ready to go. "Wait, I have more questions for..." I floundered, realizing I didn't know his name.

"Emrys," he answered, grinning wickedly at me.

"Emrys," I repeated, rolling the unfamiliar word off my tongue.

"It means *immortal*," Haniel said, dragging me quickly across the sand toward the steps that would lead us to the parking lot.

Other Works by

Tiffany King

The Saving Angels Series

Meant to Be (Book 1)

Forgotten Souls (Book 2)

The Ascended (Book 3)

Wishing For Someday Soon

Forever Changed

Unlikely Allies

Miss Me Not

Printed in Great Britain
by Amazon.co.uk, Ltd.,
Marston Gate.